BURDEN OF THE ASSASSIN

A PETER BLACK THRILLER

DAVID ARCHER

VINCE VOGEL

PRAISE FOR THE PETER BLACK SERIES

PETER BLACK THRILLERS

ONE

VERMONT, 1999

THE CAR SCYTHED THROUGH HEAVY SNOW, THE FAT flakes resembling swarming moths in the headlight beams. The radio played in the background. It was one o'clock in the morning when Linda Ronstadt began singing Irving Berlin's "What'll I Do?" Recognizing the song, the woman driving the car upped the volume and started to hum along.

It was two minutes past one when St. Joseph's Orphanage loomed up out of the snowy darkness. It was an ugly five-story slab with a bell tower sticking out of the top. Stairwells criss-crossed the outside and icy mesh covered the narrow windows. Everything about it said hopelessness.

She parked in the lot beside three police cruisers and a black sedan. At four minutes past one she was marching toward the entrance. Three state troopers lounged about the doors. One sat on the curb holding a bag of ice to a busted nose, blood dribbling down the front of his uniform and shining ruby in the moonlight. Another trooper stood holding a bloodied handkerchief to the side of his face, and the third blocked the way into the building, his right hand wrapped in a bandage. The woman observed a large red blotch in the center of the palm. Something had been driven through it.

The three men were too busy chatting to notice her silent approach. "Can you believe it took four of us to subdue the bastard?"

"Darn near chewed right through my face," the one holding the handkerchief said.

Lifting it away, he revealed a set of teeth marks deeply entrenched in his cheek.

"It was like he was possessed," the trooper holding the ice to his nose added.

"What about Sully? Doc says the swelling in his balls could take weeks to go down. Dislocated testicle is what they say."

It was now that the man blocking the doors noticed the woman. He stepped toward her, his colleagues turning to see.

"I'm sorry, ma'am," he said, "but you'll have to—"

"Agent Jane Kazinsky. FBI," she interrupted in a raspy voice. "I'm from the Rutland Office."

She held up an FBI identification card and the cop's demeanor became more docile.

"Sorry, ma'am. We weren't expecting anyone from Rutland. Being that we caught the guy already."

"Doesn't matter. Who's in charge?"

"That'd be Harry."

"And where is Harry?"

"He's at the crime scene."

Seven minutes past one she was walking through the dark

corridors of St. Joseph's. It stank of boiled cabbage and sweat. The place should have been quiet as a mouse at that time, but it wasn't. It was heaving with the sounds of bellowing, cheering boys. The sounds of a riot.

"They've been like this since it happened," Trooper Moore told her as he led her into the bowels of the old building. "The nuns are too scared to go in, so they just locked the doors."

Agent Kazinsky said nothing. All she wanted was to see what he had done.

Eight past one and she was entering the doorway to the orphanage's apartment. It was where the staff stayed. Father Collins was its latest recipient. The late Father Collins.

Trooper Moore guided her into the apartment. It was neat and tidy. There were fresh-cut flowers in vases dotted about. In a bedroom a forensic photographer took pictures. He stood in the doorway facing in. The lights were off and every second or two the room would explode with the throb of the flashbulb.

"Hey, Don?" Trooper Moore called to the photographer.

He stopped picturing the dead and turned around to them.

"Where's Harry?" Moore asked.

While they spoke, Agent Kazinsky entered the room. The light from the hallway was enough to see by. A crucifix adorned the wall above the headboard. Underneath it, a priest lay on his back in bed. Multiple stab wounds swarmed his bloody throat. Tiny puncture holes, slits, no more than a centimeter across. His eyes were fixed open. They stared into the void with wide-eyed terror and Agent Kazinsky gathered that he must have awoken halfway through. Something poked out from under the bed and when she focused on its cover, she knew for sure that it was a homosexual pornographic magazine.

"Ma'am?"

When she glanced over at him, Trooper Moore told her that Harry was with one of the sisters, so they left the priest's apartment.

The man in charge of the investigation, Harry, was in his forties. Short, heavyset, he sported a head like a cabbage and was the type of guy Agent Kazinsky associated with short man syndrome. He stood at the end of a wood-paneled corridor talking with a tall, wiry nun, the sister's spindly fingers fiddling incessantly with a set of rosary beads.

"Hey, Harry?" Trooper Moore called to him, his voice echoing off the walls and filling the frigid air of that sad place.

Looking over, Harry eyed Jane up and down.

"This is Agent Kazinsky from Rutland," Moore added.

"Don't she know we caught him already?" Harry said, addressing the officer and ignoring Agent Kazinsky.

Bored already, she stepped forward and said, "I won't take up much of your time, Detective. I merely wish to ask a few questions and then I will be taking the prisoner into my custody."

"The hell you will!"

Her eyes blank, her face deadpan, she responded: "I'm afraid so. I have everything necessary here."

She took folded papers from the inside of her coat and offered them to Harry. He snatched them and read, his face gradually changing color as he did.

They weren't from Rutland. They were from Washington.

"Fine," Harry muttered once he'd finished. "Now what do you wanna know?"

"How did he get into the priest's apartment?"

"Picked the lock."

"He told you this?"

"No. He ain't muttered a peep since we threw the cuffs on."

"So how do you know he picked the lock?"

"Because we found a hair clip shaped like a pick in the bastard's pocket."

"And he used that to escape as well?"

"No. He just climbed out of the priest's window. They don't lock the grates in the apartment."

"And the weapon he used, how did he source it?"

"They had a workman come recently to fix one of the meshes in the dorms. They say the screwdriver went missing then. They searched for it, but no one was able to find the thing. He must've stashed it somewhere till tonight."

"And you're sure it was just one perpetrator?"

"Absolutely."

"Where is he now?"

"Through there." Harry pointed to the end of the corridor where a solid oak panel door had the words Quiet Room written across it.

"You mean he's in the building?"

"We caught him nearby, and with most of the troopers here rather than at the station, I thought it better to keep him close. Anyways, St. Joseph's has got restraints specially for people his size."

Agent Kazinsky's eyes were fixed to the door. "Open it. I want to see him."

Harry looked at the nun. "If you don't mind, Sister."

The nun nodded and hurried off to the door. A large rusted ring containing innumerable keys hung from her belt.

She jangled them about as she searched for the required one and when she found it, she creaked open the door onto darkness.

A terrible smell flooded out. It was the smell of feces and urine. The smell of despair and horror. Of child maltreatment.

The nun leant inside and flicked the light on. It shuddered into existence to reveal a room the size of a cupboard. Scratch marks ran down the walls and the only furniture was a wooden chair bolted to the center of the floor. On it sat a boy whose feet didn't even reach all the way. He was strapped to it at the legs, arms, wrists and neck. A thick clasp went across his throat, the buckle resting upon his larynx. A black cloth bag covered his head.

"Get him out of that thing," Agent Kazinsky said.

Harry and the nun looked at her.

"Now!"

TWO

MONTE CARLO, 2019

HIS INTERNAL CLOCK BEGINS TICKING.

One second.

Peter leaves the marina at a steady pace as the sound of the explosion rips through the air. Women scream. Men shout. Car alarms go off. He is shaking. The air is thickening in his lungs. He is running on automatic. Nothing but muscle memory, discipline and training.

Three seconds.

It must be the same reason he gives himself for why he pressed the button. That it was an automatic response based on discipline and training. Because there can be no other reason for what he has just done.

Five seconds.

Peter heads along the jetty as crowds of people stand frozen in horror. When a bomb goes off in any given civilian area, it is usual for people to have one of several immediate reactions. They either freeze and gaze toward the carnage. Duck and find cover in their surroundings. Or they run from the scene.

What they don't do is notice the guy steadily making his way through them, going in the opposite direction to where their attention is headed. He is the last thing on their minds, the last thing they spot as he dodges along the crowded jetty to the harbor wall, and the last thing they can describe to investigators later on.

Twenty-one seconds.

Peter reaches the road. The traffic has stopped. Drivers and passengers gawp open-mouthed at the flames and smoke. A group of policemen stand close to where he wants to cross. They hold radios to their lips, eyes trapped on the two-hundred-million-dollar super yacht now burning brightly as it floats out of the harbor like a viking's funeral barge.

One of the policemen is about to turn Peter's way.

Twenty-four seconds.

Another explosion, smaller but just as frightening, ripples through the air.

The policemen hunker down and swivel around, their backs to Peter as he glides past. Hands on their pistols, the men glare at the badly dented trash can that smokes profusely ten yards away.

They're still staring at it when Peter crosses the road moving north and enters an alleyway separating two multi-storey hotels.

Thirty-two seconds.

Emerging the other side, he crosses the Rue Grimaldi, continuing north, weaving through static vehicles. The drivers and passengers stare in the direction of the big bang and the midday sun shines like fire off the chrome hoods. All of which makes Peter practically invisible.

He enters another alley that is banked by tables and chairs. The waiters and patrons shield their eyes from the sun as they watch tendrils of smoke waft high above the buildings.

"*Avez-vous entendu que?*" he hears a woman ask her friend.

"*Ça ressemblait à une explosion au port,*" the other answers.

Peter hears the first sirens.

Forty-nine seconds.

Right on cue he turns east onto the Rue Louis Aureglia. A hundred yards ahead a panel van displaying the Monte Carlo city emblem is parked at the side of the road. A man in the blue coveralls of a city worker sits in the driver's seat watching the wing mirror, his foot tapping up and down in the footwell.

Another man also in the blue coveralls of the city stands on the sidewalk holding a manhole cover open, eyes peeled on the bearded man who steadily approaches. Rushing sewage water flows along below him.

Seventy-six seconds.

Peter reaches the manhole. He tosses the detonator into the rushing water. The maintenance worker drops the cover with a clang and follows Peter into the back of the van. He slams the sliding door shut behind them and the driver puts the van into gear, casually rolling out into traffic as emergency vehicles come screaming down the road in the opposite direction.

Eighty seconds.

Clockwork.

"Did it get him?"

Victor's voice is a million miles away. Peter is in a trance. Trembling. Finding it hard to breathe as he peels off the false beard and wig that have become itchy with sweat.

"Well, did it?"

Peter's fingers are hardly working as he takes coveralls from a pile on the bed of the van and starts pulling them over himself.

"Hey! Are you deaf?"

Peter stares across the van at him with hollow blue eyes. He's trying hard to breathe. Humming loudly to himself.

Victor frowns. To him, Peter looks like a freak.

"I asked you if it got him?"

Peter goes to talk but can't. Instead of words, he takes short, shallow breaths. Like a man choking on his own tongue.

All he can give for affirmation is a nod.

THREE

THEY GOT OUT OF MONACO WITHOUT A HITCH.
Now they were waiting for orders of what to do next, staying
at the Villa Florentine—a centuries'-old hotel in an opulent
district of Lyon.

The second he was in his room, Peter took a shower. The
stench of C4 hung heavy in his nostrils. He thought he
could smell blood as well. But that was impossible.

An hour after arriving Peter is still in the shower, leaning
heavily against the tiles, the powerful jet of water hitting his
crown, the sensation scrambling his thoughts, lips
murmuring the same old song: "*When I'm alone with only
dreams of you...*"

CNN is on the TV in the main room. The male
anchor's honey-smooth voice reaches into the ensuite bathroom. "*The killing today of Silicon Valley CEO David Gregor
has shocked the tech industry and the world. But not just that.
It has shocked the stock market, with the share price of the
company Gregor founded, Unity, dropping by as much as fifty*

percent on the Nasdaq as investors fear what the future of the company could be without its pioneering head at the wheel. At the site of the explosion is Jenny Mathers with more details."

Jenny's sunny voice: *"David Gregor's super-yacht Cacas was leaving Monte Carlos when an explosion ripped through the vessel killing everyone on board. This tragically included his—"*

Peter switches the television off. Water drips off of him onto the thick carpet. The late-afternoon sun is bright outside the tall windows, casting the antique furniture in gold. Children play in the street below, their sounds flowing into the room.

He closes the curtains and lies down on a Versailles-style bed. A pair of hazel eyes stare back at him from the intricate Baroque plasterwork of the ceiling. The room is cast in shadow, yet the hazel eyes shine with the sun. Peter is sure he couldn't have seen them this clearly from where he stood. Not as clear as he sees them now. At the harbor he'd been at least fifty yards away. There was no chance.

No chance.

Peter jumps off the bed and begins pacing the room. The sound of the children becomes louder, drawing him to the window, where he stands within the curtains watching the street four stories below.

A soccer game has taken over the cobbled thoroughfare. The cries and kicks of the players echo up into the room from the deep and narrow trench they play in.

The grand Villa Florentine is built atop of Fourvière Hill in Lyon's most prestigious neighborhood. The eighteenth-century stone château opens up on its eastern side into a terrace of swimming pools and spas that are built into the hillside in a series of steps, all of which overlooks the slithering waters of the Saône River. On its western side, where Peter looks down from, the narrow cobbled road, the one now acting as a soccer field, splits the hotel trench-like from a stone apartment block. On the tiny balconies of the opposite flats, spectators hang over little wrought-iron railings, watching the game, cheering on the girls and boys.

"Allez! Allez! Passez et bougez! Passez et bougez!"

The game is a tempestuous one. A young girl, ignoring the instructions from the balconies, beats two or three before being dispossessed by a boy who appears to be just as greedy for the ball. Giving up the opportunity to pass to better placed teammates, he instead loses the ball to the same girl he dispossessed. It is a tussle of a match without the discipline of the adult game.

While Peter wonders whether he was ever allowed to be that undisciplined as a child, his phone vibrates on the nightstand, taking his attention away from the soccer.

Picking it up, he sees that it's Pat Hughes. His fixer.

Pat speaks the second Peter answers, a gravelly voice thick with cigarette tar. "The money's in the account if you wanna check."

Peter has returned to the window. He is gripping the phone to his ear, shaking all over. There's something he wants to say to Pat, but saying it makes it hard to breathe.

A car slowly approaches the children. It toots its horn, forcing the kids to temporarily pack up the game and wait patiently for it to go.

"He said they wouldn't be onboard," Peter finally says.

Pat sighs. Peter can practically smell the cigarette fumes. "It was bad intel."

"No it wasn't. It was a lie. He knew they'd be on the boat."

The driver waves out of the window to the children as he ambles slowly by. A boy stands with the ball trapped beneath an arm on the sidewalk, an annoyed look on his sweat-soaked face.

"Maybe he did know," Pat says. "There's also a chance the client told him to keep it back. To make sure you pulled the trigger, so to speak."

It is Peter's turn to sigh. "I shouldn't have taken the job the second I found out I wouldn't be working alone."

The car is finally gone. The goals are dragged back out and the game resumes with a joyous cheer from the balconies.

"Still," Pat says. "Look on the bright side."

"What bright side?"

"Doesn't the four hundred grand we just got paid make it worth it?"

Peter leans his face against the warm windowpane and ponders the question. A goal is scored. A cross from the byline, low and hard. A stringy boy of around ten puts his foot through it, the ball pounding the back of the net. The others on his team go wild. Grab him as he races around with a fist held aloft. The other team slump their shoulders. Point and shout at each other. Accusations all round. The crowd up on the balconies goes wild.

"I don't know," Peter admits. "It doesn't feel worth it."

"Look, you made a difficult choice out of desperate options. Like so many you've had to make over the years. And do you know why you made it?"

Peter stays silent.

"Because you're the kind of guy who can make those kinds of decisions. The kinds of decisions that ordinary people can't."

Peter shakes his head and comes away from the window. Stepping across a Tabriz patterned rug, he enters the bathroom and stands before a huge gilt-framed mirror. Gazing into the pale blue eyes that stare back, he asks, "But what right do I have to make them?"

"Look Peter," Pat says in a tired voice, "it's too late to start getting into the existential side of what we do. You're good at it. Okay? Is that good enough for you? You do it because you're good. You're the best."

"But what if I want more?"

"What like?"

"Life, Pat. Real life."

The handler groans. He knows Peter better than almost anyone else on the planet. These types of conversations have been happening more frequently of late.

"I had it once," Pat tells him.

"Had what?"

"That thing you refer to as life. I had it and it left me with a drinking problem and only half my possessions. Can you believe my ex-wife ran off with my best friend?"

"Life's cruel."

"And there isn't a day goes by that I don't miss him."

The joke makes Peter grin. Pat breaks out laughing. Then coughing.

Peter leaves the mirror and returns to the window. He goes cold the instant he looks down and regards the road. The street soccer game has gone.

No kids. No cars.

Up on the abandoned balconies the doors are closed and the curtains drawn. To the left, along the cobbled thorough-fare, on the far corner of the building, French police usher people out of the hotel.

"Pat, I'll have to call you back."

FOUR

Peter's companions are sharing a suite made up of two rooms with a connecting bathroom. Peter knows them as Victor and Leon. Victor is mid-forties, squat, five-seven, wears a round head on square shoulders, and has graying hair greased all the way back to his fat neck. Leon is roughly the same age. Taller, six-one, leaner, broad-chested, serious-faced, buzz-cut silver hair. Other than that, the only thing Peter knows for sure is that both men are ex-Special Forces.

Victor lies in bed eating Cheetos and watching a sitcom on his laptop. Whenever there's a half-decent joke, his guffaws send wet bits of orange chips at the screen. Leon is in his own room, sitting by an open window that faces the river to the northeast, a copy of Camus' *The Outsider* in his hand.

Both men instantly cock their ears to the loud knock at their door. When they answer it, Peter stands in the corridor wearing a black ski mask underneath a Mira tactical gas mask. In his right hand is an HK45 Compact Tactical with a Banish suppressor on the end. It is Peter's pistol of choice. It can punch a hole through a car door, but with the suppressor it is no louder than a hot knife slipping through butter.

Both men immediately stand up straight in the doorway.

"We have company," Peter tells them.

It is less than a minute when all three emerge from the room wearing gas masks and carrying backpacks. Victor is holding a Benelli M4 semi-automatic shotgun to his shoulder. The skeleton buttstock is collapsed. This shortens the weapon by almost eight inches, allowing him better maneuverability around the hotel's tight corners. Fitted with an extension tube, it carries nine shells with one in the lifter. Enough firepower to turn an elephant into pink mist.

Leon lines his eye up with the sight of a Tavor CTAR-21. The all-black bullpup assault rifle was developed by Israel Military Industries back in the early '90s for their special forces. Three words sum it up: light, compact, deadly. With a firing range of 550m, it can pump out up to forty-five bullets in just a single three-second burst.

The men move along the corridors and hallways in formation, heading southeast, passing an array of oil paintings and antique furniture. The whole floor appears deserted. A service cart stands abandoned with a serving dish on top. Victor lifts the lid and hogs down half of the club sandwich he finds underneath.

Leon frowns at him.

"I haven't had lunch yet," Victor whispers unapologetically between mouthfuls.

Peter holds a hand up.

Stop!

The men take up positions at the edges, sinking into the cover of the alcoves that pit the walls. At the end of the hallway a door to one of the rooms is opening, the scratching of a key in the lock. The door is so thick that they don't hear her until it's open and she's stepping out.

She is American. Talking loudly on her phone. "My God, Maggie. The strangest thing is happening to me. I got a missed call from the hotel reception, then a text. I got it, like, six minutes ago, but only just noticed it. It says I've got to vacate my suite immediately, leave my luggage. What is there, like, a fire or something?... No, it doesn't say. Just that I have to leave the hotel by the fire exit... No. Mark never came back from the pool. That was—"

She freezes when she spots the three masked and heavily armed men standing in front of her.

"Back in your room," Peter snaps.

She nods and retreats slowly back through the door, the sounds of her friend repeatedly asking what the matter is coming from the phone.

They continue in the direction of the southeast service stairwell. Reaching the door, Peter takes out a Nokia mobile, the old type. There are only two numbers saved into it. He picks the first and gets ready to call it.

"What the fuck, retard?"

Peter glances back over his shoulder.

It is Victor who has insulted him. The short one.

"They'll be coming that way," Victor's complaint continues. "We need to take the roof. Get out through one of the rooms."

Peter ignores him. Checking the window of the door, he

spots the black body armor of French SWAT as they move cautiously up the spiraling stairs, their eyes peering through the sights of their assault rifles.

Peter turns to Victor and Leon. "Take cover," he tells them in a flat tone, holding up the Nokia.

Their eyes widen. They quickly take positions either side of the door.

Peter makes the call.

The building reverberates with four smallish explosions, one right after another, the call setting off the four bullet-sized lumps of C4 that Peter had packed into the walls of the stairwell three days ago whilst disguised as a contractor. The men feel the hotel jump beneath their feet as each one goes off on a different floor of the stairwell, packed with just enough power to demobilize a person whilst not endangering the structural integrity of the centuries'-old building. Maybe a crack or two. But nothing unfixable.

"Let's go," Peter says, shouldering through the door.

His two companions follow him quickly down the steps, the staircase clouded in smoke, the oily stench of C4 hanging in the air.

"You planned for this, didn't you?" Leon asks as they hurry down.

Peter says nothing.

A three-man team had been sent this way. The first two are unconscious, laid out on the stairs, gray bone poking out of their ripped fatigues. The one at the bottom is the only one still lucid. He lies on his back, having being thrown down several flights by the blasts. He makes the mistake of raising his pistol as Peter reaches him. He gets it no higher than an inch before a bullet shatters the glass face of his gas mask. It makes a hole of the eye and exits through the back of the skull, brains spraying the marble staircase.

As he steps over the body Peter hears the calls of the man's unit emanating from his comms earpiece. They are heading this way.

Reaching the bottom of the stairwell, Peter uses hand signals to instruct the other two to go right, through a set of double doors into the kitchen. He'll go straight ahead and meet them on the other side.

"We shouldn't split up!" Victor hisses at Peter as the latter disappears around a corner.

Leon taps him on the shoulder. "Let him go."

The kitchen at the grand old château is what you'd expect. Steel surfaces and modern appendages occupy the tall ceilings and flagstone floors of the ancient cookhouse. Half-prepared meals line every surface. On a rack, dishes await the saucier's touch. Washing up fills a basin in the scullery. A steaming mop bucket clogs up an aisle. The entire eastern wall is taken up by the gaping mouth of a brick oven, its deep domed chamber filled with metal shelves holding bubbling dishes. Toward the back, a focaccia burns. The heat makes the two men sweat as they move in the direction of a pair of swing doors on the far side. The words *Dining Room* written above them.

It is as they reach them that the swing doors burst inwards and a gloved hand makes a sock-puppet appearance, firing a spray of machine-gun fire off the walls and ceiling. Blind cover fire as the rest of his team gets ready to charge.

As the bullets ping all around them, Victor and Leon take cover behind a tall chest refrigerator that blocks them from the doors. The hollow rattle of a stun grenade skittles across the hard floor. There's barely enough time to cover their eyes before it explodes in dazzling light. Another rattle, followed by a hiss, a third, and the kitchen rapidly fills with white smoke.

The SWAT begin shouting. *"Abandonnez-vous! Abandonnez-vouz! Nous vous avons entouré."*

Surrender! Surrender! We have you surrounded.

There follows a deafening period of quiet. Then Victor and Leon nod at each other, peel off from either side of the fridge and open fire.

Victor annihilates the corner of the doorframe with the Benelli. The seven-eighth-ounce shell holds a single solid lead slug. It blows the frame to splinters, sending the SWAT reeling back. The spring hinges fall apart and the heavy oak door cartwheels away. At the same time, Leon sends three two-second bursts of the CTAR at one of the men as the falling door pushes him out into the open. The initial burst hits the Frenchman's body armor and throws him off his feet. The second hits his legs as he goes down. The third strikes him under the chin, the bullets going all the way through and hitting the underside of his helmet so that it topples off.

The remaining SWAT do not take kindly to the killing of their comrade. They throw two more flash grenades, stunning the eyes of the two men in the kitchen. Then, as Victor and Leon duck back behind the fridge, they unload their weapons on them. The room sounds like an explosion of pyrotechnics—ratter-tat-tat of machine-gun fire, metal pings, shotgun blasts. The air moves, their eardrums recoiling from it all. Then it changes. The blasts aren't hitting the fridge any longer. The guns go dead. Silence cuts the air. Then bellows and cries come instead.

The quick zip of a suppressed bullet.

A piercing shriek cut off halfway.

Zip.

A sudden thud followed by a death-rattle hiss of last breath. A man pleads in French. *"S'il vous plaît, ne le faites pas. J'ai un—!"*

Please, don't. I have a—!

Zip.

Silence reigns briefly. The fridge no longer ricochets against their backs. A black boot materializes from the haze of the kitchen. Victor looks up and Peter melts into sight within the smoke.

"Come on."

The dining room is vast. The sun shines through a huge conservatory window that makes up the whole of the back wall. It covers the red carpet in squares of light. Stretching beyond the panes is a glittering swimming pool, followed by the hillside terraces that lead down to the Saône.

The men follow Peter between the round tables toward the massive window. Half-finished meals lie abandoned. Knives and forks lean on plates. Victor lifts his mask and picks up a pork chop. Leon goes to give him a dirty look but there isn't time.

A door on the far side swings open. Smoke grenades skittle across the polished parquet. Suppressing fire follows. Shotgun blasts to disorientate. Peter flips up one of the round tables. It is at least six feet across. Thick oak. Sixteenth century. Soaked in seawater for strength. He rolls the thing, the three men ducked behind it as the SWAT send a vicious volley at them, each bullet burying itself into the two inches of stone-hard rolling table.

They make it to the open doors, emerge into sunlight and make their way around the glittering blue waters of the pool. At the back of the terrace, stone steps lead down to the lower levels. At the next one, Peter leads his companions over a marble balustrade and into the garden of a neighboring château. From there he guides Victor and Leon through a maze of gardens, up and over walls, until they are finally spilling out of a gate onto a narrow cobbled street.

"What now?" Leon asks as they follow Peter along the deserted road, sirens and shouts ringing in their ears.

Peter remains taciturn. Around a corner is a line of parked cars. A red Audi RS3 beeps when Peter presses a key fob.

"Get in," he says as he slips into the driver's seat.

Victor and Leon get into the back. The car jolts out of its parking space and accelerates quickly down the slaloming road, the tires vibrating over the cobblestones, the men pinned back in their seats.

"You had an escape plan all along," Leon says, grinning and shaking his head.

Peter does no more than glance up at him from the rearview mirror as they hit the Quai de Bondy freeway. To their right, the river Saône glistens in the late afternoon sun like a silver snake. The Audi RS3 is a fast little sedan with great performance. Not too bulky and very popular in France. It's the type of car that doesn't stand out parked down a quiet road of Fourvière Hill for the last week. Waiting for just this type of eventuality.

Police cruisers stream out of the street to their left. The

Rue Louis Carrand. Their tires shriek as loud as their sirens as they come around the wide intersection in sweeping skids to tail the Audi.

The men in the back are worried. They are right in the heart of Lyon. One of France's most populated and congested cities. It is bustling and it is packed, the late-afternoon traffic clogging the city's arteries like fat.

Peter doesn't use the horn. He just zigs and zags between the slower-moving vehicles like a cheetah overtaking wildebeest, eyes focused on the road ahead, his mind guessing the potential movement of the other cars in a series of anticipated moves like a chess game.

They reach another intersection. The lights are red. The traffic lumbers to a stop. Every lane is filled. Victor and Leon grit their teeth as Peter propels the car up the high curb of the sidewalk, sending a crowd of people sprawling back against the railing of the riverbank.

Back on the road, Peter dodges the crisscrossing traffic. More police fly off the Pont de la Feuilée bridge directly to their right, the lead car almost smashing into the back of them. Victor and Leon hold on to anything they can as Peter swerves the Audi this way then that. The clattering sounds of a car crash draws their attention to the road behind. One of the police cars has hit a truck on the junction. Peter only has eyes for the front. A hundred meters ahead he spots a roadblock. A line of police cruisers and several big blue Citroen panel vans with their lights blasting in the low sun wait behind barricades.

Peter doesn't even say *hold on*. He pulls the handbrake. The rear end of the Audi lurches to the left, the hood spinning to the right, the men in the back thrown to the side, the door buckling under their weight. Shifting rapidly through the gears, Peter straightens the car and motors north, back up the cobbled streets of Fourvière Hill. He's annoyed. He didn't think they'd manage to get a barricade together this quickly. It means he has to make quick changes to his calculations.

He gets on the phone. Speakerphone. He begins speaking French the second it is answered. *"Claude, je vais avoir besoin de toi après tout. Es-tu prêt?"*

A gruff Frenchman replies, *"J'attends au rendez-vous."*

"D'accord. Je vais prendre deux minutes."

The call ends. Victor and Leon look sideways at each other.

Peter weaves around the cobbled streets, the tires skipping along the polished stones. They emerge back onto the Quai de Bondy, having circumnavigated the roadblock. More police sirens make Peter glance up in the mirror. They're at least a hundred meters away and getting farther.

Good. It means this should work.

Police appear up ahead and try to cut them off. Peter swerves right through another intersection. Coming round the front of a huge truck, he uses the racing handbrake he's had specially fitted to come across its grille, the trucker blasting his horn, and accelerate east over the Pont Koenig bridge.

On the opposite bank of the Saône, he turns left onto the Quai Saint-Vincent, motoring around the trams that amble slowly along underneath overhead cables. The Audi skirts the river all the way to the east until the Tunnel de la Croix-Rousse looms up. It is a great concrete wall covering part of the Saône's bank. Two semicircle tunnels burrow under the river and join up with the freeway on the other side.

"Not the tunnel!" Victor exclaims. "You'll get us trapped in the tunnel!"

Leon says nothing. It appears he has learned something in the last few minutes.

Peter takes the Nokia out. He calls the second number in it.

Way inside the guts of the tunnel, on the motor level, a small explosion occurs in the electrics room. It isn't much, but it's enough to scramble the fuse board, thus knocking out the lights and CCTV in the tunnel.

The tunnel's auxiliary lights come on. Drenching the lines of vehicles in scarlet. The Audi slips into the infrared darkness. The traffic has slowed, the auxiliary power illuminating the electronic signs that issue caution to the drivers and drop the speed limit to twenty. Yellow-colored lights stud the road, marking the three lanes. Two hundred meters in, a truck that is towing a forty-foot box-trailer has stopped in the righthand lane with its hazards blinking. The back of the trailer is open. A ramp leads into the dark box. Peter patiently waits for the car in front to steer around it. He, on the other hand, drives straight up the ramp and into the trailer, the Audi swallowed by pitch black.

"Get out," he says, switching off the engine and opening the door.

With the help of the others Peter pulls the ramp up into the trailer as sirens echo around the bend of the tunnel. An old and wrinkled face leans into the back. Seeing that the ramp is up, he nods at Peter, then shuts the back doors.

The trucker's short legs move fast, carrying him speedily

to the cab, where he scrambles up the steps, gets behind the wheel and drives the hulking rig away. Within seconds, police cruisers are streaming past, completely ignoring the truck as it ambles out of the tunnel.

The three men in the back listen out in the pitch black.

"I think we're safe," Victor says as the sirens begin to fade.

"How the fuck did you plan all of this?" Leon's voice whispers in the dark.

Like normal, Peter says nothing.

FIVE

It is night when they reach Chalamot, a small town in the Alpine foothills. Its quiet streets lie deserted as the truck rumbles down a narrow passage of road. The only life comes from a bar that takes up the corner of a crossroads.

A man stands outside the entrance, underneath a blinking neon sign. While the truck waits for the traffic lights to change from red, the man nods respectfully at the driver. The trucker's name is Claude. Claude nods back and touches his temple with a finger in response.

The lights change. With a crunch and a hiss the truck is back on its way.

Toward hilly forest is a wrecker's yard. Way back from the main road, it is hidden in a curtain of pines. Claude turns off and follows a winding dirt track that leads into it. Two men in coveralls stand waiting at the entrance for the truck and its long trailer to enter. Once it's in, they drag a solid steel gate across runners, thus closing the place off so that not even the trees can see inside.

Claude pulls up. The two men leave the gate and open up the back of the trailer. Peter, Victor and Leon jump down. Dogs bark nearby. Sheet metal rattles in the wind. Towers of wrecked cars block out the moon.

The men in coveralls climb inside the trailer. They drag the ramp to the edge and lay it out. While they retrieve the Audi, Peter and Claude walk off together. The Frenchman is in his late fifties. He is short, only five-five, with jaundiced skin and fading black hair. He looks close to death but his eyes are as bright as flaming diamonds. There is life in the little opium addict yet.

They speak in French. *"Merci, Claude. Je ne pensais pas avoir besoin de toi."*

Thank you, Claude. I didn't think I would need you.

Joyfully, the Frenchman replies, *"Je suis content. Votre peine m'a fait gagner plus d'argent!"*

I am glad. Your trouble has made me more money!

The old man is laughing as he walks off.

Claude's men are driving the Audi toward a crusher when Peter rejoins Victor and Leon by the truck.

"There is a safe house close by," he tells them. "Once you reach it, you must not leave until further notice. No matter what. Someone will bring food and anything else you may need to the house."

"Wait," Victor says. "We're staying?"

"It's too dangerous to try and leave the country at this moment in time. Even though they haven't released our faces, we still can't be sure they haven't got them. Or at least some image of us. We need to lay low until it's safe to leave France."

"So how long, then?"

"A day or two. Perhaps a week tops. But that's only if they don't have anything on us."

"What if they do?" Leon asks ominously.

"It could be a month or longer before we're safe."

"You gotta be kidding me," Victor complains.

His constant bitching is wearing thin on Peter. He says, "In the time you've known me, have I ever told a joke?"

"No."

"Well I'm not starting now. We've just been involved in a major incident. We need to bury ourselves and wait. Now can you remember an address?"

Victor frowns. "We're not stupid."

"44 Rue de Cascade. It's a mountain road east of here. Very few houses. Isolated. There's a car waiting for you by the gate over there. A blue Citroen. The keys are in it."

"You're not coming?" Leon asks.

"No. I prefer my own company."

Victor shrugs and rolls his eyes at his companion. "Sure," he says. "Why not."

With that, Victor walks off, hands in his pockets, heading toward the gate and the Citroen. Leon stays behind. He is staring at Peter so much that the latter feels obliged to ask, "What?"

"You knew they'd come," Leon says.

"No. I didn't. I only planned for the eventuality. Just because it happened doesn't mean I was expecting it to."

"All that stuff you planned out. How'd you predict it would go down like that?"

Peter thinks about it. "I guess I've been around a long time. After a while, everything—even this—has a ring of inevitability about it."

It's the only answer he can think of.

Leon gazes at him in a way that Peter only now realizes is awe. It makes him uncomfortable. Leon is looking at him the same way all those agency chiefs used to look at him whenever they'd get to meet him momentarily for one reason or another. They would look at Peter the same way they looked at some new assault rifle they'd just developed, or some sort of supersonic missile. That's all he was to them: a weapon. They had no interest in the man beneath all the training. All the death.

"How do you think they found us?" Leon asks next.

"I don't know."

SIX

It isn't a fact that lasts long. That night as he lies in an uncomfortable bed staring at the cracked walls of his safe house, Peter gets a call from Pat Hughes.

"It was the vehicle exchange," Pat tells him straight away.

On the edge of Monaco they had exchanged the Monte Carlos Municipal Works van for another vehicle; the one that had gotten them to Lyon. The exchange had happened in countryside on the northern edge of the principality. A place specifically chosen by Victor and Leon. It was a road of mansions tucked behind thick hedges and fortified gates. The houses were far away on the ends of long, winding driveways and the stretch of country road was as quiet as a graveyard.

But it was watched.

Pat fumes, "Almost every one of those gates along that road has a fucking camera recording all day. The second they found the van they went to those houses and got the footage. That's how they traced you all the way to the hotel."

During the initial planning phase, Peter had wondered whether it wouldn't be useful to have a second vehicle exchange halfway north to Lyon. Deciding it was overkill had cost him a lot of money and almost got him killed.

Caution, boy, an old woman's voice sneers in his ear.

"Those fucking idiots," Pat raves. "They almost cost us the whole thing."

SEVEN

It takes Pat Hughes a week to get confirmation that no agency in France has their faces or any other details that can stop them leaving the country on false papers. Their height and builds, perhaps. But nothing substantial. No names linked to any of the men. As for the cameras that had tracked their vehicle to Lyon, none had gotten a good enough picture due to the tinted windows Peter had made sure to fit the car with.

The French ultimately lost their chance at the Villa Florence.

Victor and Leon are nervous. Not just because the hit and subsequent escape is big news all over the world, but because there's been a change of plan. Not something they wanted to hear after a stressful seven days holed up in some mildew-stinking trailer in the middle of the woods.

Last night after giving them confirmation they could leave, Pat Hughes had added one final instruction. They were to meet the "freak" in a multi-storey parking garage in Lille. One which was currently under construction.

"The security guard at the front will let you in," Pat had told them. *"Drive the car up to the fourth level and wait."*

"But why we gotta meet him there?"

"Just a little change of plan."

In other words: Don't ask, don't tell.

So the two men wait, standing together on the fourth level, plastic sheeting rattling in the wind behind them, obscuring the sun-swept city beyond.

Leon: "You think he's pissed about them being on board the boat?"

Victor: "What does it matter? There was no other way to get the target."

"But we told him it'd only be Gregor and the crew."

"For all he knows we got it wrong. Simple mistake. So what?"

"It's just he was clear. Don't involve them."

"And the client overruled him. End of. Anyway," Victor says, turning sideways to meet Leon with his shrunken eyes, "why are you so scared if he knows?"

Leon takes a few seconds. He looks to be mulling something over in his head. Finally, "I don't like dicking the guy over, is all."

"It never bothered you before."

"But that wasn't *this* guy."

Victor cocks an eye. "What's so special about *this* guy?"

"I get a feeling about him."

"Who are you? My aunt Lucy. You get a feeling. Based on what?"

"Based on something I heard once."

Victor lowers his gaze. "You gonna continue being so vague? What did you once hear, Leo?"

"A description about a guy that matches this one."

"A description of what guy?"

"Azrael."

The name drops like a lead balloon. Victor takes a few seconds. Then, "Azrael? You think this guy is Azrael?"

"Yep."

"Now, Leo, correct me if I'm wrong, but are you saying that this mumbling *freak* is the same cold bastard that pulled off Prague?"

"That would be correct."

"Prague?"

"I said yes, didn't I?"

"This guy?"

Leon just looks at him.

Victor is shaking his fat head. "No fucking way."

Leon snorts up through his wide nostrils. "Well, I think it is. That's why I don't like lying to him."

"You're shitting me, right?"

"You'll find no bullshitting here, old friend. I can assure you of that."

Victor is grinning. So absurd is the idea to him. "You think the guy who spent the whole ride from Monaco to Lyon humming that stupid tune is none other than the CIA's former number-one assassin?"

"It's the humming that makes me think it is."

Victor just looks at him.

To little avail, Leon adds, "The tune he was humming."

"So what?"

"You remember Jonny Harris back at the agency? One of Irvin's guys."

"The one that got VD in Colombia?"

"That's him."

"What about him?"

"Jonny worked with Azrael during the Hossein Hamadani assassination."

"So he knew the guy?"

"Not exactly. Jonny was part of the extraction team that got Azrael out of Syria. Him and his crew spent an afternoon waiting around at some desert runway, standing at the back of a Hercules, everyone eager to see the legend that is Azrael, when this pickup riddled with bullet holes comes flying out of the dust, pulls a skid right in front of them and out gets this five-ten mouse who looks like he ain't slept for weeks. He's wearing some muj costume over the top of a dead Marine's body armor, the jarhead's name and class still stenciled onto it. He's holding a Kalashnikov in one hand and a spent Luger in the other, covered from head to toe in muj blood. And he just walks past Jonny and his team like they ain't even there. Sits himself down in some lonely corner of the plane and spends the whole journey out of there humming this old-timey tune. The whole ride back to base he's humming it. So much so that Jonny and the others couldn't get it out of their heads afterwards."

Leon stares at Victor. Pigeons coo in the concrete roof beams. One flies across the lot in front of them, landing on a stack of ply sheets that lean against a chipboard wall.

"So correct me if I'm wrong," Victor says. "Are you saying that it's the same tune the freak keeps humming?"

"Back when I spoke with Jonny, he hummed it for me."

The frown on Victor's face deepens as he directs it at Leon. He resembles an English bulldog. "That ain't enough," he eventually says, turning away to face the lot. "And, anyway, the agency caught up with Azrael years ago. He's dead. This guy ain't him."

"No one ever proved he was dead," Leon points out. "And I've heard plenty of stories about him still working freelance."

"It ain't this guy," Victor assures him.

"He got us out of Lyon, didn't he?"

"Oh, and we had nothing to do with that? Big deal. We could've—"

He stops when Leon nudges his chest with an elbow.

"Look. He's here."

The grumbling of a diesel engine echoes off the lot. It isn't long before a panel van bumbles up the concrete ramp toward them. The driver is wearing yellow shades. Medium-length brown hair drapes down the back and sides of his head, the fringe cut just above the eyebrows. He looks like a completely different person. His chin seems more shallow that it was before. The eyes further apart. For a second or two they think it *is* a different person, and it is only when he speaks that they're sure it's Peter.

As Victor opens the passenger door, Peter says, "Hold up. I need help with something."

"Help?"

"Yeah. We gotta leave something here for the cleanup crew."

"What?"

Peter doesn't answer. He gets out. He's dressed in coveralls with a company logo stitched on the breast. *SUEZ—*

Recyclage et Élimination. He leads them to the back of the van, where he flips a tail lift down and opens the double doors.

There are two metal drums inside.

It doesn't take long for them to get the drums onto two sack bearers and off the van. After, Peter leads them as they wheel the drums across the construction site toward a door cut into a chipboard wall.

Peter is carrying a long tool bag, the zip slightly open.

"Not much farther."

"What's in these drums, anyway?"

Peter doesn't reply. He merely opens the door cut into the partition.

"Just in there," he says, pointing the way. "The light takes a couple of seconds."

Victor makes a face at Leon, who shrugs, and they both push the drums inside.

It is as they reach the middle of the room that the light shudders into existence and both men freeze where they are.

All the walls are covered in plastic sheeting. So is the floor. They wheel around just in time to see the silenced HK45 pointed right at them. Two shots, quick, efficient, and both men drop to the floor sporting bullet holes in their foreheads.

Peter kneels down beside the tool bag, placing the gun back. While he fetches things, he thinks back to last night's phone conversation.

"The client insists on the two mercenaries being eliminated," Pat had said. *"He wants to limit who knows."*

"I thought as much."

"You okay with that? He's offered another two hundred grand."

"Count it done," Peter had replied, thinking back to the bogus intel both men had provided him.

Peter slides his arms into thick rubber gloves that reach the elbows. He puts his head through the loop of a rubber apron and ties it up at the back of his waist. Next, he opens the drums he had the men wheel into the room and stands back as the acrid stench rises up at him.

Taking a box cutter from the tool bag, he removes both men's clothing and drops it into one of the drums. He removes their jewelry. Wedding bands. Army tags. Knocks out Leon's gold tooth with a hammer. Then he uses a medical circular saw to cut their arms, legs and heads off. Each piece he places in the drums.

As he holds the head of Victor over the acid, he looks him in the squinty eyes and hears his voice say, *"I told you. Leon and I have been watching him all month. The kid's at some Swiss boarding school. Neither the boy nor the wife will be with Gregor when he comes to port."*

Peter drops the head. Bubbles cover the flesh like piranhas as it sinks to the bottom.

EIGHT

VERMONT, 1999

HARRY THE DETECTIVE TROTTED AFTER AGENT *Kazinsky as she left St. Joseph's with the boy. The latter didn't have a coat, so her own sat over his thin frame. He was filthy and ragged. Bruised skin circled his eyes. Pale skin covered the rest of him. A rash lined the edges of his chapped lips. He was nothing but a stunted, anemic skin-and-bones boy. Jane Kazinsky knew all too well the signs of prolonged malnourishment.*

As he dragged his feet across the snowy asphalt, the boy's right side drooped, his cuffed hands sticking out the front of the coat at an angle, the metal hoops hanging off his bony wrists like bracelets.

The state troopers, who were still lingering about the entrance, watched them as they entered the lot. Behind Harry, State Trooper Moore followed like a lost dog, feeling the need to continue with the others as a threesome. Being as that was how they'd started.

"You can't just take him," Harry was saying.

"I can and I am, Detective. Didn't you read the paperwork?"

"It may have escaped your notice, but tonight that little demon killed a man. And not just that. He managed to knock the shit outta the four troopers that caught up with him."

Stopping suddenly, she spun on them, a pair of cold eyes aimed at the detective. "I also see what your troopers have done to him," *she seethed. "His collarbone is broken, is it not?"*

Trooper Moore explained, "We did that trying to subdue the little brat."

With a widening of the eyes, Harry added, "And yet he don't make no peep. Don't that seem weird to you? Boy his age not crying or howling with an injury like that. It's like he's on PCP or meth."

She felt the need to remind him that he was an eleven-year-old boy.

Trooper Moore piped in: "I seen 'em as young as ten on that shit." He stared at her with an honest expression.

"That ain't no eleven-year-old boy there, Agent Kazinsky," Harry raved. "That there is a demon incarnate."

Rolling her eyes, she turned back around and continued across the lot until they reached her car.

"Take these handcuffs off him," she barked when they did.

"You got your own pair?"

"No."

The two cops looked at each other. Frowned.

Harry turned back to her. "Then you can have the ones he's got on. Trooper," he said over his shoulder, "give her the key. I'll make sure to bill Rutland in the morning."

"I won't be needing them," she told him. "All I want is for you to get them off of him."

"I wouldn't advise that, ma'am," Trooper Moore said, coming forward with the keys, a look of forewarning on his face. "His current serene demeanor is most likely nothing but a cunning ruse."

Harry pursued the matter. "He's likely to go nuts the second they're off."

Agent Jane Kazinsky stepped right up to the detective. A pair of gray eyes burning in her skull. "I said take them off."

NINE

HIS NAME WAS PETER BLACK. THOUGH HIS surname wasn't important. He wouldn't be needing it from now on.

Five minutes after leaving the orphanage, Agent Kazinsky stopped at an all-night diner that sat on the side of the highway. The converted boxcar shone in the snow like a beacon. Peter sat forward the second he spotted the big ol' sign on top proclaiming Glen's Diner in blinking yellow lights.

They sat opposite each other by the window. A radio played gently in the background. The chef mopped behind the counter. A waitress sat at the end by the register reading a romance paperback.

Agent Kazinsky's and Peter's reflections shone back at them from the dark window. She was thin faced and stern. He was pitiful. Every so often headlight beams fanned across them as a car went by. While she smoked, he polished off his third bacon cheeseburger. Glen made a good one by the looks of things.

Blowing smoke into the air, she said, "We'll have to see to that arm before we reach the airfield. Can't have you flying with it."

Peter looked up from the hamburger. "I'm going on a plane?"

"Yes."

"Ain't never been on no plane before."

"Then it will be new experience."

Peter continued eating. But after a while he stopped, as if caught by a thought, and looked across at her. "So is this my last meal or something?" he asked.

"Your last meal?"

"Yeah."

"Last meal before what?"

"Before I go to the electric chair."

She grinned. The silly imaginations of little boys.

"Who said anything about going to the electric chair?"

"Ain't that where I'm going? For," he sighed, "what I did?"

"No, Peter. You are not going to the electric chair."

"Then where am I going?"

"Alaska."

The boy narrowed his eyes at her. "What's in Alaska?"

"Your new home."

"Jail?"

"Perhaps you'll find it even worse."

"What's worse than jail?"

"That all depends on you. Now eat up. We need to see doctor about your collarbone."

TEN

DOGS BARKED MERCILESSLY IN THEIR CAGES WHILE *in a darkened corner a sleepy-eyed vet stood alongside Agent Kazinsky. Peter sat on the edge of a table, his legs hanging off, naked from the waist up.*

"You're lucky it's not a compound fracture," the vet said, scratching the back of his neck. "I would have had to wake up my nurse if that were the case."

Agent Kazinsky didn't speak. She was staring at the scars and bruising covering Peter's body.

"Who is this kid, anyway?" the vet asked out of the side of his mouth.

"You know not to ask," she said sternly.

"Yeah. Sorry. Anyway, let's get this shoulder reset. I can give him a little pain relief, but he looks too malnourished to take anything strong. Shouldn't matter, though. The pain doesn't seem to have bothered him so far."

He is eleven, *she was thinking.* He is eleven and already

he is desensitized to pain. *It took her years of training as an adult to reach that point. This boy has reached it all by himself through nothing but the horror of experience.*

ELEVEN

AGENT KAZINSKY DROVE THEM THROUGH THE snowy night, the wipers stacking the flakes at the sides of the windshield. She would put one smoke out and light another, and this had been continuous since they had left the vet.

"Your name's not Jane, is it?"

She swiveled her neck to eye Peter curiously. "What makes you say that?"

"The nameplate on your bracelet. It has the initials K.I.B. No J for Jane."

She glanced down at her wrist. "How do you know it doesn't stand for something else?"

"Maybe. But then why do you have all those other IDs?"

"What other IDs?"

"The ones inside your purse."

She narrowed her eyes at him.

He went on. "There are two more for the FBI. One for the Washington office, another for New York. Your picture is on each one, but with different names. Eileen Walsh on the

Washington one and Daphne Porter on the other. There's also an ID for military intelligence. That one says Susanne Chalmers. So which is it; Jane, Eileen, Daphne, Susanne, or something beginning with K?"

She couldn't help staring across the car at the boy in amazement. The IDs were tucked inside her purse. He had never been alone with it. She was sure of that. Glancing to her left, she could see that the purse was now safely in the side of the door. In her mind, there was no possible way he could have gotten into the purse and studied its contents. No way.

The only time she could think that he might have seen into it was the one occasion she'd opened it in front of him. This was when she'd paid at the diner. It must have been open for no longer than a couple of seconds as she'd slipped a ten out. It was the only way he could have caught a momentary glimpse of what was inside. But, then, how in the hell could he have read all that information in just a few seconds?

Unless.

Turning back to the road, she smiled. "Very observant, Peter. What else can you tell me?"

"That you ain't American. Or at least weren't raised here."

"What makes you say that?"

"You mispronounce words and vibrate your tongue too much when you speak. Also, every so often you drop the and a from sentences. It makes you sound foreign like some of the kids at the home."

"Which children?"

"Their parents come from places like Russia mostly. You Russian?"

She was grinning. "I was Russian. A long long time ago."
Her face went a little sad.

He observed that, too.

"What else?" she asked.

"We've traveled sixty-eight miles since we left the orphanage. Eight to the diner. Sixty since. We spent twenty-four minutes at the diner and an hour and thirty two minutes driving. That means we've been traveling at an average speed of roughly 44 miles an hour. Which is understandable in the snow."

"Keep going."

"You're left handed. You chew your nails. The waitress at the diner has a tattoo of a dolphin across her ankle. The chef had two of his front teeth missing. And the weatherman on the radio said the snow's expected to keep on until early March."

He turned back to the window. He was beginning to feel like a freak. Just like he did when the other kids at the home made him do sums while one of them checked on a calculator. Beat him up and got him to tell them how many punches and how many kicks he'd had. The poor boy cursed to remember everything.

Everything.

"So, anyway," he said, "you never did say your name. What do I call you?"

Turning to face him, she replied, "You call me Mother."

TWELVE

THREE HOURS OF DRIVING AND THEY WERE CLOSE to the military airfield. There, they were due to grab a C-130 Hercules to Fairbanks, Alaska. Peter had fallen fast asleep not long after their conversation. "Mother" couldn't help continually checking on him. The boy curled up in the seat like a cat, her coat acting as a blanket. It looked like the most peaceful sleep he'd had in a long time.

He started to murmur, his limbs fidgeting underneath the coat. His lips began twitching, like he was trying to say something, and his mouth suddenly opened wide like he was shouting. But only a hiss came out.

Mother thought he was about to scream when his eyes snapped open. Rabid, bulging eyes that darted about the car, searching for some way out.

He sat forward with such force that she feared he might go through the windshield. Then he threw himself back into the seat, holding his throat like he had something stuck in it.

"No... (Huh!) No... (Huh!)" he gasped at her.

His face was wrought with terror, the fingers of his good hand gripping the dashboard. The hand came away and began scratching at his seat belt. The buckle popped. As he tried to open the door, Mother slammed on the brakes. On the icy surface the car went into a semi-spin. She controlled it and brought them to a sideways stop.

The door flew open and Peter flung himself down into the snow. Choking, gasping, trying to pull himself up off his hands and knees. His face going blue. Colorless lips struggling to open.

Thankfully there were no other cars, the road deserted.

Mother reached him. Got down onto her knees, placed an arm beneath his shoulders, cradled him onto her lap, the waif looking up at her with eyes about to pop.

"You are having a panic attack, Peter," she calmly told him, her face as soft and composed as it could be. "You need to take your mind off it. I want you to sing with me."

His own face screwed up even more.

"Sing with me, Peter," she urged.

"I... can't... breathe."

"Peter, it is only panic attack. All in your mind. It will end if you can take that same mind off it. So sing with me. It will help."

He stared up at her as she began warbling softly. She had a nice voice. She had a nice singing voice that he would remember forever.

"What'll I do, When you are far away, And I am blue, What'll I do?"

She stopped. Told him to sing along.

"I don't... (Huh!) know... (Huh!) the words."

"Then listen to me and hum along." She went on singing.

"When I'm alone, With only dreams of you, That won't come true, What'll I do?"

Peter began humming along. Soon he was calm, his breathing back to normal, the color returning to his face. There, in the dirty sludge of a winter highway, he learned for the first time that a lot of life is all in the mind.

THIRTEEN

PARIS, 2019

THE HAZEL EYES HAUNT PETER'S SLEEP. THE
white-toothed smile gleaming in the Aegean sun. The
captain letting him wear his cap. Steer the boat. The boy
smiling wildly as they leave port. Calling back to his father.
"Look, Papa. Look, I am steering. I am steering the boat out
of the—"

The world ends in a flash. The delayed bang. The
midsection exploding from within and sending a massive
fireball upwards through the deck. Incinerating all that
innocence.

Rule Five has been broken. *Never hurt an innocent.* No
coming back from this.

PETER WAKES up in pitch black. He can't breathe. So he
murmurs the song.

"What'll I do?" seethes from between his teeth.

Three minutes later he is able to shower. When he gets out, he changes himself. A goatee beard is applied. He doesn't wear a wig with this one. He uses his real hair, which is shaved to a grade two. A pregnancy belt is harnessed to his torso to make him look fat. A vest is rolled down over the top of it. A polo shirt over that. Black so people get the impression he's trying to hide the belly. He transfers a fake tattoo to his upper left arm, some generic Celtic band. A Lakers baseball cap tops his head and Oakleys hide his eyes. Completing the look are cargo shorts, white socks pulled all the way up, and sports sandals.

Finding a passport under the name of Dwayne Peterson, Peter pockets it and begins packing the rest of his things away, tossing his former disguise in a trash bag which he'll get rid of on his way to Charles de Gaulle Airport.

Before he leaves, he calls Pat Hughes.

"I'm going back stateside," he says the second Hughes picks up. "Returning to the wind for a while."

"I understand."

"Monaco... It wasn't..." Peter trails off.

"No need to explain," Pat says. "Call me when you want another one."

"Sure thing."

FOURTEEN

CALIFORNIA, 2019

A DAY LATER, PETER WALKS TOWARD A SILVER pickup on the long-term level of the LAX multi-story parking garage. It's early morning. The sun has only just risen over the Sierra Nevada mountain range and the vehicles bask in golden light. Airplanes roar overhead.

The pickup is in a corner away from the outer edges of the concrete structure. The security cameras here are broken. As are many of the lights. Sitting in shadow, it is only when he gets close that Peter can clearly make out the Ford Ranger.

He doesn't walk straight to it. Instead, he heads to a concrete pillar that is five or six yards directly behind the pickup. He kneels at its base, looks about.

This level of the garage is deserted.

Free from a watcher's gaze, Peter uses a pocket knife to prize out something stuck in the pillar. It is no bigger than the head of a thumbtack and practically invisible in the low light. When he gets purchase on it, he pulls out a tiny, cylindrical camera, retrieving a length of wires that trail behind it.

Two years ago, disguised as a workman, Peter carved a cavity into the pillar and cemented inside a lithium polymer battery with a life expectancy of five years. Plugged into that are a hard drive and a night-vision camera. Motion sensors placed on the pickup activate the camera remotely whenever something comes too close to it.

The cautious rabbit always checks his burrow for the scent of predators before entering.

Peter pulls a USB wire from the cavity and plugs it into his phone using an adaptor. There's a total of three-and-a-half minutes of footage that he watches in fast-forward. Highlights include: a plastic bag carried on the wind hitting the driver's door, where it stays for thirty seconds before slipping up the car and continuing on its journey. A stray dog that spends the night underneath the pickup, intermittently setting the camera off. And a drunk that pisses up against the passenger door.

That's it. The pickup is safe.

FIFTEEN

HAVING DRIVEN NORTH ON INTERSTATE 5, PETER crosses Bakersfield to Breckenridge Mountain, entering remote, hilly woodland. It is nine thirty. The mid-morning sun strobes between the tall pines that border the winding road.

Close to the top, where the terrain becomes rocky, Peter pulls onto a track that takes him up past boulders and trees, away from the main road. In a clearing stands a severely run-down trailer and a car shrouded in blue tarpaulin. At the edges, Douglas fir trees crowd around it all like a protective cape.

Peter parks the Ford Ranger and checks a fencepost that sticks out on the corner of the lot. It faces the trailer and the car. Like in the parking garage, he pulls a camera from it, links the USB to his phone and watches.

It is mostly wind that sets off the motion sensors. A deer comes through. Beautiful and full of grace, it sniffs about, then bolts. Only once is there anything interesting. Two hunters come across the trailer. Try the door. Check the windows. But when the door won't easily budge, they decide to leave it. Don't even bother looking under the tarp at the car or breaking a window.

They're just inquisitive. Not thieves.

After returning the camera to its hiding place, Peter pulls folded tarp from underneath the trailer and throws it over the pickup. This done, he opens up the trailer.

There is nothing of interest inside. Even if those two hunters had broken in, they would have found no more than a bunch of rusted gardening tools.

Peter takes a shovel into the woods. Summer is ending, so the air is cooler. Somewhere deeper down the valley a campfire burns and the smell of smoke mixes with the soapiness of the pine.

In a clearing, Peter stands listening for a moment. Circling eagles shriek above him. The wind rustles through the trees and a car engine rumbles gently in the distance.

When he is certain he is all alone, Peter clears the ground of broken branches and other debris, using the shovel to flick the dross away. The earth underneath is hard. He has to strike it several times to break it up, but soon he is scooping it aside, the latex pregnancy belt becoming soaked with sweat.

About four inches down, he finds the corner of a sheet of tarpaulin. Pulling it up and across, the earth comes away, exposing a hatch buried within the hillside. It is a set of metal doors about the size of a manhole cover with an electronic keypad in the center. Peter keys in a code and the bolt locks slide automatically to the side. Down below is a cellar about the size of a small garage. Strip lighting jumps into action the second he's inside, the buzz filling the cramped space.

A weapons rack fills the end wall of the excavation, but he ignores the layout of guns. He's not here for that. He's here for the wardrobe next to it. He's here for *Paul*.

Fifteen minutes later a very different man lifts himself out of the cellar. Gone is the belly, the goatee. Now he has blond hair shaped like a bowl and a full beard. He likens himself to Benny from ABBA. He's wearing an Atari T-shirt, a sleeveless purple hoodie and denim cut-offs. The socks and sandals stay.

Peter looks every bit the dot.com hipster wannabe he's trying to portray.

He covers the hatch back up, returns the shovel to the trailer, and uncovers the other car. It is a marine green Saab 900. Dwayne Peterson drives the Ford. Paul Adams drives a Saab.

Tradecraft is so important for hunted men like Peter. Vital for him to fade into any given setting. Because everywhere people are looking for the one they call *Azrael*.

Over the years he has set up a series of identities which are dotted along the West Coast. All with their own documentation, vehicles, houses, clothing, hair, faces, voices, lives. Ready to be used at any point. Because it's not just about a safe house: it's about a safe identity. Therefore, each house has its own identity attached to it. Los Angeles has Dwayne Peterson. Monterey has Paul Adams. Other names live in other places. Each safe house with its own pretend version of Peter. A multitude of personalities. All with one thing in common: they are reclusive males in their thirties living entirely alone.

Quite often, Peter gets the natural urge to lower his guard. To lessen the lengths he goes to for all this subterfuge. But Peter knows that he may be able to survive six months, even a year, in a less cautious state, but eventually they'd get him. Over those six months, that year, they would be receiving sightings and reports, and after a time they would have gathered enough intel on his movements to predict a pattern of behavior that leads them to catching him.

One day Peter would return to a safe car, a safe house, or some drop spot, and there would be a man with a gun waiting for him.

SIXTEEN

AT THE TOP OF MONTEREY LIES THE SPRAWLING suburb of Pacific Grove. A crisscross of neighborhoods, it is the home of Paul Adams.

The houses are a mixture of bungalows and two-stories built in the colonial style. All of them have long porches that are perfect for watching the world go by. 24 Green Street is a nondescript two-story, nestled in a nondescript lower-middle-class neighborhood.

"Oh, Mr. Adams?" his elderly neighbor Mrs. Harrison calls out from her porch.

Peter is retrieving a box of groceries from the trunk of the Saab. His driveway is on the same side as her porch. The one she spends practically all day sitting on, her old eyes studying all that goes on in Green Street.

Creaking old bones climb up out of a lawn chair. Placing a detective thriller down, she waltzes across her lawn to meet him at the short hedge that divides their properties.

Peter leaves the groceries and walks over.

"Mr. Adams," she says breezily, "how was your trip? Texas, wasn't it?"

"Yes, ma'am," Peter replies in Paul Adams's emotionless voice. "It was very productive, thank you. How have things been here?"

She studies him a while.

He avoids contact with her eyes as if they are the sun.

Margaret Harrison is seventy-two. She is tall with a crooked back. She used to dye her wavy hair black, but since her husband passed she has let it go pale silver. Peter thinks it actually looks better. She doesn't wear anything with color anymore either. Now the only thing that is black is her clothing.

Peter doesn't think this is better.

"Oh, just the usual boring days of suburbia," she replies to his question. "Quiet. Except for perhaps the other week."

"What happened the other week?" comes automatically from Peter's mouth.

Mrs. Harrison smiles as she recounts the tale. "The yard kids caused a stink when they shattered the windshield on Bert Chambers's car while playing street hockey." She smiles a set of veneers at him, using a hand to shield her eyes from the bright sun. "Apart from that," she concludes, "it's been a pleasant few months. A good summer by all accounts."

Peter notes in his head that it is only her second without her husband.

As though thinking the same thing, her smile turns sad.

"Well," Peter says, "it's been nice talking, Mrs. Harrison. I'd better get these groceries in."

The old woman says nothing. She continues to stare at him. It is like she has become frozen. Peter goes to walk away when she touches his arm from across the hedge.

Their eyes momentarily meet when he glances back at her.

"I worry about you, Paul," she says softly, motherly.

"You don't..."

"You're always alone. You go away for months on end. Working all alone in foreign places."

"Texas isn't foreign."

"You know what I mean. You work in places far from home. I imagine you stay in some sort of motel. All alone. Then you come back and spend a week or two here by yourself. Don't you get lonely? You've lived here all this time and I've never seen a girlfriend, a friend, or even any family come to your house."

He wants to tell her he was born alone and he'll die alone. Just like her. But he doesn't want to bum her out. So instead he says, "I have hobbies. Along with work, they keep me busy."

She glances over his shoulder at number 24.

"You know, a family used to live in your house," she says. "A family with four boys. Always making a racket." A nostalgic smile curves her lips. "They're all grown up now. My Tommy keeps in touch with the eldest. Frank, I think. Oh, that house used to be so alive with noise. Just like..."

She trails off. Meets his eyes. An apologetic look on her face.

"I'm sorry," she says, the sad smile back.

"It's okay, Mrs. Harrison."

He gently pulls his arm away, retrieves the groceries from the trunk. She's still gazing at his house as he opens the front door.

Peter realizes it's her own loneliness that she sees in him.

SEVENTEEN

Inside the house, Peter places the box of groceries on the kitchen sideboard and begins putting them away. Afterwards, he opens all the windows and shutters, letting the cool ocean air flow through the place. Going from room to room, his footsteps echoing on the hardwood floor, he removes sheets from the furniture, dust billowing up into the air, the motes sparkling in the sunlight.

It is twenty minutes later while vacuuming that Peter checks his wristwatch and sees the time is four in the afternoon. He switches off the noisy machine and heads upstairs. In the master bedroom is a tall window that leads to a balcony. It overlooks Peter's backyard. The house stands on a hill. It is higher than the houses at its rear. This gives it the perfect view of the street behind, Palm Avenue.

Peter takes a position a couple of meters back from the window, so that he can see out of it but remain hidden in the relative darkness of the room. His gaze travels along the length of his terracotta patio, the striped lawn, past the cherry blossom trees at the end, and past the Hendersons' place beyond his back wall. Scanning a hundred yards to the right, his eyes finally settle on the corner of Elm Drive and Palm Avenue, where a big yellow school bus is pulling up.

When the doors hiss open the only person to get off is a boy of twelve. The kid is small and skinny. He's teased for it, the other kids calling him runt. His mousy hair pokes up at the front in a cowlick. He's wearing glasses that make his left eye, which is lazy, much larger than the right. It can't help with asking girls to the prom. Peter is sure of this. Even though he only knows what a prom is from films and TV. *Carrie* being the most prominent in his imagination.

The kid scuttles along, watching over his shoulder; a cautious rabbit far from the warren—naked, in danger, sensing predators. The distance between here and the safety of the burrow is only a block and a half. But to his electric senses it may as well be miles.

Peter imagines the kid's whiskers twitch.

There's a shout. It comes from across the street.

The kid is running before they've even gotten out of the alleyway. Three older boys. Neighborhood bullies.

The same game is played out most school days. The high school bus gets back ten minutes earlier than the junior one. It gives those three vicious dogs prime time to hide up and wait for the rabbit, getting hungrier by the second as they loiter around smoking cigarettes stolen from their parents and playing with a flick-knife they robbed from a store.

The kid reaches Palm Avenue, heading east in the direction of number 37. Castle Henderson. The kid's burrow.

"Will he make it today?" Peter asks aloud.

The chasing pack split up. As the Henderson kid heads

down the sidewalk, the fastest chaser runs around a line of parked cars and heads him off, the vehicles acting as a wall on the kid's left, while fencing and front yards block the right.

This trick has worked for them before. But today the rabbit has planned in advance and pulls a trick of his own. He drops a shoulder and darts suddenly right, ducking through the Jamesons' gate.

Good old lazy Mr. Jameson. He still hasn't fixed the catch since last autumn's storm, and the kid knows it.

The bullies, annoyed that they've lost their chance to end things early, race after him through the gate and Peter has to use field glasses to see them as they head down the side of the house and into the Jamesons' backyard.

Frank Jameson is barbecuing a belly of pork on his patio, holding a sauce brush in one hand, a bottle of Coors in the other. He's all beer gut bursting over shorts, Hawaiian shirt open onto a sunburnt chest, his bald head shining like a diamond in the sun.

"Hey! Y'little shits!" he yells after them as they run past.

The kid's a good jumper. He vaults over the wall at the end, avoiding Mrs. Jameson's flowerbeds, and drops down into an alleyway that backs onto the houses. Here is where he's real smart, and Peter realizes that the kid has figured a new escape route since he last watched.

The boy travels left, reaches the open gate of the next house, number 20, and ducks through as the property's owner Mrs. Murphy stands at the back door. She is holding her Yorkshire terrier Sandy in the crook of an arm and ushering the kid toward the bungalow, the old lady obviously in on the trick.

The kid closes the gate behind himself with silent

caution and runs to her. Once he is inside, Mrs. Murphy checks to see if the ploy has been witnessed, and when she is sure all is safe, she closes the sliding door.

The three bullies are in the alley searching up and down. One searches one way. Another goes the other. But the head boy stays in the passage, close to Mrs. Murphy's back gate. It's like he can sniff where the kid has been and senses the trick.

His name is Danny Palmer, a great lump of a kid with a mean alcoholic for a father and a stepmother more interested in his younger half-sister. Only fourteen, he is already cruel and hateful.

On Palm Avenue, the Henderson kid is waving back to Mrs. Murphy and her dog as he jogs across the street holding a cookie. Safe from harm, he enters number 37 Palm Avenue with the casual air of a winner.

Today was yours, kid, Peter thinks as he stands in the shadows watching. *Today was yours.*

EIGHTEEN

WITH THE SUN ALMOST DOWN, PETER STANDS AT the front of his house watering the yard. A local gardening company sees to it while he's away. While here, however, he always makes a point of maintaining it himself.

Rule Three: Don't stand out.

Not looking after your house makes you stand out. It brings attention and causes friction with neighbors. The last thing Peter wants on Green Street is friction.

The Ronsons go jogging by. Jack and Kenny. Husband and husband. They live at 47 Green Street. Jack's an orthodontist with his own practice. Kenny is a real estate agent.

They wave as they pass. "Hey, Paul."

They remember his name. Or at least his alias.

Peter smiles and waves back. He doesn't call out "Hey" in return because it's not the type of thing the introverted Paul Adams would do. Ironically, it's not the type of thing the introverted Peter would do either.

In the front window of the house opposite, number 16, the curtains keep twitching. They've been at it ever since Peter first pulled the hose out and began. A nose like a beak pokes out. It belongs to Larry Jenkins. Larry and his wife Pam don't like Peter. Or at least they don't like Paul Adams. They ignore him. Often in front of others. Like the time Peter spotted Pam Jenkins in the local 7-Eleven. She was standing with Kenny Ronson and Judy Chambers. The Chambers live at number 12. Walking into the store, Peter said a polite hello to each of them. No chitchat. Just polite.

Kenny and Judy smiled and said hello back. Pam Jenkins just stared at him. Like she could see right through his stupid Paul Adams getup. The blond hair. The fake beard. The clothing of a man who's never had a woman to guide him.

Had he gone too far? Tried too hard to look like a nobody? To fade right in?

Peter waves at the Jenkins house and the curtain drops.

He doesn't mind the hostility. No one on the street likes the Jenkinses anyway. Their lawn is ratty and their house is falling apart. This causes friction with the neighborhood. And if Peter can avoid friction while the Jenkinses cause it, he is sure that their hostility won't spread to the others.

NINETEEN

PETER LIKES TO TAKE HIS EVENING MEAL ON THE balcony with the surrounding neighborhood spread out around him. In the darkness the lit windows twinkle like stars. A single candle burns on the table, illuminating in flickering shadow a plate of filet mignon and new potatoes cooked in rosemary and butter.

Every so often he glances at his rear neighbor, number 37 Palm Avenue. The Hendersons.

The curtains are open on the expansive window of their dining room. They sit eating dinner around an oval table. The Hendersons are made up of Carl, wife Kate and son Michael: the kid. Carl is a high school teacher—and yes, he does teach Danny Palmer, his son's tormentor. Kate is a legal secretary working at a small law firm in the city. They are a handsome couple. Kate has long, frizzy blonde hair and the type of face that still makes high school boys swoon. Carl is dark haired and athletic, but in the jogger sense.

Their evening meal contrasts strongly with Peter's.

Carl Henderson is telling his family a story. He is an arch raconteur and always so animated when spinning yarns, his arms waving about to illustrate his many points. From where Peter sits he can't read his lips, and doesn't dare to use field glasses while in the open, but he's sure that the story is funny by the way Kate and Michael keep bursting into giggles, wriggling around in their chairs.

Peter ponders whether the family aren't producing enough warmth amongst them to illuminate a lightbulb. Benevolence seems to glow out of them, and regardless of Michael's earlier close shave with the bullies, the kid looks, for all intents and purposes, to be happy now.

His burrow is a kind place.

Watching them, Peter finds that he cannot finish his food. The steak has gone dry in his mouth and the whole meal now looks strangely unappetizing. Sighing, he places his knife and fork down and pushes the plate to the side.

TWENTY

INSTEAD OF FINISHING THE FOOD PETER DECIDES to do a job. A Paul Adams job.

It's 7:30 on the dot when he arrives at the door to 18 Palm Avenue. The yellow stucco bungalow is directly opposite the Henderson place. The bungalow to the right belongs to Mrs. Murphy, Michael Henderson's earlier accomplice. On the driveway is a panel van with Hernandez Gardening Company written down the side.

Peter rings the doorbell. While he waits he can't help glancing across the street at the Henderson place.

The door to number 18 is answered by a tanned woman in her early forties. Her forehead sparkles with perspiration and she is dressed in a black jogging suit. Underneath the thin fabric she is athletically built. Her name is Rosa Hernandez. She speaks with a slight accent, but unless you were looking for it, you wouldn't notice.

"Paul," she says, smiling the second he turns to her from the Hendersons, "how are you?"

"I'm good, Rosa," he replies in his Paul Adams robot voice. "Is Carlos home?"

"He is. He is."

She guides him into the hallway, then left into a living room. A man with thinning brown hair sits on a leather chesterfield watching soccer on a TV that practically covers the whole of the opposite wall. He is roughly the same age as his wife. Just like her, he looks after himself physically. His name is Carlos Hernandez.

The second he sees that his guest is Peter, he gets up, a broad smile on his face.

"Paul," he says, "you're back."

Rosa calls into a bedroom further down the hallway. "Hey, Nikita. Your uncle Paul is here. Come see."

"It's okay," Peter says shyly. "She doesn't have to."

"No," Rosa insists. "She'd like to see you."

A little girl, nine years old, emerges from a room dressed in a pink tutu. With a smile as big as her parents' across her face, she bounds up to Peter and hugs his legs.

Like always, he is rigid to the child's touch and doesn't hug back. Neither he nor Paul Adams has the capacity to do that.

"Come away from Paul, sweetie," Rosa says, pulling the girl off him, sensing Peter's embarrassment.

"Bye bye, Paul," the girls says as she returns to her room, giving him a cute little wave from the door.

"You wanna square up out back?" Carlos asks.

"Sure."

The Hernandez backyard is the most beautiful in Pacific Grove. It is filled with tropical plants from all over the world. Carlos Hernandez's specialty—his business's specialty—is an ability to create hybrids of tropical plants that survive in the cooler climate of northern California. Spotlights illuminate a feast of colors that burst from the edges, the vegetation permitted to go a little wild in order to give the garden a more natural feel. A true living space, rather than sterile order.

Carlos Hernandez's chief complaint in life is that people are obsessed with cutting their gardens into geometric shapes, trying to impose order upon the wild. He once told Peter that it was no good trying to tame a thing completely. You had to let it have a little of its wild side. Otherwise you kill what it is.

That was why within the Hernandez garden you always felt swept away to another place.

"Thanks for taking care of the yard," Peter says as the insects chitter in the bushes.

They sit at a small table close to the house.

"My pleasure," Carlos replies. "You'll need to water the irises within a day or two and the laurel will need trimming in a few weeks. You think you'll be around that long?"

"I plan to be."

Carlos nods and the two men watch the garden. In the center is a kidney-shaped pond filled with koi, their orange shapes swishing about underneath the water. Koi can live up to a hundred years. Peter can't help wondering who will look after these when the Hernandezes are gone.

"Did you receive payment?" Peter asks.

"Yes. The money's in the bank."

"Good. How about the family?"

"Family's good," Carlos replies in an unemotional voice. "They went away to Disney World Florida for a week over the school vacation. Had a grand time from what I heard. Kid just needs to learn to stick up for himself. Can't always run."

Peter agrees. You can't always run. Eventually you've got to just let things catch up with you. Let whatever it is happen and face the fallout.

"And you, Rosa and Nikita?" Peter asks.

"We're good. Just enjoying the sweet simplicities of a normal life."

A normal life, Peter thinks. He wouldn't even know what to do with one.

TWENTY-ONE

It is 9:00 when Peter stands at the open door of the balcony watching the Hendersons. Michael is playing his racing simulator. It is made up of three computer monitors, a steering wheel, bucket seat that reacts to the game he plays, gear stick and pedals. It is as close to real life driving as you can get in the comfort of your own home.

The kid is good. Peter could watch him maneuver the twists and bends of the virtual racecourse all night. He wonders whether Michael could have gotten them out of Lyon. He thinks that so long as the kid had of kept his cool, he would have made it.

The door opens a crack and the head of Carl Henderson leans into the room. Peter can read their lips from here. Carl tells the kid it's time for bed. One look at the clock on the wall and Michael agrees. He finishes the game with little fuss and, already in pajamas, jumps into bed.

After saying goodnight, Carl attempts to leave.

"Dad?" Michael says.

Carl stops at the door, a finger hovering over the light switch.

"Yeah?"

"Were you ever picked on?"

Carl waits a beat. Then, "Why d'you ask, Mikey?"

Another beat. The kid doesn't say anything.

"Is Danny Palmer coming at you again?"

Michael sits in bed. The light glints off the boy's wet eyes. He's looking away from his father, ashamed.

"I'll speak with his dad," Carl says.

"No, don't," Michael snaps, twisting to face him. "His old man kicked his ass last time. Then he just takes it out on me even worse."

"Then I'll speak to Danny myself."

"No! Please, Dad."

An imploring look consumes Michael's face. The father can see the tears staining his cheeks.

"Then what do you want me to do about it?"

"Just answer the question."

"Which was?"

"Were you ever bullied?"

Carl breathes in, then out. "Yeah. Once. It was at middle school."

"What happened?"

"This kid, Tommy Randall, took a disliking to me and started giving me hassle. Staring me out across the playground. Shoving me in the hall. That kinda thing."

"What did you do?"

"What could I? He was a year older and a lot tougher. I

was smaller and had no older brothers to kick his ass for me. So I mostly avoided him."

"And did it work?"

"No. Toward the end of the semester Tommy and some friends of his cornered me after school. Then, while his cronies cheered him on, he beat the shit out of me."

"Was there a reason?"

"Yeah. There was." Carl lowers his eyes to the carpet.

"What was it?" Michael asks.

Sheepishly, Carl says, "Turned out I'd kissed his younger sister at the junior prom and given her a hickey. The family were real religious and took umbrage with it. The dad had given the older brother one simple instruction: find out who did that to his daughter's neck and kick the guy's ass."

"And was that it?"

"Yeah. His sister's honor was restored and for the rest of junior high, we were cool. Not friends, but cool. I mean, I should be the one who was upset. I lost a tooth. All his sister got was a couple of marks on her neck."

Michael is smiling.

"That's better," Carl says.

Michael nods.

Carl adds, "In the end, the Palmer kid will move on to something else."

"I hope so."

"I can assure you. Just wait. Now get some sleep."

"Night, Dad. Love you."

"Love you too, son."

The light goes out.

In number 24 Green Street, Peter sings softly to himself.

"When I'm alone,
With only dreams of you,
That won't come true,
What'll I do?"

TWENTY-TWO

ALASKA, 1999

Eleven years old, Peter stood in the middle of a frozen barn opposite the woman who insisted he call her Mother. A gale howled through the wooden-slat walls. It was minus four outside. Inside, a diesel-powered space heater did its best to warm the chill air. There was a stench of earth and sweat that the heating brought to life. Icicles dripped from the ceiling beams. A well-used punchbag hung from one. On a wall there were outlines of men drawn onto the butchered wood. He saw old, rusted blood blotching many of the grooves and splits. Fist-shaped marks. A testament to the countless strikes that had beaten that thick oak wall into an array of splinters.

"Are we going to learn fighting?" Peter asked.

"Not yet," Mother told him.

"Then what?"

Peter had been there two weeks. After Vermont, an

Army plane had taken them all the way to Fairbanks, Alaska. From there they had traveled north into the wilderness, into hills, trees and snow. There were no roads that close to the Yukon River, so at the airfield Mother had retrieved a Tucker Sno-Cat which she affectionally called "Kitten."

Kitten was a bad-tempered hunk of rust made up of a cab on top of caterpillar tracks, a plow shovel at the front. It was just about big enough for two people if one of those people happened to be an underfed eleven-year-old. Worse than that, Kitten had taken an eternity to heat up and had bumbled along at an average speed of eleven mph, plowing through deep snow for fifty miles. Seven hours it had taken to reach the farm.

Mother's farm consisted of a two-story stone and oak cabin and several outbuildings, including the large barn they stood in now. All of it was weathered and beaten by a thousand snowstorms. Twenty miles south of the Yukon River and the Arctic Circle, it was the absolute definition of the middle of nowhere.

She didn't even need to lecture him on the futility of escape. It was obvious from the ride there that making a break for it wasn't an option. No houses, buildings or shelter of any kind had broken up the monotony of the endless white landscape during their journey. There would be no running away, because only death from exposure awaited him off that farm. Not freedom.

All she had told him on arrival was not to wait for summer.

"You mean you don't get summer up here?" he'd asked.

"It doesn't reach this far. So don't go thinking the weather will ever be good enough for you to survive the two nights walking south to Fairbanks."

Over the coming days he couldn't help thinking back to the diner. Back then she had said that what awaited him in Alaska was perhaps worse than prison. She had been absolutely right except for the perhaps. It was worse.

At least in prison there were other people to talk to, kids his own age for company. Not here, where all you had was some spiteful old bat that yells at you to shut up the second she senses you're on the cusp of speaking. In prison they'd let you watch television or listen to music or the radio. Here there was nothing but reading books and training. Endless training. And God, what training they did. First there was what she ambivalently termed "discipline." This basically meant that from now on he would be doing all the chores and maintenance of the house except for the cooking. She wouldn't eat anyone's food except her own.

The eleven-year-old spent the first night laying rat traps throughout the barn and outbuildings. His first morning was spent retrieving the bodies, the rats frozen stiff, their tails like wire.

"What do I do with the bodies?" he'd asked her.

"Place them in larder."

"You're joking, right?"

The look told him she wasn't. Then what she told him next made him dream whimsically of prison even more. Especially of the food.

"How you think we get food here, huh? You think we drive for week to nearest Walmart?"

"No. But..."

"You see wegetable patch? Livestock? The only meat we eat

is that which we catch. Being that there's not much around this time of year except rats and bears, we eat those."

"But rats?"

"Yes," she'd answered sardonically. "Rats. I tell you, man can eat anything." She lowered her face to meet his and repeated, "Anything," before baring her tobacco-stained teeth.

The daily ritual was a bitch. After rat duty it was time to fetch the firewood she chopped. This was made all the worse by having to listen to her constant complaints with every swing of the axe, moaning that soon it would be solely his job and if he knew what was best for him he would hurry up and grow so he could do the chopping himself, being that she was feeding him enough already.

Following firewood, with it all gathered and placed neatly beside the fireplaces, wood stove and pantry, there would be more chores. In the first week, Peter fixed several leaks on the roof, doing the work in freezing, whipping winds that had scoured the skin off his cheeks and threatened to pick him up and hurl him into sightless tundra. Yet that paled into insignificance compared to what she'd had him doing this week. The past six days had been spent repainting every one of the rooms in the house. Painting them the exact same color that they already were. He could understand if they were dirty, but the place was spotless. He should know—it was him who had been cleaning it.

Peter had begun to think he'd merely been sold into slavery to a cruel psychopath. That was until today. Today, after he had finished painting the last room, she informed him that his technical training would now begin.

In the barn, Peter was freezing but cautious to show it. A fortnight had been enough time to learn that the slightest hint of any whining or whinging and you were screwed with this ice witch. She hadn't hit him. At least not yet. But there were other punishments. Like standing on one foot with his arms held out when he had dared to complain about her rabbit stew. Or having to make and remake his bed over and over when he left a corner of the sheet exposed. Or the day he spent digging a hole in the frozen yard, filling it in, and digging another next to it when he stupidly informed her that it was a waste of time to repaint the rooms the same color.

"You think it waste of time now?" she had asked while standing over his latest hole.

Therefore, Peter did his best to control his body. To stop it trembling. Wondering all the time how she *did it*. *How* she stayed so perfectly still in this chilling air.

Her breath flooded the space in front of her mouth as she coldly told him, "It is too early in your training for fighting, Peter."

"Then what are we doing here?"

"Before fighting," she said, "we learn pain. Only once we learn how to control pain, can we overcome our fear of it. Once we overcome fear, we can learn to fight freely without the crippling weight of apprehension. That is when we will move on to fighting."

Behind this rigid, steel-haired woman stood a table with a sheet covering items on top. She turned to it and dragged the sheet away. Metal blades and other tools sparkled in the electric light.

"You do know pain, Peter," she said. "I have seen it on you."

His breathing increased. For all the suffering he'd gone through these past two weeks, he hadn't yet feared her. But now he did. Now she frightened him and fear ran its fingers through his hair. He tasted it; sour metal between his teeth as they started to itch.

"In your short life," she continued, turning to him with a scalpel that shone in her hand, "you have experienced terrible pain."

His chest tightened. He swallowed down gulps of breath.

"Fear has also stalked you. But I am going to teach you how to control it. To control your pain and control your fear. Like you did the night you killed the priest."

Peter was shaking all over. "I told you," he shivered. "I don't... (huh!) remember any of that."

"And I told you, the memory will come back one day and you will need to be prepared for it when it does. In this place," she spread her arms to express her words, "I will teach you how to subdue both pain and fear. How to run on pure discipline like a machine. How to control your heart rate. Breathing. Control your senses. Your feelings. In this place you will learn control through the mind."

She tapped the scalpel to her temple.

Peter began humming. What'll I do? In the week he'd been there, she'd had to lie with him almost every night at some point. Cradling him and cooing the song into his ear. The boy murmuring along.

"Already you are learning techniques," she observed.

The song calmed him down, his chest loosening, his fists unfurling.

"Now," she said, "have you ever been cut?"

She knew the answer but wanted him to go to that place. Return to the trauma.

He glanced down at his forearm. A thick scar ran across it.

Her plan worked. He had a flashback to the orphanage: two boys holding him, holding his arm out, another holding a pocket knife in front of his face.

"You fucking ratted on us, didn't you?"

"No."

"Yes, you did."

The boy ran the knife along his arm. "Cut him to the bone, Benny," *one of the others yipped excitedly.* "Cut the freak to the bone."

Peter lost his cool completely. He turned to run—but bumped straight into a huge body that had seemingly been there the whole time, having crept out of the shadows to block his path to the door.

He looked up a formidable body to the unsmiling face of a woman with long black hair tied in a bun. She was at least six-and-a-half-feet tall and almost as wide. She was dressed in overalls. Her eyes were hard and her face was mean.

"This is Magda, Peter," Mother said. "She and I are going to teach you about pain."

TWENTY-THREE

MONTEREY, 2019

"I hope you like pain, runt," Danny Palmer snarls into Michael's face. "'Cause you're gonna get it."

It took them three weeks but they'd caught him at last.

While his two goons keep watch, Danny has Michael up against the wall of a garage, the four boys up an alleyway and out of sight from grown-ups.

One of Danny's hands holds the scruff of Michael's shirt.

The other holds a penknife to his face.

"Please, Danny."

"Your old man keeps leaning on me in class. Gave me detention twice already this week. Took my phone away. My old man went apeshit."

"I'm sorry."

"You been telling Daddy tales again, runt?"

"No, Danny. I promise."

Michael has begun to cry. Danny turns back to his pals and grins. They smirk back, loving the games they play. They once watched Danny pull this trick on a kid behind the bowling alley. That time the boy pissed his pants. Man, they laughed their asses off after that. What did he think? That Danny would really cut him? But then they'd stopped laughing and looked at each other. Because sometimes Danny really did look like he was getting ready to slide that knife across their face.

"You think you're so darn smart," Danny hisses in a cruel tone. "Don't you, runt?"

"No."

"Mommy works at some fancy law office in the city. Daddy's a teacher. You on the honor system. I bet you think you're hot shit compared to a dingus like me."

"No, Danny. I don't think any—"

It is a quick movement. The hand leaves the scruff, balls into a fist, strikes Michael in the gut. The kid screams, or howls. It is short and girl-like. And before he can drop from the searing pain that winds him, Danny once again has him by the scruff with the same hand, preventing him from falling to his knees, holding Michael's weight one-handed with ease. All of it done in a few seconds. Bullying being the one thing that Danny Palmer excels in.

Choking, Michael pleads. "Please... Danny... Please..."

"I ought to cut you for snitching last time. Make sure that the next time your faggot dad speaks to mine, I at least get some pleasure before the beating my old man puts on me."

Danny Palmer presses the knife to Michael's cheek, the sharp tip right beneath the eye, pressed against his bottom eyelid. Michael imagines himself blind and it makes the tears pour out over the steel blade.

"Please, Danny…"

It is then that a man's voice fills the alleyway behind them.

"Don't you think the knife is overkill?"

Danny grimaces, takes the blade away from Michael, and turns to see who has interrupted their fun.

Mr. Adams from 24 Green Street stands dressed in his jogging clothes, a big white sweatband across his forehead, skin shining in the morning sun.

"What I mean is," he adds, "isn't the fact that you're much bigger and that there's three of you enough already? Why d'you need the knife?"

Danny presses the blade back into the handle, slipping the knife into a back pocket. He moves away from Michael and faces Paul Adams, the one his dad calls the freak at 24. Some of the locals joke that he's a pervert. That he spends so much time away because he's in the Philippines or somewhere like that running an underage sex trafficking ring.

Michael goes to creep away. Danny grabs him. "Stay," he sneers. Turning his attention back on the freak at 24, Danny says, "What's it to do with you?"

The two friends grin at Danny's absolute lack of respect for his elders.

But Peter knocks the grins off their faces when he comes back with: "Nothing your old man won't kick your ass about when I go tell him."

The two friends stop grinning and turn to Danny. Even Michael is looking at him.

Danny is staring lasers at Peter. "Maybe he'll kick *your*

ass instead," he says, stepping forward. "After I tell him what you just said."

Peter smiles at him. It is not a friendly smile. It is a dead one that goes well with his glazed expression. "Your old man only beats women and children," he tells the fourteen-year-old.

There is such cold impassivity in Peter's voice that a deep, preternatural fear runs through the neighborhood bully. It is the same fear that runs through him when he gets home late and his old man is sitting in front of the TV, having finished the whiskey off. Those glazed eyes glowing in the dark. That terrible look down his face. No expression at all. Like a mask. It was when Danny knew well to avoid him. When he'd creep past the open door of the living room, praying he got to his room before being spotted.

Mr. Adams is wearing a similar look. The look of murder.

"You shouldn't say that," Danny says half-heartedly.

"Leave and take your girlfriends," Peter says firmly.

Danny points a finger at him. "Fuck you." He practically whispers it.

Peter remains an immovable statue. "Come here," he says coldly.

Danny shudders. Turns over his shoulder to the mouth of the alley. It seems so much sunnier on the street than it does here in this passage. Here it feels like there's shadow cast over everything.

"Whatever," Danny breathes, turning back to the freak at 24. This time he doesn't make eye contact. This time he just looks Peter in the chest for a second before turning back to the street and moving off, snapping "Come on," at his buddies, the three of them skulking out of the alley.

Michael watches them go, still backed up against the garage. Then, as one fear dissipates and another replaces it, he turns to the man now sharing the alley with him.

The kid's spilled schoolbag is scattered about the cracked concrete. Peter is gathering up the contents, Michael watching him cautiously. He too has heard the stories about Mr. Adams at number 24 Green Street. His parents had told him not to listen to such malicious gossip, that there was nothing wrong with a man living alone and keeping himself to himself. But still. There was a feeling you always got whenever Mr. Adams was nearby. A shiver that ran through you. The breeze picking up. The clouds closing over the sun and the air turning cold.

"Are you okay?" Peter asks, handing Michael his school-bag, having scooped everything into it.

The kid looks terrified as he takes it. Even more than he had with the knife to his cheek.

"I have to go," Michael stammers, eyes bulging.

"Are you sure you're okay?"

"Yes. Please. I really have to."

Peter realizes the boy is scared of him. "That's fine," he says softly. "You go."

He steps back.

Michael walks away, footsteps accelerating into a jog as he reaches the alley's end, never looking back.

TWENTY-FOUR

THE REST OF HIS JOG IS UNEVENTFUL. THAT IS
until he gets home.

Someone is snooping in at his windows, their face
pressed to the pane. Confused as to why they can't see
through the heavily tinted glass.

"Can I help you?" Peter says, coming up silently behind
them.

The woman jumps and spins around. It's Pam Jenkins.
The one who ignored him in the 7-Eleven. The one who
lives opposite with her husband. He of the beak.

Tall and built like a coat hanger, she stares at Peter with
terror-widened eyes that bug from her narrow head. Over
her slender body she wears a long-sleeved gray dress that falls
to her feet, ragged and frayed at the hem.

For several seconds Pam Jenkins stares at him, her
spindly fingers feeling the crucifix hanging at her throat, as
though she is witnessing an apparition.

"I asked if I could help you," Peter says. "Pam, isn't it?"

"It is," she mutters.

"Were you looking for something?"

"I called at the door."

She hadn't. His phone would have vibrated to alert him if she'd gone anywhere near the buzzer.

"So it was me you were after," he puts to her.

"My cat."

"Your cat?"

"Yes. She escaped. I saw her come over here. I think she's in your backyard."

"Then let's go take a look."

Peter moves off toward the gate.

"No!" she gasps.

He turns back to her. She looks genuinely afraid.

"Just you go look," she says quietly.

"What's her name?"

"Dixie."

Peter plays along, going into the backyard, where he calls the cat loud enough so Pam Jenkins can hear. When he returns to the front she is already gone. Across the street the front door of the Jenkins' house is slamming shut.

This is the third contact Peter has had with the Jenkinses. The first was when Pam ignored him in the 7-Eleven. The second was three months ago, the last time he was staying on Green Street. He had gotten back home one evening to find a note posted under the door. On it was scrawled a simple message:

We know WHAT you are.

TWENTY-FIVE

THE FEELINGS AND SENSATIONS RACING THROUGH him as she smiles are beyond words. Everything is complete now that he is back with her. Sitting up in bed, the smile so bright it sets Peter's soul on fire, she holds out a hand and he brings it to his face, feels it against his skin, feels her, a need to consume every detail of this moment, to remain in it for as long as possible.

If he had known back then that their time together was to be so brief, he would have told her that he will never again be as happy as he is now with her in this room.

He sits with her on the bed, her lying across him, head rested on his legs, blue eyes gazing up at him. He can smell her, feel her, breathe her. But inside he knows it will end. That this is merely a lucid memory. It is not like back then, when he deluded himself that he had all the time in the world.

He finds himself in the garden looking into the room through the door. She's sitting up in bed again, but the smile has dropped. A fear has enveloped it and darkened her countenance. She is pointing at something behind him.

Peter wheels around.

There is the boy in the captain's hat. But this isn't Monaco or Greece. This is Green Street. And the boy isn't Gregor's kid. It is Michael. It is Michael and he is standing across the street from Paul Adams's house waving to Peter. He is standing there and he explodes—

Peter bursts up in bed, clutching his heaving chest, the song rising up from his throat, the words acting as waves of calm that wash over him.

He staggers to his feet and opens the blinds to the balcony.

Everyone is sleeping at the Henderson house.

TWENTY-SIX

EARLY ONE EVENING PETER IS IN THE LIVING ROOM, sitting at his laptop. At the same time every night, he spends a few minutes scrolling through an internet site where people share pornography.

Today is the sixth. So it'll be John Holmes. The Jade Pussycat.

Johnny Wadd is getting deep and dirty with some blonde as Peter scrolls the comments section below. He spots one from GushingGapes69: *What a gush!*

This is bad.

Peter slams the laptop shut and leaves the house. He drives the Saab south into Monterey, the sun lowering in the sky and casting the Pacific in bright orange so that the water looks like it's on fire. At the Old Fisherman's Wharf he takes a table in a far corner of the walkway where it overlooks the ocean. Children and parents stand at the wooden railings, watching the leathery seals that lounge about on the rocks below, their camera phones twinkling in the lowlight.

Peter sits drinking coffee. He uses his Peter phone to call Pat Hughes.

"You got my message then," Pat says when he answers.

"What's happened?"

"Something interesting came up."

Peter wonders whether it is something to do with Monaco.

"What?"

"I got a call today from some English lawyer. He wants to hire you."

"I'm in the wind. No jobs, I said."

"He asked for you personally."

"By name?"

"No. By reputation. Asked right out whether it wasn't possible to hire the guy who did Prague."

Peter doesn't like it. "What was your answer?"

"Standard denial." Pat's gruff voice rattles in his ear. "I didn't know what he was talking about. I've never heard of what he's referring to."

"And what was his response?"

"The limey was coy as hell. Just said he understood and all he wants is to talk to you."

"In person?"

"I told him about Rule Six. He says it can be done over the phone."

Peter waits a beat. Then says, "Call him back and tell him I don't want it."

"But here's the thing. He's offering your usual price just to talk."

For the first time Peter is interested. "He's willing to pay a hundred grand for a phone call?"

"No obligations, he said."

Gulls squawk and loop through the air above. The ocean rolls onto the rocks below with a hiss. The seals laze about the seaweed, their dark skins glinting with the copper sun. Children smile and play in the sand, their parents proudly watching on.

"It doesn't feel right," Peter finally admits. "I don't want it."

"Look," Pat comes back with, "a hundred grand is a hundred grand. If you want my advice, just call the guy from a secure line, away from anything sensitive, and have a little chat. Take the money. Tell him no thanks."

Peter doesn't feel right. But still, there is something about it that has laid a hook into him. Not the money. Something else. He doesn't want to admit it to Pat, but he's intrigued to know more. A hundred grand just to quench his curiosity? Why not. After all, he doesn't have to take the job. In fact, he already knows that he won't.

"What's his name?"

"Hugo Davenport. I'll send you his number."

TWENTY-SEVEN

ALASKA, 2000

By the end of a year small wounds, as well as old scars, covered his young body. Once a month he would spend an entire hour testing his ability to control his responses to pain and once a month Magda would spend another hour silently sewing up the cuts.

As she pushed the needle through his flesh, she and Mother would watch his eyes and face for any expression of pain. The slightest sign of register and the hulking woman would rip the stitches out and start again from scratch.

Days were a never-ending cycle of chores and training and discipline. Mother would time him as he took apart handguns. The boy stating the gun's classifications and answering questions whilst his dexterous fingers worked away at lightning speed.

"With a 9mm Parabellum, what would be the approximate aim reduction in a southwesterly 32-mile-an-hour wind?"

"A reduction of sixteen percent would be expected."

"How would you counter this?"

"To compensate from distances longer than fifty yards you would have to aim the weapon accordingly."

Though she always did well not to show it, Mother was amazed at his memory. He rarely got one wrong. Even when he was being distracted.

There were more nights than he wished to remember spent in the barn being bombarded with questions while the giant Magda circled like a hungry bear, whipping Peter at inopportune intervals with a length of rubber, creating an interrupted rhythm that didn't allow him to prepare for the next strike by tensing his muscles, always catching him unawares, thumping his torso and winding him, hitting him again if he got a question even remotely wrong.

His body was no longer malnourished. It was sinewy. Hard as mahogany. There were not many thirteen-year-olds in such good shape.

"What is the mission directive?" Mother asked while Magda orbited.

"To eliminate the target within a crowded area without collateral."

"What is the expected mission outcome involving a sniper?"

"With use of surrounding vantage points provided by local buildings, the outcome is predicted as seventy percent."

"Potential obstacles?"

"Access to the buildings themselves. One is a federal tax office. Government. Security would be tight. The other *building is commercial. However, it has several banks within it. This makes security again a problem."*

"What floor are the banks on?"

"Three and four."

Mother watched him. Waited.

"Shit! There's another one in the lobby."

Whack!

For the first six months, he was trained exclusively by Mother. Then a firearms expert came to stay with them for eight weeks. The morning he left, Peter watched him and Mother from the house. He lip read the guy telling her that Peter was the best asset his age that he'd ever seen. It was the first time that Peter had ever known himself to be referred to as an asset. It was also the first time anyone had ever said he was the best at something.

"It's not about being able to shoot on a course," Mother was fond of barking at him. "Anyone can play for sport. It is about doing it whilst your life depends on it. Whilst you've already got a bullet in you and you're bleeding out. It is about doing it as accurately when you haven't slept for days as you do when you've had your beauty sleep."

To make the point Mother and Magda would keep him awake while running him ragged with countless drills. Darting about the woods with a paintball gun while both of them hunted him. Back in the barn he would be bombarded with questions and whacks. Out in the cold there would be more shooting drills. At the end of four days without sleep he would be breaking apart, feeling like he was someone else, not even real.

At the end of six days he found himself standing in the

middle of the frozen woods dressed in body armor. Mother's voice echoing in his head.

"Today we will be performing a shooting test different from what you have done so far."

He realized straight away that the main difference was that he didn't have a gun.

"One day," she went on, "you will be shot, Peter. Nothing will prepare you for it but at least this will give you some idea."

She carried with her at all times a SIG Sauer P226 which she kept in a hip holster. She lifted the gun out and aimed it at him.

Peter flinched.

She smiled. Shook her head. Lowered the gun.

"No. You're cringing," she said. "Expecting it. When a bullet finally gets to kiss your flesh, it will come when you are not anticipating it."

"So we're not doing live fire yet?" he said, relaxing.

"Not from me."

"Not from you?" Peter was frowning.

"No."

"Then—"

It was at that point that he was shot from behind. The .38 caliber round hit the armor where the back of his ribs were. He heard the bones crack like dried sticks. All the wind shot out of him instead of the words he was about to utter. He wanted to scream, but the only sound that came was a helpless gasp. He fell to the ground, twisting onto his side.

There, behind a tree, was Magda holding a silenced pistol.

Mother stepped over him. "Rule One," she said. "Never drop your guard."

TWENTY-EIGHT

CALIFORNIA, 2019

PETER DRIVES TWO AND A HALF HOURS TO FRESNO. Passing through the city, he heads east toward the Sierra Nevada Mountains. Taking the winding roads upwards for another forty-five minutes he reaches Courtright Reservoir. It is a wide stretch of black water surrounded by white rocks that resemble bones in the headlight beams. A dirt road takes Peter to a hill overlooking the water. There, he parks and makes the call as the reflection of the moon meanders on the surface of the reservoir.

A man answers in a plain English accent. "Is this who I think it is?"

"You have two minutes, Mr. Davenport."

Peter clicks the timer on his wristwatch.

"Then I shall be prompt," the man on the other end replies. "I represent a man who wishes to hire your services."

"Who?"

"Like yourself, my client doesn't wish to meet in this matter or have his name or title used. Thus, he has endeavored to hire myself to be his representative in this rather precarious affair."

"And what is this affair?"

"I believe in your trade it is called a kill list."

"You mean multiple targets?"

"Yes."

"How many?"

"Three in total."

"Who?"

"I'm sorry, but no names until agreement of the job and terms."

"Where are the hits to take place?"

"I can only tell you the country at this point."

"Which is?"

"It would be here in America."

Rule Seven: No jobs stateside.

"Then I can't take it."

"I'm sorry, but you must. My client has given me strict instructions to make sure the man who performed Prague is the one in charge of this. He is willing to offer you a million dollars for each target. That makes three million."

"It's not the money. I just don't work on home soil. It's a rule."

"Then allow me to offer you something which may facilitate a change of heart, so to say. My client, being a very powerful man, isn't just offering you money. He is offering you freedom."

There is silence. A beat. Then, "Keep going."

"You are currently a hunted man, are you not?"

"How do you know that?"

"We know a lot of things about you, *Azrael*."

The name cuts through Peter. Tightening his chest.

"Who are you?"

"I told your handler. My name is Hugo Davenport. You can look me up."

"I have. You're some limey lawyer. Went to Eton with all the other privileged limeys. Did your degree at Oxford, as well as your Masters and PhD. A true Oxford blue. You worked eleven years in corporate finance at James Mills and Partners. You became a partner in 2010. Then, five years later, you had your partnership dissolved with no explanation from either yourself or the law firm. That was when you went underground. Supposedly living in Dubai as a tax exile. Is that where you found your client?"

"I'm afraid I couldn't tell you."

Peter can sense the slimy smile on the other end.

"But to the matter in hand," Hugo Davenport proceeds. "My client is offering you amnesty from your current prominent position on a certain CIA hit list. The very reason you spend your life hiding behind masks, Azrael."

"Don't call me that."

But Davenport isn't listening. The Englishman goes on. "Living a collection of closeted existences all over America until you get a call from Mr. Hughes. Get a job, so to speak. It must be a terribly sad and lonely existence."

Peter's wristwatch starts to beep.

"Your time is up."

"So what do you say? Will you take my client's offer of freedom?"

"No one gets off that list," Peter tells him. "It can't be

done. Not by your client. Not by anybody. Find someone else and don't ever try contacting me again."

Peter puts the phone down. Gripping it, he stares at the silver light undulating upon the calm waters of the reservoir.

This is going to be a problem. He just knows it.

TWENTY-NINE

ALASKA, 2003

BY FIFTEEN PETER WAS AN ACCOMPLISHED fighter.

Men and women were shipped in from all over the world to train him in various fighting techniques. They came, stayed a month, then departed, before returning at a later date to carry on where they'd left off. There would be a revolving door of six trainers throughout the year. His favorite styles were Wing Chun, which was taught by a Chinese man whose diminutive body hid an exceptional strength. And Krav Maga, which was taught by a tall Israeli with a pony-tail, whom Peter caught smiling once when the son of a bitch had broken the then fourteen-year-old's jaw with an elbow strike.

Peter liked both styles because they were relatively natural fighting techniques. Rather than attempt complicated assaults, they merely taught the combatant to use their instincts and *initiative. To do only what was necessary to defeat your opponent as quickly as possible.*

Tonight in the barn Mother stood before him. Like always, Magda stayed silently in her corner. A waiting spider.

"Your fighting teachers tell me that you are coming along nicely."

Peter said nothing.

"I would like to see how you do against a seasoned opponent who will not show the caution and mercy your teachers do."

"Who, Magda?"

"No. You're no good to me dead. And that is what you will be when Magda picks you up and crushes your ribcage into your lungs and other organs." She paused, cocking an eye at him. "You're smiling. You think I joke. It would not be first time I see her do it to a person." Raising her chin, she added, "The popping sound still haunts me to this day. No. Tonight you will fight me."

Peter couldn't help smirking. Mother was wiry. She ate little, and often he found himself worrying about her health. Though he was sure she was strong, she was old, wrinkled, and meatless.

"Is this a joke?" he asked.

"How long you have known me, Peter?"

"Sometimes I think it is all my life, Mother."

"Well, in that time have you ever known me to joke?"

Peter shook his head.

"Come here," she said firmly.

He came before her. Loose and not taking it seriously.

"Get into fighting stance."

"Really?"

Mother looked past his shoulder at Magda. It took less than a second for the whip to reach his back and snap upon his spine.

He knew it was coming. The split second before Mother even made the look. Still, it didn't stop it hurting.

So, not wanting another, Peter got into fighting stance. He already had a strategy. He would get the old woman into a hold and subdue her. He was sure that she would be skilled; he wasn't that stupid; but just look at her.

Mother didn't get into stance. She merely stood with her arms behind her back.

"Come at me," she said.

Peter rushed forward with the intention of blocking whatever strikes she tried, whipping around the back, and getting her into the chokehold.

It was when he spotted the knowing grin that he realized she knew this.

With a lightning movement, she ducked under his arm and swooped to the side, so fast he didn't even notice her hands whip out from behind her back and strike him below the ribs in a one-two of rabbit punches. Pain stabbed his kidneys. He pushed it away, used the change of balance in his favor. The gymnastics lessons coming in handy. He wheeled around like a cat, but she was right there. He blocked. Countered. She ducked again. Two bodies dancing around each other in the middle of the room. Bursts of breath and rapidly shuffling feet.

At one point he lost her and couldn't believe it. Couldn't believe that this old woman was quicker than him. She got a palm strike in that hit him just below the sternum as he was leaning forward. The hand retracted at just the right moment in a whip-snap movement, giving the blow a thunderous crack.

Pain balled up in his lungs, traveled rapidly up, expanded in his throat, and he couldn't breathe.

Peter staggered back.

In Krav Maga they call it anatomical targeting. The blow was designed to rupture the gall bladder. The prick with the ponytail would have been proud of her. She had performed it perfectly.

Peter, exhausted, winded and in severe pain, was kneeling in the dust clutching his chest. He looked up and she was standing right over him. Hands back behind her back.

"Rule Two," she said. "Never underestimate your opponent. Even if he looks like old lady. Otherwise you are dead."

THIRTY

MONTEREY, 2019

THE MAN IN THE PINSTRIPE SUIT AND BOWLER HAT makes an odd impression on the residents of Green Street as he strolls along the sidewalk, whistling a tune to himself. He sweats profusely. Dark patches swarm the collar of his white shirt and his hair drips underneath the hat. A double-breasted waistcoat is fitted tightly around his torso. It adds to the absolute unsuitability of his choice of outfit with today's muggy weather of 82°.

He passes Danny Palmer and his two goons. They're huddled around a street corner in the shade of a sycamore, leaning on the handlebars of their BMXs. The goons spot the stranger first, one of them tapping Danny on the arm. The bully looks up from his phone and joins his pals in grimacing at the latest freak to pass through Pacific Grove.

"Look where he's going," one of them whispers in Danny's ear.

Under the shade of Mrs. Harrison's porch, the old woman sits with fellow Pacific Grove resident Mrs. Murphy, Sandy the Yorkshire terrier snoozing on the latter's lap. Both women pause the drinking of their ice teas to inspect the strange man waltzing up the drive of number 24 Green Street. Mrs. Harrison has never seen her next-door neighbor receive anything remotely resembling a guest before. When the stranger reaches the door, he stops, turns to the old women and smiles in a way that makes both suspect the grin is put on. It is the smile of a toady ingratiating his master. He practically curtseys at them.

The grin drops when he re-faces the door of 24. Business is in order.

Peter is in the backyard digging up a flowerbed of daffodils when his phone vibrates in his pocket. There is a camera above the front door, hidden within the stucco. It relays video to the phone.

A face under a round hat fills the screen. The bridge of the stranger's nose is flat, but the end pokes up at an angle, so that the nostrils face forward. His black pupils sink into the middle of dark brown irises, making his eyes look like holes in his face.

He knows he is being watched, because those shark eyes suddenly fix their attention on the camera. A mouthful of yellow, jagged teeth smile at it, sweat trickling down skin the color of over-boiled ham.

Peter answers the door. His own eyes as dead as those of the uninvited caller.

"May I help you?" he asks in Paul Adams's drawling voice.

The man shines him that ingratiating smile and, cool as

you like, says, "You must accept my sincere apologies for breaking one of your rules, *Azrael*."

Peter goes cold. He glances left.

Mrs. Harrison and Mrs. Murphy are watching. Even the dog seems to have woken up especially for this.

Right. Danny Palmer and his pals stare from the handlebars of their BMXs.

Directly in front. The Jenkinses curtains are open a few inches. The fat nose of Larry Jenkins practically all the way up against the pane.

"I think you have the wrong address, sir," Peter says when his eyes are back on the man at Paul Adams's front door.

"Ah," the intruder pronounces, the smile lifting his red cheeks. "You even sound different than you did on the phone. Such tradecraft, Azrael."

Peter makes himself look confused. "I think you have it wrong, mister. There's never been anyone with that name living here. My name is Adams. Paul Adams."

Hugo Davenport gives Peter a coy look, his black eyebrows raised almost all the way to the rim of his hat. "Are we really going to dilly-dally?"

"Dilly-dally?"

"Waste time going around in circles."

Peter narrows his eyes. "Are you feeling okay?"

"I'm fine."

"Because I think you might have heatstroke. You shouldn't be walking about in this weather dressed like that. Would you like me to call you someone?"

Davenport lowers his voice and leans toward him. Peter staying exactly where he is.

"I really don't think we should continue wasting time," he says confidentially.

"You have the wrong address," Peter seethes back.

"No. I have the *correct* address. 24 Green Street, Pacific Grove. Owned by one Paul Adams. Except Paul Adams isn't really Paul Adams, is he? Paul Adams is someone else." He brings his lips to Peter's ear, the two old ladies watching from across the hedge. "Oh, and I like how you've changed your body shape," he hisses. "The way you hold yourself as though you're a much smaller man than you are. The dumb expression to go with the drawn-out vowels of your speech. It's always the little things with you, isn't it, Azrael? The way you *live* these people as though the real you never even existed. That you've never been anything other than an asset."

He steps back as he adds this last part, grinning in a self-satisfactory manner that wrinkles his chin.

Peter's expression has changed. He is imagining grabbing ahold of the man opposite, dragging him into the hallway and breaking his neck before he even gets the chance to scream.

"There. You see," the man in the suit says. "That's the cold look of a killer."

"Get in."

Peter steps back from the door and the man smiles in his face as he walks inside. Peter takes one last look at the street. There are no vehicles or people that don't belong.

"Hi, Paul."

Peter turns left. Mrs. Harrison and Mrs. Murphy are waving.

"Hi, ladies," he says back with a crooked smile before ducking inside and shutting the door.

Hugo Davenport stands in the hallway with his hat in his hands. His wispy black hair is soaked with sweat that dribbles down his forehead. He doesn't have a gun. Otherwise Peter's phone would have vibrated in his pocket, triggered by the metal detector hidden within the doorframe.

"You're a very brave man coming unarmed and alone," Peter says in his normal voice.

"Would a team of gun-heavy thugs have done me any good?"

Peter says nothing.

"I thought not," Davenport continues. "That is why my client is most insistent I acquire you and only you."

Peter has only one question. "How did you find me?"

Instead of answering Davenport sniffs the air, glances over Peter's shoulder, and asks, "Is that coffee I smell?"

Peter continues to fix him with his eyes.

"Would you mind pouring me a cup?" The ingratiating smile makes a return. The disgusting yellow teeth opening like the bellows of an accordion.

"You're not a guest," Peter tells him. "You're an intruder. One who is playing a very dangerous game."

The smile drops and the eyes lose what little luster they had. "I sincerely mean you no harm, Azrael."

"People who want to harm me often say that."

"I only wish to hire you," Davenport says, bending his face into a genteel expression. "That is why I am alone. That is why I am unarmed. I certainly do not intend to spoil what you have here. I only wish to offer you a future of living it peacefully."

The two men stare across the shadowy hallway at each other. A wedge of sunshine plays with the lawyer's face. It makes his eyes blink with light as though they're on fire.

"Now," Davenport says in an upbeat tone, "what do you say about that coffee?"

There is a view of the backyard from the kitchen. The cherry blossom at the end sways in the breeze. Beyond that is the Henderson place. Michael is practicing diving at the edge of the swimming pool. He continually splashes into the water, gets out, and tries again, asking for his mother's opinion each time. Kate lies on a sun lounger reading a book. Every so often she looks up from it to comment on her son's technique.

Peter and the unwanted guest sit at a breakfast table, a mug of coffee in front of them both. Davenport faces the window. He sits back, staring across at Peter, the ingratiating smirk hovering over his steaming mug.

Sipping his coffee, he glances out the window.

"Such a fine view you have," he says.

"Get to your point."

Retraining his gaze on Peter, Davenport says, "I wish to finish the negotiations we started yesterday."

"I ended them for good. I told you. I won't..."

Davenport holds a hand up. His face is screwed into a grimace, cheeks shriveled up to his slick eyes. "Yes. Yes," he barks gently. "I'm well aware of your rules. But I'm here to tell you that if you perform this delicate task for us, you won't need to live by rules anymore."

"No one gets off that list," Peter says firmly.

"Luther Bryce did."

Peter grins at him. "Luther Bryce got off the only way anyone ever does. By taking a bullet from some CIA sniper."

"No," Davenport says with a shake of the head. "You're wrong. Luther Bryce is living in Hawaii with a wife and young child. He no longer goes under the appellation Luther Bryce, but he does get to live a life without fear of a knock on the door."

The grin on Peter's face is threatening to crack it. He sips his coffee, puts the cup down and says, "Now I know why your teeth are so green."

Davenport doesn't take the bait. He merely stares dead-eyed at him.

Peter gives him the punchline anyway. "It's all the bull-shit that slides out of your mouth."

Davenport shrugs. Sips his own coffee, places the cup down, says, "Do you have a computer or smartphone to hand?"

Peter takes his phone from the pocket of his cargo shorts.

"May I have it?" the lawyer asks.

"No."

"Then you'll have to make the call yourself."

"What call?"

"Mr. Bryce is currently on the end of a Skype ID that will cease to exist in fifteen minutes. He has been especially kind to donate part of his day to receiving a call from an old CIA pal. He looks forward to speaking to you, Azrael."

Davenport gives him the Skype ID and Peter makes the call. It is answered within the first few rings and there before Peter's eyes is a man he's not seen in seven years. Not since Luther Bryce became public enemy number one in the agency for selling secrets to the Russians. He supposedly died last year when the CIA caught up to him in Dubai.

Luther is almost a decade older than he was the last time Peter saw him. The lines creasing the ebony skin of his forehead are now a little deeper, and gray peppers the tight curls of his black hair. Some plastic surgery has been done. The jaw is squarer. The ridge of the nose flatter. His cheeks higher up. But Peter never forgets a person's eyes.

In Luther's left iris there is an imperfection. An orange ring in the brown no bigger than a pinhead that sits just below the pupil.

"Peter, is that you?" The voice is unmistakable.

Peter feels his face. The fake goatee. The fake teeth. The face of Paul Adams.

Instead of answering, he asks a question. "Raqqa 2012. Second hit. What was the color of the target's headscarf?"

Luther nods. He's been expecting this. "Easy," he says. "Blue. You put a bullet through it."

"Kyiv 2009," Peter fires at him next like some seasoned gameshow host. "What was written on the poster in the dental surgery where you had two bullets removed from your left arm?"

Luther grins all over at the memory. "It said, 'Keep smiling and keep brushing.'" He announces it while holding his left arm up. "I still got the scars."

There they are. Two dents in the back of his upper arm. In the triceps brachii. Exactly where the contact had removed the slugs put in him by a Russian FSB agent. He lost twenty percent strength in that arm and it almost retired him.

"How?" Peter asks, amazed to be speaking to the dead.

"I just did a job for Mr. Davenport. Not the easiest of jobs, but one which required my rare expertise."

"You know who the client is?"

"Nope," Luther says. "All I know is that he's got friends in all the right places. I got paid a clear million and—Bang! —I'm free. Got me a nice place by the ocean here in Oahu. Not far from Honolulu. Got a nice little wife and a little girl aged six months. You'll have to come over and see us sometime. That is if you ever get the agency off your ass."

While he speaks, Peter is imagining previously undreamt of possibilities. Visiting Luther Bryce in Hawaii. It doesn't feel real.

For the next five minutes, he and Luther talk, Peter more sure by the second that this is his former colleague at the CIA. They talk mostly about old jobs, people who are long gone, people who are still around. When Peter asks him about the job he did for Davenport, he gets nothing. All Luther says is, "Can't tell you, man. And don't go asking me any other questions about it either. I'm on strict orders never to repeat any detail of it."

He tells Peter only two things about the mission. That it almost killed him. And that it was absolutely worth it. "I'm a free man, Peter. A free man."

For some time after the conversation's end Peter is stunned. He sits staring into space. The phone still clasped in his hand.

"A hit list?" he says.

"Yes," Davenport says.

"Three names?"

"Yes."

"How will it work?"

"Are you interested?"

"I asked first."

"Three names. Each name comes one at a time."

Peter frowns. Fixes the Englishman with his steely eyes. "You mean I don't get all three names at once?"

Davenport shakes his head. "Afraid not."

"How will that work?"

"One name at a time. My client is most insistent on this. The first will come twenty-four hours after you accept the job."

"What's the duration?"

"A month in total from tomorrow. That gives roughly ten days per target."

"Does the client just want them dead?"

"No. This is where we need your own specialist expertise. While you were with the CIA, you took part in many assassinations that were designed to look like accidents."

"Did Luther Bryce tell you that?"

"It doesn't matter. What does is that you can make death look like nothing more than the natural course of a person's life. This is what will be required of the three targets."

"Are they civilians?"

"Civilians, yes."

"They're not politicians, spies, foreign agents, celebrities?"

"No."

"What sex?"

"Two males. One female."

"What's the reason your client wants them dead?"

"That can never be divulged." Davenport stares at him with a resolute hardness writ on his face.

"Children?"

"All three are adults. I can assure you of that. Their deaths, if made to look accidental, will not go particularly noticed by anyone that will matter."

Peter muses out loud. "One month. Three targets. I get this done and I'm free?"

"Yes, Azrael. Get this done and your little secret here will be kept all between us. And not to mention the three million."

"Okay. I'll take the job."

THIRTY-ONE

THE NEXT DAY, HUGO DAVENPORT IS PERCHED comfortably in the back of a luxury Bentley Mulsanne. Sitting in the front are two ape-sized men who fill every stitch of their slate-gray suits. While one drives, the other sits in the passenger seat, his sharp eyes honed on their surroundings.

Downtown Monterey slips by the windows. Hugo Davenport sees none of it. His mind is too busy thinking in chess moves not yet made to see the tourist gaggles stacked up on the sidewalks. He is wondering which piece to move into place next. Currently he holds a knight. One which he will need all his skill to manipulate into place so that the game can end in the client's favor.

The Littmann Building is the tallest in the city. Which isn't very tall being that Monterey is a city of dwarfs. Six stories of yellow stone with a blue mansard roof, it takes up the corner of Franklin and Pacific Street in downtown Monterey.

They pull left off Franklin and dip down into the shadows of the Littmann Building's underground parking garage, using a pass card to get through the barrier. The garage is no bigger than two basketball courts. Its low ceiling of running pipes and exposed wires give it a claustrophobic feel. Only three other cars take up the badly lit space, being that the offices above are largely empty.

They park away from the other cars, which are crowded around the elevator. The men in the front get out first. Arriving at the back door, the driver pulls it open. Meanwhile, the passenger waits for Davenport to get out before handing him his briefcase.

The three men move off in formation, Davenport making up the rear of a triangle. Juddering strip lighting leads them across the lot to the elevator door. The air is oily with the stench of gasoline. Nearing the elevator, the Englishman senses movement above them in the ceiling cavity. By the time he looks up the lights are already out.

The darkness is momentary. Several suppressed gunshots zip past his ears. Two short groans and there's movement on both sides.

When the lights come back on, his two companions lie dead, their heads wearing a litany of .22-caliber bullet holes. There is little time to ponder their demise. Feet land behind Hugo Davenport and he raises his hands. The hot end of a suppressor is pressed to the back of his neck, the skin hissing, the Englishman too scared to flinch.

In a voice like a whisper, Peter says, "You have an office in Monterey. How long have you been watching me?"

Glancing down at the men either side, Davenport says, "Your reputation proceeds you, Azrael. Nevertheless, let me point out that Mr. James to my left is—or was—my firm's head of litigation. And as for Mr. Taylor to my right, he was no more than my driver. The men you have so callously murdered were in fact mere employees. Innocent of any crimes relating to myself or my client."

Peter lets him have his fun for a second. Then he asks, "Is that why they're armed?"

Davenport smiles green teeth. "Well spotted."

"On your knees."

Peter pushes him down.

"You don't have to do this," Davenport says as he lowers himself, the pistol nestling into the back of his crown.

"Who are you working for, Mr. Davenport? I will ask only a set amount of times. After that, you'll be joining your friends."

"So do I take it that you have decided to renege on our deal?"

"Who do you work for?"

Davenport takes in air through his nose, making it whistle. Exhaling through his teeth, he explains, "I'm afraid if I told you that I would be in more trouble than you."

"I'm not the one with the gun at the back of my head."

"No. But you *will* be the one with the gun at the back of your head. After all, we know where to find you."

"I'll never go back to Monterey."

"We found you once, Azrael. We surely will again."

Peter presses the gun into him. "Tell me who you work for."

"You think by killing my client you can get yourself out of this?"

"Tell me."

"It would do neither of us any good. My advice, one professional to another, is to walk away from this car park and take the job. Then you can be a free man. I promise you."

"You're lying. You can't offer me anything."

"You believe that even after speaking with Mr. Bryce?"

"I don't like being threatened into things. It may have worked with him, but not with me."

"We have tried to be polite in our negotiations. It is you who have used intimidatory measures, so to speak." The lawyer widens his arms. "For instance, our current predicament."

"Tell me," Peter growls.

"Not even the threat of death will make me give up my client."

"Then," Peter snarls, cocking the barrel and getting ready to make two dead bodies into three, "I'll wait for him to come to me."

Davenport shudders. Gasps, "Wait!"

Peter gives him a second, ready to send the limey's brains all over the oily concrete.

"Before you send me shuffling off this mortal coil," Davenport says, "do me the favor of letting me call my secretary Mrs. Henderson so I can tell her not to expect me today."

Peter has gone cold all over. "What did you say?"

When Davenport speaks, the fear is gone from his voice and he talks in a tone as cold as the blood coursing through his reptilian veins. "My secretary," he says. "Mrs. Henderson. She's expecting me at nine. I believe it is five past now. She's such a darling and does worry herself over me. I wouldn't want her to be consumed with angst on my part."

THIRTY-TWO

Upstairs on the fourth floor of the Littmann Building Peter stands at the back of Hugo Davenport. The two of them are positioned at the rear end of an office space. On the other side is the glass wall of an anteroom, inside which Kate Henderson sits at a desk. She is dressed in a flowery blouse with a navy blue suit jacket over the top. Behind her is a door with the nameplate of Hugo Davenport, Partner in Law. Close to her is another desk. Behind it a heavy pretends to work. Underneath his suit jacket is a gun.

Busy on the phone, Kate is oblivious to the pair of eyes closely watching her from across the vast open-plan office.

"You see, Azrael," Davenport hisses like a snake, "we know so much about you. Even the things you won't admit to yourself. Ah," he says, relaxing and straightening up, "you've taken the gun away. I am most grateful."

Hugo Davenport smooths out his pinstripe suit jacket, running his greasy pink hands down it. He is relieved and satisfied. This move has gone to him. A carefully positioned pawn has defeated the knight.

When he turns to Peter, he has one piece of advice which he gives in that hollow voice of his. "Go back to Green Street. We'll clean up downstairs. Expect the first name by nine o'clock tonight. Get this done and you can be free. You can *all* be free."

THIRTY-THREE

ALASKA, 2003

Having emptied the rat traps and chopped the wood, Peter packed in silence. Finished, he loaded the backpack onto his shoulders and placed a Steyr SSG 69 bolt-action rifle across his back. He joined Mother in the hallway, where she awaited him, fully packed.

Peter was fifteen. By then a strapping adolescent. Athletic and strong. Not overly bulky. Nothing showy about Peter's physique. His body exactly where it should be. Shaped not by steroids and excessive exercise, but naturally through training and hard work. The likes of which no longer existed in the life of the average American teen. It was quick, strong and accurate. Almost four years of focused muscle memory locked inside. Tens of thousands of hours. Like a tool crafted by a master, his body had been perfectly honed to perform its future work with maximum efficiency.

The colossal Magda was hanging laundry in the yard as they passed.

"Goodbye, Magda," Peter called to her.

She gazed after them, shading her eyes with a callused hand, a peg held between her teeth, her charcoal eyes following them until they sunk out of sight into the trees.

Birch Creek, Alaska, is an area of woodland the size of the state of New York. They trekked through thick forest all morning. At midday, beside a small waterfall that trickled down a rock face, they ate lunch. It was while they sat on the trunk of a fallen tree that a bird glided down from the canopy and settled on a rock not far from them. It had white plumage on the belly and turquoise feathering along the back. Peter wished he could ask Mother what it was. But he knew she would only scold him for ruining the hush. Snapping at him with something along the lines of, "Whatever the bird's name, it prefers silence to the sound of your whining."

So he didn't ask.

They proceeded through the uneven terrain with the soundlessness of migrating deer, Mother having long ago taught him how to move without sound. They lived such a silent life, the three of them. No television. No radio. No conversation. Just the wind and the crackling fire to keep them company.

By fifteen, sinking into the background had become as natural to Peter as ostentation was to his more socially refined peers.

You will never know he is there until you do.

Then you will be dead.

The weather worsened. The wind hurrying through the tall trees, ripping off branches and bark, tossing it about. Using the roots of a fallen spruce to shelter, they set up camp for *the night. Not that it was dark. This time of year so close to the North Pole, there are only a few hours of twilight for darkness.*

An hour later, they lay awake, the wind rustling the sides of the tent, the pair of them unable to sleep in the noise, even if their bodies desired it from the thirteen-hour trek.

"Mother?" Peter said, breaking a silence that had lasted since morning.

She sighed. "What do you want, boy?"

"Remember before when you said you and Magda have trained many boys and girls?"

"Yes."

"Who for?"

"I told you. Government."

"But what part of it—CIA, military, who?"

"Government within government within government. Like Matrioshka."

"What's that?"

"Dolls within dolls."

"You mean Russian dolls?"

"I mean, Matrioshka," the old woman snapped.

They fell silent. She was glad. Once more they lay there trying to focus out the sounds of the weather.

"Mother?"

"My patience won't last forever," she growled beside him.

"Why does Magda live with us?"

"Because she helps train boys and girls for program."

"But why? Doesn't she have a family somewhere?"

"I am her family. She is mine. When you leave here, you will never again see me. And I will never again see you. But Magda will still be here."

"Is she your friend?"

"She is my best friend."

"How do you know her?"

Mother breathed in and then out, the air whistling through her tight nostrils, mirroring the sound outside. "We saved each other," she finally said in a voice tinged with sadness. "Now no more questions. Go to sleep. We have busy day tomorrow."

In the morning they ate a breakfast of army preserves. There was little time for R&R. The dry food eaten, the garbage buried from bears, they continued through the trees until they reached a ridge where the forest floor rose sharply.

Mother got low. Gave a hand signal for him to follow suit. They crawled the last twenty meters to the edge of the trees. In the icy valley below there was a herd of caribou. They dotted a wide river that snaked through the lowland, grazing on the lush grass that had thawed on its banks.

Peter carefully removed the Steyr SSG 69 from his back and positioned it in the scrub before him. But as he flicked the lens cap off the scope, Mother placed a hand across the optics. When he glanced sideways at her, she was shaking her head.

"I don't want you to shoot it," she whispered. "I want you to kill it without firing single shot. Do you think you can do that?"

Peter glanced back at the caribou. "Maybe."

"Well, I hope you can. Because we're not going home until you do."

THIRTY-FOUR

NEW YORK STATE, 2019

PETER TAKES THE JOB. HE TAKES IT BUT WILL BE enthusiastically looking for a way out.

The first name on the kill list comes in: James Wilson. There is only the name and an address in East Hampton, New York. No other details. They leave all intel to Peter. So he spends his first days gathering data and watching.

Wilson is a forty-two-year-old architect. He is very successful. It helps that he is *born money*. Success is always much easier when you have the never-ending lottery ticket of extreme familial wealth for support.

You can smell money on him. Whether it's the black Ferrari F8 he drives or his sprawling mansion. It makes the poverty you see in some parts of the US seem all the crazier. This guy could sell off half his classic car collection and secure the mortgages for at least a hundred families facing eviction because they can no longer afford the bills.

But such is life, and who can blame James Wilson for playing by its rules? Even if they've always been stacked in his favor.

Peter made sure to read up on the family. Research being easy when wealth is celebrity in today's world, and whoever has it is well documented. Or at least the side of them that they want you to see. Well, until the tabloids sniff out something dirty.

Peter wonders whether someone hasn't already smelled something on James Wilson, and that is why he has to die.

The Wilsons are New York royalty, part of the exclusive Manhattan property developer clique. The one that includes the Dursts and the Trumps. Or at least used to.

James is the youngest of four brothers. The other three work in the family company. The oldest is vice president. James is the only son who doesn't work for the Wilson Organization, branching off alone as an architect. Still property, but another side of it. Away from Daddy.

Peter gets the sense of a man wanting to escape the vice-like grip of a possessive patriarch. As well as having to make himself heard above the competing dins of his older siblings.

James Wilson wants to be his own man.

The *New Yorker* has done several background pieces on the Wilson family which Peter has read. James's great-grandfather, Ted Wilson, began the company in the 1940s when he bought a modest apartment block in the Queens borough of New York City. The previous owner had lost it due to unpaid property taxes and Ted Wilson bought it for a snip at auction using money he'd made trading on the Stock Exchange. His main profession had been in construction, his trading a mere pastime that he'd hit the jackpot on. Using his knowledge of building work to run the redevelopment of the apartments himself, he had then saved thousands from not having to hire contractors. That, of course, was after he got rid of the previous tenants. Something made easy when a fire tore through the upper floors and made the entire property uninhabitable. The remaining slum tenants were then removed by the NYPD when Wilson got the building temporarily condemned pending repairs.

The source of the fire was never confirmed. Electrical fault was listed in the official report, but the article in the *New Yorker* insinuated it may have been started by someone representing Wilson himself. It wasn't uncommon during the period for slum apartment blocks to suddenly *go up* in New York City.

Whatever the reason, the Wilson Organization went from strength to strength. Once they developed the Queens block, rather than invite back the black and minority tenants that had previously filled it, Wilson invited white professionals. This would become a theme of the organization. Buying buildings filled with black and minority tenants. Having the building condemned. Then redeveloping it and filling it with white middle-class.

The trick worked and by the time his son John took over the company, he was a multi-millionaire.

James's grandfather John Wilson then built the company up further through construction. Instead of just renovating buildings, he decided to build them. Thus began the Wilson land grab, where they no longer developed buildings but land. Constructing casinos, shopping complexes, apartment blocks, skyscrapers. It was James's father, Frederick "Fred" Wilson, who then took them into Manhattan.

As for James himself, he's a successful man in his own right. A partner in one of New York's largest architecture firms, he already has several buildings throughout the eastern seaboard to his name. Hotels being his thing.

James Wilson's life is the exact opposite of Peter's. It is a life lived in the light, whereas Peter has always dwelled in the shadows. He watches Wilson like he watches the inhabitants of Pacific Grove. He is an expert at watching the lives of others. James Wilson looks like he's living a good one, and Peter can't think what he could have done to have someone want to pay a million to end it.

It is now four days into his surveillance. Peter is sitting in a small boat on Georgica Pond. It is a 290-acre coastal lagoon in East Hampton. He's surrounded by fishing rods. Across the sloshing waters, James Wilson plays tennis with his nine-year-old son on their private court. It takes up a lonely corner overlooking the water.

Wilson lives in a sprawling, 18,000-square-foot house in Wainscott. It covers more than 2,000 feet of frontage on the secluded lagoon. Peter read an article about it in the *New York Times*. The interiors are enhanced with custom millwork, Cotswold stone and state-of-the-art technology. Whatever any of that means. The eighteen-room main house has five bedrooms, two elevators and six stone fireplaces. The plank floors are 200-year-old oak, and the kitchen and family room have vaulted ceilings with antique wooden beams. Upstairs, the master suite has east and west terraces and an opulent bathroom. The lower level has a screening room, a full gym, a billiards room, and a wine cellar with tasting room. A guest wing with three bedrooms and its own kitchen is connected to the main house by a Cotswold stone breezeway. Adjacent to an indoor heated pool is a screened porch with a limestone floor, a dining area and a built-in barbecue. There are views of the water and landscape from almost every room.

Peter watches Wilson teach his son backhand. He comes across as a patient tutor. Never does he scold the boy and through a pair of field glasses, Peter can read their lips. Read the tips and gentle encouragement the father gives his boy.

Watching the father and son, he can't help thinking about Carl and Michael Henderson. He is already certain that he doesn't want the Wilson boy to see it. Even if it's made to look like an accident. He'll make sure it happens when the son is well away.

Peter's phone chirps. It's Pat.

"What did you find on our English friend?"

"Not much," Pat replies. "I called up a couple of people I still speak to in the agency. Had to be real delicate about it."

"What did they say?"

"They've never heard of him, but they're contacting some guys they know in British intelligence to see what they say."

"When do you think they'll get back to you?"

"A week tops."

"Okay. Keep me posted."

Peter is about to end the call when Pat asks, "How's the job going?"

"It's going, Pat. It's going."

He ends the call. Continues his watch of Wilson and his son.

Just like all those years ago with the caribou.

THIRTY-FIVE

OTHER THAN BEING NUMBERED, JAMES WILSON'S days are varied. He appears to hit the office when he feels inspired. Spending a few hours working heatedly before the creative impulse evaporates and he leaves the study. It makes his work hours move around a lot. Adding to this, he passes arbitrarily between the city and the mansion. Often leaving on a whim, jumping into one his fine cars and going for a long drive.

Nevertheless, after ten days, Peter has noticed certain patterns of behavior. James Wilson always wakes up at six and goes for a jog around the neighborhood. He always finishes work at five no matter what. Even if his inspiration only gets him to the desk at four. If he's at his office in New York, he makes sure to leave early enough to be back home by five. He switches his phone and computer off and returns to his family, devoting the remainder of his day to them.

Peter imagines James Wilson spending a childhood waiting up for his father to return home from work. Only to go to bed each night without so much as a goodnight kiss. Maybe that was why his brothers joined the firm. It was the only way they could get some daddy time.

With his own family, it is different. James always makes sure to spend his evenings with his wife and son. Some evenings he drives them into town to a restaurant. Others are spent staying in watching movies in the screening room. Another night Peter watches them go out in their boat, James showing his boy all about the sails.

Wilson has one other thing he does routinely. Once his son is in bed, he goes for a swim in the indoor pool. Sometimes with his wife. More often on his own.

Peter has already spent many a night watching him from the darkness of the lagoon as James Wilson swims continual lengths for forty-five minutes. Then gets out and showers.

It is one of his rituals.

THIRTY-SIX

It is Friday when Peter follows James Wilson into Manhattan.

At Times Square, honking horns jar his eardrums. Roadworks block several of the lanes up ahead. The dirge of a pneumatic drill chatters away, echoing off the tall buildings.

Peter glances at the passenger seat where his phone sits. He has placed a tracker on Wilson's car. The map on the screen tells him that the target lies six car lengths in front.

Wilson leads him to West 86th Street. A gigantic gray block grows out of the sidewalk. The bottom floor is stone facade and the rest is brickwork. A green awning and a doorman mark the entrance. There are parking spaces free for visitors. Wilson takes one, gets out of his silver Mercedes-Benz 300SL and walks into the building.

This is new. Peter hasn't seen him come here before.

While circling the block, he looks up the building. It is filled with psychiatrists. He thinks how much he'd like to be a fly on the wall while Wilson bleeds his heart out to his shrink. He ponders waiting a week. Seeing if he visits here again. Have something set up by then. A bug in the wall of the office. Maybe then he'd be able to find out why someone wants the guy dead so much. It would give him an idea who Davenport's client is. Then Peter could end this the way he wants to.

It is less than useless thinking like this, though. Wilson probably only sees the shrink once a month. That would use up too much time.

It is an hour and a half later that James Wilson leaves the building. Peter notes that his eyes are puffy and red when he emerges from under the awning. Like he's spent much of the time up there crying. He doesn't return straight to his car. Instead, he heads east down 86th until he's crossing the road and walking into the western side of Central Park.

Peter follows him on foot.

Inside the park, Wilson takes a seat at the edge of Central Park Lake. Joggers amble by. Dogs bark. Children play. The sun skips off the tranquil waters of the lake. Peter moves past Wilson and takes up a position a hundred yards along the bank on a bench. It gives him a great view of the target through the draping canopy of a weeping willow. Close enough to read Wilson's lips if he has to.

Wilson gets his phone out. There is a short conversation. Though Peter has no chance of knowing what the other person is saying, he does know what Wilson is saying.

"I've made up my mind. I want to make a full confession." Following this, James Wilson listens to whatever it is the person on the other end has to say. He appears to interrupt when he blurts out, *"I don't care about immunity."*

More listening. Then: *"I can't look my family in the eyes if I don't do this... I just can't."*

After the call he throws his head into his hands. That is the moment Peter spots the humungous man. He is some way beyond Wilson, looming in the background. His face is shaped like the skull of some ancient ape. He is a phenomenal example of man. At least seven feet tall with a chest like the grille on a truck, he is dressed in a suit that must have been stitched onto him. And the worst part is that his lifeless lizard eyes are staring directly at Peter.

He is absolutely certain of it.

THIRTY-SEVEN

IT'S A WEEK SINCE PETER LAST SPOKE TO PAT Hughes. As he follows James Wilson's Mercedes back to East Hampton, the fixer's voice fills the car over speakerphone.

"All I got was questions and no answers," explains Pat.

"Meaning?"

"Meaning that Hugo Davenport is a red flag. My contact at the agency called me half an hour ago. It's taken me that long to get rid of him. He wanted to know exactly why I'd asked about the limey lawyer."

"And what did you tell him?"

"That I'd had a chat recently with a friend who'd had some dealings with Davenport in Dubai. All I wanted was to know how legit he is."

"And what did your guy come back with?"

"Straight out accused me of lying. Said like fuck it was about business dealings in Dubai. Then he grilled me. Said he'd heard rumors I was running a freelance consultancy that went beyond the operations of my company."

"Anything about running me?"

"I don't think it would have been as polite as a phone call if he knew things went beyond consultancy. Do you?"

Peter inwardly agrees. It wouldn't have. It would have been Pat in a hot room with a bag over his head.

"What else did he say?"

"Asked me whether I was working for Davenport."

"Working for him?"

The freeway rounds a hill and the early evening sun pokes out from behind it. Light cascades off of Wilson's silver car, making it blaze incandescent.

"Yeah," Pat says. "I replied, 'Why would I be working for him?' And, get this, my guy says nothing for a few seconds. I can hear him breathing down the phone, calming himself. Then he tells me that he called a London contact he had who told him to leave it with him. The next he's in his boss's office at the agency getting his ass handed to him. He had to lie that he'd heard the name over the wire and wished to see what was up."

"So Davenport is something."

"He certainly is. Just what that something is, we can only guess."

Neither man speaks for a while as the freeway joins the coast. The Atlantic Ocean looks like it's on fire and so does Wilson's beautiful car.

What does he want to confess?

Pat breaks into his thoughts. "How far are you away from completion of the first target?"

"Tomorrow night," Peter replies. "I hacked his wife's email. She's taking the boy to Martha's Vineyard for the weekend. Her parents live there. James is staying at home.

He has a meeting with a client planned for Sunday in the city."

"And would I be right in thinking that he won't be attending?"

"You certainly would."

THIRTY-EIGHT

ALASKA, 2003

THEY WERE OUT THERE ALMOST A WEEK BEFORE HE did it. For the first four days he was obsessed with reaching the caribou while they hung about on the grass. Crawling along in camouflage, bit by bit, eking his way to them. He had even gone so far as to coat himself in their dung to hide from their expert sense of smell.

Four days of this had gotten him no closer than twenty feet before they'd sensed him and run.

It was on the day that God usually rests that Peter came up with his plan, and instead of going out in the morning, he went out in the middle of the night while it was still relatively dark, risking a run-in with bears.

At dawn the sun came up over the white crest of the snow-flecked hills and the caribou returned to their favorite grazing spot. Slowly they filled up the valley and stood as one great herd when—Bam!—Peter launched himself from his hidden place buried in the mud of the riverbank, having spent the last six hours under a hatch of reeds torn from the edge of the water and sewn together. Patiently waiting for one of the caribou to come close.

He grabbed ahold of a strapping male with huge antlers. Plunged a knife into its chest. Accurately finding the heart, he twisted the blade while pulling the bucking beast to the ground with all his weight, an arm wrapped around its long neck, the antlers swinging from side to side, the other animals dispersing, including the scattering birds.

The whining caribou dragged Peter along for some way, his feet skidding in the mud, scrambling to find anchorage. The animal finally dropped, its legs folding underneath, and Peter held it to the ground until it breathed its last groaning breath, the teenager watching his own reflection in the animal's eyes all the way until they went blank.

THIRTY-NINE

NEW YORK STATE, 2019

It is Saturday. James Wilson is kissing his family goodbye as they get into the car on the carriageway of their multi-million-dollar East Hampton mansion.

It is the last time they will ever see him alive.

He hugs his son. Gropes his wife's behind when the kid isn't looking. And when she simpers back, they fall into a kissing embrace. They are all smiles and kisses and waves and joy. It is a happy moment and Peter is glad that the couple got to spend their last night together making love. Unaware, thankfully, of the night fisherman watching from Georgica Pond.

In the morning James brought her breakfast in bed and the son joined them, pouncing onto the mattress, James tickling him. The boy turning into a bundle of giggles and writhing limbs.

It will be a loving memory that she and her son will hold

for the rest of their lives. They deserve that. Not like some when their last moments are an argument. The surviving partner issued a lifetime of guilt for one heat-of-the-moment indiscretion.

Peter is glad that the last thing the Wilsons say to each other is "I love you." Not, "I hate you."

James Wilson waves them off, only going back inside when the electronic gate closes at the end of the drive.

The rest of the day is filled with the monotony of everyday existence. Wilson works in his study. Speaks to a friend on the telephone. Cancels the call when he gets one from his wife saying they reached her parents safely. Later, he eats dinner alone. Calls his wife and son to say goodnight. Then it's time for his laps.

Wilson makes his way to the swimming pool. Amongst the sparkling white tiles of the changing room he gets into his swimming trunks, places goggles and a cap on, then travels up a set of steps to the pool.

James Wilson dives in and starts with front crawl.

Upstairs the loft hatch moves quietly to one side and a shadow gently touches down onto the landing. A body extending from the attic.

Peter sneaks soundlessly downstairs as if he is nothing more than a gentle breeze drifting soundlessly through the house. In the hallway, he picks up a framed photograph of the family. They look so happy posing at the back of their boat, the lagoon spread out behind them, an expanse of glittering turquoise. It is such a shame that he has been forced into this. The only condolence he can offer the family is that if he ever finds out who the client is, he will murder them.

Placing the picture back in exactly the same place, he

continues onwards through the house. In the kitchen, he takes a bottle of dishwashing soap from under the sink. Like a shadow, he moves toward the echoing splashes of James Wilson.

He reaches the back of the swimming pool. It is a long room surrounded by windows. The black night is unseeable beyond them. Light reflects off the water, undulating off a tall domed ceiling. Peter stands at just the right spot. Far enough away so Wilson won't be able to see him from the water. But close enough to watch from a standing position.

No going back, he thinks as the hazy image of the target cuts through the water.

Peter moves in the direction of the changing room. It is at the back of the pool down a set of steps. While James Wilson swims, Peter squirts the floor leading to it, including the steps, with the soapy liquid. He empties the entire bottle. Then he uses the floor squeegee to spread it and coat a runway section of tiles leading from the pool.

Two glass-fronted shower cubicles take up the end wall of the changing room. In front of them is a bench that faces the steps. Peter takes a seat on it and waits.

Soon James Wilson is out of the pool and making his way toward him. The second his foot touches the soapy floor, it rushes forward at a terrible velocity, dragging his body with it. His legs fly up into the air and his head comes crashing down on the tiles with a terrible crack. Then, with the motion of his body, he slides forwards down the steps, a trail of blood going with him.

He comes to a stop not far from Peter's feet. Lying on the wet ground moaning, he doesn't writhe or move in any way. He just lies still on his back, legs twisted to the side.

Peter thinks it's because his neck is broken. It had made a loud snapping sound as he'd gone down the steps.

James Wilson lies groaning and staring up at the ceiling lights. Peter leans over him. Meets his eyes. Wilson doesn't flinch because he can't. Just as he can't stop Peter sliding his hands beneath his shoulders and gently lifting him into a sitting position, making sure not to leave one mark or impression on the body.

James Wilson gazes at Peter while trying to mumble something. Peter doesn't try to listen to what it is. All he does is say, "I'm so sorry." And drops him hard, the broken skull cracking heavily on the tiles one last, fatal time.

Three minutes later his heart stops and Peter leaves the body. He uses a hose to spray down the soap, before taking one last look at the dead man.

What did you want to confess? he can't help thinking.

In the kitchen Peter places the empty soap bottle in the trash. He is sure it won't be noticed. He is sure it will take Sherlock Holmes to figure this one.

Peter is thankful that the Baker Street detective is no more than the figment of a long-dead author's imagination. New York State Troopers will have to do.

Peter is about to leave when he hears something that makes his heart stop. The locks on the front door are clicking into action. Someone is coming inside the house.

Peter is trapped in the kitchen. There is only one door out. The one leading to the hallway where the entrance is.

Footsteps close in on him as he ducks behind a breakfast bar that occupies the middle of the room. His suppressed HK45 is drawn. By their sounds, he calculates two men. One tall and heavy. The other shorter and more nimble.

The footsteps come to the kitchen door and stop. Then a man speaks in a voice so devoid of emotion that it could have been emitted from a machine trying to imitate a man.

"It's okay, Azrael," he drones, "you can come out. Davenport sent us."

Peter's whole body goes cold. Slowly, with the gun down by his side and out of sight, he raises himself.

Two men stand in coveralls. One is five-ten with sharp little eyes and a nondescript face. It literally looks like someone has cut a mouth, two eyes and some nostrils into a white rubber mask. He has black hair that looks dry and rough; a sign that it has recently been colored. Peter also spots a rash at the corners of his mouth and on his cheeks. It comes from the adhesive used for fake beards and moustaches.

The other man is a giant. But not in a steroid-experiment-gone-wrong kind of way. More in a genetically gifted way. He looks like he comes from a long line of giant men going back to the gladiatorial arenas. His head is at least twice the size of his companion's. And not just that.

He is the man from the park.

"Look at his face," the shorter one says, ribbing the giant with an elbow. "He was getting ready to ice us. What did I tell you, he's one cool, cool bastard this one."

"Who are you?" Peter asks.

"From Davenport."

"You said. But why?"

"Cleanup crew."

Peter goes to speak but the dead-mask places a finger over his lips. "Best we keep things as simple as possible," his blank voice says. "No need for details. You've done your job. Now let us do ours. Okay?"

They stare at each other a while. The tension is thick enough to cut. Peter cautiously begins to leave the room. Keeping them within his peripheral the whole time. Finger on the trigger. Gun down by his thigh, his body keeping it out of sight.

The two men eye him all the way. "It's okay," death-mask says. "We ain't here for you."

A black hold-all dangles from the giant's shoulder and Peter wonders what's inside. He doesn't ask. Instead, he leaves the house. The first target down.

FORTY

PETER WAS SEVENTEEN AND HANDCUFFED TO THE
back of a van that was being driven into the night. Nothing
could be made out beyond the black hood that covered his face.
The air was thick with wet heat and it made him sweat all
over, his skin itching.

The van came to a rapid halt. Skidding on the blacktop.
Peter tipped to the side and then back again.

The back doors creaked open. A rough hand grabbed him
by the shoulder and tilted him forward. The handcuffs were
released and the hood plucked off.

He was instantly blinded by white light as someone
dragged him from the van, having to use an arm to shield his
aching eyes. The harsh light went out. His eyes recovered, and
when they did, he found himself standing in the middle of a
residential street for the first time in a little over six years.

Rows of bungalows with little lawns and lighted windows lined the street. Bugs chirped in the neat hedgerows. He felt like he was going to cry. Because it was the first time in half a decade that he saw something other than woods and endless mountains. There were houses. There were people. There was life.

A happiness welled up in Peter that threatened to overwhelm him. Through a window, he observed an elderly couple cuddled up on a couch, the man's arm strung across the shoulders of his gray-haired wife. They were watching TV and looked immensely content. A dog barked in a backyard and Peter could hear its chain rattle. He wanted to breathe in every sound, every smell, every sight.

"Turn around, boy."

It all went gray. Mother had a habit of doing that.

By the time he faced her, the grin that had begun to grow was gone. Replaced by the placid expression he has worn now for practically his entire life.

"Home is 4000 miles north," she told him. "You have no weapons, no food, no money, no friends. I hope to see you within two months."

The engine of the van was still running. She got in the passenger side, the door slammed, and Magda tooted the horn. As Peter stood there watching them disappear, he recalled the ride from the airbase, during which Mother had told him how it would be.

"You must not kill anyone of authority. Stick to Rule Five."

"Never hurt an innocent," he had stated automatically while sitting there handcuffed and hooded.

"Yes. That means that you can't hurt them in the course of stealing. But that doesn't mean you can't steal. Just be careful. Remember the techniques I taught you. Pickpocketing is an art. As is breaking and entering, so long as you don't get caught. Don't get greedy or cocky. If the security of a home is too good, leave it. Move on to something smaller. Never steal anything worth any serious money. Nothing over a hundred dollars. Only food, clothing and medical supplies. Some money."

She called it a "walkabout." Apparently when Australian Aboriginal males reach adolescence, they are left in the outback for up to six months to fend for themselves. Forced to survive on their own wits. It is a rite of passage. The same was true for Peter. He needed to survive two months in the outback of the United States. Prove that he could survive cut off in the field.

"What if I'm threatened?"

"Then you must do what you must. Just try your best to avoid it, Peter. Use the fact that you are a teenage boy to deflect their aggression. Try to look innocent. It will be a powerful weapon."

"What about vehicles?"

"I would like you to vary your approach. You may use a vehicle, but only for a hundred miles at a time. Then you must dump it and use another technique for gaining the next hundred."

"Trains, planes and automobiles."

"Precisely."

The owner of the barking dog came to his door, the locks scratching, the porch light going on, illuminating the front yard. The shadow of a man stepped into it as he emerged from the house, his dressing gown open on stripy blue boxer shorts.

He eyed the deserted street.

Peter was long gone. Staying within the shadows of the sidewalk, he moved with purpose, as if he had somewhere to go.

"If you are caught and incarcerated," Mother had said, "you will be brought straight back to me and you will have failed."

"I won't get caught."

"You think so? You are a seventeen-year-old boy who looks even younger than that. You will be on your own without an adult. Every cop or person of authority will want to speak with you. If they spot you at night, they will take you for sure. Want to know where your parents are. Where you live."

"I've run from cops before."

"Yes. In orphanage you escaped many times. But if I recall correctly you were also recaptured many times. I remember night I find you. You tried to escape then. Got as far as trying to break into man's shed. He called police and so here we are."

Peter could tell without seeing that she was grinning that devilish little grin of hers.

"Of course," she added, her voice going deeper, "there are worse than cops. There are people who hurt young man such as you. People who prey on hitchhikers and poor boys with no home to go to. You must remember Rule One."

"Never drop your guard," Peter said automatically.

Walking the suburb, Peter kept to the darker side of the street, where the bushes overhung the front yards. He didn't hurry. He moved like he belonged there and had somewhere to go. Just another neighborhood kid leaving a pal's place having spent the evening playing PlayStation. He used to live in a neighborhood just like this. Before Mother. Before St. Joseph's. Before he became a killer.

It was with his real mother. The one he lived with the first nine years of his life.

"Do not even think of running," Mother's voice came back to him. "There is no life out there for you, and you will be hunted to the end. I won't lie to you, Peter. There is a GPS tracker sewn into your skin. If you remove it, you will become the most wanted seventeen-year-old in the world. The same goes if you do not return within three months. Run away and there will be nowhere where you will be safe. The American government will hunt you until they have confirmation of your dead body."

"I won't run, Mother."

"I hope not. You have a purpose here, Peter. Out there you will only become lost. You may think that you can live amongst those people, but you are wrong. You have a gift, Peter. Most are born to be sheep. But you, you are a wolf. And a wolf cannot live amongst sheep."

While meandering down a back alley, Peter found himself drawn to the rear window of a yellow stucco bungalow. A mother sat with her son reading him a story, the boy sitting against his headboard holding a teddy while she took up a bottom corner of the bed, the book open on her lap.

It brought back memories of his own fleeting childhood.

Mesmerized, Peter found himself creeping over the fence and wandering toward the window until he was practically up against it.

He got too close.

The mother spotted his garish face staring from the darkness. It made her scream. She got up sharply, the book flung onto the floor, and rushed out of the room, calling out, "David! David! Come quickly."

The kid turned to the window from his bed. Spotting the ghoul in the shadows, he too screamed.

Peter was over the fence by the time the husband rushed out with his shotgun.

FORTY-ONE

MONTEREY, 2019

P<small>ETER CHECKED LOCAL</small> H<small>AMPTON NEWS THE</small> second his plane landed at SFO. Whatever they cleaned up, it wasn't James Wilson. He was found by police the next morning as they performed a routine welfare check. His wife had called after James hadn't answered multiple calls. Which was very unlike him. The two state troopers who attended the property had found him sprawled out in the pool room. Having apparently slipped and hit his head.

The report in the *East Hampton Globe* claimed that falls account for 26 percent of all deaths in the home and are the second biggest domestic killer after poisoning.

James Wilson has merely become another statistic.

"And they said they were there to clean up?" Pat Hughes says down the phone.

Peter stands at the end of Old Fisherman's Wharf, Monterey. It is night. The cafés are closed and the pier is abandoned, the tables and chairs locked away inside. The tide is in and the waves crash over the rocks beneath the wooden walkway. The moon and stars shiver on the black water. The seals are somewhere else.

"I think they were there for his computers."

"Were they American?" Pat asks.

"Yeah. The short one was New York. Brooklyn if I had to guess. The big guy looked Latino. He didn't speak, so I didn't get an accent."

Pat goes silent a while. Then he says, "This is getting hot, Peter. You need to get it done as quickly as possible."

Peter isn't listening.

As his eyes trace the silhouette of a bird gliding over the water, its wings stretched out, he says, "You know, I sensed from the second I arrived in East Hampton that I was being watched. I thought I saw the same guy driving three different cars behind me on three different days. It was the little one. The one with the dead man's eyes. I also recognized the big guy from Central Park. He was the one staring at me."

"Looks like our man Davenport likes to keep a close eye on things," Pat says.

Both men don't talk for a moment. Then Peter asks, "Have you checked the second name yet?"

"Yeah. Ken Knight. He's some two-bit lawyer in San Jose."

"Local, then."

"Yeah. A real ambulance chaser. I looked hard and could find no connection between him and James Wilson. They exist in completely opposite planes. Wilson is rich Manhattan royalty with a PhD in architecture from MIT.

Knight grew up the son of a bus driver and a homemaker. Got his law degree from community college in Santa Cruz."

"Nothing in his law practice?"

"Nope. Nothing involving anything remotely relating to James Wilson. Like I said, they are on completely different planes."

"What about anything that might relate to Davenport?"

"Nothing. Except that they have law offices in the same state, there's nowhere where I can see their lives overlapping."

Peter hears giggling. A young couple have spilled out of the bar across the street. Their silhouettes skip across the beach, the two flinging off their clothing, a line of crumpled garments littering the sand in their wake. They reach the waves in their underwear and dive into them.

Peter asks, "You any closer to figuring out who the client is yet?"

"I'm tiptoeing around it," Pat says. "But so far I've gotten nothing but a big fuck you."

"Keep looking."

The couple kiss within a pool of stars.

"What are you gonna do?"

"The same."

FORTY-TWO

It is almost ten by the time Peter reaches 24 Green Street disguised as Paul Adams. Emerging from the Saab 900, he feels as close to home as he ever has. The crickets chitter loudly in the grass and somewhere a dog barks in a backyard.

"Only a short trip this time," comes a woman's voice out of the darkness.

Peter pauses. Turning to his right, he see Mrs. Harrison's wrinkled face illuminated in the dull glow of a candle that flickers by her side. She is sitting within the shadows of her porch.

"Yes, ma'am," he says.

"Where to this time?"

"Albuquerque, New Mexico."

She cocks her head. He realizes from her droopy eyes and slurred speech that she is slightly intoxicated. The open bottle of merlot beside her confirms it.

"Did you meet anyone interesting in Albuquerque, New Mexico?"

She hiccups immediately after speaking.

"Just work."

"Just work," she repeats, staring at him with big glazed eyes.

It is awkward.

"Goodnight, Mrs. Harrison."

"Goodnight, Paul."

As he reaches his door, she adds, "Don't be a stranger."

He pauses on his doorstep.

Don't be a stranger?

He's never been anything else.

Inside the house he hooks his phone into 24 Green Street's security and checks the camera footage from the eleven days he has been away.

Day five. Pam Jenkins stands at the end of the drive staring at the house. No more notes under the door. Just staring. Does she know there's a camera?

Day eight. Carlos and Rosa Hernandez come around. They tend to his lawn. Water it. Trim back the hedge. They take a moment to talk with Mrs. Harrison. Peter guesses that they're speaking about him.

Apart from that, there has been no other action around his house while he's been away.

The basement of 24 Green Street is practically empty except a washer-dryer twin tub, his weight training equipment, and a few other things hanging about gathering dust and cobwebs. Three units of shelving line the end wall. He walks straight up to the very left of the shelves and pushes the unit back into the wall. It sinks in soundlessly and when it clicks, he slides the shelving unit to the right so that it disappears behind the next one. This reveals a metal door with an electronic lock.

One of the reasons Peter chose this particular house on Green Street was the fact that it has an underground safe room built into the existing basement. Having always been more of an attack-them-hard-and-heavy kind of guy, as opposed to a hide-in-a-room kind of guy, he hadn't needed a safe room. What he needed was a communications epicenter. A listening post plugged into the heartbeat of Pacific Grove. One so powerful it is rigged directly into the city's power supply to hide its energy needs. One that, for security reasons, he had built by several different companies. Each building a separate part to one of the biggest StingRays the world has ever seen. At least on a non-military scale.

Otherwise known as an *international mobile subscriber identity-catcher*, or IMSI-catcher, a StingRay is a telephone eavesdropping device used for intercepting mobile phone traffic and tracking location data of mobile phone users. Essentially a "fake" mobile tower, it acts between the target phone and the service provider's real towers. Considered a man-in-the-middle (MITM) attack, IMSI-catchers are used in a number of countries by law enforcement and intelligence agencies, their use having obviously raised significant civil liberty and privacy concerns.

When Peter first arrived on Green Street three years ago, he wanted to know everything about his neighbors. How better to do this than to turn their mobile telephones into listening bugs?

The StingRay gives him access to all mobile telephone

devices within a thousand-meter radius. It can manipulate phones to use their cameras and microphones remotely. Essentially giving him the power of sonar.

Peter takes a seat in an ergonomic chair before a bank of computer monitors. He places a set of headphones over his ears and fires the StingRay up. He has only used it a few times since his arrival in Pacific Grove. When he had initially gathered all the intel he could on his local community. When he learned that the Jenkinses were always badmouthing their neighbors. Even each other. And that their neighbors returned the favor by badmouthing them.

He had learned, too, that Mrs. Harrison's husband Bert had gone to see the doctor about a lump under his armpit one day and had been dead within the month. "You know what I miss the most?" she had said to her sister Gwen over the telephone.

"What, sis?"

"I miss having his presence beside me on the porch. Just sitting there with me and watching the world go by. It's so lonely on my own."

Jimmy Palmer's drinking problems had also come to Peter's attention back then. As well as the position of terrorizing authority he holds in his house. The way his family, especially Danny, creep around him.

As for the Hendersons, they hadn't always been the perfect family. Another lesson of Peter's eavesdropping. Three years ago, they had been suffering marriage difficulties. The counselor they still see has helped. So too do the pills Kate takes.

The StingRay comes alive, casting its net over the neighborhood, and Peter begins listening to the airwaves. Looking for something that can tell him how Hugo Davenport and his people found him here on Green Street.

FORTY-THREE

THE LOWER FORTY-EIGHT, 2005

THEY HAD DROPPED HIM IN THE *WELLS BRANCH* suburb of Austin, Texas, and he decided to leave pretty soon after being chased out of the backyard by a shotgun-wielding Texan.

As he spent the first days of his walkabout wandering the Lone Star State, Peter spotted a lot of guns. Every homeowner appeared to have one, and he observed plenty of cowboys getting out of their pickups carrying a sidearm. It made him edgy, so he decided to leave.

On the fourth day, having jumped a boxcar out of Austin, he was chased off it six hours later in Oklahoma City. He had been hoping to get as far as Wichita, Kansas, but the huge Rottweiler that woke him up, as well as the club-wielding security guard on the end of its leash, convinced him to get out of there.

The first weeks were spent meandering northwest across the

country, observing the life that existed around him. He began pickpocketing. House breaking. Stealing clothing and food. He got lost watching people. He watched them go to work. Followed them to school. Listened to them. Hung about the strip malls, the Walmarts, the shopping centers, the bars and the alleys— the places were everyday life happened.

A few times he was approached by police officers. In Wichita a cruiser pulled up sharp coming around a corner, its headlights burning his eyes. The two cops inside signaled him to stop. That screeching half-siren honk.

He was gone before they even got out. Rounding a corner, he skipped up a dumpster, jumped straight up four feet, grabbed a ladder hanging down from a fire escape and was on the building's rooftop by the time the cops were entering the alley, the two men breathing heavily and shining their flashlights about at nothing but trash.

In the taller cities he used the deserted rooftops to get along at night, making his way without even touching so much as a paving slab. He played games with people. Played knock-and-run on their windows as he made his way up the wall of their apartment building. Breaking and entering became a habit. Not for stealing. More for seeing how people lived. Balconies were the best. More often than not they were left unlocked, the residents never expecting someone to scale the outer walls to reach them.

There were times when Peter attempted to hang out with others his own age. To socialize and be part of a group. But it wasn't long before he discovered that he was inadequately trained for the cut and thrust savagery of the average American teen.

At a skate park in Idaho some kids made mincemeat of

him. They laughed and joked at the way he spoke and the clothes he wore. The way he was there on his own. Like that was a crime. As well as the fact he knew absolutely nothing about music or pop culture. "Where the hell have you been the last ten years? The North fucking Pole?!"

They began picking on him. When one of the larger kids tried to grab him, he broke the guy's arm in two places. Several skateboards were swung at him. He dodged each one and got out of there, the kid's howls echoing off the smooth concrete.

In Casper, Wyoming, he foolishly trusted two guys who were a little older than him. They invited him back to their apartment. But the moment he was inside, they pulled a flick-knife on him. The attempted robbery turned out to be fun. They had absolutely no fighting skills and soon the knife was sticking out of one of their ass cheeks, while the other guy lost most of his front teeth when Peter grabbed a beer bottle from a nearby table and pounded it into the guy's mouth. Both were lying on the ground groaning less than a minute after pulling the knife.

Peter avoided the desert states. Arizona, Nevada, Utah and New Mexico. He kept to the relative greenery of the Midwest. He went north from Oklahoma. Up through Kansas. Entered Nebraska. Into Wyoming. West into Idaho. Then Northwest into Washington. That was how he ended up in the suburb of Port Gardner, Everett.

Washington had less guns than Texas. The voyeur was safer, and the suburbs of Everett were like dung to a fly. Watching the people in their daily lives, Peter became fixated on one particular family. A father, mother and son. Max, Sara and Joey Roswell.

To Peter, the Roswells seemed like such a great family.

There was a closeness, a bond, between Max and Joey that Peter had never seen between father and son. Probably because Peter had never seen a father and son together. But, still, when he imagined what he would have loved his relationship to have been like with his own father, this would come pretty close.

As he watched the Roswells from the dark recesses of their backyard, Peter couldn't help thinking back to his own short-lived home life with his mother.

It had lasted only seven years, but he remembered practically every second of it. The burden of his spiteful memory. Everything recalled with the accuracy of a camera. Then played back over and over on a loop.

The early years had been happy. Joy, that was his mother, had been enthusiastic at first. She wanted to prove them all wrong. Her mother who insisted she get an abortion. Her father who told her that he wasn't about to raise some stranger's bastard so she had better get out. Or the man who never returned another phone call after the one where she told him she was pregnant.

In the end, though, at eighteen and with no one to help her, Joy began to feel the weight press down on her. That terrible weight that saps the muscles and grays the day. The one that starts in your head and presses every thought down. Joy got low, and when people are low, they turn to anything for help.

Drugs offered a hand. Or at least the illusion of one.

At first, during the honeymoon of addiction, she tried to be functional. She would make sure Peter was cared for before she took a hit. But after a while the delusion of functionality dispersed completely and Peter became just another background noise to her. He watched—he still watches—her waste away; the family home getting worse and worse, decaying along with her, anything of use being sold, everything else misused and abandoned. Even Peter.

There were days without food, and even before Mother, he had learned to forage. It was partly why he had adjusted so easily to Alaska and its life in the cold. He'd never really known anything else.

The Roswells were different. They were warmth. The all-American family—or at least how Peter imagined it. They had house meetings to discuss things. There was a system of voting. No substance abuse and no abandonment. Monday, Max coached Joey's baseball team. Tuesday was date night, when Joey was left on his own while Max and Sara had some husband and wife time. Usually it was a movie and a meal at their favorite restaurant, DeMarco's. A meal they usually spent complaining about the movie. Wednesday was family movie night. The three of them huddled on the couch watching some no-brainer action movie. Peter watching it with them from the bows of a sycamore at the end of the yard, holding a pair of stolen binoculars to his eyes. Thursday, they went for dinner together as a family at DeMarco's. Friday, Joey went out with his pals while the husband and wife visited a bar with friends, singing hard-rock anthems on the karaoke stand. Saturday, they went to the lake where they had a sailboat they took out. Sunday was lazy. Church followed by a big meal with their extended family. Back home, they lounged in front of the TV, Joey up in his room doing homework.

The obsession grew and, like most voyeurs, Peter couldn't stop himself at watching. While they were away, he began to visit the house. He would sit in their chairs and lie in their beds. He would make himself useful. He fixed things. Mended Joey's broken chest of drawers. The stiff hinge on the shower cubical in Max and Sara's ensuite. The one she'd been on at him to get done for the past two weeks.

At first they didn't realize, but when he rewired the attic lights so that they worked, they called in the police.

The cop stood in their house frowning, pencil hovering over his notepad, Max and Sara pointing to things. The toaster that miraculously now worked on both sides again. The kettle that managed to descale itself.

In the end, the cop had returned to his cruiser and burst out laughing. Someone was breaking into their house to fix things. He'd never heard of anything so ridiculous in all his life.

Peter was a ghost haunting the family. Watching their every move. Dreaming about being introduced to Max and Sara as Joey's friend. Or perhaps the kid next door. Like some side character in a sitcom.

Then one night Peter got caught.

As he stood at Joey's doorway watching the teenager sleep in front of his glowing TV, a voice made every muscle in his body jar.

"Just hold it right there, kid."

FORTY-FOUR

MONTEREY, 2019

For four days Peter listens to the gripes of Pacific Grove. Initially he hones in on the Jenkinses across the street. But they never make one call, and of the four they receive, every one is a cold call.

He hacks into their computers using a malware he sends through an email telling them they've made an overpayment this year on their taxes. They fall for it and he watches their computers for three whole days.

Nothing but true crime and pedophile hunters. So he casts his net wider.

Janine Felmann at 17 Green Street is stealing from her employer at Dan's Lumber. She's been writing checks to herself from petty cash and now they're asking to do an audit on all the offices expenses. From her panicked phone calls to her sister, Peter can tell that she won't last five minutes in an interrogation room. Not five minutes before she's crying her eyes out and begging for mercy.

John Grayson at 37 Palm Avenue is still having an affair with his cousin. Peter had found out about it three years ago during his initial spy operation. It's been happening since they were teenagers and apparently no one has ever suspected. The affair has been kept totally secret in all that time. Once a month they arrive at a motel in separate cars, make love, hold each other in bed for an hour, then leave fifteen minutes apart. She goes back to her husband. He goes back to Palm Avenue and the family that love him.

Kate Henderson complains a lot about working for Hugo Davenport. She finds him an absolute slime bag.

"It's like his creepy little eyes are always watching me," she tells her friend over the phone, "following me about. And they're so dead, Cathy. Like there's no life behind them."

Cathy is laughing. "You can't be serious, Katy."

"I *am* serious. If it wasn't for the fact that he pays three times as much as anyone else, I would quit."

"He can't be that bad, can he?"

"It's not that he does or says anything. It's just *him*. Some impression he gives off that just runs shivers right through me. You know?"

"Not really, Katy." Cathy chuckles. "I'll have to believe you on that one."

Michael Henderson spends time talking with his best friend Charlie.

"Is that prick Danny Palmer still waiting for you when you get off the bus?" Charlie asks.

"Not for the past week. He's been in detention so I've only had to avoid him at weekends."

"What a dick! I wish one day someone would beat the shit out of *him*."

"Someone does: his dad!"

The two boys laugh. Peter can't blame them. It's hard to find sympathy for someone who terrorizes you.

Carl Henderson is planning something big for Kate's birthday. "I got it all lined up," he tells his brother Sam. "I rented the boat and everything. They'll sail us right out of the bay. We'll have dinner with the sun going down below the ocean. With any luck we might get dolphins. It'll be beautiful."

"You know what, Carl?" his brother says crossly.

"What?"

"You're an asshole."

"Why?"

"You know when Suzy finds out what you're doing for Kate's birthday she's gonna want to know why she only got a sweater for hers."

The two laugh. Life at the Hendersons is as warm as ever.

In other news on the street, Mrs. Murphy's dog Sandy had fifteen teeth removed. The old woman sat up all night with the little dog whimpering in her lap. The anesthetic still in her system.

Mrs. Harrison begs her sons to come visit her. But they're too busy with their own families and their own lives. One lives in Seattle. Another in Denver. They both continually invite her to come live with them.

"I can't," she says.

"But why not, Mom?"

"I can't leave this place. It's my place. My home. Where your father and I raised you. I can't just let that go."

A sigh on the other end. "Okay, Mom. I'll try to get out by fall."

Peter should go and sit with her on the porch. He really should. But he can't. He doesn't know why but he just can't bring himself to.

Lastly there are the Palmers at 78 Elm Drive. Jimmy Palmer, his wife Joyce, nine-year-old daughter Hannah, and Danny, the street bully. Jimmy Palmer is a cruel man. He is a cruel husband to his wife. A cruel father to his daughter. But most of all, he is cruel to his son Danny. It is not just violence that he wreaks upon the fourteen-year-old. It is something even more evil. It is the ultimate act of debasement.

Tonight Peter is listening to Danny. He's talking shit to one of his pals when his father bursts into the room.

"Grab your shit, we're leaving," Jimmy says.

"Where to?"

"You fuckin' kiddin' me?"

"Sorry. Where to, sir?"

"Out. Now get off the phone and grab your shit."

The call ends, but Peter continues to listen through the phone's microphone while they leave the house. A feeling rises up in him and he too leaves, taking with him a smaller, portable StingRay unit that he places on the Saab's passenger seat.

He follows Jimmy Palmer's black Ford Edge SUV as it drives east toward Salinas. Activating the microphone on Danny's mobile, he listens to the conversation in the car.

"Please, sir, where are we going?"

"Don't you say a fucking word, boy," Jimmy Palmer angrily snarls. "Just not one word. Where we go and what we do is my business."

"Please, sir," Danny begins to sob. "Not tonight."

"Don't you fucking say a word. You see this?"

There's a pause. Gazing through the back windshield, Peter sees that Jimmy is holding up a pistol to his son.

"Yes, sir."

"I will put one bullet in you and drive right back to the house and put another in your sister while she sleeps. You understand me?"

"Yes, sir."

"You love your sister, don't you?"

"Yes, sir."

"Then I suggest that for the next hour you simply comply with me, boy. You get me?"

"Yes, sir."

They drive to a trailer deep in the woods. Peter watches from trees as Jimmy Palmer opens the door and shoves his son inside. Slamming it closed behind them.

FORTY-FIVE

PETER IS WATERING THE FRONT YARD OF NUMBER 24. All the time he is staring across the street.

On the opposite sidewalk Danny Palmer walks his little sister Hannah to her junior Girl Scouts meeting.

I will put one bullet in you and drive right back to the house and put another in your little sister while she sleeps.

Danny looks smaller than usual. Hunched over. The color faded from his face. His sister skips along in front. Danny carrying her pink backpack for her. Spotting an ice cream van, she stops, twists around to him and points. Smiling just for her, Danny reaches into his pocket before placing a handful of quarters in the tiny hand that reaches out to him.

Peter only ever sees Danny Palmer smile when he's with his sister. He never gets the impression that Danny is jealous of Hannah getting it easier at home. He doesn't appear to take any of his own ills out on her. Just Michael.

No, Danny Palmer is a good big brother.

"I know what you are, Paul Adams," a rasping voice says in Peter's ear.

He turns to his left to find Pam Jenkins standing at the end of his driveway. She wears a scowl on her face.

"What am I, Pam?" he can't help asking in Peter's voice.

Sneering right at him, she says, "A monster is what you are, Paul Adams. A damned monster." She spits on the ground.

The hose drops from Peter's hand. Lands in the grass. Water pools into a puddle as he strolls toward Pam, his cold eyes fixed to her.

Fear replaces the conceited smile. She turns, begins hurrying away, checking over her shoulder when she's halfway across the road.

He catches her at the sidewalk the other side. Takes her roughly by the arm. She freezes. Petrified eyes meet his as she spins her bony body to face him.

"Was it you?" Peter growls at her. "Did you call them here?"

A defiant smile. "So it's true," she says in a tone of self-satisfaction. "The guy that visited you the other day. He was from *them*, wasn't he?"

The blood runs cold in Peter's veins. Never did he really think it could have been her. But here she is admitting it.

All he can say is, "You have no idea what you have done."

His fingers are vicelike. They begin digging into the flesh of her upper arm like the talons of some hungry bird. She cries out, buckling under his grip, falling slow-motion to the curb.

"Ya hurtin' me!" she yelps like a trapped bitch. "He's hurting me! Please, somebody!"

"Who did you call, Pam? Who?"

"Help! Ah!"

Her face is a wince of pain. Her husband is watching through the curtains. Peter looks up from her with malevolence flashing in his eyes. Daring the man with the ugly nose to come out and face him. Face Paul Adams and find Peter. Find Azrael.

"What the hell are you doing?"

Peter's blood goes from cold to ice. He recognizes the voice immediately. He turns around and there she is, standing out of her car, Michael watching from the passenger side.

"Let go of her arm," Kate Henderson says.

Shame ripples through Peter. He does exactly what she says. Pam Jenkins rips herself away, gets up from the sidewalk and scuttles back toward her house like a chased beetle.

"Damn creep," she mutters.

Kate Henderson is right there. She is right there and she is beautiful. Everyone agrees. All the men in Pacific Grove whose phone calls he's listened to. Peter dares not lift his eyes to look her in the face. He would rather die.

"What was all that about?" she asks him.

"I'm sorry," he whispers.

He can think of doing nothing else but walking away.

As he does, Pam Jenkins shouts after him, "Monster!"

"Okay, Pam. That's enough," Kate says.

Peter gets inside his house. Slams the door shut. He can't breathe. He collapses onto the floor. Lies in the fetal position. Hums the tune. *"What'll I do?"*

FORTY-SIX

WASHINGTON STATE, 2005

PETER STOOD RIGID, WIDE-EYED, HIS HANDS IN the air.

Max Roswell was a large man. Six-four. He was large and he was holding a pistol in his hand, the barrel trembling ever so slightly. He was also blocking the hallway.

"Max, put that gun away," came Sara's soothing voice.

She stood behind her husband in the bedroom doorway, dressed in a silver nightie.

"He's just a boy," she added. "Can't you see that he's no older than Joey?"

"He's some gangbanger, Sara," Max said over his shoulder. "They send the young one in first, then the older ones follow." Turning back to Peter, he says, "You gonna call your buddies to rob me and my family, kid? Hablas inglés?"

"I speak English."

"You gonna answer the question, then?"

Sara stepped forward, touched her husband gently on the shoulder and said softly, "Max, put the gun away."

She pushed his aim down.

"Sara, it's okay," he whispered out of the side of his mouth. "The clip ain't in it."

"Also the manual safety's on," Peter interjected.

They turned to him. Narrowing their sleepy eyes.

"The sidearm you're using," Peter went on, "is a SIG P365. The thumb catch at the top of the grip. It's down. It needs to be parallel to the barrel."

Max checked the side of the gun.

"But of course," Peter added, "it doesn't matter without the ten round clip."

"You learn that from your gang pals?" Max asked, eyes back on Peter, the gun down by his side.

"No, sir."

Sara asked, "Where're you from?"

"Alaska."

Max snuffed. "Alaska?! Yeah right."

"I can assure you that is true, sir."

"No gangs in Alaska."

"Not that I know of, sir."

Sara asked, "You're a long way from home. Where's Mom and Dad?"

Max: "Sara, come on! Alaska? Really? He's talking out of his ass."

"I really am from Alaska."

"Then how'd you get all the way down here?"

Peter thought about it. Then: "It's a long story."

"Yeah," Max said with a doubtful expression. "It would be. Wouldn't it?"

He turned to his wife. Rolled his eyes and frowned.

She was still looking at what she termed a boy. Her mother's instincts picked up on the loneliness in his eyes and a part of her wanted to wrap him in her arms.

"You didn't answer my question," Sara said.

"No, ma'am."

"So—Where are Mom and Dad?"

"Dad I never knew. Mom's all the way in Anchorage."

He didn't tell them that in truth his home was over 400 miles north of Anchorage, closer to the Arctic Circle than the city. He didn't tell them because he sensed that they definitely wouldn't believe him.

Sara's tone became harsh. "If you belong in Anchorage," she said, "then why are you in my home all the way down here in Everett?"

Peter made his eyes go large and his bottom lip stick out. It was a rehearsed response. There was not one part of this situation that scared or worried him. His heartbeat was ticking over at a cool pace. He was only pouting because his biggest advocate had just lost her patience, and he felt he had no other choice but to express deep remorse in order to win her back.

"I'm so sorry," he practically whimpered.

"It's too late for that, kid," Max said. "Why're you here?"

"I was hungry," he whispered, his sad blue eyes pointed to the carpet, shoulders hunched forward, back bent, making himself smaller, younger, feebler.

"Then perhaps the cops will feed you. Sara, call 9-1-1."

Instead of fetching the phone, Sara whispered in her

husband's ear, "Look at him, Max? He's obviously sleeping rough."

Max gently rolled his eyes at his wife's inevitable softness. "You telling the truth when you say you aren't from some gang?" he put to Peter.

Seizing on Sara's words, Peter replied, "All I wanted was something to eat."

It wasn't true. He'd eaten at some mom-and-pop burger joint about three hours ago. Bought and paid for on money he stole from some woman who'd gotten out of a Mercedes convertible holding a mean little chihuahua that went crazy when it saw a ginger tabby on the sidewalk. While the dog writhed and wriggled in the woman's arms, Peter had had time to slip eighty dollars out of the Gucci handbag swinging from her shoulder.

"Come on, kid," Max said. "I'll make you a sandwich."

The next thing, Peter was sitting at their breakfast bar eating a turkey sandwich. Doing his best to push it down on top of the two bacon cheeseburgers congealing in his intestines.

"Can we call your mom?" Sara asked.

"We don't have a phone."

The Roswells looked at each other. Suspicion was back in their eyes.

Max asked, "How come you're all the way down here?"

"Traveling through."

"Traveling through? What're you, like, fourteen?"

"Seventeen."

"That's still not the kind of age people go backpacking, kid. You a runaway?"

"You could say that."

Sara asked, "So you've run away from your mom in Alaska?"

"Sort of. Have you got any more of those pickles?"

"Sure," Max said, trundling off to the sideboard.

"So what's your name?" Sara asked.

"Peter."

"Peter what?"

"Black."

"Peter Black?" Max said as he handed him the pickle jar.

"Yep."

Peter went on eating. Sara couldn't help watching him with sad eyes. When he wasn't looking, she signaled Max with a nod of the head that she wished to speak confidentially with him, and they went into the hallway. They thought he couldn't hear them, but he could. Even over the sound of munching chips he could hear them whispering.

"This is messed up," Max twittered.

"Surely his mother must be worried sick. I know I would be if it was Joey sneaking about people's houses looking for food."

"We gotta call someone, Sara. They could be looking for him."

"You're right. I'll go get the—"

"Don't call the police."

They turned. Peter was standing right there holding a bag of Doritos.

"Please," he said. "I'd only run away if you did."

"But you can't just carry on living rough," Sara put to him.

"What's going on? Why's everyone talking?"

Everyone turned in the direction of the voice. It was Joey.

He was ambling out of his bedroom wiping sleep from his eyes. He was sixteen, a little taller than Peter, and had messy hair with a purple-colored streak running through it.

"Who's that?" he asked the second he spotted Peter standing behind his parents.

"Please," Peter begged them.

It was not the police that he feared. It was what he'd have to do to get away. Max was a big man. He might get Peter into a hold. Or at least try. Then Peter would have to hurt him. He didn't want to hurt him. Especially with Joey and Sara watching.

"Joey, go back to your room," Sara told her son.

"But, Mom, who is he?"

Max turned to his son. "Joey, get the sleeping bag and set up the camping bed on your floor."

"That didn't answer the question. What's his name and why's he here?"

"He's your cousin."

"My cousin?!" The boy cocked his head and narrowed his eyes at his father.

Sara glanced sideways at Max with a frown.

"Second cousin," Max added. "Removed. He's your second cousin removed. From your aunt Renee's first marriage."

The frown was deepening on Sara's face. The same was true of Joey, whose confusion only grew.

"Whatever," Max grumbled. "It doesn't matter. He's family."

"Who turns up out of the blue," Joey added dryly.

"So what?" Max said. "I always say to family: drop in any time."

"Even if it's three in the morning?"

"Okay, Joe," Sara said, hustling her son toward the open door of his room. "Time to go set up your second cousin's bed."

As she guided him by the shoulders, she glanced back at Max, gently shaking her head.

When they were gone, Max turned to Peter. In a whisper, he told him, "I'm trusting you with my family, kid. Don't misplace it."

"I won't," Peter assured him. "I promise."

That night he slept on a cot on Joey's floor, gazing around at all the posters and things; the weight bench, the pile of magazines, the sports stars and musicians glaring from every wall, the set of tall speakers, the games console with a semicircle of beanbags grouped around the TV, a telescope pointing out the window.

Back in Alaska, his own room consisted of a footlocker, a bed and four bare walls. Since the age of seven he'd never had anything that wasn't absolutely necessary. No toys. No games. Nothing but what was essential for the undertaking of his day-to-day existence.

While he lay there, Joey snoring on the other side of the room, Peter could hear the muffled sounds of Max and Sara talking in bed several rooms over. He focused his hearing until he could tell what they were saying.

"Do you believe that he's from Alaska?" Sara was asking.

"I don't know. Maybe. Whatever it is, you can see in the kid's eyes that he's had a rough time."

"What sort of world do we live in when a boy as young as that can be homeless on the streets?"

. . .

PETER MEANT to leave before they got up. But he fell into a deep slumber. In the morning he awoke to find Joey already gone. The radio was bleating in the kitchen and the sound drew him to it. Standing in the doorway, he watched the Roswells.

Sara was busy making pancakes that she stacked onto a plate. Max sat at the head of the table reading a newspaper. Gruffly snorting out of his nostrils every so often when he read something that annoyed him.

This was Peter's dream.

"Hey, you're up," Sara said when she noticed him. "Come sit down. I made pancakes."

"Where's Joey?"

"Joey left for school."

The next thing, Peter was at the table eating a stack of pancakes with a side of crispy bacon. He couldn't be happier. His dreams of finding a way into the family had been unexpectedly realized. He felt so good in that moment that he could have burst. He forgot about Alaska, Mother, Magda and his future as a killer. For the first time, he imagined a normal life without it being so obviously a fantasy.

It made it all the more painful when the police arrived. Sara having quietly let them in through the front door. It was so intense, that feeling of betrayal, that his stomach twisted into knots when he turned to see the two Washington State Troopers coming into the kitchen, having heard one of their radios crackle as Sara guided them along the hallway.

Peter was off the stool, facing the officers as they slowly approached. Max had risen from his own seat. He was standing at the back door, blocking that way out.

"Please, don't," Peter said as the officers came slowly forward.

"It's okay, kid," said the cop nearest to him. "Just come with us. We'll get you placed somewhere nice. A foster home or something. You can't live on the streets no more."

"I don't want to hurt you."

The cops grinned at each other as they split up and moved around the breakfast table from opposite sides, trying to trap him between them, Max at his back.

Peter already knew exactly what he was going to do—it had to be quick, decisive, terrible—and when the nearest one reached forward to grab him he performed it with exceptional accuracy.

Slipping to the side, kinking his body, he took hold of the hand firmly by the wrist and forearm. He ducked down, twisting with the limb, bringing it with him at a sideways angle from the elbow, popping the joint and tearing the ligaments, making it useless for at least the next three months.

The guy screamed in horror. Peter let go right as the other cop moved around the table. He patted away the grasping hands, ducked and intercepted a swing, brought the arm up and around the guy while pirouetting. Then, with the arm tucked behind the cop's back, Peter took hold of his face and used the man's heavily imbalanced step to slam him headfirst into a cupboard door.

The cop staggered back and Peter performed the trick again, repeatedly, viciously, relentlessly, until the guy went limp, the cracked door smeared with blood by the time he fell unconscious onto the checkered floor.

The other cop was sitting with his back to the cupboards, groaning with pain. Holding his flopping arm.

Max wasn't at the door anymore. He had gone to his wife. He was holding Sara tight. They both stared at Peter with wide, shimmering eyes.

"I'm so sorry," he said.

They were looking at him as if he were an animal. A wild animal.

No, not an animal. Something worse.

They were looking at him as though he were a monster.

FORTY-SEVEN

MONTEREY, 2019

THE GRASS WAS MUD BY THE TIME HE TWISTED THE tap off.

He did it under the cover of darkness, having hidden in his house the rest of the day. At one point, Mrs. Harrison had rung the bell. Standing at his porch for almost ten minutes, calling his name—Paul's name—through the letterbox.

It had made him feel terribly ashamed. To be so frightened of a seventy-two-year-old arthritic widow.

For the whole of yesterday and most of today, Peter has shut himself inside 24 Green Street, his heart skipping beats, the song humming from between his clenched lips. To take his mind off yesterday's drama he has spent the last six hours in the basement. Locked inside his communications vault.

It is now nighttime. A hard rain falls outside, a storm

coming in off the Pacific. Every so often, thunder shakes the house, the vibrations even reaching as deep as the vault.

He has become fixated on the Palmer house.

Jimmy Palmer comes home from work the same time each day and gets straight on the sauce. The next thing he does is get straight onto his family.

Peter grinds his teeth as he listens, humming the tune. At one stage, he even manages to push his short fingernails through the skin of his palms, he is gripping his fists so tight, and he constantly wonders what he is going to do as he listens to them through the microphones in their smartphones, Hannah's and Danny's, getting them in stereo. They have become his new Hendersons. His new obsession.

WHAT WILL I DO?

The image of Danny being led into the trailer haunts him. It has marked his sleep. Joining the Gregor boy on the yacht and all the other faces that stare incriminatingly at him from the darkness of his own worthless soul.

Peter is half asleep in the ergonomic chair when his senses bring him into an alert state.

"What the fuck, Hannah?" Jimmy Palmer unloads.

This man hates his family. Peter is sure of it.

He is a miserable little creature.

"What, Daddy?"

"You burnt the fucking cookies. See."

The creak of an oven door opening. Then the fire alarm goes off.

"Ah!" Jimmy Palmer shouts like it's the end of the world.

The clatter of metal hitting the floor.

"You spilled them!" Hannah cries out.

"Fuck!"

The hiss of running water. He's burned his hand.

"Hannah, you'd better go to your fucking room," Jimmy shrieks.

"But you spilled them. And look, you burned a hole in the floor."

Linoleum covers many of the cheaper kitchen floors in Pacific Grove. Peter imagines the tray melting through the canvas as it lies there surrounded by burnt cookies.

"No fucking way!" Jimmy screams louder than ever. "I just paid for that."

Peter bolts up out of the chair. He thinks he knows what's coming.

There is the sound of a slap and the girl is screaming. Jimmy has never hit her before. He's hit his wife and he's certainly hit Danny, but never the seven-year-old. It's a new low.

"Dad, what the fuck?!" Danny cries out.

He's out of his room, down the hallway and in the kitchen.

"You hit her! You fucking hit her!" he bawls.

Hannah is sobbing uncontrollably in the background.

There is the sound of a coming together. Muffled breath. Things being knocked over. *The kid's doing it. He's fighting his old man.* Never has he ever stuck up for himself. But for her, for her he finds the strength.

Peter knows, though, the fourteen-year-old doesn't stand a chance. And soon that becomes painfully obvious when Peter hears him thrown to the other side of the kitchen.

"You attack *me?!*" the father screams out. "You fucking attack *me?!*"

"Daddy, no!" Hannah screams.

The sound of meat slapping meat, the dull thud of a one-way beating, Danny crying out, trying his best to get away, the door banging. Peter guessing that he'd run for it but Jimmy had slammed it shut before he could escape, because the sounds of him being hit continue.

Hannah cries out. "Daddy, leave him alone! Leave him alone!"

In all the years Peter has watched people, he has discovered that, to a varying degree (the spectrum is quite wide), there are people in this world who either give or take. The givers walk into a room and they, believe it or not, give. They make that room brighter by offering it any type of succor that it requires. They help people when they need it. They are an ear that listens. A voice that gives advice. Or they are just simply able to share the weight of burden. They offer compassion, sympathy, a rosey smile that lifts you up. They inspire.

The takers are the opposite. They are vampires who bring with them shadow. They suck from people. Drain energy from them. They seek sympathy, but are incapable of giving it. They wish to blame all their self-created ills on anyone they can pin them on, any excuse, any reason why they're not where they supposedly deserve to be. They bring the people around them down. Their wives, their children, their work colleagues, their communities. All they want is to take and never give.

Again, this exists in people to differing degrees, and it is possible to have someone who is neutral—right in the middle of the spectrum. But Jimmy Palmer isn't neutral. He is about as far down in the dark depths as you can go. He is a sociopath. A psychopath. A man who has no feeling for those of his fellow creatures. He sees his family as his own to do whatever he wants with.

Peter can't let the boy be beaten like this. He runs from the vault and marches out of the house. The rain drums on his head as he reaches the end of the driveway. Mrs. Harrison is absent from her porch, but he can see her shadow in an upstairs window. The widow still watching the vacant street.

He is passing her gate when someone steps out from behind a parked car and Peter is face-to-face with the man from Wilson's house. The one with the death mask for a face.

"What are you doing?" he says over the hiss of the rain.

Peter stares at him. His fists balled. Chest pumping in and out. Saying nothing.

The man continues. "Why haven't you started reconnaissance on the second target yet?"

"Get out of the way," Peter growls.

The man remains blocking the sidewalk. His own fists balled at his sides, the rain dribbling down his chalk-white face.

The Palmer house is left down an alley that cuts between Mrs. Harrison's and the place next door. It empties you out on Palm Avenue. Crossing that is Elm Drive. On the corner of which are the Palmers. From the elevated position of Green Street it is possible to see their bungalow.

"We've given you some R&R to reestablish your focus," Ghost-Face tells him. "But that's at an end now. Now it's time to go back to work, Azrael."

Peter goes to move around him. But the guy isn't playing. He attacks Peter with a form of pencak silat, an open-hand Indonesian fighting style. Feinting left, he goes to thunderclap the right side of Peter's head with a palm-heel ear smash. But Peter is quick, avoiding it by kinking his body and leaning away, his balance kept by the colossal discipline of his muscle fibers, the smash narrowly avoiding him.

Peter gets in three rabbit punches to his ribcage. He feels him cringe back just in time, getting away from the worst of the damage with his own acute discipline of muscles.

The two enter a dance of moves and countermoves. Peter comes around him, waiting for him to lash out defensively, then sidesteps, parrying with an elbow the four-fingered spear-punch aimed for his esophagus, a blow that could have killed him. He counters by pushing him in the back as he avoids the blow, trying to unbalance him. As Ghost-Face reorganizes his feet, Peter goes to sweep the left leg away, but it is as if Ghost-Face is reading his mind, because he jumps it, then uses Mrs. Harrison's fence to vault in the air and come at Peter with a blur of hands, throwing punch after punch from every conceivable angle, his feet hitting the sidewalk and moving him closer and closer as Peter backs off, parrying the blows and looking desperately for an opening.

With no break to capitalize, he creates one.

Using the blade of his forearm, he whips it upwards like a club, pushing the punches away and giving him the opening he desires.

But the headbutt misses. The guy jumping away from it.

Nevertheless, the break allows Peter to get away,

He springs up Mrs. Harrison's fence, leaps onto the branch of the tall sycamore standing in the corner of her front yard, drops down, and springs over the fence the other side, running onwards.

A sharp left takes him into the narrow dirt alley that runs between numbers 26 and 28. It is almost too late when he spots something huge step out of the shadows and blot out the night. It looks like a prize bull in the darkness; not so much a man as a vast shape.

Peter ducks under the grasping shovel-hands. His parkour skills get him up the wall of the Peterson place. Gripping onto their drainage, he lifts himself onto the roof and moves across it, dropping down into the next alley.

Inside the house, the Petersons frown and gaze up at the ceiling as they sit watching *Saturday Night Live.*

It is while emerging at the end of the alley onto Palm Avenue that Peter stops dead.

Innumerable red dots swarm his chest. Laser pointers that shimmer in the rain. They come from multiple directions. Rooftops where armed men lie ready. Five red beams coming from the darkness.

Ghost-Face catches up with him. Joined by his huge friend.

Across the yards Peter hears the side door of the Palmer house slam. Through the trees and hedges, he sees Danny Palmer riding off on his BMX, the rain washing the blood down his face.

"See," Ghost-Face says. "There was no need for you to get involved."

He holds a hand up and the lasers disappear. He then comes right up to Peter.

"Come back when this is done," Ghost-Face hisses. "Then you can act the good neighbor."

FORTY-EIGHT

SAN JOSE, 2019

"THEY'RE ALL OVER PACIFIC GROVE," PETER TELLS Pat Hughes down the phone. "Hidden up. Watching me. How did they know I was there, Pat? How?"

"It has to be that kooky pair across the road. The Jenkinses."

"But who did they call?"

Peter is leaning against the tall window of an empty office. It is only him and the carpet tiles on the entire floor. No one else. Not even furniture. The morning traffic trundles slowly along the street below. Only three floors up, he can see the dejected looks on most of the motorists as they cruise to work.

Pat asks, "Where are you now?"

"Watching the next target."

Peter glances down between his feet. An open laptop displays hidden camera footage of a man in a blue discount-store polyester suit. He sits in an office behind a huge oak desk, puffing on an e-cigarette. Meanwhile, on the other side of the desk, a middle-aged woman sits angrily remonstrating. Earlier on, Peter heard the beginning of the meeting. The sobbing woman has found out that her ex-husband, and father of her three kids, has recently come into some money. He hasn't paid a penny in child support or alimony in the ten years since the divorce and is now refusing to share any of his newfound wealth. The man behind the desk, Ken Knight, is going to help her get her chunk. Explaining that he can get the man's bank accounts frozen.

"How is our good knight Kenneth?" Pat asks.

"*Good* would probably be a stretch. But then he's not exactly swimming with the sharks."

"Who is he swimming with?"

"Bottom feeders mostly."

Ken Knight runs a trips-and-falls racket out of a second floor office in a largely defunct block in downtown San Jose. Surrounded by emptiness, Knight's waiting room is filled daily by people in neck braces, on crutches, or wrapped in plaster casts—bad cough, laid off, wants to get paid off. Trips, falls and any other form of bad luck is Ken Knight's coin. He is a magnet to it. Like a drain in a sewer, he just keeps on sucking all the shit toward him.

It doesn't escape Peter's attention that Knight must have spent so much time hanging out with bad luck that it's finally rubbed off on him. Being that Peter now stands over the lawyer like the Grim Reaper.

Arriving in San Jose two days ago, Peter had considered renting an office above Knight's. But when he saw that the whole of the third floor was empty, he simply picked the locks, overrode the security (which was basically no more than motion sensors rigged to an alarm) and let himself in. After that, he drilled a hole through the concrete floor in the middle of the night when no one was about, and fed a camera and speaker down the hole so that they hung just above the false ceiling in Knight's office, the eye of the lens poking from a broken corner of one of the fiberglass tiles.

"What about Wilson?" Pat asks. "Any sign they're connected?"

Peter explains that there is no sign Ken Knight has ever met James Wilson. That they've ever spoken or been in the same room.

"What about any reasons you think Davenport's client would want him iced?"

"Nothing," Peter tells him. "Knight's cases are so low profile that there could never be anything that would bring him to the attention of a million-dollar bounty. All the work they're putting into it. For what? Some insurance company that got burned in one of Knight's cases? No. There has to be something more. Something outside of anything to do with his practice."

On the screen of the laptop the woman leaves Knight's office. The lawyer beckons his secretary to invite the next poor wretch in. Out on the street, there's a traffic jam. The day is sunny. Peter thinks that everyone should be sitting in the park or on the beach. Not in their cars being slowly poisoned by carbon monoxide.

"How long do you think before you finish with this one?" Pat asks.

"Not long," Peter replies. "Maybe a day or two."

FORTY-NINE

PETER IS FOLLOWING KEN KNIGHT'S RED HYUNDAI
Accent through a San Jose suburb of wood-slat bungalows
with neat gardens. It is night and the lawyer is going home.
It has been a long day of hustling the unlucky.

Peter's phone goes. It is Carlos Hernandez. Paul Adams's
gardener.

"Hey, Paul," his voice says over speakerphone.

"Hey, Carlos."

"I managed to locate those weeds for you. Got everything ready for when we rip them out and replant the
flowerbed."

"Good. What about weedkiller?"

"Oh, I got plenty. It's all ready."

"Thank you, Carlos."

"You're welcome, Paul."

There is a short silence. Peter wonders if Carlos expects
small talk. In the end, he says his goodbyes and the call ends.

Ken Knight reaches home. It is a white stucco bungalow

on the bottom corner of a hill. Its porch faces an intersection of residential streets. Knight parks his car on the sloping driveway and gets out carrying a black suitcase.

When he opens the door, a snowy white West Highland Terrier comes bounding up to him, reaching his knees when it stands on its hind legs, tail wagging frantically. Its attention is easily taken when it spots a cat behind its master and bolts from the door, down the slope of the drive, barking repeatedly as it scurries across the street.

"Ricky!" Ken yells as he chases after it.

He steps blindly into the road. A car screeches its brakes on. The driver punching the horn.

Ken holds his hand up as he steps back onto the curb and waits for it to pass. "Sorry," he mouths to the irate driver.

The dog is on the other side of the road, leaning its paws against the fence of a neighbor, barking at a black cat that sits on top, its tail swishing side to side.

Knight scolds the little dog as he carries it back inside the house, throwing the pooch onto the floor once he's shut the door. His wife is waiting in the kitchen. She is reading a book at the table. He warms dinner up and sits with her while he eats, the two of them chatting, an open bottle of Shiraz between them.

Peter has bugged the house. Something he did the other night while they were away at the bowling alley with friends.

"How was work?" the wife eventually asks.

"Got some shitty news today," Knight replies in an undertone.

"What?"

There's a pause in the conversation. Ken Knight is

chewing his food. He swallows. Sips his wine. Then starts up again.

"You remember that client of mine that slipped over in the cold stores at the Walmart he works at—the one that fractured his spine?"

"Yes. You said you expected six figures."

"Make that no figures."

"Oh, Ken. What happened?"

"I found out today that the son-of-a-bitch got the injury in a drink driving accident that he hid from the cops. Put his car into a tree coming home from the bar juiced to the eyeballs."

"What about the two colleagues who witnessed the accident?"

"They were in on it. The bastards planned it together after the accident. My client—Huh! Client!—he ditches his car and manages to partway walk, partway crawl home, get into bed, and go to sleep. Wakes up with a huge hangover and the worst back pain ever. His friends fetch the wrecked car before anyone notifies the authorities and that's when they come up with the plan. They're about to take him to hospital when one of them says, 'Hold on. We could turn this in our favors.' The age-old get-rich-quick scheme. As old as money itself. My client decides instead of making his way to the ER, he'll make his way to that evening's night shift."

"How'd he get there with a broke back?"

"Took two OxyContin and did his best to look breezy as he walked inside under the security cameras. Of course he didn't have to look breezy in the warehouse. They knew the camera outside the cold storage had been broke for months. It was perfect until the mooks got caught."

"How did they get caught?"

"How else? The usual."

"The usual?"

"Yeah. They couldn't keep their traps shut. Started bragging to people. Telling their neighbors and bar buddies they were gonna get rich. Another Walmart employee happened to eavesdrop on a conversation they had, recorded it, and sent it to management. All three have been arrested for fraud. My client with drunk driving, reckless abandonment of a vehicle, and leaving the scene of an accident added to his rap sheet."

"Oh, Ken."

After the meal, the two sit together in the lounge at opposite ends of a couch watching TV. They're just about to go to bed when Knight gets a call on his mobile. He places his glasses on, glances at the phone, and widens his eyes behind the lenses.

He peeks sideway at his sleepy wife, then answers it.

"Natalie?"

There's a pause. Peter turns the volume up. He can only hear enough of the person's muffled voice to know that someone is speaking.

"Hold on hold on," Knight says. "I'll meet you. Yeah. Same place as last time."

The call ends seconds after it began.

Knight kisses his wife goodbye, leaves the house, and gets in his car.

FIFTY

Peter follows the Hyundai across San Jose to the red-light district. Along a wide stretch of road lined with electronics superstores and minimarts, women linger under streetlights in skimpy clothing, trotting about on stilettos like gazelles in some urban Serengeti.

Ken Knight pulls over at the corner of a closed-down Safeway. That particular corner seems to be primarily taken by members of the trans community. Their hipless bodies twisted into provocative outfits.

A young, meatless one dressed in a red boob tube and skinny jeans trots out to the Hyundai balancing on a pair of eight-inch heels. She hasn't had any surgery. The boob tube is empty. The jeans not. Her face is heavily made up. White cheeks and black lips. Hair combed back into a thick pompadour.

She looks like a female Elvis impersonator.

The second the passenger door is shut, Knight pulls away. They don't go to a motel or somewhere quiet in the car. They go to an all-night diner on the edge of the city. The only other patrons are a young couple holding hands across a table in the end booth. Absolutely ignorant to the rest of the world.

Knight and the trans order coffee and sit down opposite each other in a booth by the window. Peter does the same, seating himself in the next one. A radio plays gently in the kitchen. It can barely be heard. The lovers whisper in confidential tones. Peter easily filters the outside sound out and hones in on the conversation in the next booth.

"How is she, Natalie?" Knight asks, sounding concerned.

"She thinks she's being watched," replies Natalie.

Peter spies on their reflections in the dark glass of the diner. The street light outside the door is bust and clouds close out the moon. The lack of exterior illumination turns the pane into the perfect mirror.

Natalie huddles over her coffee. She looks terribly nervous under all that makeup. Knight leans back in his chair, a perturbed look narrowing his brows.

"Have *you* seen anyone?" he asks.

"Yes," she says, looking up and meeting his eyes. "There was some guy outside the apartment the other night. I took his picture. Look."

She hands him her phone.

Knight scrolls through several pictures. "You can't see much," he comments, then hands her back the phone and concludes, "It won't be of any use."

"I was too scared to get any closer shots of him," Natalie mumbles. "That's why it's so blurred."

They sip their coffees in silence for a moment.

"Anyway, you never said," Knight says.

"Never said, what?"

"How *is* she doing?"

Natalie widens her eyes. "How do you think? With the guy showing up outside the apartment, she's terrified. You said that there was no way they'd know. Not until the DA serves the papers."

Leaning forward and coming over the table, Knight says in a low voice, "I can assure you there isn't anyone watching either of you. You're both being paranoid. They still think we're going to take the money, remember? Why would they come after us if they expect us to take their offer?"

"Maybe they guessed it. Maybe your guy in the DA's office tipped them off."

"Robert is a stand-up guy. There's no problems there."

"Then I don't know, Ken. Maybe you've talked to the wrong person."

"Why would I talk to anyone before we've presented everything to the DA's office?"

Natalie just stares across the table at him.

"Look, Nat," he says softly. "Didn't I get your cousin Rico that settlement?"

"Yeah," she says begrudgingly.

"I did your family an honest then. So just trust me on this one now. No one's watching you or her. Okay?"

Natalie shrugs, sniffs up a stuttered breath. She turns to the window and catches the eye of her own jaded reflection.

Peter gazes at it too. She looks so scared. You can see it in her petrified eyes. He wonders what it is that is scaring her so bad. He wants to go around to their table, bring his fist down on it and demand they tell him what the fuck they are talking about. Tell him what they are going to take to the district attorney.

But he must be prudent. After all, Hugo Davenport's men are currently occupying Pacific Grove. Best not kick the hornets's nest too hard.

"Look, I know I've already been through this," Knight says, making Natalie turn to him from her reflection, "but are you sure there isn't a chance she'll take the offer? I mean, it'll be so much easier."

"She won't. I've tried. She says she can't stand the idea of Marie growing up in a world where men like him get to do whatever they want. She's tired of seeing powerful people crush everyone beneath them for sport. She wants to change it."

"Change what?"

"The world."

"Oh, so she sees herself as a crusader, then?"

"I guess."

"Wouldn't it be easier to take the lifetime on easy street? Maybe invest some of the settlement into a charity?"

"She says she couldn't live with herself if she let her life be bought like everyone else."

"Then I hope she's ready for one hell of a fight."

"Why would she need to worry? She has the truth on her side—as well as undeniable evidence. Remember?"

"I do. But these are not the type of people who will allow themselves to be exposed. And think what kinds of connections they have here in the United States. I mean, all I'm doing is preparing everything for the DA. After that, I'm out of it. It's you and her who's going to have to contend with this. They're going to come at the both of you any way they can. If you really were her friend you'd convince her to reconsider."

"I told you, I can't," Natalie insists. "Believe me, if it was my choice, I'd take the money. Screw the hassle. But, then, I'm bad. She's different."

"What is she?"

The transvestite looks up from her coffee. "She's good. I guess that's why I love her. Because no matter how shitty the world is to her, she always believes in doing the right thing. You want to know what I think?"

"What do you think, Natalie?"

"I think she's one of God's angels."

FIFTY-ONE

APART FROM DISCOVERING A BUNCH OF NEW characters, Peter doesn't really have any additional information to guide him. A woman is involved. One who has a daughter named Marie and a friend named Natalie.

Oh!—And she is an angel.

Something happened to her. Something that Davenport's client is trying to pay her off for. Buy her silence. But this woman, this mother, this angel, is refusing. She wants to bring justice crashing down on the head of someone powerful. In Peter's experience, powerful people don't take kindly to justice.

Natalie leaves the meeting after her bold declaration. She doesn't get back into Knight's car. Instead, she leaves the diner by herself, swinging those square hips from side to side as her heels clack along the sidewalk.

It is easy to trail someone who makes so much noise. Peter leaves Ken Knight for now and follows the staccato beat of Natalie's step. The trans taps her way across the city.

Leading him into the run-down part of San Jose. The tramps. The drunks. The addicts. The prostitutes. The pimps. The horror.

Natalie makes it to a ramshackle apartment block that overshadows a busy railway. The cracked white stucco is smeared in coke. The main door is broken, swinging loosely to the vibrations of the passing trains.

Peter stands in the shadow of a busted streetlight. Natalie enters a stairwell at the block's end. He watches her emerge shortly after onto a balcony that runs along a line of front doors. At number six, she stops and checks over her bony shoulder.

Peter steps further back into shadow. A freight train rumbles by, shaking the neighborhood windowpanes. Natalie enters the apartment. A wide rectangular window covers the lounge, which the front door opens straight into. Peter observes Natalie being met by a young woman in her early twenties. The woman is pretty with sad eyes. Her milk-white face looks worn out underneath a mop of frizzy black hair.

She leans to the side, allowing a little girl no older than five to squeeze past her legs and run at Natalie. The trans lifts the toddler up in her arms and the girl becomes a mess of giggles.

The young woman comes to the window. She gives the ugly streets one last survey. As her gaze reaches Peter, she pauses, staring right in his direction. He is sure she can't see him. He's too well shielded in darkness. But her fixed gaze insists that she can, and he begins to sense a need to get away from there.

In the end, she shakes her head and shuts the curtains.

Leaving Peter to wonder whether he hasn't just witnessed an angel.

FIFTY-TWO

HE'S STARING AT THE KID. AT MICHAEL Henderson. The kid playing captain on a giant yacht. Smiling brightly as he steers the boat out of Monte Carlo harbor. Kate and Carl Henderson laugh in the background, sitting back and drinking champagne, encapsulated in glorious sunshine.

Kate spots Peter standing on the jetty. She places her glass down and gets up. Coming to the yacht's railing, she begins waving at him, calling his name.

"Peter? Peter?"

Her joyful expression suddenly fades. Horror replaces it. She is no longer waving in a friendly manner. Now she is waving at him with both arms, pointing frantically at Michael.

Screaming: "No! Peter! Please! No! *NO!*"

He presses the button and a ball of flame rips through the deck and consumes them all.

FIFTY-THREE

PETER WAKES UP IN THE CAR CLOTHED IN SWEAT. He is already having a panic attack. He hums but it's no good. Tries hard to breathe.

The boy on the yacht. Gregor's kid. He was probably vaporized. Not even enough of him left for a coffin. What had he ever done to deserve that?

What is wrong with me?

The panic attack eventually subsides, but Peter is worried. Ever since Monaco they have been steadily getting worse. Harder to bring under control, easier to trigger.

He cracks the window to let some air into the car. The night is cool, the breeze chilling the droplets of perspiration on his face. He is parked outside an empty bungalow with a For Sale sign in the front yard. Around the corner is Ken Knight's white bungalow. A mobile StingRay unit sits in the trunk. It is wired to a laptop that glows on the passenger seat. A beeping sound indicates that Ken Knight is receiving a call. So Peter slips the earpiece in.

Knight speaks first. "I tried one last time to get her to take the money. But it's no good. She's already arranged the DNA test. She thinks I'm going to the DA in two weeks. I can't delay it any longer. If I don't go, she'll just take it all to someone else."

A chill goes through Peter when a familiar voice replies, "We can't allow that to happen at any cost."

It is the voice of Hugo Davenport. Ken Knight is playing both sides.

"But if she doesn't take the money and sign the agreement, then what?" Knight splutters.

Peter already has a pretty good idea what the answer to this is. In fact, he's sure it's already in motion.

Of course Davenport lies. "There's no need to worry yourself about that," the Englishman deludes Knight. "Just stay as her council and we'll advise you of what to do to bring this to an amicable settlement."

"But she's out for blood. The way the sissy was going on about it, she's looking forward to dragging— *KRRAKAAKK!*"

Peter jumps out of his skin, head jolting, feeling like it's about to explode, the earpiece shrieking from interference.

He rips it out. Looks up sharply to his left.

Standing at the window is Ghost-Face. He is holding what looks like a black plastic wand. From the pounding static, Peter gathers it is some kind of magnetic distortion device that scrambles electronics. The screen of the laptop is flickering.

"Unlock the back doors," Ghost-Face says in his usual monotone hum, the thin, colorless lips hardly moving.

Peter pops the locks. Ghost-Face takes a seat right behind him.

"Eyes front, Azrael," he says when he catches Peter glancing at him in the rearview mirror.

There's a few seconds' uncomfortable silence. Peter registers that the guy smells faintly of disinfectant. Like a hospital mortuary.

"You've watched him long enough," the voice wheezes. "I know you. You don't need much time to guess a person's rhythm."

Peter is sure this fucker is agency. Or at least was. It's possible he could even have been part of the program. Hell, he may have been trained by Mother.

"Stop eavesdropping," he advises Peter.

"Davenport said I have to make this look like an accident. Surveillance is how I find where to position one in the target's life."

"It's also how you start poking your nose into things that don't concern you. Think about Pacific Grove. Think about freedom."

Peter glances up into the rearview mirror. "Can we be candid for once?" he asks the snowman-faced ghoul in the back. "One field agent to another."

"Knock yourself out."

"I hope you're not dumb enough to think your boss is going to let me go free when this is done."

"Luther Bryce is free."

"For all I know Luther Bryce is currently dead. Capped in the back of the head the second he got off that video call."

Ghost-Face says nothing.

"And you and your large friend," Peter goes on. "How

do you know there isn't someone waiting for *you* as well? Davenport's client is willing to off Knight even though he's on the same team. It could be the same for all of us."

"You're being paranoid."

"Am I? All this trouble and you couldn't be bothered to do the job yourselves? Surely you can make someone slip down the stairs?"

The goon runs a hand down his featureless face. He turns to the left. Moonlight shines through a gap in a fence, casting him in garish silver light. Peter spots tiny indentations and blemishes on his face. Around the jawline. Behind the ears. The marks of plastic surgery. Like Peter, he has had work done to change his appearance. The face probably wasn't always so featureless. Peter is even sure that Ghost-Face has had the pitch of his voice changed, something he's considered doing himself, because there's a half-inch line of discoloration running horizontal across the larynx.

"Just get the job done," the guy grumbles. "Stay out of things. Go home. Stop putting them in danger."

And with that final warning, he leaves the car.

FIFTY-FOUR

"JUST THINK OF ALL THE SHITTY THINGS WE'VE done in the past," Pat tells Peter over the phone. "This is just one more."

Clouds overhang the Knight residence. The white stucco turned gray by shadow.

"I don't like being strong-armed into it."

A single car sits on the Knight driveway. A cream Mini that belongs to the wife, the hooky lawyer having left for the office hours ago.

She's late getting ready for a brunch date. The friend she spoke with earlier over the telephone will be annoyed. She had specifically insisted, "Don't be late." But apparently tardiness is a habit of Mrs. Knight's, and habits die hard. Hence why, with five minutes to go and ten miles to drive, she's still applying makeup.

"Just try to think," Pat tells Peter, "of coming out of this with the money and off that list. Think what you can do with the rest of your life."

Peter does think about it. All the time.

"I don't believe it," he says.

"You always were a pessimist."

"Realist," Peter corrects as he watches the haggard image of Mrs. Knight beyond the frosted glass of her porch. He glances at video playing on his phone and memorizes what he sees, before adding, "I can see no other reason I've been chosen for this except one."

"Which is?"

Mrs. Knight walks out her front door carrying the little dog in the crook of her arm.

"I gotta go," Peter says. "Speak soon."

"Keep me in the loop."

"Copy that."

The phone goes dead. The Mini reverses out of the driveway into the road. It swings around and then she's gone, the Highland Terrier gazing out the back windshield as the car drives away.

Peter jumps out of the panel van he's sitting in and makes his way across the street toward the rear of the Knights' property. The side of the van carries the same logo that is on the left breast of his gray coveralls: *S&W Home Security* written in red across a blue oval. The gray baseball cap he wears also has the logo. A thick black beard hangs from his chin. His skin itches underneath from the heat and the adhesive.

Like the Jamesons in Pacific Grove, the Knights don't lock their back gate. Peter waltzes right into their yard carrying a red toolbox. The back door is easy to pick. Inside, the alarm beeps its thirty-second warning and he makes his way through the kitchen to the hallway where the keypad is.

1-2-3-4 is the code.

The alarm dead, he dumps the toolbox on the floor. Opposite the keypad is a shelving unit stuffed with framed pictures. One shows the Knights at some Fourth of July celebration. It is nighttime. They are holding each other as fireworks go off behind them. The picture is at the end of the unit, facing the keypad at an angle so that the person keying in the code doesn't block the view.

Peter removes the back of the picture. Tucked inside is a tiny battery. It is flat, rectangular and no larger than a stamp. Wires flow from it around the photograph. A small section of one corner is folded in so they can pass to the micro camera he's placed in the blackest corner of that Fourth of July night sky. A camera smaller than the head of a thumbtack, yet able to send a signal as far as 200 yards.

Last night, he had placed it there while the Knights were asleep. There was no chance to do the rest then. For that he'd need them out of the house.

Having retrieved everything, he replaces the picture in exactly the same space. The camera is tossed into the toolbox. Next, he pulls out a screwdriver and opens the front door.

No one is outside on the street, the neighbors all at work. Somewhere far off a lawnmower groans, but apart from that there's no sign of life.

He kneels at the door edge and uses the driver to remove the screws from the latch plate. He then pulls out the locking mechanism. Thankfully the Knights only have a single deadbolt. The chain, he's never seen them use. If they had been the paranoid types with multiple locks, he would have had to think of something else. But they're not.

On an earlier visit to the house, he discovered which type of deadbolt they use. It is a Yale P-5211. An easy model to replicate. It took him all of yesterday afternoon in his garage at Monterey to modify the same model for his purposes.

He fits it into the door, replacing the lock he pulled out.

He feels better now he knows Knight is working both sides. The lawyer's probably been promised a huge payout. A few more brain cells and he'd probably figure out that the client has no intentions of paying. Like most people, Knight has allowed money to cloud his judgement. Because if he just flexed the old gray matter a little harder, he'd see that he knows something that the client will do anything to keep hidden. There is no way they'll let Knight live whether the angel signs or not. The promise of money is nothing more than them stalling whatever it is this woman wants to take to the district attorney. Giving Peter enough time to work his black magic.

With the door finished, he gives it a couple of dry runs. Then, happy that it will work when the time comes, he leaves the house the way he came.

Across the street from the front porch of the Knights is a streetlight. Peter the workman uses his tools to open the back cover and pulls the fuse. Lastly, he squirts a pheromone spray all over the sidewalk, emptying the bottle onto the concrete.

That done, he leaves in the panel van. S&W's work complete for now.

FIFTY-FIVE

Rain clouds entomb San Jose, making it a pitch-black night. Ken Knight sits in an easy chair watching some crime documentary on Netflix. He looks bored. His wife is sitting nearby flicking through something on her phone. The dog barks incessantly at the door, standing with its paw leaned up against it.

Outside, on the opposite side of the street, several cats warble, sending the dog crazy as their shrieks reach into the hallway.

The Knights keep telling the dog to shut up. But it keeps going. Yapping and scratching at the door. Desperate to get out there.

Knight lifts a beer bottle to his lips and rolls his eyes when he finds it empty. He carries it out of the room, asking his wife if she'd like anything as he goes. She waves him away and he moves into the hallway.

Peter presses the key-fob.

Just as Knight is passing the front door the lock pops open and before he can stop it, the dog is flying outside.

Peter drops the clutch.

The streetlight is out. The dog disappears into darkness.

"Ricky! Ricky!" Knight shouts as he bolts from the door himself.

Peter is already in fourth and flooring it.

Knight gets halfway across the road. The electric engine is so quiet, he doesn't even hear the Tesla Roadster. He wheels around right at the moment the car smashes into him.

He spins through the air. Lands hard with a loud slap.

The air flies out of him and he chokes to get it back.

The dog is standing on the sidewalk watching him. Knight hears the sounds of shrieking brakes and then the Tesla shifting into reverse.

Red lights explode in the dark like eyes.

Lying broken in the road, all Ken Knight can do is watch the back wheel reverse over him.

FIFTY-SIX

ALASKA, 2006

P ETER WAS EIGHTEEN. H E WAS EIGHTEEN AND HE
was ready.

He stood upright in the cabin, the fluttering light of the
crackling fire playing on his face. Before him were Mother and
Magda. The latter was smiling. The former was not.

This was as close as he'd ever get to a graduation ceremony.

"Peter," Mother said, "you have worked so hard and for so
long. You have been good student. Soon you will be good asset.
You will serve your country invaluably in the coming years
and you will do so without ever receiving any credit or praise
for it. There will be no medals. No parades. No books written.
If you are ever caught in a foreign country, your existence will
be denied. There will be no negotiations for your release no
matter how many body parts they send. You will always be at
work. Placed where we tell you. Doing what we tell you to do.
Ready to be triggered at any time. To hit any target. You will

never live any other life than this. This," she pauses, her gray eyes shining, *"solitary one will be the only life you will ever know. There will be no family. No friends. You will be on your own until you are killed in the line of duty. No one will mourn you. There will be no funeral. No recognition for your valiant services to your country. Only denial and death. You were born alone. You will live alone. You will die alone. This is the burden of the assassin."*

Peter said nothing.

Magda had made cake. A fruit one. Dried figs circled the top.

Peter hadn't had chocolate since his days slumming it through America and Canada almost a year ago.

They ate in silence, the sound of the old cuckoo clock that never cuckoos clicking in the background. With her cake half eaten, Mother got up from her armchair. At the bureau she pulled a drawer open. When she returned to Peter, she was holding an envelope out to him.

"Take it," she said when he did no more than look at it.

Peter placed the dry cake down and retrieved the envelope from her slender fingers. She told him to open it. Inside were plane tickets. London to Athens. Athens to the island of Mykonos.

"You always did love reading Homer," she said. "I thought as a treat for all your hard work we could visit the places described in Odysseus's adventures. A little something before you leave me forever."

Peter was shaking. Tears welled in his eyes and a lump formed in his throat.

"I know I never say it," the old woman added softly. "But I am proud of you, Peter."

"Is this real?" he asked, his wet eyes looking up from the tickets. "Not another trick?"

"No trick. We leave tomorrow. Take Army plane from Fairbanks to London. From there we fly like normal people. Have beautiful week in luxury villa."

Peter got up unsteadily from his chair. "I don't know what to say."

"Then don't," she said, holding a hand up to him. "This is just one week of niceness before you go to work. Then your life will be very different."

FIFTY-SEVEN

GREECE, 2006

"Mykonos is part of the group of Greek islands known as the Cyclades," Peter told Mother while sitting in the passenger seat of a convertible holding open a travel book.

She drove them down a narrow strip of gray that bent and twisted through sun-drenched towns of white stone. He'd been nattering away ever since they'd driven out of the airport parking garage in the cherry-red Ferrari Portofino, and usually she would have told him to shut up a long time ago. But today she had decided to indulge him.

"It lies," he went on, "between the islands Tinos, Syros, Paros and Naxos. In Greek mythology, it is said to have been the site of the Gigantomachy. Do you know what that is, Mother?"

"The battle between Zeus and the giants," she said disinterestedly.

"Yes. It's where Hercules killed the invincible giants, having lured them from the protection of Mount Olympus. According to myth, the large rocks all over the island are the petrified corpses of the giants. Look."

He was pointing out of the car at a gigantic black volcanic rock that poked out of the long stretch of beach they drove past. It was the size of a small office block and shaped like a jagged egg. He imagined it alive and raining fire on all those sunbathers lining the white sand around it.

The villa they were staying in was incredible. It was built into the cliffs of the bay, part of an exclusive neighborhood. A one-story stone bungalow perched on the edge, it dropped several floors through the excavated rocks until it opened up into a terrace that took you all the way down to the clear blue water.

Peter removed a box of sundries from the trunk of the Ferrari while Mother opened the door. Following her into the hallway, he exclaimed, "This is amazing. Wow!"

White and blue patterns meandered along the mosaic floors. A domed skylight illuminated paintings of mythical scenes. Grecian vases overflowed with pink bougainvillea. On the way there all the white stucco buildings had been covered in the bright flowers.

"Come," she said, leading him to the kitchen.

They passed a mirror that covered a wall and Peter couldn't help gazing at his reflection. He couldn't believe how sophisticated he looked. How they looked.

Mother was dressed in a black Chanel dress. It was V-necked, armless and ended at the knees. She wore pearls on the outside of it. In the kitchen, she removed a red scarf from her head and her medium-length gray hair stayed perfectly straight.

She resembled the rich and famous, some grandee of the silver screen, and Peter couldn't believe the transformation that had taken place in her with just some makeup and a set of expensive clothes. He blushed at the idea of Mother as attractive.

"Place those things on the counter," she told him. "Let's take a look around."

Back in Alaska, their clothing was practical and for the purposes of their hard life there. Barring his two months walkabout, he had never dressed himself. Being that he had never had anyone to show him the fashions.

In London, Mother showed him. And he was astounded at her expertise. Never in their seven years together had he once seen her read a fashion magazine or heard her take an interest in clothing. She could sew and stitch, something she had taught Peter, but apart from practicality, she appeared to hold no interest in the vogues of dress.

Once they touched down in Europe, that changed. She took him to all the best boutiques, kitting him out in the best fashions. At Savile Row she had him measured for a number of suits. All of them for different occasions, which she explained while a rake-thin Englishman moved around Peter with a measuring tape. Then she took him to Selfridges and Bond Street. To all the designer stores.

"The only thing you need to know about fashion," she had told Peter as he tried on a black Alexander McQueen sweater covered in white skull prints, "is that it is merely another way for people to show they are wealthier and therefore more powerful than others. It is the uniform of a person's particular class. Of caste. Of socio-economic position. Trends are merely what you can afford. And if you are beautiful, you can pull anything off."

"Am I beautiful?" Peter had asked cheekily.

"Yes," she answered frankly. "It is one of the reasons why you will be so good at what you do."

A day later in Greece the pair descended marble steps that traveled through the middle of the villa like an escalator through a shopping center. Peter was wearing light blue Dolce and Gabbana shorts and a black and gold baroque print Versace silk shirt, opened on his ripped torso. She was right: his own beauty did make him feel powerful.

A bedroom door was wide open on a lower floor. Mother took a position to the side.

"Take a look," she told him.

Peter walked into the room. The whole back wall was floor-to-ceiling glass paneling. The blinds were drawn. The first thing he did was open them. Sun flooded the room, illuminating antique furniture, a four-poster bed—and a telescope. Not a cheap one either, but a heavy, long range Celestron. The second he saw it, he was drawn, reminded instantly of Joey Roswell's room.

He applied an eye to the telescope and gazed out along the expanse of sun-dazzled waves. Across the same sea that Odysseus sailed to get home to Penelope and Telemachus. To the yachts and the boats and the people and the frolics and the fun.

This is life. Real life.

"Is this my room?" he asked, looking up from the eyepiece.

"Would you like it to be?"

Peter just smiled.

"Come. There is more."

"Who's is this place?" Peter asked as he followed her along the intricate patterns of mosaic.

"It belongs to friend of United States. This is all you need know."

The rear of the villa was a single panoramic expanse of glass. The crystal blue Aegean Sea spread out beyond it, specked with boats and activity.

They walked out onto a stone terrace that had been carved out of the volcanic rock. Walls rose up to the left and right, shielding them from the neighboring villas. Passiflora climbed the stonework, their flowers resembling purple jellyfish.

Peter followed Mother down a set of sculpted steps. They led to a jetty that stuck out into the water. A speedboat was tied to its end, bobbing gently on the lapping waves.

"What do you think?" Mother asked.

"It's perfect."

"It won't all be bad out in the field. Sometimes you will stay in places like this."

Fishing boats and expensive yachts glided about the glinting water. A speedboat flew by pulling a water skier. A group of young women came paddling around the rocks in canoes. Spotting Peter, they began smiling and waving, giggling to each other.

He smiled and waved back.

Mother rolled her eyes. "Come," she said, stepping down into the speedboat. "Let's take a look around island. I'll let you drive."

Peter smiled with boyish joy and jumped down into the boat. Soon, they were cutting through the water. Peter standing at the controls and Mother sitting behind him. The runabout was a classic Riva Super. Wood finish, white leather.

"Not so quick," she scolded him as they slalomed between two yachts. "This is a pleasure cruise, not a race."

Groaning, Peter pulled the throttle back and brought the boat to a steady jog over the water.

"You see that rock ahead?"

She was pointing. He followed her finger's direction.

About three hundred meters in the distance a rock the size of a two-story house poked out of the water. A cave ran right through the middle of it, meaning that the boulder was shaped like an archway. Peter couldn't help wondering if it too wasn't a dead giant. The upside-down U looked, to Peter at least, like part of the tentacle of some goliath sea monster killed as it swam toward the mainland.

"You mean the arch?" he said, not mentioning mythical beasts.

"Yes. I want you to take us to it."

The cave in the middle was just about wide enough for the boat. Once they were consumed within the shadows of it, she told him to cut the engine.

The static boat tipped on the water, the waves slapping the sides, the sound echoing inside the hollow. Mother took a pair of field glasses from the boat's trunk and joined him at the front.

"Here, take these," she said, handing them to Peter.

He was still smiling as he applied them to his eyes. "What am I looking at?"

"The huge yacht close to the horizon. Eleven o'clock."

He spotted what he thought she meant. It was one of those

oversized super yachts. Long and slender. Like a big silver spear hovering sideways on the water.

"The Mermaid?" he said, having just read it on the side of the bow.

"Yes."

"It's beautiful."

"I didn't ask what you thought of it."

Her voice was flat. The earlier playfulness gone.

A sudden feeling spread over Peter. It was like a black cloud covering the sun. His whole being sunk.

"You see the fat man sunning himself on the top deck?" she asked.

Peter moved his field of vision across the polished deck of the boat. A tanned man with the body shape of an egg, the sun glinting off his bald head, sat in red trunks too small for his ass and too big for the rest. He was being fed by a young man in his early twenties who was completely naked. His athletic body holding an unkind mirror up to the slob.

"I see him," Peter answered in a flat tone.

"His name is Giovanni Destro. An Italian. You may have noticed, he likes young men."

A certain realization hit. Peter said, "This isn't about treating me one last time before I go out into the field. This is the field."

"You should have guessed as much. Rule Four."

"Never assume. Only plan," Peter muttered in a deadpan voice. "I'll try to remember that in the future."

"See that you do. Now. It is time for you to prove that Magda and I haven't wasted the past seven years. Tell me how many men are on board?"

Peter gave the yacht a quick scan.

"There are two in white ship's uniform," he told her. "One is the captain and the other is his deputy. On the deck, spaced out, are five men. Three are dotted around the deck and two stay within close proximity to Destro and the boy."

"Armed?"

"Pistols. Concealed under their suit jackets."

"Surely you can't see from here. How do you know?"

"Because otherwise they wouldn't be wearing jackets. It's at least a hundred and eight and they're sweating."

"What else?"

Peter observed one of the men touch his ear.

"They're in radio communication."

"What does that tell you?"

"They're organized. Probably ex-military. Special Forces."

"Good. Now watch the fat man while I explain who he is."

Destro lay on a lounger, being fed salmon by the young man and resembling a hungry seal, his flipper-hands busy groping the guy's behind.

Mother explained, "On the surface our friend Mr. Destro is one of the world's biggest shipping magnates. Underneath he is one of its biggest arms traffickers."

The salmon finished, the young man sat down next to Destro on the lounger. They kissed, sweetly. Then something in Destro appeared to snap. Sweet no longer did it for him. He grabbed his concubine violently at the back of the head, balling the blond hair up in his fist. He began forcing the young man's head down toward his groin, using the other hand to pull his undersized shorts down his fat thighs. The boy tried to get back up but Destro's weight pressed down on top of him.

"In the past he has come in handy," Mother went on. "Helped us get weapons into the right hands when under *international law ours were tied. But now he is threatening to leak several of these deals to the United Nations if the US Government doesn't release his son from prison."*

"He has a son?"

"He is still married to the mother. If you can believe that."

Destro gripped the young man's hair, suffocating him. With his other hand, he hit the boy, beating his head and neck like an angry gorilla.

"What's the son in prison for?"

"He murdered his American girlfriend while in Florida. Tried to escape punishment but was caught leaving Tampa onboard his private jet. Destro wants the whole thing quashed or he's going to leak everything to the world."

It looked like the boy was choking. His arms flailed about. Destro let him up. The boy rose, breathing in and out, his mouth open and wet like a fish. Destro laughed at him. Slapped him. Kissed him violently. Then pushed him back down.

Peter got the impression Giovanni Destro didn't do consent.

"Won't that cause him more trouble than it's worth?" Peter asked.

"His son is facing the death penalty or the rest of his life in prison. There is no getting out of it by conventional means. Even for a man as wealthy as Destro. The evidence is too overwhelming."

"How overwhelming?"

"Hotel CCTV tracked the couple arguing in the lift and then entering the room. Outside CCTV then caught the young Italian throwing her over the balcony on the seventeenth floor to her death. It's clearly him."

"So the father's desperate?"

"Yes."

"And that's why I've been dragged all the way out here to be the next guy he tries to force his dick into."

She turned her hawk eyes sideways at him. "Don't look so glum. I told you right before I handed you that envelope: You will always be at work. Placed where we tell you. Doing what we tell you to do. Surely you knew this wasn't going to be a real holiday. Now come. There's someone I want you to meet."

FIFTY-EIGHT

BACK AT THE VILLA A MAN WAS WAITING FOR THEM inside the bedroom, all the blinds once again drawn. He was tall, jaundiced, and smelled of cigarettes. His brown hair was shaved to stubble and his thin cheeks sunk in. A pair of lazy eyes stared out from behind yellow shades that matched the color of his skin.

"This is Patrick," Mother told Peter. "We call him Pat."

"Nice to meet you, Peter," Pat Hughes said, grinning. "I look forward to working with you."

They shook hands.

"Pat will be your handler from now on," Mother said. "He'll take you through everything. Including the required tradecraft."

"Take your shirt off," Pat said.

Peter looked at Mother.

"Do as he says."

Peter undressed.

"And the rest," Pat added once the Versace was puddled on the floor.

Peter was soon standing butt naked in front of them.

"We need to get him more tanned," Pat remarked. *"Destro likes them tanned. The hair will need to be a little lighter, too. He's a fan of blonds. We won't have to change the eyes, though. He likes them blue. Have you ever kissed another man, Peter?"*

The question stunned him. He regarded Mother.

She turned her eyes away.

"No," Peter mumbled, dropping his own to his feet.

"Then we'll have to go through that, too."

"I'll have to kiss him?"

Mother frowned. "Isn't that obvious?"

"I don't think I can."

Peter's guts were twisting up.

Pat said, "We're not asking you to fall in love with him, Peter. Just kiss him. Touch him. Let him touch you. Make the pig think he can fuck you."

"But I don't know how."

Pat turned sideways to Mother. "His inexperience could actually work in our favor."

"Why so?"

"Our intel shows that Destro likes them shy. Likes the chase."

Hearing Pat say this, Peter couldn't help recalling the rape he'd witnessed earlier.

FIFTY-NINE

Destro would be in the area for another week. He wasn't staying on Mykonos, even though he owned one of the largest villas, he was staying on the Mermaid. It was only at night under heavy guard that he left the super yacht and visited the island.

Inside the villa the blinds were drawn. Peter was walking from one side of the room to the other then back again. Watching him were Pat Hughes and Mother. Their eyes studying him closely in the dim light. Back and forth. Back and forth.

"Don't walk so stiff," Pat advised him. "Be more loose."

Peter tried but it looked ridiculous. Put on. Not natural.

Mother came into the middle of the room, practically pushing him out of the way.

"Swing your hips out. Like this," she barked, doing her own little walk on the catwalk. "See," she added, moving seductively before them. "Your feet should step inwards with the heel out. Like this."

Her hips swayed like the ocean. Her face had changed, too. The way she smiled was sweet. Innocent. The smile of a baby lamb. Even in her late sixties it made her look pretty, and Peter could tell that she must have been phenomenal in her day.

It made him wonder what Mother used to be before she trained boys and girls. What she was before she was Mother. When she was KGB.

A slap round the face brought Peter back.

Mother was standing before him. Her eyes pierced.

"Are you paying attention, boy?" she snapped. "This is important. Life and death. Not a game. You daydream in this business and you are dead. Do you hear me? Dead!"

In between the sealed-off lessons, Peter spent intermittent hours out on the terrace lying on a sun lounger. Then, while he bronzed himself, Pat Hughes would sit beside him going over mission protocols.

"Every Friday, Destro visits a local gay club. Under the cover of darkness, he comes to shore with a five-man security team."

"Can't we just set up a sniper to hit him as they come in?"

"Destro stays within the cabin until they secure the boat. Added to this, they pick a different entry point every night and never at the same time."

A group of paddle boats came splashing by. Boys and girls on their college vacations having fun. The girls squealing in the arms of their holiday romances. The boys clinking beer bottles. Winking at each other and nodding their heads at the beautiful ladies they'd picked up. There would be no murders for them tonight. Only fun.

"Not forgetting," Pat went on, "that we've promised the

Greeks we won't do the hit on their territory. They were kind enough to leak us his travel itinerary. The least we can do is repay the favor by not making it a problem for them."

For Peter there would be no fun. No time to go for a swim. No time to eat a meal in the clifftop restaurants. No drink in the bars. No lounging on the beach. Dancing in the clubs. Chatting to the beautiful girls who would adore his company. And he theirs.

There would be only work.

"Are the five he takes to shore his entire team?" Peter asks.

"No. There's two more left on the yacht. Seven total. All well trained."

The party people stopped their convoy right in front of them. The girls and boys stood up and began diving into the clear blue water, swimming around their pedalos like water nymphs, as if purposely to get underneath Peter's skin. To make him feel even more of an excluded freak than he already did. To show him that even though he might be able to look like one of them, he would never actually be one of them.

"So back to the nightclub," Pat pressed on. "Destro has his own private booth in a far corner overlooking the dance floor."

"What if he doesn't like me when he sees me in the club?"

"Don't worry," Pat said with a wry smile. "He'll like you."

SIXTY

PETER WALKED THE LATE-NIGHT STREETS LIKE A catwalk model, strutting his hips, camp as hell.

"True tradecraft," Pat Hughes had informed him a day before, "should never be dropped until the target is down. You're like De Niro out there. As a true Method actor, you should live the role."

He approached Adonis nightclub via a narrow passage of tucked away bars. All the buildings were painted white in this part of Mykonos and they shone in the neon glow of the bar signs, becoming a blinding alleyway of light and noise.

It was a warm night. The constant din of the cicadas was only beaten by the honking moped horns, pumping bass of the bar music, and shouts of the revelers. People littered the outsides of the saloons, their eyes getting trapped on Peter as he passed by. A woman stumbled away from her friends and temporarily blocked his path, speaking to him rapidly in Spanish, asking him what his name was, whether he'd like to join her and her friends.

He declined the pretty girl politely and moved on.

He reached Adonis. Colored lights flashed from the doorway. Techno music throbbed the white stone. A long procession of people trailed out the entrance.

Peter joined the end. Now it was the turn of the queens to look him up and down. Some smiled. Some blushed. Others went purple with envy.

These were the young men looking for wealth. For the VIPs. Competition this hot was not welcome.

Peter returned their glares with death in his eyes.

They shivered and turned away.

A minute into his wait, a well-built man in a tight black T-shirt moved along the line toward him, scanning the faces as he went along. Peter became nervous when he stopped right beside him.

"You," the bouncer said.

"Me?" Peter replied, lightening his voice the way Pat had showed him.

"Yeah. Follow me."

Peter's nerves jarred. Was this one of Destro's men? Had they guessed what was going to happen? The guy had the nightclub logo on his left bicep. Adonis. But he could have still been working for the Italian.

"You can go straight in," the bouncer added.

"I can break the line?"

"Yeah. Don't worry about paying entry, either. Adonis is always looking to fill its dance floors with the brightest talent."

Brightest talent, Peter thought as he entered the nightclub, the queens glaring after him with envy. Then he stopped sharp and looked around. This was the first time Peter had ever set foot inside a full-blown gay club. In all the exhaustive intel *they'd been over these past six days, Pat and Mother had mentioned nothing of what he was seeing now. No warnings. Nothing. And Peter guessed the reason for this was because it would have been pointless to explain. No description could have prepared him for this.*

The first thing he noticed as he pushed through the swing doors were the men aggressively dancing and gyrating inside giant birdcages that hung from the ceiling on chains. Scantily clad in tight latex, or nothing at all, the dancers' skins glistened with oil as they wriggled to the thumping sounds.

Next, it was the men walking around in leather and rubber that freaked him out. A full-on fetishist party going on. Black walls covered in neon graffiti glowed under UV lighting. On the dance floor, which was in the shape of an oval and sunk deep into the center of the club, the strobe was constant, animating the writhing dancers in stop-motion jittering images.

The pumping techno came from everywhere, as if the building itself was producing the frantic noise that beat the air, causing a panicked feverishness to flow through the bodies.

At the bar, he ordered a bottle of Bud and a whiskey chaser. He had never drunk alcohol before. Not even during the walkabout. The only reason he ordered these drinks was because he'd seen people order them in films. The ones he used to watch from the Roswells' backyard. The reason he chose Budweiser? Easy: because of the incessant advertising he'd witnessed during that time.

Just like the films, Peter necked the short at the bar in one.

Not like the films, he almost coughed it all straight back up, the barman having to step back.

He kept it down, just. Croaked a thank you to the barman

and departed with the Bud, hoping it didn't taste as bad as the whiskey.

He began to walk the club. The whiskey warmed his stomach and focused his attention. The lights shone off the oily torsos squirming in the cages. As he made it to the dance floor, he passed a podium where a full-blown sex show between three men was going on full throttle.

The display brought back the queasiness of the whiskey and he faced away, doing his best to ignore it.

The VIP area of the nightclub was on a mezzanine overlooking the dance floor. Peter entered the writhing, stop-motion masses below. The music shook his teeth, the bones of his skull. The dancers were too preoccupied with the thunderous sound to notice him sidling through, exerting every muscle in their bodies as if they were pent-up with unused energy, having to get it out of them tonight, whatever happened.

Peter gazed up at the balcony of the mezzanine and began watching the target.

Giovanni Destro looked out from his high position with hungry eyes. He sat in a white leather booth with his arms spread out along the back of the seating, a gold bottle of Armand de Brignac champagne on the table in front of him.

Sitting beside the fat Italian was a young man. He wasn't the one from the yacht, though he was the same type: slim, athletic, feminine facial features. A swipe of bleached white went through his black hair. He sat pressed into Destro, chatting in his ear, giggling, Destro's shark-smile making momentary appearances on his plump lips.

The billionaire casually scanned the dancers. The instant he caught Peter's blue eyes staring up at him, he froze. For several seconds their eyes locked and the two were staring right at each other, Destro lifting up his Lugano diamond-encrusted sunglasses to get a better look.

Peter turned away. He didn't want to give the impression he was staring particularly at the Italian. He continued through the crowd, making sure to keep within Destro's line of sight. When he turned his eyes to the scene again, the Italian was speaking into the ear of one of his men—a large specimen squeezed into a suit. The pretty boy was now standing several feet back, a sore look on his face.

The henchman left Destro's booth and Peter watched him descend the winding metal steps that stretched down from the VIP area. He waded through the dance floor and came right up to Peter. The blank look on his granite face didn't make it clear whether he wanted to kill him or invite him up.

Thankfully, it was the second.

"The boss invites you to have drink with him," he said in a thick Slavic accent that was drowned out by the music, Peter having to read his lips.

"Sure."

The goon's name was Dimitri Dzuba. Peter knew because of the intelligence they had on him. Dimitri led him up the winding stairs to the VIP area. There were another four well-built men standing around the booth. Destro had already told the skinny boy to scram. He was leaving with an indignant face, eyeing Peter haughtily as they passed each other at the top of the stairs.

A lascivious smile bent the Italian's fat-lipped mouth the second Peter met his eyes.

"Siediti, ragazzo mio," he said, patting the seat beside him.

"Grazie," Peter replied timidly as he took it.

The letch was on him immediately, placing an arm around his shoulders and bringing him in tight. His overpowering cologne and breath wafted at Peter. He had recently eaten oysters and his sweaty face reeked of them.

"Sei stato a lungo a Mykonos?" he asked, blowing hot breath into Peter's cheek with each word.

"Non molto. Sono qui con la mia famiglia."

"You are American?" Destro asked in English.

"Yes. You could tell by my…"

The words dried up in Peter's throat as the letch slid a hand up his thigh, brushing his penis. Peter couldn't help shaking as Destro grabbed the top of his leg.

"You have strong legs," he breathed in Peter's ear. "I like athletic boys."

Peter was struggling to breathe. The shaking got worse. He wondered whether he was about to have a full-blown panic attack. He hadn't had one in years, but he felt the all-too-familiar sensations. The shortness of breath. The dread building inside.

What would happen when he started humming Irving Berlin?

"It's okay," Destro said, letting go and sitting back. Giving Peter some space.

He was able to breathe. Just in time.

"I see you are shy," Destro said. "Maybe some champagne will loosen you up. After all, why else would you come to my table?"

"Champagne," Peter muttered. "Yes… Thank you."

He did his best to regain his composure.

Destro nodded at Dimitri. The gorilla came forward and poured Peter a glass of the Armand de Brignac. As Peter picked the drink up, Destro shuffled back up to him, sniffed at his neck with his pig's nose.

"You smell so pretty. So fresh."

Peter was staring at the champagne flute in his hand. He imagined breaking it, using the stem to stab Destro's neck, repeatedly. Lunging at Dimitri while Destro choked on his own blood. Taking the pistol he's got hidden under his suit jacket. Shooting the other four men positioned around the booth. Everyone screaming and fleeing the nightclub.

"So what is your name, my handsome companion?"

"Joe," Peter told him.

Destro smiled. "So, Joe, what do you know?"

The shark's grin increased. Peter gripped the stem of the glass. Then drunk some.

"You said you were here with your family," Destro pursued.

"Yes. The trip to Greece is a present from them."

"A present? Have you achieved something for this present?"

"Yes. I got accepted at Harvard on their classics course."

"Harvard." Cue faux astonishment. "Wow, Joe. So you're not just a pretty face."

Peter simpered. Just like Pat taught him. He was feeling more relaxed. It might have been the champagne.

"So where are your family? Not here, I hope."

He playfully looked about.

Peter giggled. Made his cheeks go red. "No. They don't know that I've," he went bashful, "you know, come here."

"A secret?"

"Yes."

"Oh, well, I can believe that, Joe. Coming from a Roman Catholic family, I also must keep a secret. Would you believe it that my mama is eighty-six, and still she doesn't know my true tastes?"

"It's hard, isn't it?" Peter said, trying to make an empathetic connection.

"Yes, Joe," Destro said, lowering his voice. "It is very hard." The old man looked sad. And with it, not so ugly. A little more human. But the cocksure machismo soon returned. "No sadness, Joe," he announced with reanimation. "Only life tonight."

He topped up Peter's glass. Then, as he placed the bottle back down, he asked, "Why did you come to my table, Joe?"

"Your man asked me."

Destro smiled at the innocence. "He didn't force you, though, did he?"

"No. But I was intrigued."

"Intrigued, how?"

"I thought that someone who has other men fetch him companions must be worth meeting."

"Is that all?" Destro said, displaying that big shark's grin. "Be honest now."

"I like older men," Peter said firmly as Destro's hand returned to his thigh, the old man loving the way he made Peter squirm, getting off on it.

"But you can have any other older man," the Italian said. "You can have any man in this whole nightclub. You are beautiful. Why me?"

"You have an aura."

Destro rolled his eyes.

"No. I mean it," Peter assured him. "It's not just the fact you have your own booth, men serving you, fetching companions, protecting you. It's because you emit power on an anatom-

ical level. Some scent you give off." He budged closer to Destro, so that his penis touched the Italian's hand. It's just tradecraft. Brought his lips close to Destro's ear. *"It tells me you are power,"* he purred. *"Not just rich power, but apex predator power. King of your ocean."*

Destro's eyes lit up. *"Oh, Joe,"* he growled, *"you have no idea."*

SIXTY-ONE

THE AEGEAN SEA WAS SO TRANQUIL THAT IT HAD *become a watery black mirror. A vast carpet of stars spread out across it, so that Destro's luxury cabin boat looked like it was traveling through the cosmos.*

Not everything was tranquil, however. On the horizon a bruised bank of cloud grumbled and flashed with purple veins.

The fat man was like a sleazy octopus, touching and groping Peter all the way to the super yacht, his men acting as though ignorant of it. The lead man, Dimitri, sat in the cabin with them, his back turned so he didn't have to watch.

To those burly military men Peter was just another of the boss's boys. As harmless as a schoolgirl.

Their underestimation was a useful weapon.

"What's this?" Peter said in between the grotesque kissing.

He was holding up a medallion that hung from Destro's neck.

"You like it?"

"It's shaped like the moon," Peter remarked.

"It is the cat's-claw moon that hung in the sky the night I shot my very first elephant."

"Really?" Peter said, his blue eyes sparkling, trying to look as intrigued as possible.

"Yes. I had gone night hunting and the moon was beautiful. Have you ever been to Africa?"

"No. But I've always wanted to."

Well, Joe did, at least. Peter had never really given it a second's thought.

"In Kenya," the Italian droned on, "you are much closer to the Equator than here in Europe or in America, and, as such, you are closer to the orbit of the moon. At certain times of the year, it is so close that you feel like you can reach out and touch it."

He articulated the sentiment with his hand, Peter following its movement with his eyes, acting fascinated by the man's tale.

"I remember that it hung right behind the elephant as I took the shot. As if the great gray beast could step back and sit on its edge. Such a perfect memory, and when we took the ivory, I had them carve a piece into a cat's-claw moon so I would always remember killing that elephant."

"It's a beautiful story," Peter lied, running his fingers along the crescent medallion. "It's sharp," he added delicately.

"Yes. Just like my teeth." The Italian grinned widely. "Now come," he added, taking Peter's hand and getting up off the cream leather. "I would like you to see my most beautiful possession in the whole wide world."

Destro led Peter out onto the cockpit of the cabin boat and the two stood beside the pilot, the billionaire pressing himself into Peter from behind.

"You see her?" Destro called out, pointing toward the horizon.

The Mermaid *rose up before them like the craft of some mythical sorcerer, the storm rumbling and flashing in the background. The 80-meter-long super yacht's polished aluminum hull and aluminum superstructure shimmered with the reflection of the star-spangled water, making it look like a trembling mirage.*

It was decadence personified. A floating mansion with eighteen bedrooms. Italian interior design. A sauna. Bar. Gym. Indoor swimming pool. A main apartment at the stern. A helipad at the bow.

A temporary dock lined its starboard side. Pontoons held up a floating wooden walkway. The pilot parked the cabin boat next to two smaller speedboats that were moored to the platform and they disembarked.

A gangway led up the side of the yacht. Two men stood at the top. Dimitri was first up. He stopped and talked with the two while Destro, Peter and the other four men continued onto the yacht, the Italian's heavy arm strung across Peter's shoulders.

The two men at the top of the gangplank made seven. That was everyone. Intelligence had each of their pictures and a list of details. Pat Hughes had showed them to Peter. One after the other like playing cards. Making him mentally record each man.

They were ex-Russian Special Forces.

"Some say still are," *Pat had suggested.*

The leader, Dimitri Dzuba, was a veteran of covert operations in Chechnya, Georgia and Ukraine. Some suspected he'd performed certain tasks for the Russians in the European

Union, but that was as of yet unconfirmed. He apparently ran his own securities company these days.

The two men at the top of the ramp were Andre Tarkovski and Afanasy Bulgarin. Both veterans of operations in Georgia and Chechnya.

Pat Hughes thought Dzuba's company was just a front for the Russian Federation. "It would make sense for the Russians to be protecting Destro," he had told Peter back at the villa. "Being that the Russkies would be one of the highest bidders for anything damaging on the US. They'd certainly be willing to offer him a platform. Fucking Rus—"

"Okay, Pat," Mother had snapped. "Stick to the facts as we know them."

She had gone red. As she always did whenever someone badmouthed the Motherland. After all, she was born there. Made of it. Her stoical forbearance forged within its harsh crucible. It made no difference that the USSR had turned on her.

Over the years, Peter had learned to understand enough of the Russian spoken between Magda and her to discover that she had once been KGB. Its best assassin. Somewhere along the line, though, her own people had gone against her or she against them. He was never sure which. Whatever it was, it was bad enough that she had no choice but to turn to the United States for protection.

They offered her a deal:

Asylum in exchange for all her technical knowledge.

Peter tried to forget Mother as he walked the vast ship. The four Russians that remained with them formed the corners of a square around their boss and his latest lover, the six of them ascending a wide staircase illuminated by blue *footlights. It led to the very top deck of the gigantic* Mermaid, *the superstructure resembling a multi-storey villa made out of shiny metal.*

"I like to make love under the stars," the Italian purred in Peter's ear as they stepped onto the top deck.

The center of the floor was taken up by a huge double-king-size bed that sunk into the polished wood. It was surrounded by candles that flickered in the steadily increasing wind.

"I had it custom made," Destro told him.

As they proceeded toward it, the bed rose soundlessly on some type of motion-triggered mechanical system. It made the Italian grin, but Peter didn't notice. He was too busy looking toward the horizon. The storm was closer. A heavy wind passed over the water. The waves gathering steam.

Destro sat his round body on the bed, his thick legs dangling off the edge. He patted the mattress beside him.

"Come, boy. I promise to be gentle."

Peter tentatively approached.

The four men kept their square formation as they came to a stop around the bed, turning their backs to them. Their names were Pavel, Sergei, Igor and Arkady. In a few minutes they would all be dead.

"Don't mind my men, Joe. They won't watch. They're just here to make sure no one hurts us. Okay?"

"Sure," Peter said shyly.

A faint murmur of thunder reached their ears. Almost at the same time, frigid air ran over the deck, unsettling the candles.

Peter took a seat on the bed. Destro hustled up behind him, taking hold of his shoulders within claw-like fingers.

"So tense," he remarked as the fingers worked the firm muscle. "Full of knots."

Peter tried to relax. Tried with all his might to stay in character. But it was difficult.

The thunder rumbled. Giovanni Destro brought a rough hand down on Peter's chest.

The massage was over.

Just as he did when Peter and Mother had watched him from the rock, he turned from passive to aggressive, grabbing Peter by the right breast, gripping it in his claw.

"You are mine," he roared with the weather.

He brought his mouth down on Peter's neck. It felt at first like he was going to break the skin, but it was just a love bite, the fat man sucking away like a leech.

Peter's gag reflex almost kicked in. He did well to hold it back. Before he could get his composure, however, Destro shoved a hand down his Ralph Lauren pleated wool trousers. Gripped his penis and testicles. Peter went rigid like he was in shock.

"Are you a virgin, Joe?" Destro growled.

Peter noted that the men kept their backs to the scene. Ignoring—or too embarrassed to pay attention to—the rape going on behind their backs.

That was good.

Thunder crackled and purple threads reflected off the yacht's shiny surfaces. Peter decided that enough was enough. He twisted around, wriggling out of the letch's grip. Jumped backwards across the bed, smiling playfully at Destro as the fat man made a renewed grab for him, Peter playing hard to get, but really getting him where he wanted him.

Destro grinned sharkishly. Followed him into the middle

of the massive bed. He tried to pin Peter but the latter outma-
neuvered him, slipping away from underneath.

Destro appeared annoyed that his weight was not enough.

"You like to play, Joe," he said breathlessly. "I like a man
who plays. A man with fight. With passion. It makes it all the
more glorious when I take from him."

"I didn't come out here to be raped," Peter said.

"Then what did you come out here for? You said it your-
self. I have an aura. I reek of power. Men with power don't just
wait for the fruit to fall. They pick it themselves."

"Isn't that rape?"

"Not out here it isn't. We're in international waters.
There is no law except mine."

He pulled his shorts down to reveal a mushroom-shaped
penis that was not much bigger than one, either.

"Now I want you to suck my cock."

"Only if you kiss me first."

"A kiss before the fuck. I'll let you have your little win."

"Very gracious of you."

They came together in the center of the bed. Peter checked
the surroundings.

The men remained with their backs to them.

A thunderclap shook the boat. The storm was almost upon
them. A heavy wind gusted over, making the curly strands of
the old Italian's hair flap about the sides of his sweat-glossed
head. He came in for the kiss, pressing his grotesque body into
Peter, his tongue reaching right inside Peter's mouth—

Destro's eyes widened in horror. Peter's teeth were
clamping down on his tongue, trapping their faces together, the
Italian tugging back, until he feared he would sever the organ.

He stopped struggling. Held his face there, wondering what was going to happen next.

If he thought his one-night lover was playing, the thought didn't last long. Peter whipped the ivory necklace off the old man's neck. He pressed himself right into Destro. Hooked a leg behind the Italian and flipped him onto his back. Pinned him to the bed. Secured his legs before they could even start to flail. Then, with the blade-shaped necklace, he reached down the thigh—eyes glaring into Destro's—and dug the sharp end of the medallion deep into the flesh, hacking through the fat, and dragging it down the leg until he felt it slice across the rubbery hardness of the femoral artery.

Destro's screams were eaten up by their clamped mouths. Hot blood pumped over Peter's hand, and all the Italian could do was beat at his back, the sounds of the kill hardly making it over the approaching storm, Destro's men, with their backs turned to the scene, ignoring the gentle sounds of struggling, thinking it no more than their boss raping another poor wretch.

Peter was back on the muddy bank with the caribou. With his entire body one rigid piece of flexed muscle, he contained Giovanni Destro beneath him for the next three minutes, pressing him into the bed, a continuous flow of blood slipping out of the fat leg, and with it Destro's strength. Peter's mind and emotions completely detached from the scene. Running on training, discipline and muscle memory, fading into the last seven years of instruction.

Peter was covered in a slick of red by the time he got up from the dead man, the sticky necklace gripped in his hand. The men covered the corners of the bed at a distance of seven feet. None of them had even flinched during their boss's death.

Peter snuck silently up behind the nearest one. Pavel was his name. With his right hand Peter came up and around the man's throat, stabbing into the left carotid with the medallion and dragging the blade down at an angle across the artery. Much the same as with Destro's thigh. His left hand, he slipped into the guy's gun belt and removed the Glock.

While Pavel collapsed to the deck clutching his neck, Peter let off three shots. Sergei. Igor. Arkady. In that order. Three bullets: three head shots.

Pavel was still choking and spluttering on the ground beside him, so Peter let off a fourth shot. Blowing the Russian's brains all over the polished deck.

Five down. That left three.

Peter scavenged the bodies, changing the clip with one of the others. Tucked another two in his pockets. They were all holding standard third generation Glock 17s.

He left the bodies and moved cautiously along the deck to the stern. On a lower level, he spotted shadows moving about: men coming to investigate the gunshots. So he searched for an alternative route.

SIXTY-TWO

THE THREE REMAINING MEN EMERGED ONTO THE second deck. Speaking in Russian, Dimitri tried over and over to reach the others via their comms.

"Pavel? Sergei? Do you copy?"

There was no answer, so he gave his two companions the signal to go up. Staircases lined both sides of the deck. Arkady took the left, Andre took the right, and the two men moved cautiously upwards through the decks.

They reached the top at the same time, approaching the scene from opposite ends. Lightning struck close to the yacht, illuminating the dead men, the blood-soaked bed, Destro splayed out on his back, his wide, staring eyes facing the heavens as they rumbled overhead.

"They're all dead, Dimitri. All of them."

At that moment the sound of a speedboat engine roaring into life made them turn. Spotting the blond boy driving away in one of their boats, the men narrowed their eyes and gritted their teeth, so tightly that they creaked.

PETER RACED INTO THE STORM, *the wind rustling his hair and the choppy water tossing the boat from wave to wave, wrestling with the wheel as he zigged and zagged between them.*

Gunshots crackled the air. Something hot flashed past an ear. He chucked a glance over his shoulder. The cabin boat and the other speedboat rapidly cut the distance between them.

The boat Peter used was unfortunately the weakest of the three. It was, nonetheless, the easiest to hot-wire. Hence the reason it had been the only one that Pat Hughes had had time to teach him how to bypass the ignition system on. One advantage it did have, however, was that with it being smaller it was more nimble in maneuverability. It was also black, which meant it sunk into the dark background more readily.

Of his pursuers, Andre was in a standard speedboat. Dimitri and Anatoly in the larger cabin boat. While Dimitri drove, Anatoly leaned an AK-74M on the windshield, firing off volleys at the swerving speedboat as they raced after it.

A spray of bullets caught Peter's boat along the back. Gathering that Anatoly now had his range, Peter ducked down, right at the moment another volley struck.

When he stood again, the windshield had a line of shattered bullet holes arcing across it.

Another shot whipped overhead and his eyes snapped right. Andre was coming up alongside. As Peter skimmed off the ramping waves, the Russian heaved his steering wheel and rammed into him.

The speedboat almost flipped, the waves lifting it. Andre wedging his larger boat underneath. Peter forced to swing the speedboat in a hairpin turn to get away. Except now, he was heading straight at the cabin boat. The muzzle of the AK flashed, lighting up the night. Peter swerved 90 degrees, cleaving right across a long rolling tubular wave, bullets raking along the water in a series of splashes that chased the surfing speedboat.

As Peter steered into the wave and jumped it, Andre managed to get back alongside. Steering one-handed, the henchman attempted to aim his Glock with the other. It was awkward, being that he was right-handed and Peter was on his left. He had to bring the right arm across his chest to make the shot as the waves viciously tossed both boats about, and consequently threw his aim all over the place.

He shot once.

Too high. The bullet heading for the storm clouds.

Again.

Missed.

Two shots in quick succession.

Closer, but Peter still had a head.

The teenage assassin decided he'd been playing defense long enough. He too took the wheel with one hand, the thing bucking and tugging, the waves battering the speedboat, and lined up his own shot. Breathed in. Focused on making it.

Went to pull the trigger.

The boat jumped. Throwing Peter forward, the gun leaping out of his grasp, skittling along the front of the speedboat and into the water.

Peter was now unarmed.

Another shot rasped the air above his head. He swerved left, cutting across the bow of the cabin boat, which was about to ram him. The AK barked and snarled as Peter skimmed across the black water, the pack snapping at his heels like wolves chasing a deer.

He led them into the storm. Into the rain. Where the sky and the sea merged into inky blackness, hoping to fade into it with his pitch-black boat.

The waves grew larger, rising up around the boats, cracked with tendrils of white foam. He weaved in between them, hiding within the towering water, the speedboat hacking its way along, snaking through a rolling gorge of lofty kahunas.

"HEY!" Anatoly shouted over the storm. "He's disappeared."

He was right. Peter couldn't be seen anywhere in the thick rain, their three sets of eyes scanning the rough sea around them.

Lightning illuminated the air in incandescent purple.

It was Dimitri who spotted Peter; the light reflecting off the black speedboat about a hundred yards away.

"There," he shouted, pushing the throttle all the way. "Twelve o'clock."

"I see him!" Anatoly shouted out, lining up the AK.

Andre spotted him also. Teeth gripped together, he pushed his speedboat to its very limits, flying ahead of the cabin boat, his craft the fastest. He got in the way of the shot, Anatoly crying out, waving him out of the way. But Andre ignored him and raced ahead regardless.

It was then that something odd happened.

On the cabin boat, Dimitri blinked his eyes when Peter's speedboat vanished into thin air. Not like before. Before they had lost it in the waves. This time, the boat was literally there one second. Gone the next.

Lightning shocked the world awake.

"Watch out!" Dimitri shouted.

It was too late.

Andre hit the black rock before he even saw it. A few feet to the left and he would have traveled straight through the cave. Just like Peter did when Dimitri thought he'd vanished.

Water and pieces of wood exploded into the air, the front of the craft torn into splinters. Andre was thrown forward into the rocks. There was no way he could survive the impact.

Two left.

Dimitri corrected the cabin boat's course just in time and veered into the cave, scraping the side and speeding through the giant rock. The one shaped like part of a tentacle.

They followed Peter into the bay, where he led them into a field of anchored yachts and fishing boats, zigzagging his craft down the narrow alleyways of water in between, the cabin boat longer and more cumbersome, unable to work its way through the labyrinthian gaps at the same rate.

They lost sight of him for a third time.

Dimitri went slowly. The engine putting. The hissing rain canceling out the sound. Anatoly was standing at the bow like an oversized figurehead, wielding the AK and scanning the area with pierced eyes.

He suddenly went rigid like a hunting dog and began pointing to the bow of a hefty sailing yacht they were taxiing past.

The black nose of Peter's speedboat poked out ever so slightly from it. Dimitri pointed at a ladder hanging down the side of the twenty-meter boat. He further signaled for Anatoly to climb up on deck and ambush Peter.

Anatoly nodded his approval to the plan.

Dimitri pulled beside the yacht and Anatoly clambered up onboard. He then crept over the deck, the rain beating hard, his long blond ponytail heavy at the back of his head. He stepped down into the cockpit, moving past the open door to the cabin. Oblivious to the man hiding in the darkness just a few feet within. Still oblivious as the man silently emerged and snuck right up behind Anatoly with the silence of a praying mantis.

Lightning.

An arm came around Anatoly, trapping the AK against his chest. Destro's necklace made its second appearance of the night, hacking at Anatoly's throat, right across the windpipe, cutting the vocal cords, so that his wet, clucking gasps couldn't be heard over the beating rain and the imminent thunder.

THE CLAP CAME RIGHT *at the moment Anatoly dropped from Peter and the latter was grabbing the falling Kalashnikov from his dead fingers.*

One left.

As the thunder died down, Peter listened out for the putting motor of the cabin boat. It was close. He ran to the bow just as it passed by underneath. Aiming the AK downwards, he got ready to fire. Only to end up frowning.

Not a single soul stood on the boat.

Peter had had his own trick played back on him.

He dived for cover just in time. From the yacht anchored in front came multiple shots. They sparked and pinged and—hit.

Peter let out a yelp as he landed on all fours, covered by the cabin, for now. It gave him time to check his abdomen, which was on fire. The bullet had ricocheted off the boat and hit him, taking part of its power, but also making it spin as it struck and therefore increasing the size of the entry wound.

He lifted his shirt and blood fell onto the wet decking.

Mother had been right. Nothing could truly prepare you.

A second or two of panic—the very least that should be afforded to all persons shot for the first time—and Peter was back at it, the pain ignored, discipline and training kicking in. What else had he been preparing for all these years in Alaska?

More gunshots blasted the wet air.

Peter was back on his feet. Skidding along the deck toward his speedboat, which had drifted away. He calculated that Dimitri would by now have moved far enough along the opposite yacht to have come around the cabin and got sight of him.

Peter flung his body around 180 degrees, feeling his guts tear in the process, and spotted the Russian straight ahead. He pulled the trigger on the AK and the thing bucked in his hands. He didn't hit Dimitri, but the short burst did the trick. It forced the Russian to throw himself to ground and find cover, winning Peter enough time to drop into the water and swim to the speedboat.

He didn't think the landing would hurt so much. The pressure of his feet hitting the water jerked his hip and tugged on the wound. He lost his grip on the AK and it sunk through the water. There was no time to swim after it, and he wasn't sure he'd have the strength anyway.

Peter pulled himself into the speedboat, screaming at the effort. If he thought he had enough time to lie on his back panting breath back into his lungs, the nature of the circumstances had other ideas. The sound of the cabin boat roaring into action made it over the pelting rain and he realized that Dimitri was already back onboard.

With energy he didn't have, Peter launched himself up, took hold of the controls and accelerated the speedboat rapidly out of the anchored vessels.

Guiding the craft one-handed into open water, he grasped the wound with the other, blood pooling through his fingers. He took the hand away and lifted the shirt. The wound was a deep red, the skin turning purple around it.

More gunshots made him flinch and he gritted his teeth. Training kicked back in. Discipline. He went cold all over. Concentrating on steering the boat toward the island, he managed to remove the silk Armani shirt he was wearing. With his teeth, he ripped it into strips and used the cloth to plug the wound, balling the silk up and forcing it into the hole, the bullet still smoldering inside.

A weakness attacked him. He was nauseous and in need of help. More gunshots rang out behind him. Dimitri closing in.

"This fucking guy...never quits," Peter complained breathlessly to himself.

The storm had made landfall when he reached the jetty. Lightning illuminated the terrace and the back of the villa in garish detail. None of the lights were on and Peter found this odd.

He limped up the steps of the terrace, hearing the chugging engine of the cabin boat as it approached the wooden platform. Peter was unarmed and severely injured. He needed immediate medical attention. Not a fight.

Reaching the villa, he expected sanctuary.

All he got was a locked door.

Peter hammered his fist on the glass, already feeling the

last of his energy drop out of him. Not a single movement happened inside. No sound. Nothing. All the blinds on the windows drawn.

"Mother?!" he cried out desperately as thunder beat at his ears. "Where are you?!"

He flashed a look over his shoulder.

The cabin boat was almost at the jetty.

Peter grabbed a rock from the terrace. Returning to the glass door, he bashed the pane with all his ebbing strength. The first blow merely cracked it. So he hit it again and again, the wound screaming with pain, until the window shattered apart and he was staggering into the villa.

DIMITRI CAUTIOUSLY LEFT the cabin boat.

Lightning.

It illuminated the drops of blood leading along the wooden walkway, the rain gradually washing them away. The Glock grasped in his hand, he followed them upwards, moving slowly toward the back of the villa. The rain was fierce. He stepped up to the shattered door. The blood continued inside across the mosaic tiles, disappearing into the darkness of the villa.

The boy was in there somewhere. Lurking in the darkness. Wounded and unarmed.

On the verge of stepping inside, Dimitri heard bare feet rapidly beating the stone to his right. The little punk had tricked him. Making it look like he was inside the villa when he was actually hiding on the terrace.

Dimitri twisted sideways. It was too late.

Peter brought the telescope crashing straight down on top of the Russian's nose with such incredible force that it sent bone fragments into both frontal lobes of the brain.

It didn't immediately kill him. More like lobotomized him.

He stumbled backwards, eyes rolling into the back of his skull, the Glock falling from his fingers, and Peter finished him off almost as a kindness. Using both hands on the heavy telescope, he brought it down on the same spot, the center of the Russian's face, sending the man's forehead caving in.

Dimitri fell heavily onto his back and Peter made sure of it, bringing the telescope down repeatedly until it was as broken and bent as the man's face.

Breathless, Peter picked the Glock up. Checked the clip. There were only two rounds in it.

He stumbled around the villa. The electric was out. None of the light switches were working. The rooms were empty. All their things gone.

Reaching the upstairs hallway, he froze when the frosted glass of the front door was illuminated by blue flashing light. It was a police patrol cruiser, called by the silent alarm, the vehicle pulling up in front of the place.

Peter pushed the fresh panic down. He glared at the gun. It was practically useless. He attempted to think things through as the police got out the cruiser and made their way to the door.

He was there under the name of David Foster. A Canadian. Not that that mattered. Even the documents were gone. It was like they'd bailed on him the second Pat had dropped him in town.

Peter had little choice but to run. He was holding a Glock 17. There was a dead man downstairs. Another two in the bay. *Another five on Destro's super yacht. Including the billionaire himself.*

This is bad, *he thought as they began pressing the doorbell, the sound echoing throughout the lonely villa.*

Peter left via a side door. The two police officers were busy at the front. He waited on a corner before leaving it hurriedly and joining the street. He thought he had made it when one of the cops yelled through the rain, "Hey! Hey, you. Stop!"

Their flashlight beams were on him. And soon so were they.

The clifftops in that part of Mykonos were a cluster of villas and small apartment blocks that faced the crystal water. From the sea, they resembled a cemetery of white tombstones. Peter turned right into an alleyway. Steps led down to the beach. The rapid clacking sounds of the cops' shoes placed renewed vigor inside Peter. He couldn't run. He could only hobble, seized with pain every time he lifted his right leg.

One of the cops fired a warning shot.

"Stop!"

There was a wall to his immediate left. Peter screamed as he vaulted over it. Dropped into the yard of a small villa. The landing knocked the wind out of him, and while he spent a few seconds getting his breath back, he scanned his surroundings.

A whole row of backyards led onwards.

He heard the cops. Catching a look over his shoulder, he spotted a pink hand landing on top of the wall above him.

Peter screamed a second time. Vaulting a second wall. Dropping into the next yard. Then a third. Pushing the pain away into the corners like Magda and Mother had taught him all those years ago in the barn. Pushing his body to move faster and to ignore the burning injury.

As he dropped into the fourth yard, the bloodstained cloth fell out. It landed on a bed of pebbles that decorated the edge of a jacuzzi. Warm blood ran down his thigh.

Moments later the two policemen dropped down into the yard with the jacuzzi. They hadn't seen him since the second garden.

"Where is he?" one of them said in Greek as they moved cautiously through the beating rain.

The other was about to answer when a clang alerted them to the next yard.

"Come on."

They vaulted over the wall, across that yard and over the next.

Peter emerged from his hiding place. In his hand were some pebbles. He threw them as far as he could, over the heads of the running cops. Then, when he could no longer hear their panting, he once more scanned his surroundings.

He was standing in the backyard of a villa. Not as fancy as the one he had been in with Mother. Newer. Smaller. Just a bungalow. A swimming pool and a jacuzzi in the yard.

A sliding glass door led into it. He felt so sickly weak that he couldn't even bear the thought of climbing another fence. He'd stuffed the cloth back in, but it wouldn't do forever.

Tugging the door to the side, he stepped, staggered, into a room.

A bedside lamp flicked on.

It illuminated the face of a young woman. She was sitting up in bed, and she was beautiful.

"Please, help me," Peter murmured at her, practically collapsing onto the floor.

SIXTY-THREE

MONTEREY, 2019

KEN KNIGHT WAS DISCOVERED TWO MINUTES after his death. Unable to see him in the blind spot under the busted street light, another motorist had driven straight over the body.

Getting out of the car and checking, initially thinking she'd hit a dog, the seventy-nine-year-old driver had proceeded to scream so loud that she alerted the whole neighborhood. Including the lawyer's wife.

"You're in the clear," Pat Hughes tells Peter over speaker-phone. "They think the old woman did it. She's already had her license revoked twice and is foggy at best around what actually happened."

Luck has always had a hand in the art of killing.

Peter drives Paul Adams's Saab 900 into Pacific Grove. Moonlight shines through the trees lining the streets, striping the roads in silver. He feels tranquil returning to this place. Even if his enemies are hiding in the shadows.

It is cruising past the corner of Palm Avenue and Elm Drive that his composure is broken. Ambulance lights flash blue outside the Henderson place.

He goes cold.

"Pat, I'll have to call you back."

Peter turns into the street, people standing about the road, and taxis the Saab slowly toward the scene. Michael Henderson lies on a stretcher that two paramedics are loading into the back of an ambulance. The kid is holding a sheet of medical gauze to one side of his face. A few feet away, Carl holds on to Kate, their pensive eyes fixed to the sight of their stricken son.

Michael looks like he's taken a savage beating. The part of the face that Peter can see is bloated, a black eye closed over.

Mrs. Murphy stands in the street with the others, the little Yorkshire terrier, Sandy, held within an arm. She smiles at Paul Adams as he drives by.

Peter waves back.

The Hernandezes are watching from their front yard. Reaching them, Peter rolls down the window and asks Carlos what happened.

The gardener comes to the window. "That God damn Palmer kid," he says, "beat the shit out of him and then cut his face with a knife. I got to them just in time. Pulled the little shit off him."

Peter turns back to the scene.

Kate Henderson sobs. Carl holds her tight to his chest.

He is looking over her shoulder. Up the street. Toward the corner of Elm Drive. Wrath burning in his eyes.

"Where's Danny now?" Peter asks.

"After I got him off, he ran away."

"Did you hurt him?"

"No."

Peter nods. Thinks about it.

Kate Henderson gets into the ambulance. She takes her son's hand right as the doors slam shut.

SIXTY-FOUR

At the hospital, a short doctor with thick glasses speaks to Kate Henderson in a corridor of gleaming white walls.

"Your son will need plastic surgery to help with the scarring. He's also sustained a fractured cheekbone. The swelling around his left eye is pretty sustained too, but the socket isn't fractured, which is good. The X-rays on his ribcage show no signs of bone or cartilage damage, but he's still bruised up pretty bad. We'd like to keep him in overnight."

"Is it okay for me to stay with him?" Kate asks in her soft voice, fingers playing with the neck of her sweater.

"Of course. I'll have a porter bring another bed for the room."

Around the corner, Peter stands before a vending machine, pretending to buy candy but really listening to everything they say. Desperate to know what the status of the kid is.

"Paul, isn't it?"

Peter jumps.

Turning to his left, he comes face-to-face with Carl Henderson. He's carrying an overnight bag, having followed in his car.

"Yes," Peter says. "It's Paul."

They stare at each other, until the other man says, "I'm Carl."

"Of course," Peter says, shaking his head. "Sorry."

More staring.

"How come you're here?" Carl asks.

Peter can tell he's only speaking to him out of politeness. That he's already regretting it. Wishing he'd just crept past.

"My mother," Peter lies. "She's at the end of this corridor. I'm just getting her a snack."

"What's wrong with your mother?"

"She fell down the stairs. Broke her hip."

"Ouch."

Even more staring.

Peter this time. "How about you?"

Carl's face clouds over. He clears his throat. Eyes down. "Michael was hurt today," he murmurs.

"What happened?"

"*Someone*," his teeth are ground together, "cut his face with a knife. Beat him up real bad."

Peter acts surprised. "Gosh. Is he gonna be all right?"

"That's what I'm just about to find out."

"I'm sorry," Peter says. "Don't let me stop you. I'd better be getting along to Mother. She can be quite stern."

Carl tries to smile. It comes off crooked.

"I hope your boy is okay," Peter adds.

"Yes. Thank you," Carl mutters in a hollow voice before walking off.

Peter watches him disappear around the corner, then listens to him and Kate.

"They say he'll need plastic surgery," she tells her husband.

"Oh God."

Kate breaks down. "You should see what he's done to him, Carl. To our little boy."

Peter stands there. Screwing up his fists.

The Hendersons don't deserve this.

SIXTY-FIVE

Pulling into his driveway at seven p.m., Peter notes that Mrs. Harrison's front porch is empty. A light is on in an upstairs window. It is still warm from the day's heat. Usually he'd expect to see her sitting outside her house watching for fireflies. Maybe she's watching something interesting on TV instead.

Peter is hit with a foul odor the second he opens the front door of 24 Green Street. He flips the light switch to illuminate a mound of dog shit that sits piled atop his doormat. It has been here for a while; the rancid stench has had time to spread throughout the house and take hold.

He glances over his shoulder at the Jenkinses's front window.

The curtains twitch.

Peter shuts the door and logs into the security. He then uses his phone to watch Pam Jenkins feed feces into his letterbox the day before yesterday.

There is nothing else from the five days he's been away.

Peter goes upstairs, lies down in bed. His mind is glowing. Thoughts are streaming through him like electrical currents.

The Jenkinses line up before him. *Who did they call?*

He wants so badly to march across there and have it out. But it's not just the fact that Davenport's men will stop him before he gets the chance; it is what his other neighbors will think of him if he does.

Nevertheless, the Jenkinses are not the main thing burning a hole inside Peter's brain.

He already knows exactly how he will get rid of Jimmy Palmer. Knows how he will make every cell of him disappear from the face of the planet. It would be just like he was never here. Nothing more than a bad dream.

But he can't. Not yet.

And the impatience of it makes Peter gnash his teeth together. Makes him hum.

"What'll I do,

"When you, are far away..."

SIXTY-SIX

It is the next day. The cops are looking for Danny Palmer. They went around his house this morning. The short and sweet of it is that Jimmy Palmer told them to get fucked. Said come back when they had a warrant to enter the property.

From the StingRay, Peter knows Danny is home. Hiding out in his bedroom. At first, he couldn't understand why Jimmy was protecting his son so fiercely. He never showed any type of protective instinct toward his children before. Quite the opposite. Peter had expected him to stand aside and let the cops drag Danny out of the house.

But then he understood.

Before Danny got inside an interrogation room with cops, Jimmy wanted to make sure he'd placed enough fear in his son so he wouldn't go getting the idea of opening his mouth about *other* things.

Tuning in to Danny's phone, Peter had listened to one of the father's threats.

"You keep your mouth shut, boy," he'd hissed so low there wasn't a chance for his wife to overhear outside the room, "or she's fucking dead. You understand?"

"Yes, sir."

After visiting the shadow of the Palmers, the police went over to the sunshine of the Hendersons. Though, it has to be said, the darkness of the Palmer world had tainted their luster somewhat.

Michael had come home from hospital first thing this morning. Peter watched his return from the high vantage point of his bedroom balcony. The kid has a huge amount of packing bandaged to his left cheek and the eye on that side is still closed over, resembling a bubonic boil.

Danny Palmer really took it out on him.

As for Michael's police statement, the kid sobbed his way through most of it. The trauma fresh like an open wound, Kate holding him throughout, the deepness of her mother's love almost overwhelming for the watching Peter.

The kid is too soft for the type of black violence that swells in someone like Danny Palmer. In his youth Peter faced that type of dark brutality many times. Taken into care at the age of nine, he'd been undersized and an easy target. The orphanage had been hard. Some of the children were already starting to resemble their abusers. The anger they'd absorbed early on in life was starting to ooze out of them in fits of violence. Life was hell. And it was there, in hell, that Peter first discovered he had an iron will that made him different from others. Very quickly he learned that if you are the smaller boy, you hit first, you hit hard, and you keep hitting. And, eventually, the bigger boys will learn to fear you, and will back off.

In the beginning he took a lot of beatings. But, soon, when his skill and accuracy improved—coupled with his utter ruthlessness, unwillingness to back down and massive pain threshold—Peter began to be the one who dished out the beatings, many of them against much older and larger opponents, kids his own age generally staying out of the way.

Michael hasn't been beaten enough yet to learn if he has the will or not. And Peter hopes he'll never have to.

He also worries about the father.

While Kate is at work and Michael in his room, Carl Henderson has spent the majority of the afternoon on the back porch, staring into space, sipping from a bottle of rum, and grappling with his manhood.

Peter watches him from the shadows of his bedroom. Carl Henderson looks like a man who is going to do something. A certain resolution has been building in him since yesterday. One which could be dangerous.

The doorbell chimes, making Peter turn from the Henderson place.

When he answers the door, Mrs. Murphy stands under his porch holding her dog, the old woman's wrinkled face wearing a concerned expression.

"I'm so sorry to bother you, Paul," she says.

"Not at all. What's up?"

"It's Helen."

"Helen?"

"Mrs. Harrison."

Of course. Helen Harrison.

"What is it?"

"She's not answering her telephone or door. Today, she

was supposed to come over for brunch, but didn't attend. There's an upstairs window open at the back of the house. I'd climb up the ladder myself, but..." She trails off and raises her eyebrows.

"Have you called the police?"

It's the type of thing he's sure Paul Adams would say.

"I don't want to bother them until I know what I have," Mrs. Murphy states.

"And what do you think it is you have?"

Her eyes shimmer. The only word she says is, "Please."

Two minutes later Peter is stepping off the top rung of a ladder, ducking through the upstairs window, and dropping onto the checkered tiles of Mrs. Harrison's bathroom.

He senses it immediately. The second he breathes the air of the house into his lungs.

Peter makes his way to the master bedroom. Unlike 24, number 26 has it at the front of the house. Framed pictures line the walls of the landing. Her dead husband Bert. Her sons. The grandchildren. A crowd of frozen faces to watch her grow old alone.

When he reaches the room, Peter stands in the doorway gazing at the back of Mrs. Harrison. She is sitting in a chair facing the window. A view of the street below. The light still on in the room.

If he was Paul Adams he'd call out to her. But he isn't. He's Peter Black, and he already knows it would be futile.

He comes around her front. The old woman's eyes are open. Staring sadly at the neighborhood. He makes sure to close them before leaving the room.

Peter meets Mrs. Murphy at the front door.

"Is she—?"

She can't say the word. Her wet eyes finish the sentence for her.

Peter nods.

Mrs. Murphy breaks down and throws herself into him. Peter isn't ready for it. He does his best to comfort her, but he is as stiff as a coat stand.

SIXTY-SEVEN

AN HOUR LATER, PETER IS STANDING AT THE window of his living room watching the ambulance take the body of Mrs. Harrison away. Early predictions are that she suffered a massive stroke which killed her instantly. She was likely dead when he came home last night and saw the light on.

Mrs. Murphy sits sobbing on the settee behind him. Sandy the Yorkshire terrier sits in her lap shivering. From her owner's demeanor, the dog senses something is wrong, but doesn't know quite what.

Having blown her nose hard into a handkerchief embroidered with tiny bluebells, Mrs. Murphy says, "She was looking forward to seeing her grandchildren next month. We were talking about it just the other day."

Peter says nothing as he watches them lift the body into the back, the old woman zipped up in a black body bag, the thing strapped to a stretcher, a strap across the shins, another across the midriff. A third he can see goes across her face.

Paul Adams had to speak with a police officer about how he found her. The cop took the details from him, then from Mrs. Murphy, told them both that someone will be in touch, and left in his cruiser only five minutes after he arrived, leaving it to Mrs. Murphy to inform next-of-kin. Peter supposes Mrs. Harrison's sons will make time now.

"I tried to see her more often," Mrs. Murphy goes on. "Her family are so far away. After Bert died, she didn't really have anyone. He was the social one. Most of their friends were couples she knew through him. She said that being around them only reminded her of what she'd lost."

"How long was she married to Bert?" Peter asks.

He knows the answer, having discovered it while doing his original reconnaissance of the inhabitants of Pacific Grove. But, still, he must play the part of Paul Adams, and he gathers that's what he'd ask.

"They were married for almost fifty years," she says. "Almost half a century with one person. I guess I look back and think I'm lucky. None of my three marriages lasted longer than fifteen years. They all ended in acrimony. Good riddance, I say." She smiles. Then it drops. "Helen and Bert, though, they were happy. Right up to the end."

The doors slam shut on the ambulance. It makes Mrs. Murphy jump. She looks past Peter and out the window.

The ambulance gives a burst of siren and it's on its way.

Peter follows it with his gaze as far as he can see. Wind rattles the leaves in the trees that line Green Street. It is getting dark and the shadows are growing longer.

Mrs. Murphy gives a shiver as she says, "It's so much harder to be the one left behind. All alone."

Peter turns to her from the window. "Would you like some more ice tea?"

"No. No," she says. "I've already taken up enough of your time."

On the way out the door she touches Peter's arm.

Turning to him one last time, she says, "She always liked you, you know. Always stuck up for you when others," her eyes move in the direction of the opposite house, "were being spiteful."

"I wish I had spent more time with her," he can't help saying.

He really means it, too. That's not Paul Adams articulating regret. It is Peter.

Mrs. Murphy pats him on the arm and leaves. Halfway up the driveway, she calls the dog and it skips past Peter's feet.

Watching them go, he feels like he is sinking into a well of shame. He has failed Mrs. Harrison. He has failed her as a neighbor and he has failed in his role as a human. He feels it deep in his soul. That even though they weren't related in any way other than geography, he still owed that women something that we all owe each other. Some small duty that he should have performed but didn't. Like simply sitting with her on the porch.

Peter once saw a homeless guy wearing a sandwich board that said *Jesus Saved Me*. It was in New York. The man was standing on a street corner proselytizing. He proclaimed that, "We are all one family. All God's children. We owe as much to the stranger on the subway train as we do to our own children."

Peter doesn't believe in God. But he likes the ideal. Everyone looking out for each other. Your problem is my problem.

SIXTY-EIGHT

A FULL MOON ILLUMINATES THE NIGHT IN GLOOM. Peter stands on Elm Drive opposite the Palmer house. He's been there for the last five minutes, staring at the yellow stucco bungalow.

Behind the curtains, the silhouette of Jimmy Palmer watches TV. Every half hour he screams at his wife to fetch him another beer from the cooler.

Peter realizes he's been there too long when a red dot hits his left breast. Right where his heart is. It comes from one of the rooftops. Peter traces the laser into the night air, where it disappears before he can locate the source.

A test. He steps into the road.

Another dot, coming due east from the first, hits his chest, practically landing on the other one.

He stops. Steps back onto the sidewalk.

He is contemplating what to do next when footsteps make him chuck a look to his right.

Carl Henderson is marching up the street with a determined expression. Peter falls back into the shadows of a huge sycamore as he reaches the front door of the Palmer house and brings his fist down on it.

Inside, Jimmy Palmer shouts for someone to answer "the God darn door!" But Lyn is in the bathroom washing Hannah's hair and Danny is hiding from the police in his bedroom. So he is forced to answer it himself.

The second the door opens, Carl Henderson launches into a tirade.

"Have you seen what your psycho son did to Michael?"

He holds his phone out, and though Peter can't see, he's sure there's a picture of Michael's injuries on it.

"So what?" Jimmy says with a shrug once he's seen it.

Peter is sure a smirk is curling the edge of his lips.

"So what?!" Carl bursts out. "So he'll be scarred for life! Have to live with the trauma of what your son did to him. Do you have any idea what that does to a person?"

Peter likes Carl Henderson a lot. He is a good soul. A giver. He has only ever tried to give in his life. But he is talking to a brick wall, and if he thinks this piece of shit will understand or even care, he has had way too much rum.

Typically, Jimmy Palmer dismisses it with a smug look.

His wife, Lyn, leaves the bathroom, having overheard the ruckus. Sensing the scene like an animal sniffing the air, she reads the vibrations of the land and silently comes to the door, bringing a pair of soft hands up to her husband's shoulders and gently rubbing them.

"It's okay, honey," she coos into Jimmy's ear.

All Jimmy does is stand in his doorway watching Carl with a pair of evil eyes.

"You don't even care, do you?" Carl slurs.

Jimmy Palmer sniggers, his wife working those tense shoulders to no avail.

"You find that funny?"

"I find *you* funny, faggot," Palmer tells him.

"What kind of a father are you?"

Jimmy's smirk drops. His eyes go black. He steps forward. Lyn tries to hold on. It's no use, she loses her grip.

"What kind of a father am *I*?" Jimmy blurts, cocking his head to the side and stepping toward Carl.

The latter is not a fighter. He wasn't all those years ago with the kid whose sister he'd given the hickey to, and he's not now. He can't help taking a step back for every one Jimmy takes forward. It's like he's spent all day on that back porch imagining how this would go. What he would say. What he would do. The first part done, he's not so sure about the second.

Jimmy Palmer is moving toward him with menace. "Are you questioning my ability to raise my family, Henderson?"

"I do when one of your family uses a knife to mutilate one of mine. What sort of a father raises that sort of—"

Carl Henderson doesn't even see the right hook whip round. It takes him off his feet and lays him out. But not out cold. Even though it'd be better for him if it had.

Carl gasps for breath while floundering on the driveway. Big-eyed and looking like a guppy on a boat deck. The punch hit him right in the temple. Peter can almost see the stars floating before his eyes.

Jimmy Palmer is on him. Straddling Carl, stopping him from getting up, taking him by the scruff and then punching him in the head, over and over.

Peter looks down his chest. The dots are gone.

He walks across the street as Jimmy pummels Carl. The schoolteacher's eyes are barely open. His face already unrecognizable.

Jimmy swings a punch back and Peter seizes it by the wrist. Pressing his thumb into the nerves and tendons with the accuracy of an acupuncture needle, he sends razors of pain rushing up the arm, causing the shoulder to spasm.

Jimmy jerks his body and cries out as Peter pulls him up and backwards by the wrist, getting him off of Carl, who just collapses onto his back once Jimmy's hand releases the scruff of his shirt.

Peter lets go. Immediately Jimmy swings an elbow behind him, followed by a right hook when he's twisted himself around. The thing is, Peter isn't Carl Henderson. This sort of street brawling might do well in the barroom, but in the field, he'd already be dead.

Peter easily avoids the onslaught, but Palmer doesn't give up. He keeps on coming, a whirl of misplaced punches. Peter bored and letting him get it out of him like a hyperactive toddler.

Jimmy eventually comes to a stop. He can barely stand. Doubled over, huffing and puffing. Fists screwed up in front of him, looking like they weigh too much for his arms.

Peter stands straight, hands by his sides.

"Go inside," he tells Jimmy in a flat tone.

"Fuck... you," Jimmy pants.

"*Go*," Peter repeats more firmly.

Lyn shouts for Jimmy to get in.

Peter: "Do as your wife says."

"Fuck you, pervert," Jimmy practically spits. "You think

everybody doesn't know what goes on in that basement of yours."

Looking him dead in the eyes, Peter hisses, "I can assure you it's not the same thing you've got going on in that trailer out at Carmel Valley."

Palmer's eyes explode. The color drains from his face.

"What the fuck you say?" he mutters.

Peter stares right though this piece of shit. "Just go inside," he says.

Palmer launches himself at Peter. He's a big guy. But he's no match.

Peter rotates 180 degrees on his hips, keeping his feet planted. This does two things. First, it completely removes the target of Palmer's flying sledge-hammer fist. Second, it allows Peter to grab the wrist out of the air with his right hand, trapping the shoulder with his left. He twists the arm around Jimmy's back, forces a knee into the upper coccyx, hitting the sciatic nerve and buckling the legs, and forces Jimmy down onto his knees.

Peter is shaking with anger as he holds on to him, the arm twisted up behind Palmer. Jimmy groaning and whining as the bones of his wrist and forearm flex and crackle within Peter's hold, the joints exploding with pain.

Peter looks sideways into the house. Past Lyn, who still stands in the doorway.

Farther along the hallway, Danny stands holding Hannah. The second his eyes meet those of the teenager's, Peter can't help it—he breaks Jimmy Palmer's arm, the bone bursting through the skin.

Jimmy screams as Peter leaves him on his back, grasping the crooked limb, the hand flapping from side to side on the end of it. Peter has broken the ulna, fractured the radius and dislocated the scaphoid and lunate bones from the joint, destroying the UCL in the process.

Carl Henderson is sitting up on the Palmers' driveway blinking when Peter reaches him.

"Here," Peter says, offering a hand.

Carl Henderson blinks a couple more times before holding out a set of trembling fingers.

"Get a fucking ambulance!" Jimmy yells at his wife. "Now!"

Peter helps Carl up and lets him rest an arm across his shoulders as they hobble all the way around the corner to 37 Palm Avenue.

Kate Henderson answers the door. She cries out when she sees her husband. His trampled, bleeding face, blood all down his T-shirt.

Peter hands him to her, Carl's arm coming around his wife.

"What happened?" she asks as she helps him across the hallway.

"I went to speak with Jimmy Palmer," Carl lisps through his bloated lips. "As you can see, it didn't go too good." He gives a little laugh. "Thankfully, Mr. Adams was there. Paul..."

He swings around to eye the front door.

There is no one there. Peter is gone. The door wide open onto the night.

SIXTY-NINE

PETER SHOULD BE ON THE LAST NAME OF THE LIST by now. He's had it three days. But he just can't stay away from Pacific Grove. It is like the place needs him right now. Needs his particular skill set.

Or maybe it's more that he needs it. He's not sure.

His run-in with Jimmy Palmer was approximately twenty-four hours ago. Almost Peter's entire day since then has consisted of sitting in the basement listening to the Palmer household through the StingRay.

Jimmy spent last night having his wrist rebuilt. It is in a protective sleeve. His health insurance doesn't cover it because the injury isn't work related. The cover not high enough on potential accidents at home. His wife suggests he sue. But, just like he did when she mentioned the cops, he shouts her down.

Jimmy wants more than his hospital bills paid or a day in court. Peter can sense it in his voice. A seething undertone that betrays a thirst for blood.

Today, the sneaking, silent life that his family has become accustomed to has grown more severe. Danny has spent it in his room, playing video games and listening to music through headphones. The teen immersing himself in anything but his own life.

Lyn went to work. Making sure to take Hannah to her sister's.

At four p.m. Jimmy tries to get inside Danny's room. The door is locked. He hammers on it. When he jars his busted wrist, he begins kicking it.

"You little prick!" he shouts before marching off.

All day long he's been washing pills down with beer. Like he's trying to subdue the rage churning away inside of him. At one point he falls asleep. Danny must have been listening out for him. He sneaks from his room and for almost three minutes stands over the snoring sack-of-shit stretched out along the couch.

The teen just stays there, stock still, staring down at Jimmy, fists balled up at his sides. It's like he wants to fill that gaping mouth with one. Shove it all the way down and choke the bastard.

But he doesn't. Probably scared that Jimmy will wake up halfway through, turn the tables, and it'll be Danny choking.

So instead, the teen leaves him, makes himself something to eat in the kitchen and locks himself back in his room.

It's when Jimmy Palmer wakes up at eight p.m. that he wanders into the garage and fetches his Smith and Wesson M&P 9mm. The StingRay intercepts Danny's texts to his friends. He tells them that their neighbor went crazy on his dad last night. Used some super skills and now his old man is sulking. Lounging on his Fatboy, drinking Coors and popping barbiturates. Playing with his pistol.

I honest to god wanted him to kill the bastard, the teen texts at one point.

It's midnight when Jimmy Palmer finally plucks up the courage to do it. He half staggers, half marches out of his house, the 9mm dangling heavily from a hand. Just another drunk idiot with a handgun.

Peter leaves the basement, goes upstairs, sits on the edge of the bed, waiting for him. If he steps foot on Paul Adams's property with that gun, Paul Adams is well within his rights to protect himself.

So Peter waits.

Jimmy Palmer crosses Palm Avenue and continues north along Elm Drive. The street slopes upwards with the gradient of the hill. Green Street runs perpendicular along the top of it, number 24 off to the right. But he doesn't take the street. Rather, he enters the alleyway that runs along the backs of the properties, separating Green Street from those on the adjacent Palm Avenue. It is the same route Peter took eight days ago. Jimmy's plan is to get into the backyard and gain access that way. Maybe knock on the back door. Wait for Paul Adams to come to it. Then— *Blam!*

He enters the alley. The fences and hedgerows are drenched in darkness. Jimmy's face is a fixed mask, the gun gripped tightly in his hand, so mad with hate that he doesn't immediately spot the huge shape stepping out from behind the short wall of the Graysons' place.

Before he knows it, he's swallowed up by a giant that blots out the moon.

"Go home," a deep, guttural voice growls from the great buffalo of a man.

"Fuck you, wetback," Jimmy tells him.

The skull-shaped face leans down to him, the eyes consumed in black. "Go home, little man."

"You picked the wrong night to fuck with me," Jimmy cries out, bringing the gun around.

The big man is out-of-this-world quick.

He captures the hand holding the pistol before the aim is anywhere near him, consuming it in his massive paw, gun and all. He instantly begins to squeeze like an industrial vice, the pistol facing upwards. He lifts Jimmy off his feet, so that he dangles, Jimmy tugging desperately at it, trying to use all his two hundred pounds to get away. But it's no good. His hand may as well be trapped in some type of factory machine.

As the bones begin to buckle and crack, Jimmy goes to cry out and the big guy's other hand grabs his mouth, cupping the whole lower part of his face right back to the ears, shutting the sound off at the source, Jimmy's faint murmurs getting no farther than the alley.

He desperately struggles, pulling at the hand, the bones breaking apart like dried twigs. He goes to pull the trigger—to alert help if anything—but the finger is too broken to do anything. Even with all that booze and barbiturates inside him, Jimmy is nauseous with pain. He feels faint. The air goes cold as a sheet of sweat pours out of him.

He loses consciousness, flopping on the end of the big guy's arm, and just hangs there like a pair of dungarees on a clothesline.

A third person enters the scene. Ghost-Face. He is

holding an aluminum baseball bat. As if Jimmy Palmer were a piñata, he smashes him several times in both knees before shattering his hips, the bat giving off a hollow ping with each hit.

The big man releases Jimmy from his fist and he pours onto the dirty ground as though he has no bones.

Inside number 24 Green Street, Peter sits at the end of his bed waiting for Jimmy Palmer.

His phone goes off.

"Palmer has been neutralized," comes Ghost-Face's corpse voice on the other end. "Now go back to work."

SEVENTY

SAN JOSE, 2019

THE ANGEL'S NAME IS THERESA DA SILVA. SHE IS
the last name on the kill list.

Theresa lives in San Jose. Residing in an apartment by a
train yard with her seven-year-old daughter Marie and best
friend Natalie (born Gustavo). Peter gathers that someone
else will deal with the roommate. But he doesn't know what
will happen to the little girl.

Following the death of Ken Knight, they've had to set up
a meeting with another lawyer. Peter has five days until that
meeting. Until another person knows whatever it is that
Theresa da Silva has on the client. Signing, of course,
another death warrant in the process.

Theresa is twenty-two and pretty. She has coffee-colored
skin and a cosmos of little black freckles that cover her
cheeks and nose. Whenever she looks at her daughter, big
chocolate brown eyes shine pleasantly. At other times, the

luster fades and they turn practically black. As though someone has rolled down the dimmer inside her head.

She reminds Peter of his mother. Not the one that trained him. The other one. It is in the way she reserves a softness in her expression and voice when dealing with Marie. The way she summons all her energy the second her daughter's gaze falls upon her, forcing a radiant glow to shine back, an enthusiasm all for her, like Theresa is keeping that strength in reserve for these moments when Marie meets her with her eyes. It is the mother's way of protecting the girl from the darkness that so clearly surrounds them.

His own mother couldn't keep it up. Especially with the drugs. In the end, she faded so far away from him that she simply didn't see him anymore.

It is now the third day of his watch. Theresa and Natalie are picking Marie up from school. As soon as the girl spots them at the gate, she bursts from the pocket of friends she is leaving the building with, arms wide, running full tilt, a recently dried painting flapping from a hand. Theresa scoops her up, lifts the child high into the air, swinging her legs about as they spin around.

"Momma!" the girl calls out.

Once Marie has finished with her hellos and goodbyes, Natalie lifts her onto her shoulders and the three walk away as one happy family. A little odd in setup, if Peter was honest, but happy nonetheless. He likes to believe that unconditional love is the biggest ingredient to a family. And this one has it in abundance.

The family enters a busy park. It's a sunny day and people are taking advantage of the good weather. A Little League baseball game takes place in one corner. Parents cheer from a small stand. Behind that is a stretch of field covered in sunshine and picnickers. Along the pathways, dog walkers are pulled along by their mutts. On one corner, a French bulldog and a Jack Russell are busy fighting, their owners pulling at their leashes to drag them away.

"Yes. They *are* bad dogs," Natalie agrees with Marie as the family sidesteps the scene.

They buy ice creams at a stall. Peter gazes from under the thick bow of an oak tree on the other side of the field, watching their happy faces as the snacks are handed out, Theresa making sure Marie says thank you to the vender.

A terrible guilt is trying to make itself known inside Peter. He pushes it down. *Discipline and training.* It's the same with emotional pain as it is with physical. Compartmentalize. Push it into a corner of yourself. Detach from it.

Still. One question keeps ringing in his skull:

What right do I have to tear their worlds apart just to save my own?

They make their ways to a playground. On the way, Marie drips ice cream down the back of Natalie's neck, the roommate cringing, Marie and Theresa laughing.

"Ah! Marie!"

"Sorry, Aunty Nat."

Natalie places her down. Theresa hands Marie a tissue from her handbag and the little girl wipes Natalie's neck.

A minute later, they all enter the playground, Marie strung between the two women, hands in hands. A giant pirate-ship-shaped climbing frame, the thing crawling with children, takes up the majority of the space.

Ice creams finished, Theresa and Natalie sit on a bench while Marie plays with the other children. Peter takes a seat on a bench on the other side of the pirate ship, trying to look like a father getting bored waiting for his child.

The two women begin conversing. Through the swarm of children, Peter reads their lips.

"You know you can still take the money," Natalie says.

"I know."

"It would be easier." She pauses a moment before adding, "Especially for Marie."

Theresa's cheeks go red. "After this is done," she says, "he'll have to pay anyway."

"But you're going to have to go through hell to get him to. Think about the media. The newspapers. The fucking internet. Imagine what it's going to be like. The stress of it all on Marie."

"I have imagined it, Nat. Many times. I'm ready. This has to be done."

"But James is dead."

"So?"

"So you'll have to do it all on your own. At least with him beside you you had someone to back you up. Now it's just gonna be *you*, Theresa. Think about that."

This is the first mention of James Wilson. Peter waits for them to say more. But instead of replying, Theresa glances up from her lap, quickly finds her daughter amongst the writhing mass of children, shivers and closes her eyes tight. Breathing out, she tells her friend she doesn't want to talk about it anymore.

"I'm scared, Theresa," Natalie says, insisting upon talking about it. "Real scared."

"Please, Nat. I don't want to argue with you."

"But think about—"

"Mommy!"

Theresa opens her eyes to see Marie running off the pirate ship toward them. The little girl wants someone to push her on the swings. Natalie volunteers, the seven-year-old dragging her away by the arm.

Theresa da Silva really should take the money. She lives in dire poverty. For one thing, she doesn't work. Only Natalie works, clip-clopping those high heels along the strip at night to make enough to pay most of the rent and bills. Welfare and food stamps just about taking care of the rest.

Peter thinks he knows why Theresa doesn't work. He thinks it has something to do with the medication she takes. On the first day of his watch, all three were absent from the apartment. It gave him the opportunity to take a look inside, go through the cabinets, look for some clue to the client.

As it went, he found nothing on that. But he did find a hoard of prescription drugs.

Along with the insulin she takes for type 1 diabetes, Theresa da Silva is on Xanax, Zoloft and Paxil. All are commonly prescribed for post-traumatic stress disorder. All three are only prescribed at the same time when symptoms are in the extreme.

What gave Theresa da Silva such severe PTSD?

Three o'clock in the morning on the fourth day, Peter's senses are awakened when a light goes on in a window across the street. He is staying in an empty apartment on the other side of the road from their apartment. Sitting in the dark and watching them. He is on the third floor, one higher than Theresa's, giving him a good vantage point. Using field glasses, he can see right into their living room, the curtains rarely closed.

Natalie, who sleeps on a futon there, is making her way to the back of the apartment where the bedroom is. She goes inside and soon emerges with Theresa, holding her by the shoulders, guiding her into the living room, seating her on the outstretched futon. Returning to the bedroom, Natalie closes the door, avoiding the possibility of Marie seeing her mother in such a state.

Theresa sits clutching her chest. Her face is pale gray. Her small breasts heave in and out, the brown eyes shimmering with desperation as she struggles to pull air into her lungs.

Natalie sits behind her, rubbing her back, calming her, cooing into her ear. It is just like Mother. Natalie soothing and singing and rubbing the panic attack out of her.

Peter thinks he knows where Theresa da Silva's panic attacks come from. He thinks Natalie knows. That James Wilson knew. Ken Knight. He thinks Hugo Davenport knows.

And the client?

The client especially knows.

SEVENTY-ONE

AFTER FOUR DAYS, PETER ALREADY KNOWS HOW he'll do it. How he'll kill this poor unfortunate woman. This unlucky nobody.

Theresa and Natalie walk Marie to school. Today, Peter doesn't follow. Instead, he breaks into their apartment.

The studio flat is a shoebox. He's been in bigger walk-in wardrobes. The front door opens straight into the cramped living-room space. A breakfast bar, three stools lined up along it, dissects the room at the back. To its left is a corridor. An archway gives access to the galley kitchen from that, and the next door on is the bedroom, which is situated behind the kitchen. Straight ahead is the closet-sized bathroom.

This is the entirety of the apartment.

Peter gazes out the bedroom window at the train yard. It's not huge. Just eight tracks where they repair and paint the units. The main attraction is a shed in the middle where they do all the welding. It stands opposite the bedroom window. He'd thought about it with regards to surveillance while doing reconnaissance, but had reneged on choosing it because of the train yard security and the fact that it was easier to work from the empty apartment.

He leaves the window. A framed photograph on the nightstand draws his attention. The frame is shaped like a heart, but it isn't that which catches his eye. In the photo, Theresa holds an infant Marie. She must be only days old and looks like a lump of wrinkly pink skin wrapped in a blanket. As Theresa holds her, she beams proudly down at the baby. It must be their first photo together.

Theresa looks like a child, and it is only now that Peter thinks about it. Thinks about her being twenty-two. The little girl being seven. Theresa was fifteen when she had her. Most likely fourteen when she became pregnant.

Peter places the picture back and heads for the bathroom. Black mold climbs the walls in there. As he stands breathing in the earthy air, he wonders what it does to the health of a little girl.

A train rumbles past, *clickety-clack-clickety-clack*, shaking the panes in the window frames. Peter's reflection trembles in the mirror of the medicine cabinet.

He opens it up. Ten vials of insulin line a plastic shelf.

Peter removes them all and replaces them with ten replica vials.

SEVENTY-TWO

IT IS NINE P.M. ON THE DOORSTEP OF THE apartment, Theresa hugs her roommate goodbye. "Be lucky," she tells Natalie.

The trans grins back. "Always am."

Natalie blows a kiss over her shoulder as she waltzes off along the balcony. Their apartment is on the very end and she passes four other flats on her way to the stairwell.

At the bottom, she skips through a gap in the fence, stretching a stilettoed foot into an alleyway that separates the apartments from a block of garages. A panel van is parked at the end of the passage. Bored, Natalie reads the company name written down the side of it.

S&W Home Security.

Farther along her route, she stops at a 7-Eleven and buys a mini bottle of cheap vodka. "Keep the change, Ernie," she says in her scratched voice as she heads for the door.

"I'll put it in the box," the old man behind the counter croaks back. "The one for the veterans."

"Put it wherever you want," Natalie replies under her breath.

She trots onwards to a bus stop, sipping nips from the bottle as she goes along. Dutch courage. Not for the night ahead, mind, but for the *days* ahead. The ones she will spend with Theresa. When everything will come their way. The accusations of lying. Of entrapment. Of being a blackmailer. A slut. Even if they do have absolute evidence, it won't matter. Social media will believe whatever it wants to. The court of public opinion could turn against Theresa—against Natalie. It could go bad. Real bad.

These are the things that grip Natalie's stomach as she makes her way to the strip.

The bus journey is short. She gets off at one end of a four-mile stretch of commercial buildings. The retail outlets and supermarkets are closing up; many of them have closed down for good. Natalie walks along a cheap cartoon background of chain stores and coffee shops. Anything locally owned is long gone.

Her workmates hang out on the corner of a boarded-up Safeway. There are greetings and kisses with the *girls* when she strolls into their cluster. A nightly ritual and the beginning of the shift.

Having caught up on the gossip and politics of the corner, Natalie gets one in quick. A regular. Tony. Flashes a picture of his wife and kids every time he opens his wallet to pay.

That done, he drops her back at the Safeway.

"Hey, Nat," calls a tall trans, humungous on heels, with gold foundation caked across her cheeks.

"What's up, Bernie?" Natalie replies, walking away from Tony's pickup whilst applying lipstick.

"You've got a request."

"Who from?"

"Don't know. But he looks money. He's over there."

She points across the parking lot. In a far corner sits a black Mercedes S-Class. Its shiny chrome skin shimmering in the city light.

"You know him?" Bernie asks.

"Not the car."

"Well, he says you came real recommended. Got a gold Rolex on his wrist worth more than my car. I told him, 'You better watch out. Some motherfucker likely to rob you.' And he says, 'Don't worry, baby. I'll be safe.' We'll see about that. Mm-Hmm."

"Did *you* recognize him?" Natalie asks, staring at the silhouette behind the wheel.

"No. None of the girls did. Maybe some of the bitches farther down know him, but we ain't seen him none."

"Came recommended," Natalie says to herself.

It could have been anyone. She's had quite a few rich johns in her time.

"I s'pose I'd better go see," she says, trotting off.

"You go, girl," Bernie calls after her.

Natalie struts over to him, one foot crossing the other, hips swinging side to side to side. Halfway there the electric window of the Mercedes begins whining as it rolls down. The man's face comes into view. He lifts his mouth into a friendly grin. Natalie senses it's fake. He looks like the type of man who rarely smiles. The type who'd have to be taught.

He isn't familiar, either. But she is sure that even if she had seen him before, if she'd spent time in his car, she'd still have difficulty recalling him later on. He is the type of man whose own mother has to look twice before she is sure it's her son.

"Hello, Natalie," he says as she crouches by his window.

His voice is so devoid of humanity that she has difficulty recognizing it as a voice at all. More like a vibration in the air. The kind of voice you'd expect to answer at a seance. His eyes are just as vacant, and it is like staring into Nietzsche's abyss.

Still, the car says money. And money always seems to say "Trust me."

"How do you know my name?" Natalie asks.

"You come highly recommended."

"By who?"

"By John."

There are any number of Johns that she knows. Hell, they're all johns in one way or another.

"You wanna party or what?" the guy's voice bristles.

"Sure. Why not."

Natalie jumps in and they drive off. The car smells of expensive cologne, but there's another smell underneath. A stench of something rotting.

It slowly dawns on her that it is him.

Later on, when the police ask Bernie and the rest of the gang about the appearance of the man who drove Natalie away, they can hardly even say. In the end, a meaningless photofit that could be anyone and looks practically nothing like the guy will end up spending a long long time stapled to the inside of a cold case file.

SEVENTY-THREE

THERESA ALWAYS TAKES HER INSULIN THIRTY minutes before she eats. Tonight, she doesn't fetch dinner until Marie is in bed.

"Goodnight, Mommy," the girl calls as Theresa blows kisses from the bedroom doorway.

"You too, sweet pea."

"Love you."

"Love you."

She switches off the bedroom light and walks into the bathroom. From the medicine cabinet she takes a vial of insulin from the ten lining the shelf. From there she walks into the kitchen. Straight ahead is a sideboard with some drawers underneath. She pulls the top one open and takes a syringe that lies amongst the clutter inside. Having performed this action uncountable times before, she does so with absolute unthinking, the act installed onto the memory of every fiber of muscle, the brain somewhere else, daydreaming. She pushes the needle into the vial, tugs the plunger, sucks the liquid into the syringe, pulls her T-shirt up, gets ready to stab the spike into her stomach, the sharp point inches from her skin, when—

"I wouldn't do that if I were you."

Theresa jumps. Wheels around. Stares wide-eyed at the man standing in the opposite corner of her kitchen.

It was he who had spoken the warning.

"It's filled with a neurotoxin," he adds. "One that doesn't show up in autopsies unless specifically looked for."

Theresa is confused. The galley-sized kitchen shouldn't be big enough for a person to hide from another. She should have heard him breathing no more than three feet behind her. Sensed him when she stepped into the room. But until his voice pierced the silence, she hadn't heard or sensed a thing.

"Put the syringe down," Peter says as she stares at him, the needle hovering over her abdomen.

"How do you know it's poison?"

"Because I put it there."

She frowns.

"I had no other choice," he goes on. "They're checking my every move. One of them broke in after I swapped the vials. Made sure I'd replaced them."

"Who's *they*?"

"I was hoping you could tell me."

A trembling hand places the syringe down on the counter. When she turns abruptly, Peter snaps, "Don't make any sudden movements."

She freezes.

"They're watching through the window," he warns. "No, don't... look."

Too late. She's already facing it. Casting her gaze past the breakfast bar, across the living room and right out of the window, staring at the black form of the opposite apartment block. Where Peter knows they're watching from his former bolthole.

She's probably eye-to-eye with them.

"You are in a lot of danger, Theresa da Silva," he tells her.

She turns back to him from the window. "Why are you here?"

"I've been sent to kill you."

She goes to move forward. About to run to her daughter.

"No!" he cries, stepping momentarily into the sight of the window to block her way.

Theresa stays still, her wide eyes fixed to the back wall of the kitchen. No, not to the back wall. To the place beyond the wall, where her daughter lies.

"Just stay where you are," Peter says. "I'm not going to hurt you or your daughter. Okay?"

"You just said you've been sent to kill me."

"I don't have time to explain. I just need you to trust that I have your best interest at heart. Now, we need to get Marie and get out of here. But to accomplish that you must do everything I say. Do you understand?"

Rather than answering, she turns to the window. "You said they're watching us. Does that mean—"

"Get down!"

Peter launches himself forward and pulls her onto the faded linoleum, just as the living-room window shatters in a shower of glass. Bullets fly in from across the street, muzzle flashes in the third-floor apartment opposite, the breakfast bar taking the brunt as they crawl out of the kitchen.

In the bedroom Marie is waking up as Peter bursts into the room. He grabs her off the bed right at the moment a muzzle flash lights up the dark air above the roof of the welding shed. The window shatters, the empty mattress exploding as a bullet hits it.

Peter carries Marie out of the bedroom, shoulders the door of the bathroom open and dumps the child on the tiled floor.

"Get in here," he commands Theresa.

She follows inside and Peter shuts them in.

The windowless bathroom is the one part of the apartment that you can't see from the outside. Even the thin door is obscured, and no matter the angle it is a sniper's blind spot.

"Now what?" Theresa asks, taking ahold of her daughter, the three of them seemingly trapped in the closet-sized room.

Peter says nothing. He simply gets down on his knees at the bathtub and rips the fiberglass side from it.

Theresa is surprised to find that the cavity is stuffed full of things. A regular drop box.

First, Peter drags two bulletproof vests from under the tub. One is specially tailored for a child.

"How did...?" Theresa stammers.

"Put them on."

If Peter is running on the mechanics of training, then Theresa is merely running on whatever instruction he gives her, ceding her own will to his. She places the small vest on

Marie and the large on herself, helping the girl do the straps up. Peter is already wearing one.

Two helmets come out. Military standard. One designed for a seven-year-old child.

"These, too," he says, handing them backwards to Theresa.

Next, he slides out an HK416 gas-operated assault rifle and shoulders it, the shortened strap keeping it close at hand. The last item he drags out is a sledgehammer.

"Get the girl back," he tells Theresa, "and cover her eyes."

"Come over here with me, sweet pea," the mother says, cajoling the little girl to the opposite corner. "Close your eyes."

"Mommy, what's happening?"

There's no time to answer. As Theresa shields Marie into her waist, Peter takes a step back and swings the hammer into the wall that divides this apartment from the next. The pounding thud makes the little girl scream.

The segregating partitions are nothing more than thick drywall and insulation. It takes Peter less than a minute to break through.

"Come on," he says, ushering them into the hole.

The couple next door are in the living room ducked behind furniture when the three strangers emerge from their bedroom, gawping after them as they run into the bathroom.

Peter sets forth his hammer on the next wall, quickly breaking through. In the bedroom on the other side, a young man is playing video games, sitting on the end of his bed with his back to the wall. With a pair of headphones clamped to his head, the volume up high on a frantic shoot 'em up, he chats away to his online pals like nothing is happening until he feels their feet stomping along the mattress behind him. He flips around to see Peter carrying the hammer, Theresa carrying Marie, the helmets, the body armor, the three of them covered from head to toe in plaster dust—and the HK416 dangling from Peter's arm.

They leave the bedroom, head into the bathroom. It's occupied by the guy's girlfriend, who sits in the bath covered in foam and surrounded by candles. She begins screaming and splashing.

"Get out," Peter orders.

SEVENTY-FOUR

HUGO DAVENPORT IS BEING DRIVEN IN THE BACK of the Bentley when he gets the call. Staring blankly forward, the Englishman plucks the phone from his suit pocket and applies it to his ear.

"What is your progress, Mr. Linton?" he asks.

"The knight has gone rogue," the dead voice of Linton says down the line.

A hollowness opens up inside of Davenport. He has feared this from the start.

"What is the status?" Davenport replies with little emotion.

"He has the girl and the child with him in the apartment. I have two men at the location. More are on their way."

"What about Mr. Castillo?"

"He's at the second site. Ready for action."

"Good. You know what to do."

"Yes, sir."

Davenport puts the phone down and makes a call.

"Status, Mr. Davenport?" a man's voice answers.

"I'm afraid the knight has turned on us."

There is a few seconds' silence. Heavy breath falls down the phone. Followed by a statement.

"Then we'd better be ready for one hell of a fight."

SEVENTY-FIVE

In the darkness of the opposite apartment, Number One watches the living room through the sight of his M4 carbine. He hasn't seen any sign of them there or in the kitchen for some time. The last sighting was when Number Two observed Azrael take the girl off the bed. He didn't come back into the living room, so he has to be in the bathroom.

"What are they doing?" he whispers into his comms.

"I don't know," Number Two's voice hisses in his ear. "Go take a look."

"Copy that."

Dressed in black body armor, eye trapped to the sight of the M4, he cautiously leaves the block, skips across the street, aim concentrated on the balcony, ascends the stairwell that end of the building, and moves toward apartment number six.

A doors flies open.

"Ay Dios mío!" the old woman screams, throwing her arms into the air.

"Get inside," he barks, the muzzle of the M4 staring right at her.

"Por favor, no dispare!" she adds in panic as she runs back into her apartment.

Taking cover at the edge of the doorway, Number One uses the butt of the M4 to crash the door in, then tosses a flash grenade inside. Seconds after it goes off, he follows it in.

Seeing everything through the sight of the carbine, he rapidly checks the corners of the living room; blind spots Azrael could be in like the one in the kitchen. Coming to the archway, he checks behind the breakfast bar, as well as the corner Azrael hid in before.

He leaves and goes to the next door.

They could be ducked below the window in the bedroom.

They're not.

Lastly, he kicks the bathroom door in. The room is covered in dust. Broken pieces of drywall and chunks of rock wool lie all over the floor. Number One steps inside, turns left, and gazes through a series of holes that lead all the way to the end of the apartment block.

"They're at the other end!" he calls into his comms.

PETER, Theresa and Marie quickly descend the metal steps. Like the stairwell on the opposite side of the apartment block, they are open to the train yard. This worries Peter.

"You knew they were coming?" Theresa asks as she carries her daughter.

Peter says nothing.

The moment they hit the bottom, shots come from the train yard, sparking and pinging off the rusty steps, making them move faster. Peter turns to the darkness, spots the location of the flashes as more shots ping around them.

"Go to that van!" he cries out, pointing at the one parked at the end of the alley.

While Theresa and Marie duck through the gap in the fence, Peter stops, turns to where the shots come from, and gives covering fire.

Theresa frantically carries her daughter across the alleyway, running on pure adrenaline.

"Get in the back of it!" Peter cries out, coming away from the corner of the building and joining them.

At the van, Theresa places the girl down. She grabs the sliding door, rips it open—

"*Mommy!*"

The door halfway open, Theresa falls to her side, panting for breath. Peter spins around, sends a volley of machine-gun fire at the sniper's position.

Marie is holding her mother as the latter stays down on her knees, grasping her throbbing flank, trying to compose her breathing. She's been shot with a heavy caliber round in the side of the ribcage. The body armor has limited the damage to two fractured ribs, but it has still knocked her off her feet.

"Breathe!" Peter says, coming to her and lifting her into the van.

Picking Marie up next, he dumps her inside, flips 180 degrees, just as he thinks the sniper has come out of cover, and sends another peppering of gunfire into the darkness of the train yard. Then, he gets in the van, grabs the door, and slams it shut.

NUMBER ONE EMERGES at the top of the stairwell. Aim fixed to the van, he warily proceeds down the steps, through the gap in the fence, and into the alley.

Within twenty feet of the van, he waits.

"Why's he not moving?" he says into his comms.

"Copy that. I've got visuals on the windshield. No activity in the front. They must all still be in the back."

"We'll both take it."

"Copy that."

Number Two gradually emerges from the darkness of the train yard. Dressed all in black, it is as if a piece of the night has broken away into a live man.

They use hand signals as they round on the van.

"Keep lively, people," their group leader says in their ears. "I don't need to remind you who this is."

Their hearts pound in their chests as they stop inches from the door. A door which hides the one they call Azrael. They push their ears to listen. But all they can hear are the crickets and the distant sirens. No movement. No breathing. Nothing from inside the van.

Number Two nods and Number One wrenches the door to the side.

There's nothing in there except electronics tools.

"What the fuck?"

It's only when they look at the bed of the van that they get an idea where they are. A big round hole goes right through the vehicle.

Both men lean over it.

Metal rungs stick out of slimy brickwork that leads down into a sewage tunnel; the van parked right over the open manhole.

"They're in the sewers," Number One calls into his comms.

"What's this?" Number Two says.

He's investigating something that is poking from a shelf built into the van. It appears to be a micro camera.

WITH THEIR FOOTSTEPS echoing off the damp walls, the stench almost unbearable, the three of them make their way through the sewer. Theresa is breathing better now, though she can no longer hold her daughter, the two moving steadily along behind Peter.

As he guides them, he stares at the screen of his phone. Number Two's face stares right back at him.

"Hold your ears," Peter says.

"Do as the man says, sweet pea."

The little girl places both hands over her ears. As does the mother. Peter presses the phone and the sewer shakes. A loud explosion in the street above. The van and the men decimated. Theresa almost loses her footing and Peter gives her a hand.

"I can take the child, if you'd like."

She shakes her head at him.

"You don't have to be scared of me," he tells her.

She nods, but she still looks terrified.

On the move again, Peter makes a call. "Raul, is everything ready?"

"Yes," the man on the other end replies.

"The whacker is ready?"

"Yes. The weeds are lined up."

"Good. Then everything is ready. Meet soon."

"With God's will," Raul replies.

"I never needed any other will except my own."

With the call ended, Peter leads Theresa and Marie up a ladder and out onto another street. A pitch-black BMW M5 CS is parked at the side of the road in the shadows of a wide oak. Peter presses a key fob and the headlights flash.

Leading them to the back door, he opens it and guides them inside. Then he helps Theresa snap Marie into a racing harness before she buckles herself into one. Once they're secure, Peter takes a bug detector wand and twists it on at the end.

"What's that?" Theresa asks as he brings it over her.

"I'm checking for tracking devices."

Marie gets scared when it comes to her turn, so he hands the wand to Theresa and makes sure she checks every part of her daughter.

Once he's certain they're clean, Peter gets into the driver's seat and twists the keys in the ignition. Seconds later, they're tear-assing their way out of San Jose.

SEVENTY-SIX

THE HENDERSONS ARE WATCHING A MOVIE together. It's *The Goonies*. A favorite of Kate's and Carl's childhoods, as well as one of Michael's, too. The kid sits in the middle, a bowl of popcorn on his lap. The swelling on both the father's and son's faces has gone down. Even if the stitches on Michael's cheek are not even close to coming out yet.

In local news, Danny Palmer turned himself in yesterday. Admitted to the whole thing. He's looking at getting sent to reform school for it.

He never even gave a reason. Just shrugged his shoulders, having explained that he jumped Michael in the alley and started beating on him for no other reason than boredom. The two goons weren't even there. Just Danny and his knife and his twisted anger.

The doorbell chimes, resounding through the rooms.

"I'll get it," Carl says, untangling himself from his loves.

It chimes again impatiently when Carl is halfway across the hall.

"Okay, okay," he says.

He puts an eye to the spy hole.

A bullet bursts through the back of his head, killing him instantly.

The door is opened externally. A black-clad paratrooper with his GSCI PVS-7 Single-Tube Night Vision Goggles in the up position comes walking in with an MDRX bullpup rifle to his shoulder. The silenced Beretta M9 he used to kill the target is holstered.

"Papa bear is down," he whispers into his comms as he steps over the body of Carl Henderson.

A halo of blood pools from the back of the dead man's head, rapidly spreading over the hardwood floor.

Kate and Michael sit blissfully watching the film. As Sloth and Chunk rescue the rest of the gang from the pirate ship, the mother and son are completely unaware that their world as they know it is over. That currently they are doing no more than enjoying the final moments of innocence before all the chaos.

When they see a shadow spread across the floor, they turn toward the doorway with happy faces, expecting to find husband and father. Instead, they find paratrooper and killer.

SEVENTY-SEVEN

THE SPEEDOMETER NEEDLE TREMBLES AT 170MPH as the BMW M5 tears down the southbound lanes of the Route 101 highway, the twinkling lights of San Jose gradually fading behind them.

Peter dodges around an oil tanker, then a cruising Hummer, the traffic rushing toward the windshield like a hail of bullets, the raging roar of the engine filling the car, the steering wheel trembling within his white knuckles, the G-force pressing all three of them back in their seats.

Glancing up into the rearview mirror, he spots the three motorcycles coming rapidly up behind them in V formation. The two at the back are Honda Fireblades. 1100cc superbikes. A rider and a passenger on each. The passengers hold MAC-10 submachine guns.

A crackle of bullets announces their arrival.

Nevertheless, regardless of the Fireblade's speed and the MAC-10's ferocity, it isn't those that worry Peter the most. What really worries Peter is the lead bike. The one that is a monster. Matte black and without insignia, he can't tell what model it is. It has only a single rider, who sits forward over a huge fuel tank, gripping the handlebars and looking through the sight of an M134 Minigun, the rotary system and five barrels poking from where the headlight would usually sit. Ammunition runs along two feeder belts that hang out the sides of the gun and connect back to a pair of giant ammo boxes either side of the back wheel.

"Get down!" Peter shouts, not sure whether the Lexan he's had fitted to the windows will stop a near never-ending supply of bullets.

The gatling roars into life, the rotary revolving faster and faster, a sudden burst as the cluster of barrels explode in a whirl of spinning muzzle flashes, tracer rounds lighting up the nighttime highway.

Peter veers wildly around a Winnebago, the back of the camper taking the brunt of the bullets that skirt across the lanes in pursuit of the BMW. The red brake lights of the Winnebago burst into life, screeching tires, a great smoke cloud erupting from the back, the thing tipping and bucking as it attempts to come to a rapid halt.

One of the Fireblades makes it down the outside of it before the camper loses control and careens left, straight into the concrete central reservation. With the road erupting into chaos behind them, the Fireblade gets alongside the BMW, the vehicles separated by two lanes. The passenger aims the MAC-10, tugs the trigger, and the gun starts spitting rounds, a four-leaf clover of muzzle flash lighting up the end.

A stitch of bullets cascades down the side of the BMW's ballistic steel plating. Inside the car, their ears throb with the sounds of metal on metal. Peter fights with the steering wheel as he comes around a dumper truck, using it as a temporary shield, then cuts across the front of it, trying to ram the bike, the Fireblade dodging him, falling back.

The M134 opens fire behind them. Bullets sparking and jolting the BMW. Sounding like coins rattling in a washing machine. Marie screaming, "Mommy! Mommy!"

SEVENTY-EIGHT

KATE AND MICHAEL ARE BEING MARCHED FROM their house at gunpoint, their wrists zip-tied behind them. Two men flank the mother and son front and back, corralling them toward a black Chevy Express.

"Mom, is Dad dead?" Michael keeps repeating.

She hasn't answered him so far and she doesn't answer him now. What she does do is desperately search the street for any sign of a savior, a neighborly face she can cry out to. But, to her bitter disappointment, the street is deserted, everyone tucked up safe and sound inside their houses. Just as she had been only moments ago.

She thinks about screaming, but doesn't because of Michael. Not sure what they will do to him if she does.

"Please," she stammers, "tell me... what is happening. Where are you... taking us?"

The man at the back tells her that if she wants her son to survive the next hours she should keep deathly quiet.

So she does.

A third man, Team Leader, stands at the open back doors of the van. A fourth waits in the driver's seat, the engine running, ready to depart. Six men in total. Four on the ground. Two more up on the adjacent rooftops, watching the scene through the scopes of their sniper rifles, the lasers switched off.

"How we looking, Sniper One?" Team Leader asks over his comms.

"Looking good, Team Leader," Sniper One comes back. "No sign of the neighbors."

"What about you, Sniper Two?"

"Everything's clear my end, Team Leader. Let's get Dorothy and Toto out of Kansas."

SNIPER ONE PACKS away his C14 Timberwolf. With the rifle on his back, he gently lifts himself up off Mrs. Murphy's roof without making so much as a rustle of clothing.

Once he's on his feet, he turns around. Freezes.

A man stands right there. A man whose face is painted in black camouflage, the whites of his eyes glowing in the dark.

Before Sniper One can do anything, a double-edged Gerber Strongarm survival knife is shoved straight through his throat, his attacker grabbing him by the scruff of the hair, forcing Sniper One onto the blade until it bursts through the spine.

The camouflaged man lowers Sniper One soundlessly to the roof, retracting the knife. Then he snaps down the night-vision goggles sitting atop his head and gazes eastwards across the rooftops, the nighttime neighborhood drenched in green phosphorescence.

Three houses over, Sniper Two is busy having his throat cut from behind by another camouflaged assassin.

So begins the rescue.

IN THE BACK of the Chevy Express, long benches occupy both sides. Kate and Michael sit along one, and on the other are the two men who flanked them.

"Mom, is Dad dead?" Michael sobs.

So many thoughts cram her brain right now that she is unable to articulate a single one. All Kate can do is shake and stare into space, everything gone numb. She can hear her son speaking, but his words mean nothing to her. It is as if she has forgotten their common language. Soon, it will all catch up, like an elasticity reaching its peak and snapping back. Then she will be confronted with the horrific turn her life has taken.

Team Leader slams the back doors shut. He makes his way to the passenger side, jumps in the front, turns to the driver and says, "Let's get—"

The window shatters, the driver's head explodes. Team Leader scrambles out of his seat, falling backwards out of the door, bringing his MDRX bullpup to his shoulder.

"We are under fire!" he barks into the comms as he crawls for cover behind the van. "Sniper One, Sniper Two, do you copy?"

Only silence comes back and the seconds creep over Team Leader's back, making it itch.

"I said: do you copy, Sniper One and Sniper Two?"

More itching.

When his comms does spark into life, it is one of the men inside the van.

"What are our orders, Team Leader?" he asks.

"Stay with the family. Shots came from the south. Use them as a shield, if you have to."

Team Leader creeps to the rear corner of the Chevy. He uses a telescopic inspection mirror, extending it out past the van, rotating it until he has a view of the opposite rooftops.

He spots something. A person. Muzzle flash.

The mirror bursts into shards, a bullet hitting it.

"Fuck," Team Leader hisses to himself.

The sounds of a dog barking and a door opening. "What in the hell is going on?" Mrs. Murphy cries out as she stands on her porch holding Sandy.

Team Leader takes the opportunity. He runs from the cover of the Chevy Express toward the wide truck of a sycamore, power sliding on his knees to reach it, the sidewalk chipping up around him, Mrs. Murphy screaming and running back indoors.

"I need covering fire," Team Leader pants into his comms from behind the tree. "One of you keep close to the family. One of you come out."

There's a short exchange in the back of the van.

"Okay. Where's he at?"

"Shooter is at Sniper One's position. You ready?"

"As I'll ever be."

"Go," Team Leader says.

The back doors of the Chevy burst open. The guy flies out firing his MDRX bullpup in a scatter pattern, bullet holes dotting Mrs. Murphy's rooftop.

Team Leader emerges from the sycamore. Through his

scope, he spots the target sitting up on the rooftop, further back from where the covering fire hits.

"Got you now, you son of a bitch."

He fires a neat string of bullets into him and the guy falls forward, sliding off the roof and dropping limply into the front yard.

"Check he's dead," Team Leader says.

His colleague leaves the van, steps across the street and enters the front yard of Mrs. Murphy's green stucco bungalow, the old woman hiding inside, the dog going scatty. A short hedgerow borders the lawn from the driveway and porch. The body fell onto the path, so it isn't until he gets around the hedge that he can see the dead man.

His heart thuds to a stop, he twists his body sharply to face Team Leader and shouts, "It's Sniper—"

The explosion tosses his body high into the air. Mrs. Murphy's windows shatter. Pink mist fills the space where he stood a second ago. His torso lands with a slap in the middle of the street, followed by a rain of dirt and body parts.

Sniper One had been boobytrapped.

With his one surviving team member trapped in the back of the van with the family, Team Leader is all alone. Not even during his days in the US Marines was he ever alone like this. Not even those darkest of days out in Fallujah.

He jerks his head so that an eye peeks out from the tree.

Bark flicks up, Team Leader feeling the vibrations through the trunk.

He's breathing heavily. He throws a glance at the van.

"What do we do, Team Leader?" the man in the back asks.

"Orders are to stay with the family. Repeat, do not leave them."

The only plan he can think of is to use the Hendersons as leverage. A human shield. Because whoever this is, is here for them.

"Wait for my signal," he says. "We'll move them into the front of the van. The mother can drive. We'll place guns to their heads. Anyone stops us, we'll shoot."

"Copy that, Team Leader."

"On my mark. Go!"

Team Leader bursts from cover but gets no farther than a foot. Someone has stepped sideways from the other side of the tree and intercepted his path. Before he knows what is happening, the hunting knife is plunging through the gap in his body armor, stabbing him just below the left armpit, and sinking through the ribs into his heart. She holds him close, making sure to trap the assault rifle between their bodies as he shivers the last of his life out of him, his mouth guppying, no sound emerging except a choking hiss.

He stops breathing and slowly slides from the knife.

The guy shut in the back of the van stands close to the family, his Beretta aimed at their heads.

"I'm gonna fucking waste them, man," he shouts in a panic. "You hear me?! They're dead if you don't let me out of here."

His voice reverberates inside the Chevy. Kate still doesn't quite understand what's going on. All she does is hold her son.

"You hear me?! Get back or I'll fucking shoot them. The woman, then the kid."

A man's calm voice replies, "You're not going to kill them."

It makes the soldier spin in the direction of the voice. "I will, man. Trust me, I will."

"Then what will your bosses say? Especially when they need them."

The soldier whips around, aiming his Beretta in the other direction. "I don't give a fuck," he says. "You let me leave or they're dead."

Kate suddenly sits up. Everything crashes in on her. A sudden realization hits.

She recognizes the man's voice.

He suddenly cries out, "Hendersons, *tírense al suelo.*"

Hendersons, get on the ground.

Kate knows Spanish. She grabs ahold of Michael and pulls him onto the bed of the van with her. The soldier glances down at them as they lie there between the benches and frowns.

No time to ponder things.

Bullets burst through the sides of the Chevy, hitting him repeatedly from both directions, his body spasming as it falls to its knees, where he remains, head bowed as though in prayer, the last air wheezing out of his lungs in a whining death rattle.

The back doors creak open. Two people stand outside in camouflage.

"Carlos? Rosa?"

SEVENTY-NINE

AT BERTA CANYON THE 101 ENTERS RURAL LAND. Rolling hills spread out either side. Peter ignores the scenery. He only has eyes for the onrushing gray band of road trapped in his headlight beams.

He checks his mirror for the innumerable time.

"Get down!" he shouts.

The minigun bursts into life, the car exploding in clinking, clattering metal, Theresa covering her daughter's ears as they both scream.

Slaloming across the lanes to make himself as elusive a target as possible, Peter isn't concerned by fear or angst. He is the definition of absolute calm. His heart rate is as passive as an ordinary person's while they wait in line at the grocery store or fill their car with gasoline. This is his natural domain. Much easier to him than normal life and its ever-evolving puzzles. Where you are forever learning the rules, only to find out those ones are wrong or no longer count. *This* is merely a matter of will, dedication, and planning.

Two things work in their favor on this stretch of the 101. One is the road itself. It is narrow and only two-laned. A concrete central reservation barrier runs down the middle— certain death for any colliding biker. The outer edge drops off in a gravel bank. Traveling at the speeds they are, those bikes will slide out of control the second they hit the stones. This gives them minimal space to avoid things; the road becoming a treacherous gantlet.

The second thing in Peter's favor is the complete lack of traffic in Berta Canyon. On a Sunday the rural highway is practically deserted at this time of night.

He presses a button on the wheel and the passenger footwell begins mechanically opening; a panel sliding back to reveal the rushing whir of gray asphalt speeding beneath them. Next, he opens the middle console. Foam lining holds a row of what look to the untrained eye like hockey pucks. He takes one and tosses it into the hole.

The remote bomb doesn't bounce. It sticks straight to the road. A red light blinks: Armed.

Eyes on the mirror, Peter watches one of the Fireblades reach it and flicks a button on the steering wheel.

Rider and gunner are blown high into the air.

A crash helmet slams down on the BMW's hood, bouncing off and falling into the road. Peter isn't sure if there was a head in it.

One down. Two to go.

EIGHTY

KATE HENDERSON IS IN SHOCK. SHARP BREATHS jerk through her chest. Every inch of her body trembles. Michael holds on to her, still trying to process the image of his father lying dead on the hallway floor. Unsure if any of this is real or not.

Having cut them free, the Martinezes hustle the mother and son across the street toward their own house: number 18. Car alarms wail. Dogs bark. Neighbors stand in windows or on their porches. Most of them are on the phone to police.

"Get inside," Rosa commands the Hendersons, holding open the front door to her home of the last six years. Tonight being the last time she or her husband will ever see it.

As they enter the house, Kate stops. "Rosa, please tell me what is happening?"

"My name isn't Rosa," comes the cold reply. "It is Marta. Now come on. We need to keep moving."

. . .

Now is probably about the time to stop calling the residents of Number 18 Palm Avenue Carlos and Rosa Martinez and start calling them by their real names:

Raul and Marta Lozano.

It should be pretty obvious at this point, but the Lozanos haven't always been gardeners. Once upon a time down Mexico way, they were the head assassins of two warring narco families. Raul with the Durango outfit. Marta with their bitter enemy, the Sinaloa gang.

With the families at war, both Raul and Marta were sworn enemies. Under orders to kill the other on sight. This was written in the blood of a decades' old conflict, taken to a spiritual level—to disobey such a blood oath was a level of blasphemy Santa Muerte can never forgive.

But love is an odd thing. It develops in the strangest places.

Fortunately (or unfortunately, depending on your view), when Raul and Marta first met, they were on neutral ground —America. For one, though they knew the other's name, knew their reputation, they had never seen one another or met in person. They were only ever acquainted with pictures, none fresher than ten years old, and, with their gang affiliations hidden underneath clothing and both using false names while traveling in America, neither recognized the other as an enemy.

All they saw was *attraction*.

Marta was in California visiting family. Raul had been seeing to some business for the bosses. When they met in a bar on San Diego's Fifth Avenue, neither allowed their conversations to drift toward gang affiliations. Why would they? They stuck to their false names and their cover stories. After all, tradecraft is as necessary for the criminal as it is for the field agent.

They hit it off over cocktails. Told the truth about where they were from, but not what they did. Good lies always sticking as closely to the truth as they can. Change the details that get you into trouble, but keep the rest.

Having hit it off, they met every day over the next week. Raul walking Marta to her hotel each and every night. The two kissing in the dim illumination of the lobby. Marta waving her gentleman off.

It wasn't until their last night together that they finally made love. It had gotten dark and they'd gone for a drive. Under moonlight they visited a small bay area south of the city. They made a fire on the beach and sat cuddled up in front of it.

Slowly and surely, as if it was always meant to happen at this exact moment, the two fell to making love in the sand, gradually building into the violent throes of sexual ecstasy.

Within the haze of darkness and lust, neither of them noticed the details of the tattoos inking the other's back and chest. They were too busy reading the movement, scent and feel of the other to register anything beyond their lovemaking.

It wasn't until they finished and lay panting in the sand that both jarred in shock. There before their eyes was the enemy's mark: the tattooed insignia inked over both bodies. Raul's Durango panther snarling at the Sinaloa eagle spreading its wings across Marta's breasts, the bird's talons outstretched toward the cat.

They held each other tight after that. Then, with trembling voices, they admitted that they couldn't see each other ever again. They kissed with hot tears running down their faces and went their separate ways.

That was until Marta got back to Mexico and discovered she was pregnant. Pregnant with a child of the enemy.

She got word to Raul and they began meeting in secret, talking over burner phones, covering their tracks, meeting in neutral places whenever they could. At night, in whichever hotel they ended up in, Raul would hold Marta, hold her belly, and wonder what their future held.

Countless nights were spent like this. Until the night they were awoken in their latest hotel room by a man loudly humming an odd tune.

Both shot up in bed the second they saw the stranger sitting on a chair at the end of it. They immediately began threatening his life. Then, once they'd finished, he put forward a proposal.

"I have been offered a significant sum of money," he said, "to kill the heads of both your families. Don Carlos and Don Ignacio."

"Who is behind the contract?" Raul asked.

"The money will be provided by nine other families with the agreement of the other thirty-five. You see, they have become tired of the endless fighting between your factions. They already have far more peaceful successors in line to take over. All they need is these two men's heads. You give them to me and—the gun you're reaching for, Marta," he interrupted his own speech, "I already have it here."

Marta was leaning over the side of the bed. Her hand feeling between the mattress and the base. When she lifted her gaze, the man was holding out her mono-black Desert Eagle.

With pierced eyes, she retracted the hand from the bed.

"You give me the heads of your bosses," the man finished where he'd left off, "and I will give you the life you desire."

"Why should we do this for you?" she asked.

"Because if your bosses knew about this, they would remove both your heads with machetes. Cut the child from your belly."

"What do we care—you said yourself you've been paid to kill them. So go kill them."

The stranger shook his head at them. "They're not the only ones I've been commissioned to kill."

Both Raul and Marta narrowed their eyes at him.

"Both your names," he continued, "are on the list as well. Don Carlos, Don Ignacio, Raul Lozano, Marta Aguirre."

"Why are *we* on there?"

"The bosses believe you're too loyal to the dons. They want both of you executed along with the bosses in order to limit future repercussions."

"So," Marta said, "we have no choice but to take this deal you offer us?"

"Essentially, yes. I'm taking great risk coming here and revealing this to you."

"You want us to kill our bosses?" Raul said, wanting to be sure.

"Not just that. I will also require your future employment thereafter."

"What employment?"

"I will protect you and your unborn child. Get you both

out of Mexico. But after that, I will need you to protect something of mine."

And so a deal was done. One that brings us to the current situation.

Raul and Marta guide the Hendersons out of the house and through their backyard.

"Please, Rosa?" Kate shivers.

"I told you. That's not my name."

"What is going on? Who were those people?"

Reaching the end of the garden, Raul uses a hunting knife to cut away the vines that run down the wall there. Marta helps him and the two quickly clear them away from a door with a digital keypad.

Marta fingers the code in and the door clicks. She pulls it open in a whining creak.

"In here," she says, ushering them inside.

"Please," Kate mutters, "what is going on? Where's Carl? Shouldn't we wait for Carl?"

Marta grabs ahold of her by both shoulders.

"Get a grip for your son," she barks at Kate. "The time for questions is later. There are more of those men on their way. Now come on."

The door leads into a concrete tunnel. Strip lighting runs along the ceiling. It is an escape route that spreads underneath Pacific Grove. They emerge three streets over, where Raul and Marta lead them to a Mercedes R63 AMG. A very quick minivan. Especially when it's been tuned up like this one. Though, what's been fitted in the trunk may slow it down a little due to the weight.

They get inside, the family in the rear, Marta driving. Raul leans into the back from the passenger side, "Stay down. Stay low. This van is armored, but that doesn't mean it's invincible."

Kate holds Michael tightly as Marta fires the engine and drives them away from Monterey forever.

"Mom," Michael shivers, "is Dad dead?"

"I don't know," she sobs.

EIGHTY-ONE

OCCASIONAL SPRAYS OF BULLETS HIT THE BACK OF the BMW. The Fireblade and the gatling gun keeping their distance to avoid getting hit by the explosions as Peter tosses more pucks through the footwell onto the road. Keeping at least 100 meters back, they make it impossible for him to judge accurately whether they're close enough or not. So all he's really able to do is buy time, keep his pursuers at arm's length and out of range.

It isn't long before Peter is down to his last remote mine.

They enter the old farming town of Salinas, a place where the buildings don't grow any bigger than four stories and the streets are deserted this time of night. As they race past a strip mall a call comes in and Peter puts it on speakerphone.

"Everything good?" Raul asks.

"Everything is on schedule. How is the package?"

"The package is shaken, but otherwise good."

"Carl?"

"Afraid not. They eliminated him before we had a chance."

Peter grips the steering wheel so hard the leather squeaks. "Okay. I'll—"

Rapid fire hits the back of the car, the minigun getting within range as Peter rushes through an intersection of traffic lights. Two police cruisers sit parked in the shadows of a Dunkin' Donuts, almost spilling their coffee when the convoy zips past.

Their lights and sirens flare up and they accelerate after them.

"Raul, I'll have to call you back," Peter says, canceling the call.

He crisscrosses town, taking a left then a right, the MAC-10 and the M134 constantly bursting into life and spitting lead at them, sparks flying off the tailgate. A bullet punches through the Lexan in the rear windshield, ricocheting through the car and embedding in the back of the passenger seat, where it smokes in the leather. Theresa and Marie scream out, their eyes closed tight, the car throwing them around.

Peter spots what he's been waiting for.

"Hold on!"

He pulls the handbrake and spins the wheel right, locking it, the car screaming sideways on its tires, Theresa and Marie thrown against the door, the BMW cutting across the street at a 90-degree curve, the hood lining up with the mouth of an alleyway that splits two streets of commercial buildings in downtown Salinas, Peter twisting the wheel rapidly left, bringing the car straight and heading right into it.

The bikes just about make it, the gatling gun having to take a wide loop around, losing some distance on the BMW, but soon motoring into the alley after the Fireblade, the fierce sounds of their engines echoing off the tall brick walls of the buildings. The police cruisers are so far behind they don't even spot the maneuver and instead whiz past the alley, missing it altogether.

The passage is narrow. With the Fireblade leading the gatling gun, the passenger lets off trails of 9mm rounds from the MAC-10.

"Momma! Momma!"

"Just hold on!" Peter cries.

He kisses the last puck before tossing it out.

The Fireblade is no more than twenty yards behind. Peter has to be quick. He hits the button just as the motorbike passes over it.

The God of War is smiling on Peter.

The edge of the blast radius pushes them violently forward, flipping the bike over and sending both men crashing to the ground at 110mph. The passenger hits the deck headfirst, his spinal column compacting like the crushed bellows of an accordion, dead long before his ragged body rolls to a stop.

The rider goes down with the bike and skids along on his leathers. He hits a divot in the uneven ground and cartwheels, breaking both legs in the first of four heavy somersault landings. The last of which lands him so hard on his coccyx that he shatters the bones.

He lies across the alley when the gatling gun comes motoring toward him. Raising a weak hand, he can do little to stop the inevitable as the heavy motorbike rides straight over his midriff, crushing his pelvis and finishing him off.

Two down. One to go.

EIGHTY-TWO

County Route G17 is a rural road that passes the Monterey Zoo and runs alongside the Salinas River. Raul and Marta Lozano keep their eyes open and wide as they speed down it in the Mercedes minivan. In the back Michael and Kate tremble into each other, their eyes staring vacantly into space. In the passenger seat, Raul reaches forwards into the glove box and takes out a long plastic wand. He's about to twist the end and turn to the Hendersons when he notices something in the mirror.

"We got trouble," he says, placing the wand back in the box. "Ten o'clock."

"I see it," Marta says.

An MD 530G attack helicopter looms in the air behind them, its searchlight moving quickly toward them, eating up the road. Twin machine guns hang either side of the cockpit. They explode in circling muzzle flashes, the blacktop cutting up in stitches of bullet holes all the way to the Mercedes.

"Get down!"

The van is hit, pinging metal. Marta pulls sharply to the right, the tires shrieking as they cling to the road, the Mercedes tipping, the Hendersons crying out, their voices swallowed by the sounds of bullets crackling the bodywork.

Turning to her husband, Marta says, "You know what to do."

"Yes, I do."

Raul slips between the seats into the back. He politely asks the Hendersons to move over and pulls the middle seat forward when they're clear of it. Following this, he slides on his front into the gap until his legs and nothing more stick out down the middle of the van. Lying there, Raul takes hold of the handles of an M2 heavy machine gun. A hatch the size of a cat-flap slides to the side in the tailgate and he pushes the brutal gun a foot on runners until the muzzle is sticking out the rear of the Mercedes.

The M2 or Browning .50-caliber machine gun is a heavy machine gun that often carries the nickname "Ma Deuce" in reference to its M2 nomenclature. It is effective against infantry, unarmored or lightly armored vehicles and boats, light fortifications, and low-flying aircraft. In other words, it punches big holes in big things. The back of the minivan is fortified, with armor plating protecting the gunner as he lies behind the scope mounted on top.

Raul lifts the aim of Ma Deuce, sets it on the helicopter. The heavy gun bucks and kicks as he pulls the dual triggers. Tracer rounds light up the black sky. The chopper pulls up, lurching to the right. Bullets hit one of its miniguns, the thing exploding in sparks.

Smoking, the chopper totters out of view, switching its spotlight off so that it's swallowed by darkness.

"How we looking up front?" Raul asks through his comms.

"Not long now," Marta says. "We're almost there."

EIGHTY-THREE

THE REAR OF THE BMW IS ON FIRE AND SMOKE fills the inside. Theresa and Marie lie in the footwell continually screaming. The gatling gun comes alive every few moments, bullets shredding the car. Peter zigzags, brakes sharp, tries to get alongside or behind the bike so he can ram it. But the rider is skillful. He keeps within range but doesn't come too close, expertly judging the BMW's maneuvers and adjusting his own position on the road to suit.

Peter fears that eventually the powerful gun will break through the ballistic nylon and steel polymer armor plating and pierce the fuel tank.

About two hundred meters ahead is an on-ramp that slopes down the right side of the 101 before joining it. Seeing it, Peter scans the top with his eyes.

Perfect.

The rider holds fire for a moment. The end of the minigun is glowing orange. Continual fire will cause it to overheat so he has to be careful to give it time to cool down. He has opened up a hole in the armor plating on the rear corner of the BMW where the fuel tank sits. He's sure one more sustained burst of fire will give him a direct hit. The throttle pulled back, his thumbs resting on the triggers, he waits for the temperature light on the dash panel to go green.

Peter, meanwhile, keeps his lane position straight, speed steady, all the time checking the top righthand corner of his peripheral vision.

Excellent.

The second they pass the end of the down ramp the light changes on the bike and the rider's thumbs stab the triggers. The gun takes a few seconds to get spinning and then engages. The handlebars vibrate in his hands and a line of fire begins smashing the back of the BMW.

Oddly, the car stays perfectly straight, not maneuvering to get away, making the rider wonder why he doesn't dodge the lethal barrage—then, suddenly, the BMW veers violently to the left, revealing the back of a Mercedes minivan.

One with something sticking out the back.

The rider's eyes widen as the end of Ma Deuce explodes and the front of the bike is hit by a storm of .50-caliber rounds that slam straight through the gun, the handlebar column, and the fuel tank.

The gatling gun goes up in a flash of fire, the rider swallowed within.

"Yeh-ha!" comes Raul's voice, yipping like a cowboy over the speakerphone.

"Just in time," Peter breathes.

"Best time to be, ese," Raul adds.

The steering wheel shakes in Peter's hands, the car on its last legs.

"I'm gonna need to stop," he tells Raul and Marta. "Transfer to your vehicle. This one's not gonna make it."

"There's still that chopper somewhere," Marta informs him as Peter approaches a T-section where a road feeds in from the left.

"Then we need to be careful," Peter says. "There's a truck stop just past Dean. We'll change over into the Mercedes there."

"I know it," Marta says.

"Peter?" Kate Henderson's voice says in the background.

His heart shrinks to hear her call him by his real name.

"Yes, Kate," he says, his mouth going dry.

"Is that really you?"

A tear rolls down Peter's cheek. "Yes, Kate. It's me."

"Peter, what is happening?" she sobs.

"I'll explain everything later."

"I think they killed my husband."

"I know, Kate. I'm so sorry."

"Is this... Is this you?"

Peter swallows. "I'm so sorry."

His eyes are fixed on the Mercedes as it crosses the junction. Through the rear window he can see her silhouette on the backseat, and it fills him with— Something moves rapidly from the left.

"Watch out!"

By the time Marta sees the black Hummer speeding at them it is too late. The all-terrain military vehicle smashes into the side of the minivan and bowls it off the road, the thing toppling down a steep embankment—the sounds of crashing metal, screams and hollers coming over the speakerphone.

"Kate?!"

EIGHTY-FOUR

GREECE, 2006

"PLEASE, HELP ME," PETER BEGGED AS HE stumbled into the villa clutching his blood-soaked stomach.

Dressed in naught but a pair of shorts, his bone-white torso shone in the moonlight. He looked so washed out and pitiful that the girl whose room he had just trespassed into felt compelled to rush from her bed and come to him. He practically fell into her arms, only just managing to catch himself on furniture and keep relatively stable with her help.

"What happened to you?" she asked.

"I was shot," he replied, his voice sounding far away.

Whatever he did, he mustn't lose consciousness. He must keep control of the situation.

The girl guided him to the bed. Sat him down.

"I'll get my parents."

"No!" he snapped, grabbing her arm and stopping her, shaking his head when she swiveled around to meet his eyes.

"Please, you can't," he begged. "They'll kill me if they find me."

He softened his expression, channeled a lost little boy in the look, shrinking before her.

His shimmering eyes, the wound—they terrified the girl.

"Who will kill you?" she asked.

He didn't dare say. "Please, hide me. I'm begging you. Please."

A blade of moonlight fell across his stomach and she got her first glimpse of the winking hole in his guts. Dark blood oozed from it like leaking engine oil.

"You need the hospital."

"No, I don't," he assured her, swallowing and lifting himself off the bed via a bookcase. Halfway up, his arm went weak, he slipped, fell down, the girl grabbing him back up as a fat copy of Middlemarch dropped onto the floor with a thump.

She guided him once more to the bed. He leaned back and lay across it. Closing his eyes, trying to steady his swirling head for a moment. Then a voice hit him, coming from his own head.

"Get up, Peter." It was Mother. "Get up and fix yourself. Don't just lie there and die. GET UP!"

His eyelids snapped open like blinds and he dragged himself up into a sitting position.

"Where's the bathroom?" he asked with sudden composure.

"The ensuite is there," she said, pointing to a door on the other side of the room.

"Does it have a bath?"

"Yes."

"Good. Because this is going to be messy."

She helped him stumble into the bathroom, his leaden feet

shuffling along the tiled floor. A pink bathtub took up the far corner and she assisted in lowering him into it.

"Run the water."

Transfixed and half asleep, the girl leant over him to twist the taps. She was so close that he could feel the heat of her body. Smell the sweet scent of her perfume. Watch a bead of sweat up close as it glided down her windpipe.

The wound twinged violently to remind him what was more important.

With water running underneath him, Peter used all his energy to wash it over the bullet hole.

"Do you have a first-aid kit?"

"It's in the kitchen. I'll fetch it."

She went to dash off, but he stopped her before she reached the door. "Have you got a sewing kit as well?"

"Yes."

"Good. I'll also need a very sharp knife. Not the type you chop things with. More the type you'd peel a potato with. Paraffin if you have it. And a cigarette lighter. Oh, needle and thread."

"You can't be serious?"

"Please, I'm in a lot of danger. I promise you, I will be gone the second I'm well enough. I just need you to get me through the next twenty-four hours."

His face bristled with helplessness.

"You're so young," she breathed.

"Please, help me."

It was like the year before with the Roswells. Using those blue eyes, those boy band looks, to pacify someone into helping him.

"Who's after you?" she asked in a soft voice, a hand on the doorframe.

Peter was about to answer when the doorbell chimed, echoing throughout the whole building, making their hearts throb in their chests and their blood freeze in their veins. Both their sets of eyes fixed in the direction of the front door.

Who could be calling at two o'clock in the morning?

The bell went again, sending another shudder coursing through them.

"Please," Peter begged when she glanced back at him.

A third chime awoke her parents, the sounds of movement coming from the other side of the villa. A bedroom door opened, muffled complaints.

"Okay okay," a man grumbled as he made his way to the front door and answered it. "Hello?"

"You are English?" a Greek voice asked.

"American. What's up?"

"I'm sorry to disturb you. Bu—"

"Look, buddy," the father interrupted. "My wife and daughter are asleep. You woke us up. So is it cool if we do this outside so we don't disrupt them even more?"

"Of course, sir."

They stepped onto the porch, closed the door a fraction, dousing their voices. Peter couldn't hear what they were saying over the sound of his own heartbeat and the rain outside.

It couldn't have been much, because it wasn't long before the girl's father was coming back inside.

"Sure thing," he said as his footsteps begin approaching the bedroom.

He knocked and it sent a fresh chill through both of them.

"Honey?" he called through the door.

"Answer it," Peter whispered, "but please do not let him see me."

"Okay."

The boy looked so frightened, so fragile right now, that the girl couldn't let him down. Even at the expense of deceiving her parents. As she left the bathroom, she switched the light off and closed the door quietly behind her. When she answered her father's knock, she opened the door a crack and tried to look as sleepy as possible.

"Dad, you woke me," she told her father, rubbing her eyes for effect.

"Sorry to bother you, honey. The police are here. Apparently there's been some sort of disturbance. You haven't noticed anyone running through the backyard, have you?"

"No."

"Is the door into the yard locked?"

"Yes. Why?"

"It's nothing. Keep it locked and go back to bed. Night night."

"Night night, Daddy."

The girl closed the door but stayed by it, an ear pressed to the wood. She listened to her father speak to the police, for them to go, and then she returned to the bathroom.

"Thank you," Peter murmured from the tub.

Her father went back to bed. From the bathroom Peter and the girl remained frozen while listening to her parents converse in their bedroom, their voices smothered by the walls.

Shortly after the conversation ended, Kate crept out of the room and fetched the first-aid kit, sewing kit, and all the other things. Back in the bathroom, they started by soaking the wound in antiseptic. Peter visibly tensed up as he poured the searing liquid straight into the hole. Other than that, he didn't make a single sign that any of this was particularly painful.

With all the dried blood cleaned away, he could see the edges of torn flesh clearly. There was a rip across the bullet hole where he had stretched to pull himself over the wall. It would need stitching with the rest of it.

"What now?" the girl asked.

Peter gazed at her fingers. Then at his own. Then at the wound that was no larger than an eye socket.

"Your hands are smaller," he said. "I need you to reach in and take the bullet."

"No," she said instantly, shaking her head.

"It's okay. It hasn't hit anything important. It's just wedged in the tissue of the external and internal obliques. All this bleeding is superficial."

"I can't," she said.

"You have to. The slug is too big for the tweezers. My fingers are too big for the hole. I'll have to enlarge the wound with a knife." Gulping, he added, "I'm not sure I can do that without passing out. Please. All you have to do is reach in an inch and hook it out."

"Is that all?"

"I promise you. There's no damage you can do to me, and it can't hurt any more than it already does."

The girl stared at him a while, almost completely white. Then she nodded.

"Thank you," he said.

Gripping his teeth together and forcing the pain to the corners, Peter stretched himself out along the bathtub, flexing the wall of his abdomen, pushing the bullet toward the entry. The girl cautiously dipped her fingers toward the bloody hole.

Peter poured salient fluid over it to clean away the fresh blood that constantly oozed out, making the tear visible. She went to push the fingers into it when she caught him smiling.

"What?" she asked, turning to him, her hand hovering above his stomach.

"Sorry," he said. "It's just. I bet you never expected when you went to bed tonight that in just a few hours you'd be removing a bullet from a complete stranger with your bare hands."

She smiled back dryly. "You're right. I didn't. But then I did come to Greece for new experiences."

"Then," Peter said with an ever-expanding grin, "here's to new experiences."

"You ready?" she asked seriously.

"Yes," he replied likewise. "Do it now."

She pushed her fingers into the wound very slowly, glancing constantly between Peter's face and the hole. Worried. Except, he wasn't even grimacing. He was just watching her with those cold blue eyes that reminded her of a wolf.

How can he not even be making a face?

She pushed the fingers deeper. Still no reaction. Only a careful look at what she was doing.

"You're almost there," he said. "Just a little—"

"I can feel it," she exclaimed, a look of triumph on her sweat-glossed face.

"Okay, good. Don't get cocky and push it further in."

"It's so warm. Almost hot."

"That's great. Now I need you to hook your finger underneath it and wedge it out."

She went deeper. For the first time she felt him tense around her fingers as they strummed the naked nerves, the *muscle wanting to spasm, Peter using all his mind to control it, to not pass out, not scream in agony, alert her parents.*

"I've got it," she said.

A wheezing sigh of purest ecstasy seeped from the corners of Peter's mouth as she hooked the slug out. It spilled from the wound and dropped onto the ceramic bathtub with a clang.

"Thank you," he mumbled, his hair and face soaked in sweat. "Thank you so much."

"I did it," she said in awe, gazing at the bullet lying in the bloody water of the tub, absolutely astonished that she was even capable of such things.

"Now," he said, almost out of breath, "I can sew myself. You wash up and go back to bed."

Pleased with herself, the girl went off to the sink and began rinsing her hands.

"Oh, and by the way," Peter said.

"Yes?"

"My name is Peter. What's yours?"

"Kate," she told him, looking back over her shoulder from the basin. "My name is Kate."

EIGHTY-FIVE

PETER SLEPT ALL NIGHT AND MOST OF THE morning in the bathtub. Next day, the wound was bloated but healing. The skin surrounding it had gone deep purple. Under the circumstances, he was pretty pleased with the effort, the stitches tightly pinching the tear together.

When he finally got up, he was weak and aching. It took all his strength to raise himself out of the tub. Kate was sitting by the window reading a book when he entered the room proper. She put the novel down and came to him as he leaned heavily on the doorframe.

"I tried to wake you," she said. "Tried to get you out of the bathtub, get you into bed, but you were out cold."

"I owe you my life," was what he said to this, meeting her with his wet eyes. "Really," he added. "There's not many who would have done what you did last night. Especially for a complete stranger."

The sincerity of his tone. His eyes. His looks. They made Kate blush so much she was forced to look away.

He took the opportunity to observe her. She was tall, five-ten, and slender. Dressed in khaki shorts, he couldn't help admiring her legs. She was a runner. He could tell by the definition of her thighs and calves.

And she's so darn pretty!

It was the type of prettiness Peter admired most. The subtle beauty that was often missed at high school and only appreciated later on when the girl had matured into early womanhood. The petite lips, tiny nub of chin, oval eyes that weren't too large. All of those understated features made Peter's skin tremble.

"Anyway," she said, turning back to him. "We need to clean the wound and redress it."

Two minutes later, he sat on the end of the bed with her next to him, Kate delicately dabbing at the stitches with cotton wool dipped in spirit, a pile of bloodied bandages sitting on top of the nightstand.

With her hand so close to his groin, Peter had to look away, concentrate on something else, the view of the garden. It was at this point that he decided conversation was needed.

"Where are your parents?" he asked.

"They've gone sailing with friends," Kate told him. "I said I wasn't up to it. Wanted to spend the day at the beach."

"When are they due back?"

She checked her wristwatch. "Not for another four hours."

It took her a few minutes to clean the wound. Once she'd finished, both of them satisfied it was healing, she began dressing his abdomen in fresh bandages.

With her gaze concentrated on the job in hand, he couldn't help staring at her once more. Outside of the women Mother brought to him at the farm, she was the most beautiful person *he had ever been within such close proximity to. A part of him wanted to reach out, touch her face, kiss her.*

She spotted him looking. It brought more red to her cheeks and an involuntary smile pursed her lips.

"Sorry," he said, looking away. "It's rude to stare."

"It's okay. There, finished."

She got up and he watched her glide across the room. Sunlight caught her blonde hair and the world slowed down a little so he could enjoy the moment for longer.

"I got you some of my dad's things," she said, taking a pile of clothing from the top of a bureau.

Everything caught up, speeding into real time.

"You're around the same size," she added, coming back to him with the clothes. "Now you can take off those blood-soaked shorts."

"Thanks," he said, taking the things. "I'll go get cleaned up."

Kate watched him hobble to the bathroom. She took a deep breath the moment the door closed after him. Her heart was racing in her chest. Just like it had for most of the night. Except this time it wasn't from fear. It was from something else.

Shaking it off, she went back to her book, retaking her seat by the window, the blue waters of the swimming pool glittering in the sun on the other side.

It was three pages later that a shadow fell across her face and she glanced out at the garden. The gate was wide open. Sweeping her gaze across the pool, she spotted a man beside the jacuzzi, crouching at the pebbles that surrounded it.

Coming outside and closing the sliding door behind her, Kate announced in a loud and clear voice, "May I help you?"

The man turned sharply to her from the stones and stood

up. "Ah, hello there," he said in a Greek accent, brushing his hands down his jeans.

"Why are you in my garden?"

He slipped a hand in a pocket and when it came out, a shock went through her.

"My name is Detective Dominic Tzimikis," he said, holding out his police badge.

Kate went serious. Shook it off.

She felt some sort of affinity with the boy in her shower. Felt an overwhelming need to protect him. That meant she must summon all her cool.

"Is this about what happened last night?" she asked.

"You heard?"

"Only what was on the news this morning. Not to mention that the police came to the villa last night."

"Oh," the detective said, nodding, eyes fixed on hers, as if he was weighing her up, trying to bore through her eyeballs to see what she was thinking.

Or perhaps that was just her paranoia.

"I didn't see or hear anything," Kate felt urged to say.

"I know. I read the officers' reports. They spoke to your papa. He said none of you noticed anything. But it's strange, is it not?"

"What's strange?"

"That the suspect appears to have disappeared in this very spot."

He continued to stare at her.

Kate frowned. "Why do you think he disappeared here?"

"The wall back there." He was pointing to the white stone wall on her right, a little ivy coating part of it. "It was the last one the suspect was seen going over."

"Suspect?"

"Yes."

"You mean the man that the police were looking for here last night is a suspect in those men being killed?"

"He is the only suspect."

"My god," she mumbled, placing a hand over her mouth, instinctively glancing sideways at the villa. To the killer in her shower.

"As I was saying," the detective went on. "There is dried blood on the top of the wall that the rain didn't wash away, being that the storm passed over this part of the island pretty quickly. The blood is on all the walls leading up to here. A sure sign that the suspect climbed over them." He paused and narrowed his eyes, cocked his head. Like he was fucking Colombo. Kate was half expecting him to shake a finger at her when he said, "But the tops of the walls leading onwards are completely clean. No blood. No sign he climbed over."

Kate shrugged her shoulders. Played dumb. "I don't get it."

"It means that he didn't get out of this garden by that wall." He pointed to the one on her left. "So where did he go?"

"Maybe he escaped from here another way."

"Like where?"

The villa backed onto a tall apartment block. It towered five stories up at the end of the garden, a solid white wall blocking the view of the crystal sea. It was one of the reasons her father got the villa so cheap—and it was also the reason why there was no way out that end.

"The only other way," Tzimikis stated, "is through the villa."

He stared right at her.

She grinned. Kept her cool. Played it like her improv drama club at high school. "Maybe he went back the way he came. Wouldn't that explain it?"

Detective Tzimikis shuddered. He hadn't thought of that.

"You are sure you heard nothing?" he said, getting to his point.

"A hundred percent."

He gazed past her shoulder; toward the sounds of the running shower coming from the room.

Her cool dropped and she went cold when she realized where he was looking.

"Who is that?" he asked.

"My boyfriend."

"Was he here last night?"

The detective began approaching the sliding glass door.

"No," she said, quickly blocking the way.

"Can I speak with him?"

"Why?"

"To see if he—"

"He only arrived on Mykonos this morning," she interrupted. "He's jet lagged and taking a shower. He wouldn't know anything and he's really tired. His plane was delayed overnight in Paris."

The detective stared at her and she felt the touch of his eyes on her. Summing her up. Deciding whether to press on.

Deciding not to, he shrugged. "Okay." Taking a card and handing it over, he added, "This is my number. If you or your parents recall anything about last night that may help, I'd like you to call me immediately."

"Sure thing," she said, gazing at the card she held.

"Remember," the detective said in parting, "the man we're

looking for is a dangerous killer. He could return." He let this hang a short while, then added, "Ciao," and walked away, leaving the yard through the open gate.

When Kate returned to the bathroom, Peter wasn't underneath the running shower.

"Peter?" she whispered, treading further inside the room.

He emerged silently from behind the door.

Spotting him in the mirror, she wheeled around. He looked different to her. Like something had changed. A switch gone off. He was holding the knife she'd fetched him last night and his face was a mask. His eyes had lost all their life. He wasn't pitiful anymore. He was frightening.

"Who was that?" he asked in a blank voice.

"Here," she said, giving him the card.

While he read it, Peter said, "I couldn't quite make out what he was saying."

"He was curious," she told him. "There's blood leading all the way to the yard but not afterwards. He wondered whether you'd come through the house. I assured him we heard nothing. He left that in case we remember something."

Kate took a seat on the toilet pan. Peter stood glaring at the card. The knife still gripped in his other hand.

"Did you do it?" she asked.

He looked at her from the card. Swallowed. Even though he knew exactly what she meant, he asked, "Do what?"

"Kill those people. It's all over the news. Five bodies on some billionaire's yacht. Another two found in the bay. One more on the island."

His eyes softened. They weren't so hard and cold. He was no longer the killer. Now he was the boy.

"I'll clean up and be gone by the time your parents are back."

"Is that a yes or a no?"

He said nothing.

"Did you kill those people?"

When the word finally came out, he whispered it. "Yes."

Kate had prayed that his part in all this was as nothing more than an innocent victim caught up in some terrible business that had gotten him shot. Not as the chief villain.

She gasped. Placed a hand over her mouth. When she spoke, it was to say, "You're just a boy."

His hurt pride colored his cheeks. "I'm eighteen."

"My God! That's the same age as me. Holy shit! You just finished high school, Peter."

"I never went to high school."

"What do you mean you never went? Everybody goes to high school."

"I didn't."

"Then where did you go?"

"I was trained on a farm in Alaska instead. Trained to do what I did last night."

"Trained to do what you did last night?" she repeated, dumbfounded.

"Yes."

"To kill people?"

"Yes."

Tears welled in her eyes. Staring right at him, she breathed, "What are you, Peter?"

"I'm an assassin."

EIGHTY-SIX

PETER MEANT TO LEAVE AFTER THE SHOWER. BUT *when he emerged from the bathroom she'd made him a chicken sandwich and left it on the side. Having eaten it, he felt heavy. Whereupon she convinced him to lie down and rest some. He fell to sleep instantly and didn't wake up till she rocked him into consciousness many hours later.*

It was dark outside. At first this startled Peter, his eyes searching the gloom. But when he caught sight of Kate's sweet expression, he was put at ease, the girl kneeling at his bedside.

"My parents are back," she whispered.

As if conjured by her words, the sounds of them clattering about the villa reached his ears.

"Don't worry," she added. "They won't want to come in. They're pretty respectful of my privacy."

"Kate?" her mother called out.

"Coming," she called back. On her way out, she told him, "I won't be long."

She left the room.

As soon as she was gone, he staggered out of bed and pressed an ear to the door. Soundlessly twisting the lock, he listened carefully.

"Hello, honey," her father said.

"Hey, Daddy. How was sailing?"

"Your mother got seasick."

"Oh, Mommy," Kate gently cooed.

"Don't hug me, Katie. Please. I'm still icky. I had to concentrate on the road all the way while your father drove us home."

"How was the beach?" her father asked.

"It was, eh, good." Her tone was somewhat downbeat. A glimmer of hesitation in her voice.

Peter realized that Kate didn't often, if ever, lie to her parents. She was taking a massive risk for him, a total stranger, and she was doing things she wouldn't usually do.

He couldn't help wondering why. After all, she owed him nothing.

Peter decided he would leave the first chance he got. She had helped him enough. He didn't want to cause her any trouble.

He glanced over his shoulder at the glass door. Footlights around the pool illuminated the garden in a shivering glow. He came to the conclusion he should leave right now. Get dressed and go.

Yes. That's what I'll do.

Peter came away from the bedroom door. He threw on the shirt and shorts Kate had borrowed for him. He fetched his shoes and put them on. She had cleaned the blood off.

It was only as he went to leave that his plan fell apart. With his hand on the grip of the sliding door, Peter found that he couldn't bring himself to open it. Something inside wouldn't let him complete the action. It was the same part of him that couldn't leave the night of his run-in with the Roswells. That had almost cost him. Mother would say that only a moron repeats the same mistake twice.

But, then, *he thinks,* fuck Mother. Mother left me to die.

So when Kate returned to the room, he was sitting on the bed.

Having learned nothing.

EIGHTY-SEVEN

THE NEXT DAY HER PARENTS TOOK A TRIP INTO Chora for some sightseeing. While the cats were away, the mice were in the bathroom dying Peter's hair black. As he sat in the tub, Kate leaned over, perched on the edge of the toilet pan behind him, and pasted the dye into his hair with a brush.

"The only image in the newspapers or on TV is a sketch," she was telling him. "It doesn't really look like you. There are no videos or pictures."

"What about the CCTV in the nightclub?" Peter pondered out loud. "Surely they would have had my image from that."

"Maybe it's like you said; the Greeks are helping to cover it up."

Peter wasn't sure what he was going to do. For all he knew it was supposed to be a suicide mission. One where Mother and Pat weren't expecting him to survive.

Some fucking holiday.

The more he thought, the more angry he got.

Seven years and she does this to me. What was the point of any of it?

"Isn't there some sort of protocol?" Kate asked.

Snapping out of his mumbling thoughts, Peter gazed at her reflection in the mirror opposite. "What do you mean?"

"You said you're an agent of the American government."

"So?"

"Then if you go missing during a mission, won't they expect you to call in?"

"I'm to do it at the earliest opportunity."

"Then why don't you?"

"Because they left me for dead."

She stared back at him through the mirror. "What happened exactly?"

Over the next ten minutes he told her everything about the mission. By the time he was finishing, she was blow-drying his now jet-black hair in the bedroom.

"And this Mother," she asked; "is she your real mom?"

"Not my biological one. She only insisted on me calling her Mother. Magda and her trained me from the age of eleven."

"The age of eleven?"

"Yes."

"So, let me get this straight, the American government are training children to be killers?"

"I guess so. Mother always said there were other boys and girls. More like me."

"What about school?"

"Mother taught me."

"And what did you learn?"

"Fighting, mostly. Tactics. Espionage. How to read your

opponent's movement. How to blend in. How to survive. How to kill. How to be a weapon."

Kate stared at him. "What about geography, English, history?"

"I read some books on history. But never recent history. Always old. And most of them were about Russian history. I know a lot about Catherine the Great."

"What about TV?"

"We didn't have one."

She was wearing a look of amazement. "You never had a TV growing up?"

"No."

"What about a computer?"

"I was taught how to use one. How to hack it. How to crack passwords, get around firewalls, access government databases, stuff like that. But we didn't sit around watching things on one."

"Then, Peter," Kate said with a wide, beaming smile, "let me introduce you to the world."

Minutes later they lay together in bed eating popcorn and watching Netflix on her MacBook Pro. She started him off with The Simpsons. He found it hilarious, though he missed every one of the cultural references that made up around a third of the jokes. Still, that didn't stop him enjoying the other two-thirds of the humor.

"Of course," Kate remarked after their fourth episode, "it was no good after '97. Nothing more than flogging a dead horse for money. Even the film wasn't great."

Next up they watched Seinfeld. Which Kate said ended before it got really bad. "Though some disagree," she added.

Kramer made Peter laugh most. Especially the way he

entered Jerry's apartment. He found Eileen ditzy and self-centered.

"That's the point," Kate told him.

Jerry he found too cocky. George was hopeless. His life one never-ending worst day ever.

At the end of one episode Kate told Peter that people regard Seinfeld as "the White Album of American sitcoms."

"What's the White Album?" he asked innocently.

"The Beatles."

He said nothing. Just stared at her.

"You've never heard the Beatles?"

"No."

Minutes later they were dancing around the living room of the villa, listening to "Twist and Shout" through her iPod and Bose Sound Dock, yelling the lyrics at each other:

"Well, shake it up, baby, now,

Shake it up, baby,

Twist and shout,

Twist and shout."

She was amazed that after one play, he would know the lyrics by heart, so that by the second, he could sing along with her. Not just that, either. Peter was a good dancer. Natural. His athletic build, crafted from hard work, made him flexible for the dance floor. As they rolled through the songs on her iPod, they became more physical, holding hands and dancing together by "Love Me Do."

"Love, love me do,

You know I love you,

I'll always be true,

So ple-ee-ease,

Love me do."

They came together, spun around, fell down onto the couch laughing. By "Norwegian Wood" she was in his arms, the two gently swaying to the haunting melody, Lennon's voice holding them together, Kate's head on Peter's shoulder.

"I once had a girl,

Or should I say, she once had me."

They'd known each other less than forty-eight hours, but already there was something between them. Something that normally takes months, if not years, to develop.

"She asked me to stay,

And she told me to sit anywhere."

The night before last, as he'd lain bleeding in her bathtub, a bond had begun to form between the pair that had been growing ever since.

"So I looked around,

And I noticed there wasn't a chair."

Neither of them knew it then, but this moment, holding each other to the song, would go on to haunt the pair of them for the rest of their lives.

"I sat on a rug,

Biding my time, drinking her wine."

Kate cuddled deeper into him. Gripped him hard. She felt so close it was like she was a part of him. As Lennon echoed in the background, she whispered into his ear, "One of my favorite books is named after this song."

"Oh yeah?"

"It's by this Japanese writer. Haruki Murakami. It's a beautiful book."

"What's it about?"

"The narrator is a man named Toru Watanabe. He is in love with Naoko. But Naoko is still in love with her dead

boyfriend. Toru loves her so powerfully and yet she can't show it back. Slowly she is going mad; going inside herself; falling deeper into a well of despair. Toru becomes obsessed with trying to bring her back from the darkness. But it's no good because she is too obsessed with the dead boyfriend to be saved." Kate takes a deep breath. Exhales. Continues, "You can't help but feel sad for them. They are both in love with what they can never have."

A shiver ran through Peter and when she looked up, his eyes were filled with tears.

"What's wrong?"

"Nothing," he said, letting her go and arming the tears away.

"I didn't mean to upset you."

"It's okay. I just—"

They froze as the front door was suddenly flung open and Kate's parents walked in.

EIGHTY-EIGHT

"Mom. Dad," Kate exclaimed, stepping toward the open door as a wedge of sunlight flooded the living room. "I thought you'd be in Chora till six."

"It's half past six now," her mother said, coming inside and walking straight up to the Sound Dock and switching it off. "Much better," she added to herself when it went dead. "I always found that song so depressing."

Kate's mother was shorter than her daughter. They did, however, share the same curly blonde hair and both had freckles.

"What's with all the darkness?" Kate's father said, following his wife inside.

Kate got her height from him. As well as his long, narrow nose that pointed gently upwards at the end. Placing two fat grocery bags down, he picked a remote up, pressed a button and all the curtains began opening on a mechanism. It was then, as the dusk light filled the room, that they spotted Peter.

"Oh my," the mother said. "Hello there."

"Hey."

"Mom, this is Toru Watanabe."

"Watanabe?" her father said. "That sounds Japanese."

They were looking at Peter strangely.

"You don't look, uh," her father said. "I mean, you're not..."

"My stepfather is Japanese," Peter said. "I took his surname."

"Ah, I guess that explains it."

"Well, nice to meet you, Toru," Kate's mom said. "I'm Ellen, and this nosey ape is David."

David rolled his eyes.

"Nice to meet you, Ellen," Peter said, shaking her hand gently.

Stepping forward for his handshake, the father said, "Nice to meet you, kid."

"Nice to meet you, David."

"How did you two meet?" Ellen asked when the greetings were done.

"At the beach yesterday," Kate replied.

"Oh," Ellen said, before turning to Peter and asking, "Are you here on your own, Toru, or with someone?"

"I'm with my mother."

"And where's she?"

"Back at our villa."

"Where are you staying?"

"Mom!" Kate exclaimed, coming between them and taking Ellen by the arm. "Don't you think it's rude to interrogate someone you've just met?"

"I thought I was being polite. Showing an interest in your friend."

David asked, "How are you and your mother finding Mykonos?"

"It's very nice."

"Ooh, what's that?"

Peter turned to Ellen.

Kate's mother was looking at the hem of his white T-shirt. Or David's white T-shirt, depending on how you looked at it. Blood had seeped out of the bandage. He must have pulled the stitching while dancing.

"You've hurt yourself," Ellen observed.

"Cliff diving," Peter said.

"Cliff diving?"

"Yes. I was diving and hit some rocks. Cut my stomach pretty bad. Had to have some stitches."

Ellen moved forward. "Would you like me to take a look?"

"Mom!" Kate snapped, intercepting her as she approached Peter. "It's okay."

"But I used to be a nurse."

"The hospital already looked at it."

"I only want to help," Ellen said, gazing apologetically over her daughter's shoulder at Peter. "I only wanted to help, Toru."

He smiled pleasantly back.

"I tell you what," David said. "Why doesn't your friend stay for dinner? Your mother and I bought three fat lobsters. More than enough for four. You like lobster, kid?"

"Sure."

"Then it's a date."

EIGHTY-NINE

WASHING THEIR HANDS IN THE BASIN BEFORE dinner, the two stared at one another in the mirror, gentle smiles on their lips as they held the other's look. She was so beautiful to him then that somehow he already knew he was in love. Just straight-out knew it.

Alone together, they talked away from the parents.

"Toru Watanabe?" Peter put to her with a raised eyebrow.

"Yeah," Kate said, a guilty look on her face. "Sorry about that."

"You couldn't have just gone with Josh Smith or something?"

"I was thinking about Norwegian Wood. I thought it would be romantic."

Peter glanced sideways at her. He dared himself to ask. "Is this a romance, then?"

She swallowed. Her cheeks changed from cream to peach. She spoke softly and slowly. "I was..." She trailed off. Her gaze fell to her feet. "I'm sorry. I shouldn't have..."

Again she trailed off. But not through embarrassment. This time it was because he had taken her by the chin. When their eyes met, something in hers told him everything her voice was unable to.

Peter leaned forward and they kissed. Not like teenagers necking at some party, but as lovers tenderly embracing. It felt to both of them as though they had kissed a thousand times before, a familiarity to it that surprised them.

They were smiling when they parted. Kate giggled. Him too. It was all too strange. For Kate it was like he wasn't real. Just a figment of her imagination. Like she was going to walk out the bathroom now and find her parents waiting for her with a doctor. They would sit her down and explain that she's delusional. Then the men in white coats would stream into the villa. The van waiting outside, engine running.

She couldn't help repeating over and over in her head: How can any of this possibly be real?

NINETY

AROUND THE DINNER TABLE, ELLEN AND DAVID were quick to mention the killings.

"Everyone is talking about it in town," Ellen said as she passed Peter the butter. "Police were everywhere. Taking statements. Asking questions. And there were other ones that looked more like the army. These had black berets and big guns. Weren't there, David?"

"Yeah. Absolutely crazy."

"You remember Robin and Bob?" Ellen asked Kate as she received the salad bowl from David.

"Am I supposed to?"

"They're the couple we met at the restaurant the first night."

"Sure. What about them?"

"They were talking about leaving the island. Flying to Crete."

"Why?"

"Haven't you been listening? There's a killer on the loose."

"Huh!" David scoffed. "I told you, Ellen. Giovanni Destro was the target. Whoever did it has moved on."

"But still," Ellen said, a note of trembling worry in her voice, "what if he hasn't? What if the killer is still on the island? Hiding until he strikes again."

For some uncanny reason her gaze fell on Peter, who sat opposite her at the table. He smiled, looked down at his plate, and forked up some lobster meat.

"Imagine if he were to strike again and someone innocent were to get caught in the crossfire?" Ellen asked.

"He's long gone," David assured his wife, eyes narrowed as he wrestled with a claw he'd got wedged between a pair of lobster crackers.

"I'd have to agree with Dad, Mom," Kate put in, collecting up her food with dainty little pecks of the fork. "He's long gone."

"I still feel uneasy," Ellen said, lifting a hand to her chest.

"I have to, uh, say, though," David said while breaking apart the claw, "it's pretty impressive."

"What's impressive?"

"They say it was one guy who whacked the Italian and his whole security team. One guy."

Ellen narrowed her eyes on her husband. "Are you saying that the type of monster who can murder eight people in cold blood is—and let me use your words, David—pretty impressive?"

Turning a sardonic grin on his wife, David said, "I guess I am, Ellen."

Kate rolled her eyes at him. "You've read way too many Jack Reacher books, Daddy."

Holding the broken claw in his sauce-spattered hand,

David said, "So what if I happen to like red-blooded guys who can look out for themselves?" He widened his eyes at his daughter.

"That sounded so gay for so many reasons," she said with a canny grin.

He shrugged it off and continued. "It's men like that that built your great nation, young lady. Red-blooded men who fought the British for independence. The right to exist as a nation."

Kate was shaking her head. "Young lady?! Really, Dad?"

"And women, David," Ellen interjected with a hot expression aimed at her husband. "Don't forget about the countless women who fought alongside those men. Who supported them. Made sure they had homes to come back to. Lands that were still tended."

"Okay, okay, Ellen," David said with a hand up. "But still, where are those types of guys now?"

It was the father's turn to gaze into Peter's eyes. The latter felt Kate's hand under the table. It took his and gently squeezed.

"They still exist, Dad," she said.

"Yeah. On that yacht. For whatever reason Destro got hit, the guy who did it showed the type of balls you rarely see these days."

Ellen was getting hotter. Her eyes two pierced coin slots. "David," she snapped, "I won't have you talk so empathetically about a killer. Especially not in front of our daughter and her friend. Who is, lest you need reminding, our dinner guest."

Kate's dad went to open his mouth, but his wife beat him to it.

"An end, David," she hissed.

NINETY-ONE

Not long after dinner, Kate and Peter lined the back seat of her parents' rental car, their fingers entwined, her head leaning on his shoulder.

Ellen was driving, David staying back at the villa, and every few seconds, she would glance up into the rearview mirror and smile, admitting to herself that they made a sweet couple.

"Here's good," Peter said as they reached the corner of a rural road overlooking cliffs.

The part of the island he had Ellen randomly drive to was practically deserted. All there was were the odd gated driveway and occasional streetlight. The narrow road wound its way to the coast and nowhere else.

"You're all the way out here?" Ellen said, peering through the windshield.

"Yep. This is it."

"Must be real exclusive."

Peter said goodbye to the mother, thanked her for dinner, and got out.

"You're welcome, Toru. Say hi to your mom."

Kate turned a frown back at her from the road and said in a hushed voice, "You've never met his mother."

"I was being polite, Kate."

The daughter rolled her eyes and joined Peter on the corner of some stranger's driveway. There they stood within the soda glow of a streetlight, their fingers entwined, the rental car ticking over in the background, Ellen watching with a smile.

"I brought some money," Kate whispered. "It's only 200 Euros but it'll get you a place to stay if you look hard enough. There are some hostels in Chora."

As she lifted the crumpled notes from her pocket, he placed a hand on top of hers, stopping the action.

"There's no need," he said.

She looked confused. "So, what—I sneak you back into the villa later on?"

"No."

Her face turned sad. "Does that mean this is it?"

Her heart tensed, the beats falling flat, her world dropping out of her.

"Not that, either," he said, flooding her with instant relief. "I'll come by and pick you up tomorrow at noon."

She narrowed her eyes at him. "In what—your car?"

"In a car."

She could do no more than stare at him, a dubious expression on her face.

"Don't worry," he reassured her. "I'll see you tomorrow at twelve. I promise. Now how about a goodbye kiss?"

She smiled and leaned forwards.

A minute later Kate was waving to him from the back

window of the rental. All the way until he dissolved into the night. Still wondering whether he was real or not.

NINETY-TWO

PETER ARRIVED AT 12:00 ON THE DOT, SITTING IN the cream leather driver's seat of a blue Ferrari 812 GTS. The fast drive there in the convertible super car had fixed his jet-black hair in a swept-back style. Dressed in a pair of Dior tailored navy chinos and a tight Breton striped T-shirt by Yves Saint-Laurent, he made quite the impression—looking like some dream version of a millionaire playboy.

"Wow! A Ferrari?" David gasped in disbelief as he stepped out of the villa onto the driveway.

He began rounding the beautiful car.

"This is the one with the twelve-cylinder engine, isn't it?"

"I believe so," Peter said. "Or at least that's what the guy at the showroom told me."

David was absolutely mesmerized. He reached out and went to touch the car before freezing, his fingertips inches away. Looking up at Peter, he asked permission.

"Sure. Touch it," Peter assented.

Wearing a big old grin, David ran a hand along the hood as if he were running it along the hip and leg of a supermodel.

"Is this your mother's car, Toru?" Ellen asked.

"No," he said, his blue eyes gazing past her shoulder, stuck on the vision of Kate as she stood in the shadows of the porch. "It's mine."

"Wow. How did you afford such a car?"

"It was a present from my father."

"Nice present. What was it for?"

"I'd been accepted into Harvard."

Turning a beaming smile back at her daughter, Ellen remarked discreetly from the corner of her mouth, "You've really bagged yourself one here, Kate my girl," before joining her husband at the car.

"Isn't it amazing?" David asked Ellen the second she was beside him. Looking over at Peter, childlike awe on his face, he practically begged, "Can we sit in it?"

"Go ahead."

"Oh my," Ellen exclaimed as the scissor door arced 90 degrees forward on its hinge.

In the meantime, Peter joined Kate under the porch.

"Look at them," she said. "They see a Ferrari and immediately nothing else matters."

"Like what?"

"Like the fact that you left here last night in one of my dad's T-shirts and now you're dressed in the finest clothes and driving a half-million-dollar convertible."

Peter smiled. "In my experience," he told her, "people are blinded by money and the things it buys."

"They sure are," Kate remarked coolly.

Peter left her at the front door and stepped toward the car. David was behind the wheel, practically vroom-vrooming.

"You wanna take it for a spin?" Peter asked.

David's head snapped left. "Can I?" he gushed.

"Sure. I just need to grab the laptop that's in the glove compartment and you can go."

Ellen leaned forward and opened the box, pulling out the Air Mac that was inside. "You mean this?" she said, holding it up.

"That's it."

Peter took it from her then held out the keys to David.

"She's got some pickup," he told him. "So make sure to keep an eye on the clock. Other than that: enjoy."

David couldn't help laughing with excitement as he twisted the keys in the ignition. The car roared into life like a mechanical tiger. In the passenger seat Ellen was like a high school cheerleader in her boyfriend's T-Bird—all simpering sniggers and wide toothy smiles.

Peter rejoined Kate. They watched David edge the Ferrari out of the driveway. At first, he had trouble with the sensitive sports clutch, the car lurching forward bit by bit. But in the end he got it and they were pulling out of the drive, a beaming Ellen waving wildly back at them.

The second they were out of sight, Kate's smile dropped and she turned a sober look on Peter. "We dropped you off in the middle of nowhere last night without a dime in your pocket. Now you drive here in a Ferrari dressed like a prince."

Peter replied casually, "I have ways of getting things. Especially in a place like this where everyone's so rich. It's like walking through an orchid before the picking begins."

She cocked an eye at him. "You've managed to steal a Ferrari and those clothes in under fifteen hours?"

"No. I rented the car. The clothes I bought."

"With what money?"

"Money I stole."

"You robbed a bank?"

Peter chuckled. "No one physically robs banks these days, Kate."

"How then?"

"I'll show you."

Inside the villa he opened up the MacBook Air on the breakfast bar. She took a stool beside him, resting her head on his firm shoulder while he explained what he did after he left her last night.

Having stolen a car from the driveway they left him at, Peter had driven into Chora and begun visiting bars. Mykonos was full of rich older homosexual men. They were easy to rob while under the influence of alcohol and the allure of Peter's looks. Over the course of the evening he stole a number of credit and debit cards.

"It isn't just that these guys were out of it," he explained, "it's the fact that they're not gonna notice the missing cards among the rows of them in their wallets. These guys can't keep track of one account from another. That's why the tip is always to take the least used card. The one tucked at the bottom. If they've not even signed it, all the better."

When he finished, Kate said, "And did you have to—?"

She was unable to quite say it.

"Do what?"

Taking a deep breath, she said, "Do things with these men."

"No. All I needed to do was make them think something could happen. Bide enough time till I found an opportunity to take the card."

Peter further explained that once he'd collected twenty cards, he'd found an all-night cybercafé, and in a booth tucked away at the back had accessed a US Government VPN. Through this, he was able to enter a program hidden on the dark web. One that was designed and initiated by the American government, but one that they will absolutely deny if ever asked about their role in its existence.

Operating on the hidden web, it is the type of thing that can be easily explained away as some financial hacker's tool. But it isn't. It is a government tool for eliciting funds from credit and debit cards through fake online payments. It then funnels the funds along a spider's web of innumerable transfers, crisscrossing the world from one ghost account to another, until the money sits in a digital holding account.

So, having taken money from the various pieces of plastic and placed it in the holding account, Peter bought one of those prepaid disposable cash cards that you can place money on.

"Thankfully," Peter told her, "in Greece they don't require ID for prepaid cards."

"But I don't get it," Kate said.

"What don't you get?"

"Why would the government give you a means to steal money? Surely if you're an agent of America you'd have access to funds."

Peter gave a knowing grin and said one word, "Deniability."

"I'm sorry?"

"If I were caught or at least tracked, then I could be linked *to money transactions. These could be traced back to America. So wouldn't it be easier for the government to have no link to me, whatsoever? To be able to say, 'Look. Isn't it obvious he's some terrorist for hire? He's stealing money. Using the dark web. Why would an agent of the biggest economy in the world be doing that?'"*

Kate nodded. "It's so there's no obvious link between you and them. Complete deniability by making you look like a rogue agent."

"Yes."

"But," her eyes softened, "wouldn't that mean that if you were caught, the American government would just let you rot?"

"Of course," Peter replied matter-of-factly as he scrolled through the account details of the prepaid card.

"That's so sad, Peter," she said, rubbing his shoulder.

"It is. But this'll make you happy."

He tapped the return *key on the flimsy keyboard.*

Kate almost fell off her stool. "Holy shit, Peter. You weren't joking."

"I never joke."

There in front of her on the screen was the balance of €586,456. Shining a mouthful of pearly whites at her, he said, "Let's go have some fun."

NINETY-THREE

OVER THE NEXT FOUR DAYS THEY DID SO MANY OF the things Peter had dreamed of doing ever since he and Mother arrived on Mykonos almost a week ago.

Once he got the Ferrari back off her parents, Peter took Kate for a drive to the other side of the island where they rented a speedboat. The rest of that first day was spent exploring the smaller islands that surrounded the main one. On the island of Delos, they visited the ruins—the Hippodrome, the Naxian Lions, the House of Diadumenos. With the evening drawing on and the shadows lengthening, they arrived back on Mykonos and ate moussaka, fried calamari and grilled whitebait in a tiny rustic eatery overlooking the diamond waters of the Aegean. As the sun sunk into the horizon and light guitar played in the background, the two held hands over the table and every so often, would lean forwards and kiss.

"Have you ever been in love before?" she asked, her cheeks reddened by the Chablis.

Peter shook his head.

Kate took a deep breath. Gazed sideways at the silhouettes of fishing boats returning to port. She didn't understand how it could happen, but she knew it had. She was in love for the first time in her young life after knowing him barely three days.

It was crazy.

She dared. Meeting his eyes, she said, "Are you now?"

He squeezed her hand. "Yes."

He waited a beat, their gazes trapped together, the scent of the sea and the burning candles, the smoke from the grill wafting about them—then he asked, "How about you?"

"Never before. But, even though it is so crazy, I am now."

Everything appeared to be slotting into place. That night they booked themselves into a luxury $1000 a night villa close to Psario Beach. Together in their own little nest, they made love. It was neither of their first times. Kate had had a steady boyfriend in high school and they'd lost their virginities together at the age of seventeen. After graduation, she'd finished with him, knowing that they couldn't sustain a long-term relationship with him going to college in Michigan and her at California State. It hadn't upset her as much as she'd thought it would. It was more that it signaled the end of a major stage in her life. The end of adolescence and the beginning of adulthood.

As for Peter, Mother had furnished him with a steady supply of professional women who not only met his needs from the age of sixteen, but also taught him how to please a woman. "After all," Mother had told him, "sex can be a useful weapon."

Afterwards, Kate was a little embarrassed.

"That's never happened to me before," she said breathlessly. "I've never made those sounds with anyone."

She seemed surprised at the capabilities of her own body.

They rented the boat for two days. On the second, Peter guided it out to the tentacle sticking up from the sea, the black volcanic rock sheered away where Andre's boat had smashed into it.

In the watery echoes and undulating shadows of the cave, the two of them gazed at the impounded super yacht. A diplomatic struggle had begun almost the second the Mermaid's crew reported the crime; all due to Destro's love of evading the law by anchoring it in international waters. The Greeks saw it as their investigation, as three of the murders happened within their territory. However, as the yacht was registered in Italy, the Italians believed Destro's murder, as well as those of the four bodyguards, was under their jurisdiction. Therefore, four days after the killings, the two-hundred-million-dollar boat was still out there, shining on the horizon like a beacon of iniquity.

"It's crazy," Kate said as Peter held a pair of field glasses to his eyes, watching investigators skulk around the deck of the Mermaid.

"What's crazy?"

"That you have some people who can't even afford to house themselves, and then others like him living on that monstrosity."

"It's because men like Giovanni Destro are willing to fight. They may not deserve it, or even be worth it, but they fight. First to get it. Then to keep it."

When Peter removed his eyes from the glasses and turned sideways to her, he found her own eyes pierced.

"So you see a world of constant fighting, then? Dog eat dog?"

"Isn't it?"

"What ever happened to virtue, huh? Decency? The powerful using their might not to weaken others, but to preserve them? Isn't that what our forefathers wrote the Constitution for?"

Peter couldn't help it. He didn't want to upset her, but he couldn't help replying cynically, "And now the children of those forefathers in today's government send me to commit their crimes abroad in the name of protecting that Constitution. All the time defiling the constitutions of others."

She was sore with him the rest of the afternoon.

That night he took her out dancing to help salve her. They found a bar which played old music—the Doors, the Stones, Bowie, Led Zeppelin. They were having so much fun on the dance floor that Peter was completely oblivious to the man glaring at him from across the crowded bar.

As he held on to Kate's hand and jived away, a claw came bursting through the thronging dancers and grabbed his wrist, tugging him away from Kate and pulling him to the side.

"So this is what you spend your ill-gotten gains on then, Freddy."

Peter was face-to-face with one of the men he'd robbed. A short man in his sixties with curly gray hair and a pair of bushy black eyebrows. His lip pouting out and the brows on a sharp incline.

He snarled, "You took over fifty thousand euros from my account, you little shit."

Just then Kate came in on the scene.

"Peter, who is this?" she asked.

"So your name's not even Freddy," hissed the sour-faced man. "And I suppose you're not even queer." Turning his burning eyes on Kate, he added, "This must be the little cunt you spend your stolen cash on."

"Easy, Henry," Peter said firmly. "I'll promise you now that if you ever insult my girlfriend again, I will break your fucking neck."

This only worked to incense the old man. A retired stockbroker who still commanded respect whenever he was in the London Stock Exchange, Henry Carter was used to respect. It was probably this that led him to make such a terrible mistake.

"Yes. Well, how about this," he snarled before lurching forward and tossing his glass of champagne at Kate.

Peter was quick. He stepped in the way and took the full brunt of the drink in the chest. With another quick movement, he box punched Henry in the larynx and if the music hadn't been so loud, everyone would have heard the pop.

Kate didn't even see the move, it was so quick. Neither did anyone dancing around them. All they saw was the man drop instantly to Peter's feet, curl into the fetal position and hold on to his throat, his face going blue as he gasped and choked on the beer-sticky floor.

"Let's get out of here," Peter said, taking Kate by the hand and whisking her away.

They went for a long walk along the clifftops after that so Kate could get some air. She wouldn't let him touch her, not hold her hand or place his Armani suit jacket over her shoulders when she shivered in the breeze.

"I'm sorry, Kate," he kept saying.

"Why did you have to hurt him? He was just an old man."

"He was rude to you."

"But you didn't have to do that to him. You could have walked away. Shown the other cheek."

"Shown the other cheek?"

"It's the Sermon on the Mount. It's what Jesus would do if he were struck. He would offer the other cheek. Respond to injury without revenge. Allow more injury if he has to. Forgiveness and pacifism."

"And we all know what happened to Christ," he couldn't help adding.

She twisted around sharply on him. "I don't want to live in a world of dog eat dog. A world of revenge and vendettas. Of violence and counterviolence. Escalation until we're all on fire. I want to live in a world where a child dying of hunger actually shocks people. Where America attacks the tyrant instead of being one."

Her voice was carried off in the wind. Moonlight reflected off the water below. It made the night air glow. Peter's blue eyes shimmered, a hangdog expression plastered on his face.

She realized then that this boy had been taught the opposite of every moral lesson she had ever learned.

"I'm sorry," he said. It was all he could.

"It's okay, Peter." She threw her arms around him. "It's okay."

NINETY-FOUR

On the third day he took her luxury clothes shopping in the boutiques of Chora. Decked in beautiful clothing they walked arm-in-arm throughout the narrow, hilly passages, bags dangling from their elbows, the sun baking the white stone and making it shimmer in the intense light.

At one point they took a breather, seating themselves on a little wrought-iron bench. Nearby, an olive tree sprouted up from the middle of the sun-soaked alley, its thick canopy shading them.

There in the cool air, they let themselves become serious.

"What will you do?" she asked him.

The world went a little darker. He turned to her. Beheld the anxious look on her face.

"I don't know," he admitted.

"You can't just go on robbing people."

"Why not?"

"Because it's wrong, Peter."

He had no idea of the concept of right and wrong. His

moral education had been of little concern to everyone he'd ever known. His biological mother had soon abandoned any pretense of an upbringing for the preferred obliteration of drugs. The nuns and the priests only wanted what they could solicit from him. Then there was Mother. All she ever wanted was his absolute obedience. Do what she said and he would be safe. That was the unwritten rule of the farm. But he had done what she said. Had done it and had been left out in the cold.

"So what are you gonna do?" Kate asked again.

"Get a job," he said, only because he thought that was what she wanted to hear.

"What type of job?"

"I don't know."

"Well, what can you do?"

"I can disassemble and reassemble a Beretta M9 in just under twenty seconds."

She frowned at him.

"While blindfolded," he added.

Kate shook her head, looked away, the sun making her squint. "I'm sorry," she said. "I shouldn't ruin things. Should learn to enjoy the present."

"It's okay."

When her eyes were back on him, they were glazed in tears.

"I really like you, Peter," she said in a trembling voice. "I've never in my life felt this way. I've never met anyone even remotely like you. And now I'm scared that something is going to come along and take you away."

Peter didn't know what to say. She was right. Of course she was right. Something was bound to drive a wedge between *them. They were from completely different worlds. She from the light and he from the shadow. There was no chance for her to pull him into her world, and he could never do her the harm of pulling her into his. So he did the only thing he could. He threw his arms around her and held her tight while she sobbed into his shoulder.*

NINETY-FIVE

THE FOLLOWING DAY THE TWO TOOK A TRIP TO THE *tiny island of Ktapodia. There, they hiked to the top of cliffs and had a picnic in the middle of their very own desert island. On the boat ride back, Peter's free arm wrapped around her waist, Kate fell asleep on his shoulder. By the time they reached the villa, they were spent, practically falling through the front door.*

That was when they froze.

A hawk-eyed woman with hair the color of iron was sitting on a chair in the middle of the entrance hall. Dressed all in black she made a formidable sight. Standing behind her were three men. All of them wore expressionless faces like masks. Arms tucked behind their backs. Feet apart. But ready. Focused.

"Hello, Mother," Peter muttered, placing an arm out and gently ushering Kate behind him.

"It's okay," Mother croaked. "We're not here for her. Only for you."

This did nothing to set him at ease as Peter spent the next seconds processing the situation. Three men. Probably armed. One woman. More than likely armed. He couldn't see the guns, but he knew they were there. The doors were closed behind them. All exits blocked. Every scenario involved almost guaranteed harm to Kate. So all he could do was stand between them. Mother and Kate. The two worlds. Shadow and light.

"How did you find me?"

"The digital accounting program you transferred the money through. Your naivety cost you if you think we weren't watching it all the time."

She gave this a few seconds to drop.

He didn't say anything.

"It is time to come home, Peter."

He slowly shook his head at her.

"I understand that you are angry," she continued, "but you have no choice. No matter how much you wish it, you are not an ordinary eighteen-year-old boy. You will never be ordinary. You will always be an asset."

"One you left for dead."

"I had no choice."

"Obviously," he snuffed.

"Shortly after Pat dropped you in Chora, we got word that the Russians had found our location. There was risk that we were compromised. That the Russians would attempt a countermove against us. There was no way we could get message to you without jeopardizing your safety."

Peter was grinning in disbelief, shaking his head even more. "Jeopardize my safety? You mean jeopardize the mission. Isn't that what's more important?"

Her hard expression softened. She leaned forwards in the chair. "Please, Peter. Don't make this any harder than it has to be."

"What if we just leave right now? Walk out the door and go?"

"You won't be able to do that."

"Why not?"

The three men answered the question for her, fanning out from behind the chair. As they began closing in on him—Peter pushing Kate back against the door and getting into fighting stance—Mother held a hand up and the men froze.

Peter stepped forward, reducing the space between them to not more than a few feet.

"Don't be stupid, Peter," Mother told him. "You will not leave this room alive if you choose to go that way. Like you, these men were trained by me. One of them you might beat. Two, perhaps. But three?" She shook her head at him. "You'll be dead before you get to number two."

Peter spoke through locked teeth. "I am not going with you."

"Don't be so naive, you ungrateful little brat!" she shrieked, stamping a foot down with a clap of the heel, making Kate jump behind him. "You listen to me, boy, and you listen good. If you do not leave here with me alive, you leave here dead. Your girlfriend, too. Do you understand?"

"I should be allowed," Peter practically sobbed. "Allowed to do what a normal eighteen-year-old does. Live a normal life."

"But, Peter," Mother said softly, maternally, "you are not a normal eighteen-year-old. You never have been. Those people you call normal—the girl cowering behind you right now. Those normal people will never accept you and they will never be enough for you. Their world will never be your world. They are sheep, Peter. But you, you are a wolf."

He stood there staring at her, staring at the three highly trained killers who would die protecting her, die killing him, killing Kate. It was so futile. Everything. Peter was trapped like a bird in a cage. It was obvious that he had only two choices: leave willingly or lose Kate another way. A permanent way.

"Peter," Kate whispered into his ear, "what's happening?"

The face that turned back to her was coated in tears.

"I'm so sorry," he said.

And with that, he left her shivering by the door. Walking across the hallway and returning to the world of shadow. Leaving her behind in the light.

NINETY-SIX

CALIFORNIA, 2019

THIRTEEN YEARS LATER, THE DRIVER'S DOOR OF the Hummer creaks open and out steps the size 16 combat boot of Mr. Castillo. The goliath. The pitch-black body armor and helmet he wears must have been specially made for him. The chest plating makes him look like the front end of an armored personnel carrier. He heaves his gigantic frame out, an MDRX Desert Tech bullpup dangling from an arm. He starts across the highway like a juggernaut. A convoy of three men get out of the all-terrain vehicle and trail in his wake, eyes trained on the scopes of their bullpups, heading in V-formation across the wide road toward the wreck of the Mercedes, the minivan smoking on its side down the grass embankment.

Halfway across the wide highway, Castillo stops. Holds an arm up. His men freeze.

The goliath hears something. The faint murmur of a

roaring car engine that is getting louder and louder. He snaps his head to the left and his eyes search the endless band of gray. In the distance, he spots a car strobing in and out of the streetlights, approaching at wrecking ball speed.

"Take cover!" Castillo yells at his men.

The BMW hurtles toward the scene like a comet, the reflection of the streetlights blinking across the top of the black bodywork, smoke trailing from the back.

The men take positions behind the Hummer and begin pummeling the car with their bullpups, bullets skittling off the Lexan windshield, denting the hood. Their aims follow the speeding car all the way past their position, about 200 yards up the 101, where it hairpins around 180 degrees. The car comes back at them, at the Hummer, sending the men scattering round it for cover. For one of the men it's too late. As the BMW rushes at them, Peter suddenly brakes— screaming, smoking rubber—swerves around the hood of the Hummer and catches the poor bastard against the corner of the bullbar, crushing his pelvis and leaving him twisted up on the ground.

The Hummer is thrown several feet sideways with the force of the collision. Castillo shoulders it as it comes at him, stopping the vehicle dead.

"You see that?" one of the men says to the other.

"You mean at the back?"

"Yeah. The big hole in the armor. Over the fuel tank. Aim for it."

They get little time to hit the weakness. The BMW spins around again. Comes in for a second charge. Face-on with the car, they fire their 6.5 Creedmoor rounds at the space on the windshield where the driver would sit, hoping to break through the Lexan, which begins to shatter and mist with each punch from the bullpup rounds.

The charging BMW forces the men to run back around the Hummer, matadors escaping the bull. Or rodeo clowns. They aim for the fuel tank when it passes, but are given no time as the car twists around almost immediately and once more forces them to continue their game of chase.

"We're not close enough," Castillo complains as the BMW passes once more and their bullets skitter around the edges of the hole over the tank.

"We need to get it to stay still," one of his men adds.

Castillo has an idea as the BMW begins to make its move. This time Peter stops the car, revs the engine. A bull chafing the ground with its hoof. Castillo finds the moment poignant. His eyes narrow and he begins to take the stance of the bullfighter.

Peter dumps the clutch. The screeching tires grip the road and haul the metal and polymer and bullet-holes at them, sending the men scuttling around the back of the Hummer like rats while Castillo holds his ground, stands proud, chin out, the Hummer at his back, his men giving him covering fire from the sides, the BMW hurtling toward him, sparking with bullets.

Castillo watches the car grow larger as the lights blink off it, making it harder to judge when to bring the red cape flowing up, and then—he's airborne, hauling his weight upwards so that he rises above the grille and lands on the hood right at the moment the BMW hits the Hummer with an explosive clang, pushing the huge vehicle down the road, flipping it onto its side, the back tires of the BMW screeching as it pushes onwards, Castillo holding on with one hand, kneeling on the hood, firing bullpup rounds into the car. Smoke rising up.

As it whips around 180 degrees, Castillo is thrown off, the rifle flying from his hand. Tumbling across the street, the big man lands the other side of the embankment in a motionless heap.

The damage to the car is catastrophic. With the engine smoking and making terrible crunching, grinding sounds, the BMW limps past the men as though lost. They aim their bullpups at the gas tank and, from about fifty yards, let it have it.

The car goes up almost immediately in a ball of fire.

"Yee-haw!" the men yip, high-fiving in the middle of the road, the smoldering, flaming wreck of the BMW rolling onwards on its wheels, the bull slain.

"Now let's go see about the others."

"What about Castillo?"

"We'll see if he's—"

Two gunshots. One second apart. The men drop to their knees, blood pooling down the backs of their necks from the exit wounds. At the edge of the road stands Peter. His eyes looking down the scope of a smoking M4 assault rifle.

NINETY-SEVEN

Four minutes earlier.

"Kate?!" Peter cries out, eyes pinned to the image of the Mercedes bowling across the 101.

He passes behind the Hummer and carries on, before taking his foot off the gas.

"Why are we slowing down?" Theresa asks.

Peter says nothing. Checks the phone. Checks where they are. Reevaluates the plan. Evolves it in his head. Then he's ready.

Once they're out of sight of the T-section, Peter brings the car to a stop.

"Get out," he says, throwing open his door and grabbing the M4 from the passenger footwell as he leaves. Ducking his head back into the car, he repeats, "Out."

Theresa needs help opening the back door, the thing smashed and covered in pitted bullet dents. The armor is completely out of shape, the once smooth surface of the BMW now resembling the skin of an orange.

"You see those trees?" he asks Theresa, pointing at the top of a ridge that overlooks the sloping embankment.

"Yeah."

"You head toward them and wait for me there. Hide if you have to."

"But where are you going?"

"To get the others."

"Others?"

"Just do as I say. Please."

A flicker of softness comes over his hard mask of a face. It convinces Theresa to trust him enough to pick her daughter up and head for the pines that dot the crest of the rocky gully.

With his charges on their way, Peter takes his phone out and switches to an app. Camera footage fills the screen. The 101 highway as seen from the front of the BMW. There is the icon of a directional pad for steering. Icons for the gas, gears, brakes, etc. Because this particular BMW M5 can be controlled remotely via smartphone.

Making his way along the sloping embankment, staying low and using the long grass for cover, Peter keeps one eye focused on the phone as his thumbs move the BMW around the men—charging at them, the car eating up road on the screen of the phone, crushing one of them into the bullbar, heading out, 180 turns on the smoking asphalt, the stench of rubber hanging in the air.

At the Mercedes, Marta is already out. She is bent over the wreck, pulling Michael from the busted open passenger door. Apart from looking shaken up, the kid is in pretty good shape.

Peter keeps the BMW still, revving the engine, so that he can look away from the phone and find out the situation.

"Marta?" he says in a hushed voice as he closes on them.

She turns sharply, pistol aimed right at him. Then lowering it.

Peter spots tears in her eyes, lacing the dirt of her cheeks.

"Raul?"

She shakes her head.

"I'm so sorry, Marta."

"It was always the risk," she says.

The minivan is on its side. To his great relief, Kate is alive and essentially well. Shivering on the back seat and still strapped into her safety harness, she has cuts to her face, but is otherwise okay. Raul lies crumpled at the rear of the van. Ma Deuce has come off its runners and sits on top of him. There is no time to take his body. It will simply have to be left here.

"Can I leave them with you?" Peter asks Marta.

"Sure," she replies, before nodding in the direction of the road, the sounds of gunfire and the BMW's revving engine growling against their eardrums. "That you?" she asks.

"Uh-huh."

Peter is about to depart when someone calls to him from the darkness. "Hey?"

Pausing in the long grass of the verge like a creeping lion, he swivels around to see the kid's face staring at him from the bottom of the bank.

"Who are you?" Michael asks.

"I'm no one, kid. No one. Now do as Rosa tells you and keep your mom safe."

Peter continues up the slope until he's close to the edge of the 101, till he can peek over and watch. He sends the revving car at them. Castillo jumps onto the hood as it strikes the Hummer with a deafening crash of metal. The car carries on, spins, tosses Castillo off right as the engine gives in. Comes back at the men, passes them, the camera on the front destroyed, the screen of Peter's phone nothing but snowy static. The fuel tank is finally pierced. The hot bullet igniting the gas. The BMW bursting and carrying on as a moving fireball. The men yipping in the road, practically dancing. Peter coming up over the ridge, his M4 drawn and his aim on the first. A squeeze of the trigger. The gun gently jolting. Aim onto the second. Another squeeze. Another jolt. Another corpse lies in the road.

WITH PETER'S HELP, Marta gets Kate out of the Mercedes. As she passes her former love, Kate's glazed eyes come to life and she jolts as if hit by a bolt of electricity.

Going still, she murmurs, "Peter?"

He looks so much older than the boy she knew all those years ago. So much more careworn and faded. His eyes have become washed out. No longer the blue that matched the Aegean Sea. Now as gray as that old woman's hair. The one who'd taken him away from her with a warning ringing in Kate's ear. *"You share any of what he has told you with anyone and two things will happen. One, no one will believe you. Two, you will be charged in the United States with sedition, breaking the Espionage Act and treason. Go back to your normal life, girl. Forget about Peter."*

It's not just that the light has paled in his eyes. It's

the artificial changes that the years have brought about. Plastic surgery, all part of the inevitable tradecraft of the assassin, staying one step ahead of his wanted posters, has eroded him into something unreal, almost faceless.

"What happened to you?" she whispers, reaching out and touching that strange face.

"We don't have time," he tells her.

"Why can't you meet my eyes?"

"Please, Kate. We don't have time. We need to leave. More will arrive."

"They killed my husband."

"I know."

"Because of you?"

"Please, Kate."

"Look at me, Peter. At least look at me."

"Kate..." He trails off. His throat constricted by the lump forming in it. The tune coming back to him. The effects of her saying his name after so long yearning to hear it.

"Is it because of you that my son doesn't have a father?" she asks, taking hold of his chin and lifting his face to meet her eyes.

Peter shudders the second their gazes fix and he can't breathe. Every cell inside him turns to stone and he freezes in her grasp.

"Mom?"

She glances sideways at her son.

"Who is this guy?"

Kate returns her eyes to Peter. She goes to talk but stops, almost choking on the words. Tears sprinkle from her. Then, once she can, she sobs at Peter, "You get me and my son out of this alive. You hear me?"

Peter can only nod.

"Good," she says, letting him go.

The moment she moves off, he can breathe again.

Kate joins her son. "It's okay, Mike. He's nobody. Just someone here to help us like Rosa and Carlos."

The mother and son walk off, making their way up the rocky ridge toward the trees. Peter does his best to get his head together. His wet eyes stare into the distance, the tune breathing from his lips.

"You okay?" Marta asks him.

He shudders. Puts his blank "give a fuck" face back on. "I'm good," he says, holding out his phone and bringing up a map of the area. "Now," he goes on, pointing up at the ridge of the gorge they stand in, "those pine there are in the direction of this." He lays a finger on the map. "You see it?"

"Yeah. About 300 meters of trees. Another 100 of rocks and bank. Then the road."

"Good. The package is waiting in the woods about a half mile south of here."

"How is the package?"

"They're okay. Shaken but unhurt. Now if something happens, you know where to meet me."

"What's gonna happen?" she asks.

Just then something huge moves behind Marta, emerging from the corner of the wrecked Mercedes. Peter has just enough time to throw her sideways before the bear of a man grabs her—planning to break her neck one-handed. In a panic Peter unshoulders the M4, but before he has time to fill the goliath with lead, the huge creature swoops and grabs the end of the assault rifle, pointing it up at the full moon as Peter pulls the trigger, the black night lighting up and strobing Castillo's mean face.

Marta, knocked down by Peter's shove, gets up, takes the Beretta from her belt, aims it at them. Castillo is quick, he pivots on one foot, spinning Peter around as he holds on to the M4, so that he blocks Marta's shot. In the meantime Peter aims kicks at the goliath's shins and knees, but it's like trying to kick a statue off its plinth.

Castillo takes a hand from the barrel of the M4 while they wrestle over it, able to keep his grip one-handed. He plucks his own pistol from his belt and fires at Marta, all the time using Peter as a shield. Peter summons all his strength to rock the giant sideways and pull his aim away from her as she dives for cover in a drainage ditch.

"Get them out of here!" Peter cries at her.

With Castillo's aim away from her, Marta runs from the ditch to where Michael and Kate await her at the base of the ridge. Castillo ignores Peter and tries to shoot her. The ground cuts up behind her as he finishes the clip. Then she is free and the big man is tossing the empty gun after her.

Castillo turns his full attention on Peter.

"And then there were two," he growls.

Nice and cozy.

Castillo's eyes narrow at Peter. He reattaches the hand to the barrel of the M4 so that he holds it with both. As if plucking cotton candy from a baby, Castillo rips the rifle from Peter's hands and goes to turn it on him. But before he can, Peter, the skilled finger-smith that he is, manages to pop the magazine release button and take out the mag.

Throwing it far away, he dives for cover behind the

Mercedes as Castillo fires the single bullet left in the chamber. It sparks off the chassis of the minivan. The assault rifle then clicks in Castillo's hands and he glances down it. Spotting the missing magazine, he grins a mouth of jagged teeth, a pair of solid gold canines shining in the moonlight.

"I'm glad I'll get to do this with my bare hands," he says, throwing down the useless M4.

The bull creeps around the Mercedes, ignoring the shadows of Marta and the others as they clamber up the rocks of the ridge toward the pine.

He bursts around the corner and gets ready to fight—thin air.

"Up here."

Castillo raises his sight, but it's too late. A foot swings from the top of the overturned van, kicking him hard in the cheek.

It barely turns his face sideways.

Peter jumps down from the van and the two men stand apart, legs sunk in the long grass of the ditch. The man and the bear. David and Goliath.

"I've been waiting for a long time to meet you, Azrael," Castillo growls. "It's the only reason I took this bum job. Because it gives me a chance to kill you—the great Azrael."

He begins stripping the armor off his body. Peter does the same.

"You recall Mexico City, Christmas Day 2012?"

Peter says nothing as they free themselves of the constraint of the heavy armor. He's already of the understanding that offence will be useless against the brute. He'll have to wait for him to strike first and then counter.

"Of course you do," Castillo goes on. "That night you

murdered five people, including Miguel 'El Tiburón' Rosario—the Great Shark of Mexico City. Lord of lords."

"It was my job," Peter says blankly. "Nothing more."

"But you did it. Killed a man who was like a brother to me, *bastardo*."

A cloud comes over Castillo's whole face and he appears to swell. He explodes at Peter. Launches that hulking mass at him, a tree-branch arm scything through the air in a colossal right hook. Peter sidesteps, swerves around the body and ducks under the hammer arm, floats back up and twists around. Castillo pulls up, his feet skidding to a stop. He whips back at Peter. This time the left comes across. Peter sidesteps it and they're back where they started.

Castillo is panting. Peter is not.

The huge Mexican comes at Peter again. This time he feints with his left and swings in with the right. But a body like Castillo's has a way of broadcasting its every move. Peter reads it perfectly. As he passes underneath, he crashes an elbow into Castillo's ribs. It has zero effect. The giant comes around again, Peter dodging back from him, feeling the whip-snap of the air on his face as he avoids the big man's onslaught by mere inches.

Castillo takes a breather. He needs it. He's panting heavily.

He spits in the grass, comes at Peter like a truck. A swarm of piledriver fists. Peter ducks under the arms and pushes up on his heels, into a jump, laying an elbow on Castillo's cheek as he comes down. He puts all his weight behind it. It should shatter the big man's face. But the blow has nowhere near the impact Peter is expecting and Castillo connects with his forearm as Peter puts up a block. It knocks him sideways, almost on his ass, Peter falling onto one knee but springing back up before Castillo's swinging wrecking ball foot can kick his head off his shoulders. It is so close Peter gets the scent of boot leather in his nostrils.

The giant twists round with an elbow, Peter ducking under it, the arm sliding over his face. There's just enough time to arch back up before the next scattergun attack of fists comes at him. One lunge that Castillo puts all his weight into misses Peter completely and the momentum drags him past, giving Peter ample time to smash him with a right cross punch to the ear, followed by a left jab to the jaw, letting the punches go with everything he has.

Peter dances back. Takes a breather himself. Evaluates the damage.

Minimal.

Peter has hit him twice in the head with all he has and he may as well have not bothered. Apart from a cut lip, there's nothing on Castillo that wasn't there before. Not even swelling. He should have never survived those blows. Any other man would be on the ground unconscious. Or dead.

Like a bull, Castillo scrapes his foot along the ground and comes at him. He doesn't throw any punches. Just drops a shoulder. Peter dodges to the side but Castillo is expecting this. He moves over Peter like a tidal wave and lands a left hook straight into his chest. It is like being hit with a 350-pound sledgehammer. He feels his sternum flex inwards, every bit of its elasticity put to the test, and the blow explodes in his heart. He lands on his back in the grass.

Now it is about survival. Trying to stay alive.

"Get up, boy!" he hears Mother scream. *"Get up!"*

He rolls onto his front. Heaves himself up on his palms.

Turns left. Jumps out of the way as another hammer fist comes swinging by. With his chest in constant pain, Peter spends the next minute avoiding whatever Castillo throws at him. Slowly, he gets back into the fight, the giant losing energy with every missed punch, and in the midst of all this dodging, Peter gets a few elbows in. One of them flattens the Mexican's nose to his face, Peter feeling the cartilage and bone mush up beneath the arm. It means Castillo has to hold his mouth open to breathe from now on, making him lose energy quicker. Peter dances away with him, waiting for his moment. A left hook catches him in the upper right arm and for the rest of the fight he can hardly feel the limb, losing at least 70 percent of its power. A rabbit punch helps disguise a right hook but not enough. Peter recognizes the ruse and narrowly avoids the poleaxe. It gives him a fraction of a second's opening and he launches himself into an upper-cut.

The punch is a thing of beauty. Every cell of Peter's body knows what to do. Has been trained to do it. And his poise, positioning and timing are flawless. Mother would be absolutely proud of it. It catches Castillo with a crack, Peter following through, stretching up onto tiptoes, the giant staggering back. It should shatter Castillo's jaw and snap his neck.

But it does none of those things.

Castillo rocks back on his feet and stops. He shakes it off like a bucket of cold water to the face and is back into stance before Peter has time to feel the energy suck out through his feet—before he can do much about the punch that connects with his head.

It is like being run down by a tank. As he flies backwards

through the air, Peter's vision completely blacks over—his lights are shot. Landing on his back, he loses track of where he is or what he's doing as his vision gradually returns and he gazes up at the inky sky. At the full moon.

The air is kicked out of his lungs. Castillo's huge boot colliding with his ribcage. Blood sprays from his mouth. He tries to get up on his right arm but it's so dead he stumbles. Far away someone is laughing at him and it takes a while to realize it's Castillo. As he tries to get up Peter is reminded of the gas generator they had at the farm. Sometimes, especially when it was below zero, it would take ages to kick the thing over, Peter constantly pulling on the starter handle as it choked and coughed and spluttered into existence. That was him now. Trying to restart his engine. Choking and spluttering back into existence.

"Get up, Peter! Get up!"

Halfway up, he folds his feet underneath and raises himself from the grass. Dizzy and with double vision, he teeters from side to side, his heavy fists slowly coming up before him.

Castillo is beside himself with laughter. Peter had wondered why he didn't just finish him while he was on the floor. He thinks he knows now. It is because Castillo wants to take his time. Wants to pull Peter apart bit by bit like a child with a captured butterfly.

Recalling why he's there, Peter glances up the ridge. There's no sign of the others. Turning back to Castillo, he realizes that this is the place where he will die. At the side of the 101 southbound just outside of Fort Romie, close to the Salinas River. On a late summer night, he will die in a ditch, beaten to death by a giant. But at least they are away.

At least his death will mean something if they all get to safety.

Then a thought fills him as Castillo smiles, and Peter realizes that he might not die after all.

The big man lunges. Peter ducks under the blow and runs for the Mercedes. Diving on top, he drops inside and begins crawling through the middle of the overturned minivan till he reaches the dead body of Raul Lozano. Castillo goes after him, squeezes himself through the opening and grabs ahold of Peter's foot. He tugs him, hauls Peter back, almost gets him up to him, reeling him in like a fishermen with a net. But a kick to the face makes him lose his grip and Peter escapes, pulling himself into the rear of the van, where he takes ahold of something heavy and uses every ounce of strength left to heave it around and face Castillo. Only then, when staring down the barrel of Ma Deuce, does the giant realize he's dead.

"David has his slingshot," Peter remarks before pulling the duel triggers.

Can you imagine the damage done to a human body by an antitank gun from close range? It would be similar to spraying a paper target with an Uzi. Shooting butter with hot knives.

The .50-caliber rounds explode from the gun, shell casings arcing out the side of it. The huge bullets pummel Castillo, turning the bull into a joint of beef, sending him back against the windshield like a hit from a freight train, punching holes through him, busting out the Lexan windshield. The only movement from Castillo comes from the continual onslaught, his body jerking as it is quickly turned to pink mist. The rapid fire keeps him pinned, and when one hits his face, the huge skull flies apart and Peter lets go of the triggers.

By the end, Carlos Castillo is nothing but a beaten-up slab of meat. There is nothing recognizable about him. Even his black clothing is in shreds, some of it smoking.

With his ears ringing and the smell of burning flesh in his nostrils, Peter scrambles out of the Mercedes and staggers up the ridge, slipping and falling several times, his whole body in terrible pain, his vision snowy, head pounding. But alive. Still alive. Just.

NINETY-EIGHT

MARTA SPOTS PETER STAGGERING DOWN FROM THE trees, slipping on the sloping gravel before regaining traction. She thanks God he's made it. She's not sure she can do the rest of this alone.

On the other side of the ridge from the 101, the land drops all the way down to a back road that cuts through Pine Canyon. The others wait outside a second Mercedes minivan. This one lacks Ma Deuce in the back, but it's still armored. It is what Peter had pointed Marta to on the map. One of the many spare minivans he's placed along their route. It was very, very lucky that they were stopped only two miles from this one. Once more the God of war has tossed the dice in Peter's favor.

Kate steps toward him as he reaches the group.

"Peter, where have you been all these years?" She's sobbing. "Who are all these people trying to kill us?"

All he can do is stare down at his shoes. "I don't have time to explain."

"Mom, don't you think he looks familiar?"

Peter turns to Michael.

"I told you," Kate tells her son. "I knew him before."

"No. Familiar from somewhere else. Like *I've* seen him before."

"Where?"

"Pacific Grove."

Kate looks confused as she asks, "What are you talking about, Mikey?"

Panic spreads through Peter, creeping all over him, making him hum into his teeth. Michael steps right up to him. Looks right into his face as Peter does his best to avoid eye contact.

"*Mr. Adams?*" the kid says slowly.

Peter is rigid, his aching chest going in and out, fists curled at his sides, fingers pressed into his palms. Kate narrows her eyes.

"Are you our neighbor Mr. Adams?" Michael asks.

His pierced eyes burn into Peter.

"Look," Marta insists, "we need to keep moving. There's still that helicopter somewhere. So get in the van."

The twelve-year-old continues to stare up at Peter. "It *is* you, isn't it?"

Marta claps a fist against the side of the van. The clattering thump makes everyone turn to her.

"I said get in the van!" she shouts. "That is unless you wanna wait around to get shot."

NINETY-NINE

THE SECOND CAR RIDE IS MUCH CALMER THAN THE first. Marta drives them southeast toward the Sierra Nevada mountain range at a steady pace. Clouds cover the full moon, drenching the road in darkness. Michael and Kate sit behind the driver. The kid is fast asleep. Kate isn't. She stares blankly out of the window at the passing fields, the elastic starting to slowly recoil back. Peter, Theresa and Marie sit right at the back. Where Ma Deuce had sat in the last Mercedes. The little girl is curled up asleep like a cat, her head rested on her mother's lap.

Twenty minutes into the journey Peter decides to scratch an itch that's been bothering him for some time. Turning to Theresa, he says in a hushed voice, "I think it's time we spoke."

Theresa doesn't say anything. She merely nods.

"I was hired to kill James Wilson," he tells her, "Ken Knight and yourself. I would like to know why."

Her face goes solemn. She glances down at her daughter then back at him. "I have a question first," she says.

"Go ahead."

"Why *didn't* you kill me?"

He thinks about it. Then says, "Because you don't deserve it."

"But you killed James and the lawyer. Didn't you?"

Peter nods.

"Why did they deserve it and not me?"

He thinks about it. Then he answers. "Maybe they didn't. But I could switch my feelings off with them. Make it just another mission. With you, I couldn't."

"Why not?"

He says it straight away. "You remind me of my mother."

This makes her smile softly at him. There is an element of pity in it.

"Then I guess I'd better tell you," she says.

There follows a terrible tale only too common in today's decadent world. Theresa is nine when she gets taken into care. Her parents are drug addicts. She spends her early years in neglect, hardly going to school, often homeless. Though structured, the orphanages and children's shelters she ends up in are even worse because, like Peter, she discovers the world of abuse. The first chance she gets, she escapes.

By fourteen Theresa da Silva is on the streets selling the only commodity she has that is marketable: herself.

The thing that gets her tangled up with Peter happened almost eight years ago. Theresa da Silva is fifteen when her pimp drives her out to this huge estate on the edge of Beverly Hills. She and another girl of only eleven, sit side by side in the back of a sedan that is being driven up a winding carriageway to the type of stone mansion you'd expect to find some Hollywood legend living in. "It actually looked like a castle," Theresa tells Peter as the minivan climbs the hills around Bakersfield. "They said it once belonged to Howard Hughes, the really rich guy from the '50s."

Theresa and the other girl are led inside by the pimp. There is no one there to greet them but all the lights are on and the doors open. When they'd pulled up at the entrance to the driveway in the pimp's Toyota, the huge iron gate had automatically opened. Footsteps echo across the marble floor of the vast hallway and a man appears. He is in his sixties and dressed like money. Ralph Lauren polo shirt. Fawn-colored Armani chinos. His pink skin smooth as mahogany, hair as white as bone, cheeks that practically glow. "He had this really fierce look to him," Theresa explains. "His eyes were almost black and when he looked at you it was like he was staring into you, not at you. And he had no smell. Like he washed himself in bleach or something. Or he just wasn't there."

Her breathing goes hard. Peter senses an oncoming panic attack.

"You don't have to go on," he assures her.

"It's, *huh*, okay," she says breathlessly.

Theresa takes a while to collect herself. Then continues.

Money exchanges hands, the pimp leaves, and the man asks the girls to follow him. He walks them down a long corridor, their young heads filled with the wonder of their luxuriant surroundings. "He took us to what they called a rumpus room," she says. "But it looked more like the war room of some medieval king. All the walls were paneled in oak. There were bookcases so high they needed steps on runners to reach them. There were two pool tables and a snooker table. Antiques, he said. There were leather couches everywhere. More antique furniture. The type you'd expect to see at Versailles—and God knows what else. It was insane."

Another man was inside the huge study awaiting their arrival. One who was much younger than his companion. Their fierce guide told them they were father and son, and while the severe father draped an arm each around their waif shoulders like a cat with two sparrows, the son stared at his shoes, unable to lift his face, his nervous fingers peeling the label off a beer bottle.

"He looked like he wanted to get away from there just as bad as we did."

"It was James Wilson, wasn't it?" Peter says.

She nods.

"So the other man must have been Frederick Wilson?"

Theresa shudders. She goes to speak but almost gags on the word. All she can do is nod.

For the next minute Peter lets her get her breathing back to normal. Then she recommences her story. It doesn't get any better.

It just keeps getting worse.

"'I want to teach my son how to be a man,' that sour old bastard tells us. 'To be strong and to taste forbidden fruit.'"

Fred offers drinks. The girls agree. Anything to take the edge off and stop the shivering. They sit down. Try to make themselves feel comfortable. The drinks arrive. They taste bitter. "The fierce one," she can't say his name, "he did all the talking. I don't remember much about what we talked about. I think he just asked us random questions. Where we went to school. If we had boyfriends. If either of us were virgins. Stuff like that. I remember his voice sounding like it was getting farther and farther away until it was like I was listening to him from another room."

"You were drugged?"

She nods. "I thought we'd been taken there to have sex. But really that motherfucker had sold us to that rich bastard."

Tears stream down her face as Theresa tells him about waking up in a basement lined with excavated stone. The two girls in separate barred cells. A gynecologist's chair in an opposite corner. "It was like some medieval dungeon," Theresa sobbed. "And like a dungeon, it had a torture studio." She fully breaks down at this point. "What that bastard, huh, did to us down there, huh, should never be forgiven. *Never*."

Her voice changed on the last word. Like the horror itself was speaking.

The girls wake up in cages. Heavy metal dog collars are locked around their necks. Searching them with their fingers, they can't find any way of getting them off. It is then that the two men enter the scene. James Wilson trailing his father, his head hunched between his shoulders.

Theresa's face screws into hate as she speaks. "The fierce one, he stands there and he tells us straight out how it's gonna be. Tells us that we ain't the first girls he's had down there and we won't be the last. It's up to us just how long we want to live."

For the next twenty minutes the billionaire property tycoon Frederick Wilson tells those girls a secret that he hides from the world. He tells them that he is a rapist. A proud rapist. Always has been and always will be. He says nature made him that way and who was he to fight nature. Says that unlike rapists among the common man, he was able to enjoy his *hobby* ("That's what he called it.") with full impunity. He can make a place like this basement and hide away in it. Have men like their pimp bring him an endless supply of lost girls. Many years later, Theresa tells Peter, "That old sack of shit stood there telling us how he would spend the next days, weeks, months raping us in every conceivable way. He said, and these were his words"—her face is full of disgust—"he said, 'I've been doing this a long time, so I know exactly what I'm doing. I know every way to hurt a person and every way to give them pleasure. It will be up to you which one you get.' Then he turns to Gemma—that's the other girl—and says..." Theresa da Silva stumbles, sniffs, glances down at the snoozing face of her daughter. "He says," she goes on, "that 'perhaps given the chance, some of you may begin to enjoy the pain more than the pleasure.' Telling us that it had happened before with girls he had down there."

She closes her eyes and tips her head back, breathing deeply through her lips and making them tremble. When she exhales, a low, howling moan comes out with the air.

Before he knows what he's doing, Peter reaches a hand across and lays it gently on her shoulder. She opens her eyes and swivels her head sideways.

"How did you escape?" he asks.

The eyelids shut up tight once more. Her lips twist and she answers. "James."

Peter had thought as much.

"By that point," she goes on, "Gemma was dead. That bastard, uh, he, eh, he, well, he killed her within the first week. I won't even begin to explain to you how. All of it is way too fucking haunting." She cringes, swallows, continues. "Then for a whole month it was just me. In the end, bored, the bastard was just gonna put a bullet in my head. Get himself another girl. But James took pity. He came down one night and let me go. Put me in a car and drove me outta there. I got him to take me north to San Jose. It was where I grew up. He gave me some money but I can't remember what I did with it. I spent the next months wandering the streets until I got picked up eating garbage. The cops took me to a psychiatric hospital. It was there that they found out I was three months pregnant. Too late for an abortion."

She has the baby. Marie. The girl in her lap. Child of her rapist. Far from taking her further over the edge, however, the pregnancy is good for her. She has a kind of *opposite* postpartum psychosis. Rather than send her spiraling into her despairing mind, the child focuses her energies and the clouds of her psyche clear. Theresa da Silva has purpose. Theresa da Silva knows what she is. Theresa da Silva is a mother.

"So how come you decided to go after them?" Peter asks.

"I didn't. I wanted to just forget about it."

"So what happened?"

"It was James. He showed up at my apartment one night. I started having a panic attack the second I opened the door. He helps me inside, then, once I'm okay, he starts bawling his eyes out. Saying how sorry he is. How he knows that he can never make it right. How he wants the world to know the truth about his father and how he wants me to help him uncover it."

"Fred Wilson must have found out," Peter muses aloud.

"Yeah." She thinks about it. Then, with her eyes on Marie, adds, "How could a person have their own child killed?"

Peter's reply is stark and personally honest. "The wolf," he tells the young mother, "will always choose to eat its own young in order to survive."

ONE HUNDRED

IT'S NOT UNTIL THEY HIT THE MOUNTAIN ROADS that Kate's eyes come alive and she looks away from the passing hills. Whipping her head around, she comes face-to-face with Peter sitting behind her.

Her eyes shimmer. "Peter?" she whispers.

"Yes, Kate."

"Peter, did you really live just meters away? Was that you? Paul Adams?"

Peter swallows and tells her that it was.

She is stunned. "You mean that you lived right next to us all that time and never said a thing?"

"I couldn't," is all he can say.

"Why would you do that?"

Taking a deep breath, he tells her, "Because I was trapped between two states. I knew I couldn't be with you, but at the same time, I couldn't stay away."

"You watched us?"

He nods.

"I used to see you," she says. "Sitting up on your balcony."

His eyes drop. It is all too much. The lump in his throat is threatening to choke him.

"It used to make me so sad," she says. "To see Paul—*you*—up there all alone. No family. No friends. Just you."

"I should have stayed away," he mumbles.

"Is that why they came for us—to hurt *you*?"

He nods.

"Why didn't you ever say something?" she goes on. "Just let me know you were there." There's a terrible melancholic pleading to her tone. "All these years I spent wondering where you were, and you were right there."

"I'm so sorry, Kate."

"Please, Peter. Tell me why you didn't come and see me?"

She lifts his face by the chin and forces him to meet her eyes.

"I would have," he says in a tremulous voice. "But you'd gotten on with your life. Married Carl. Had Michael. I didn't want to ruin it. Carl was so much better for you than me. He's a giver. All I know how to do is take life and destroy things. I'm a taker, Kate. Every life I've ever touched has suffered as a consequence. Including yours."

"Oh, Peter," she breathes gently. "What have they done to you?"

ONE HUNDRED ONE

HIGH UP IN THE MOUNTAINS OF THE SIERRA Nevada, they pull off the road onto a sloping track that rises up through endless pine. In a clearing stands a tiny trailer. Next to it is a Ford Ranger pickup covered over in blue tarpaulin. The thick and snaggled branches of several Douglas fir trees crowd around the hideout, shielding it from the main road.

Marta parks the Mercedes beside the Ford. While Theresa and Michael help her pull tarp over the minivan, Peter checks the fencepost on the corner of the lot. The one facing the trailer and the pickup. He pulls the camera from it, plugs the USB into an adapter, plugs that into his phone.

In the eight weeks he's been away, nothing has been here except coyotes and the wind.

Peter and Marta take shovels from the trailer and lead the others into the woods. At a clearing, they begin digging and scraping the dry earth away from the metal hatch buried in the hillside.

"Mommy, I'm cold," Marie complains as she holds on to her mother's waist.

"It's okay, sweet pea," Theresa assures her. "We'll be warm soon."

"I'm scared."

"There's no need to be. Everything will be okay."

Peter and Marta pull back the tarp, revealing the hatch doors. On a hill, they're at an angle. Punching in the code and creaking them open, Peter tells the others to go inside.

They look apprehensive.

"What is it?" Kate asks.

"A safe place," Peter tells her.

Michael stands beside his mother, gazing uneasily at their strange neighbor. Then at the pitch black beyond the doors. He can't help thinking about that Austrian guy. The one who kept his daughter in the basement.

"Momma," Marie shrieks, "I don't wanna go down there."

To the child, the open hatch looks like the gaping jaws of some man-eating creature buried in the hillside.

"It's okay," Michael says gently to the little girl. "I'll show you there's nothing to be afraid of."

Marie watches the twelve-year-old step past everyone and make his way to the open hatch. Marta and Peter stand either side of it. Smiling back at the girl, Michael says, "See," and steps into the darkness.

That's when something terrible happens.

An alarm goes off. One which makes Peter feel sick.

Red light flashes in the cellar.

"Mommy?!" Marie cries, throwing herself into Theresa.

Peter grabs ahold of Michael. Wrenches him out of the cellar.

"Hey, wait!" the kid cries as Peter manhandles him, lifting his leg up, sending him down onto his back.

Peter rips his sneaker off, lets go of the leg and—as everyone watches—checks every conceivable angle of the white Nike high top.

"Peter, what are you doing?" Kate asks.

He doesn't say a word as his eyes survey the shoe, his fingers feeling it like the grasping tentacles of some blind creature, flexing the sole, until he feels something hard in the center.

Using his hunting knife, Peter cuts open the sneaker and finds what he's looking for. A small device no larger than a penny.

A tracking bug.

Looking up at Marta, he says, "You didn't check them?"

She looks distraught. "Raul was about to when the chopper showed up. Since then I forgot in all the chaos. I'm so sorry."

Blinding light rises up from the trees, taking all their attentions. A searchlight beam cuts through the black air and illuminates everything in garish white. The jagged shadows of the pine stretch along the ground, the canopies waving about, the dust and dried bracken swirling in the air.

"Into the hatch!" Peter shouts as the minigun on the side of the attack helicopter begins rotating.

"Momma!" Marie screams as bullets chop the dirt up in front of Theresa, stitching a line all the way to her.

Theresa da Silva's last act as a mother is to push her child clear. Marie falls heavily onto her front as Theresa takes the full brunt of the minigun. It chops her down in seconds and she is dead before she hits the ground.

"*Momma!*" Marie shrieks, getting up from the dirt and running to Theresa's body.

The others are in the doorway of the hatch.

"Kate, no, don't!" Peter cries as she runs from the hatch to the little girl.

"Momma, Momma," Marie is sobbing into the body of Theresa, holding on for dear life, face buried into the bloody chest, the mother's eyes open on the black sky.

The minigun charges again—its aim on Kate as she runs to the girl. The pilot's eyes narrow as he sinks the trigger.

Then those same eyes widen.

They widen because of what he's just seen in the corner of his vision. Peter has emerged from the hatch shouldering an MK 153 shoulder-launched multipurpose assault weapon. Basically, a US military-grade RPG (rocket-propelled grenade) launcher.

The pilot has time to see the thing fire, pull the chopper violently to the left, spot the rocket change its own course to match, and then—*boom!* The chopper explodes in a flash and the pine woods get scattered with innumerable pieces of smoldering rubble.

There's no time to rejoice. As the searchlight goes out and the flaming fuselage falls down through the trees, shots come from the woods. Six men in black body armor fan through the pine toward their location.

In the meantime, Kate is trying to prize Marie from Theresa. But the bloodied child has her arms around the dead body and is holding on for dear life.

Michael goes to run from the hatch but Peter grabs him, throwing him back into the cellar.

"We can't just leave her out there," the kid pleads.

"Take him," Peter says to Marta, who obliges, grabbing Michael by the arm.

Peter turns his eyes back on the scene. Bullets cut the ground up around Kate and Marie. The men aren't quite in range yet. With the MK out and not enough time to reload it, Peter drops the RPG launcher and unshoulders an HK G36 assault rifle.

As he runs from the hatch, he sprays covering fire at the trees. Kate has finally gotten Marie off her dead mother and she is hauling her toward the hatch.

That is when she suddenly falls and spills the child.

"No!" Peter cries.

He stands still and aims the HK at the shadows moving about the trees, showering their positions with bullets, forcing the attackers to retreat into cover.

"Momma!" Marie cries out as she runs back to Theresa.

Kate is on the floor when Peter reaches her. He shoulders the HK and rapidly checks her over. She has been shot in the stomach. There's a lot of blood and he prays that nothing vital has been hit. Picking her up, he carries her inside.

Once in the cellar, Peter lays Kate down, returns to the entrance, and pulls the doors shut with a bang.

ONE HUNDRED TWO

THE SIX-MAN TEAM EMERGE SLOWLY FROM THE trees, creeping cautiously toward the hatch. Sideways steps, bullpups to their shoulders, single tube night-vision goggles covering their faces. Six black cyclops coming to get them, slithering silently through the night, the wreckage of the attack helicopter smoldering in the background.

Marie lies over Theresa.

"What do we do about the girl?" Number One asks into his comms.

From his faraway command center, Operation Commander replies in his ear, "Take her with you. The client may want her."

"Copy that, Commander."

Number One nods at Number Two. He goes to the girl.

"*No!*" Marie shrieks as a black-gloved hand makes a rough grab for her. Before she knows what's happening, he's zip-tied her tiny wrists and ankles and she lies hogtied.

Facedown, Marie no longer makes a sound. She stays

still, her tear-drowned eyes staring along the dirt ground at her dead mother.

The little girl is sinking into shock.

"Take her to the van," Number One says.

"Yes, sir."

Number Two picks her up, throws the motionless seven-year-old over his shoulder and begins making his way down the hillside.

In the meantime, Numbers Three and Four place plastic explosives on the locked hatch, stand back, and detonate it. The blast breaks the doors off their hinges and sends them crashing inwards. The men then run to the opening and toss frag grenades into the cellar before tear-assing it back to the others.

The two explosions go off in quick succession—*Boom! Boom!* Smoke and debris bursts out of the hatch and the men crouch down as it rains heavily on them from above, thumping and crashing against their helmets.

Number One makes hand signals at Five and Six. The two men nod and head toward the opening in crouched positions, their single ocular scopes lined with the sights of their bullpups. Smoke billows out of the hatch. They step into it and down a set of stairs that are cut into the rock. This used to be the entrance to an old nickel mine. The cellar is the size of a small garage. Things lie blown about. Some clothing has caught fire and smolders in a corner.

"What—you—down there—Five?"

Their comms are frazzled. The two men tap their earpieces.

"Sorry, One, you're breaking up."

"What—got—see, over?"

"There must be something blocking communication," Six says.

The room is empty except for guns and other ordinance. Much of it is scattered about the floor from the blast. A weapons rack occupies the back wall. Most of the guns lie on the floor, blackened with soot. Some cupboards, the doors busted open, line part of the rack. A wardrobe is filled with disguises.

"Where are they?" Five muses aloud as he searches the rack.

"What's this?"

Five turns to Six. The latter is checking the wall adjacent to the shelving and cupboards, running a finger around the eye of something round that is set into the rock. It looks like the end of a tube about the size of a quarter.

"It's metal," he says.

"There's more," Five observes.

Six looks along the excavated stone. The holes dot it, trailing all the way along with gaps of four inches. Looking up the wall, he sees that the rows are on three levels. At one foot. Three feet. And five feet.

"They're on the opposite wall, too," Five says, gazing across the cellar.

"What are they—drainage pipes?"

"The holes are too small. Could be cameras."

"Maybe."

Number Six places an eye to one of them.

It is only then that both men realize what they are. They are gun barrels.

The bullet wrecks his eye, carries on straight through the socket, boring through the frontal lobe, snapping the brainstem and rushing out the back of his skull. Number Five follows him into death within seconds as the guns all fire at once, a scattering of bullets crisscrossing the cellar and filling the men.

The weapons rack slides open in the middle on runners. Peter steps into the chamber, over the two dead men, assault rifle gripped in his hand. He heads for the exit, fury burning in his eyes, and, as he reaches the top of the stone steps, says into the comms mic stuck to his cheek, "Now."

The trees surrounding the hatch explode with white light as innumerable LEDs attached to the pines themselves make the forest shine as bright as any supernova. All wearing night vision, the men are shocked and blinded as Peter climbs out of the bunker and turns the Heckler and Koch on them, sending one man after another into hell, fanning the bucking rifle across them as they struggle to flip their goggles up.

It is only when he kills the last of them that he realizes there are only three.

Where is number four?

Peter gives his incandescent surroundings a quick check. Marie is nowhere to be seen. Only the body of her dead mother. The woman he was supposed to save.

"Marie?!" he shouts into the woods. "Marie?!"

He listens, his heart sinking in his chest.

"Marie?!"

Nothing.

It is only when his despair is almost feverish that he hears a mouse's scream far away.

"Marie?!" Peter shouts as he heads into the trees toward

the trailer and the main road, the Heckler and Koch swinging from his arm. "Marie?!"

"Help!" comes her fading voice.

Approaching the trailer, he hears an engine idling. Then it being slipped into gear. Tires rapidly crunching across gravel, and, by the time he's there, the van is accelerating away down the track, Marie thumping her little fist against the back window until someone snatches her away and she's gone.

Peter stands in the middle of the track watching the van fade into the night. Knowing that he has failed.

That he has failed them all.

ONE HUNDRED THREE

ON THE OTHER SIDE OF THE WEAPONS RACK LIES A vast underground bunker. Peter's very own fortress of solitude buried deep in the Sierra Nevada. Though, quite how long that solitude will last now his enemies know where it is is anyone's guess. It was supposed to be a safe place for him to hide them while he got rid of the client and everyone else. But with three dead, one taken, one badly injured and their location known, Peter must think again.

Rule Four. Never assume. Only plan.

The fortified structure is around the size of a tennis court and designed to withstand a nuclear strike. It has its own power systems, water purification systems, blast valves, and Nuclear-Biological-Chemical (NBC) air filtration. It has food supplies for eighteen months, and includes a hydroponic garden to supplement the rations. It also boasts a medical clinic and gym.

"She's real bad," Marta says the second he enters the clinic. "They've hit the artery. She needs surgery."

Kate is lying on a hospital bed. She is pale and looks terrified. Michael is applying pressure to the wound, his hand shivering, blood pooling from underneath the cloth he holds to it. The bullet has gone right through her, nicking the celiac trunk on its way.

"I've got Epoetin," Peter says.

"Good. It'll help stimulate erythropoietin. But we'll still need blood as well."

Marta goes to ask Kate her type when Peter says, "She's type O negative. I have it in the fridge."

Peter is about to fetch it when Kate calls him over.

"I need to tell you something," she says weakly, her face bone white and covered in sweat.

He leans an ear to her colorless lips and as she talks, his face grows ever darker until there is nothing in his glazed eyes. For several seconds after she's finished he stands there, stunned, Kate crying and mouthing the word *sorry*.

"Peter?!" Marta snaps. "We need that blood and the Epoetin. Now! Before we lose her."

Peter shakes himself and runs to the medical cabinets lining the wall of the clinic. First he grabs the vial of Epoetin, before heading to the blood fridge.

"I got it," he says the second he returns to them.

The words hang in the air. He stops dead and all the life rushes out of him.

Michael is holding his mother's hand to his face, crying wildly, his whole body jerking, the tears threatening to wash away the bandage covering his cheek. Marta stands to the side, her own face blanched by melancholy.

Peter leaves the things on a sideboard and goes to her.

"Kate?" he says faintly like a lost child calling for its

mother, gently taking hold of her head, unwilling to believe that she's gone. "Kate?"

He checks the pulse of her neck and when he feels nothing, he howls like a wounded animal at the concrete ceiling of the bunker. He grips her tightly into him, lifting her from the bed and pressing her head into his chest.

"Kate?" he weeps.

Someone hits him and he opens his eyes on Michael.

"Get off her," the son sobs. "Go on! Get off her!"

Peter kisses Kate one last time on the forehead and lays her gently back on the bed. He staggers off into the bunker, throwing himself down onto a bunkbed, curling into the fetal position and humming through his teeth—*"When I'm alone with only dreams of you that won't come true, What'll I do?"*

For the first time in his life Peter questions everything about himself. Every decision he's ever made. And he sums it up that he is simply a faulty human being. A taker of the worst proportions.

To make it even more painful, her last words revolve around his head like a curse.

"Peter," she had whispered, *"Michael is your son."*

Inwardly, he had known it all along. But he had hoped—had despaired—that it wasn't true. That Michael belonged to Carl. Not to the terrible darkness that was himself.

"Peter?" Marta says, coming over the bed. "Peter, there will be more coming and they will come with bombs and machines. We're not safe here."

"What'll I do when you are far away and I am blue, What'll I do?"

"Peter!" Marta snaps at him, crouching beside the bed

and bringing her eyes level with his. "Now is not the time to go to pieces. They know where we are."

"What'll I do?"

She shakes him roughly. "God damn it! Listen to me. Do you want him dying as well, huh? Her son. You still have a mission, Peter. Because I can't stay here if it means death. My daughter has already lost her daddy; I can't let her lose me."

Her words penetrate his gloom. He pinches his eyelids closed, tears sprinkling over their edges. When they are open, he searches the bunker. Landing on the boy, who holds on dearly to his dead mother, Peter mumbles, "Michael," as if a new resolution is raising itself up inside of him.

ONE HUNDRED FOUR

SHE COULDN'T CONVINCE EITHER OF THEM TO leave the body. So Peter loaded it up into the Mercedes, lying Kate across the rear end under tarp, and once more they hit the road.

Somewhere outside of Merrill just over the state border into Oregon, they drop Marta off. She is changed and disguised. Loaded with false papers to get her to her hideaway where Nikita awaits.

Standing next to the open driver's window, she leans in and kisses Peter goodbye on the cheek.

"I'm so sorry, Marta," he tells her.

"Don't be. Raul wouldn't be sore. These past years have been the best of our lives."

"Say hello to Nikita for me."

"I will."

The kid is staring straight ahead. He hasn't spoken a word since watching his mother die.

"Goodbye, Michael."

He doesn't respond.

She leans through the window, across the van, and touches his hand.

Still nothing.

"Good luck," she says once she's retracted herself. "Both of you."

Peter watches Marta Lozano disappear down an alleyway that splits two buildings in the tiny town. She has her own escape plan. Her own way back to her daughter.

Peter has no such thing. The bunker was it. Now there is nowhere he can go. Nowhere. He and the boy are all alone in the world. All alone and being mercilessly hunted.

ONE HUNDRED FIVE

OREGON, 2019

Two hours. Thirty-eight minutes. Six seconds. That was how long their reunion had lasted.

Peter needs somewhere to think, so he books into a motel under the Dwayne Peterson persona. It's on an Oregon backroad in the middle of the Willamette National Forest, not far from Rainbow. Giant redwoods rise up around a collection of log cabins that are mostly used by the truckers who transport timber across the state.

"Will it be just you and your boy?" the old-timer behind the counter asks.

Silver hairs stick out of the proprietor's ears and glint in the sunshine flooding the small reception. A stuffed pike is mounted on the wall behind him and a stuffed raccoon guards the countertop.

"It sure will," Peter replies, glancing out the dusty window at the Mercedes. At his *boy* sitting leaned to the side in the front passenger seat. His unseen hands zip-tied to the steering column so he can't run away.

Dressed as Dwayne Peterson, complete with pregnancy belt, Peter takes the end cabin. As far from the reception shack as possible. He cuts Michael loose and guides him into the room. The kid hasn't slept. Hasn't eaten. Hasn't said a word. All he's done for the entire journey is stare forward as the minivan eats up road. The dead body of his mother lying in the back under a sheet of tarp.

Peter has absolutely no idea what he will do with her.

Or with *him,* for that matter.

Inside the musty room, Michael takes a shower while Peter sits on the end of a bed watching TV. The news is on, Peter staring at it blankly, certain theories being confirmed, the volume on loud so he can hear it over the hissing sound of the shower.

"A nightmare in suburbia," the stick-thin reporter says into her mic as she stands on the sidewalk outside 24 Green Street. *"This is the home of one Paul Adams. The man being dubbed the Creep. A local recluse, Adams lived among the community of Pacific Grove for four years, all the while hiding a terrible secret from his unsuspecting neighbors. Little did they know but Paul Adams was a monster of the very worst variety. One who was watching over them all. Waiting for an opportunity to strike."*

Still pictures of 24's basement fill the screen.

"These are the images of Adams's lair that police have released," the reporter explains over the top. *"This image shows the secret room Adams had fitted with surveillance equipment to spy on his neighbors, using his knowledge as a tech wiz to listen in on their telephone conversations. Even turning their*

own devices against them. Remotely hijacking the cameras of smartphones to watch them. Microphones to listen in. And not only that, but Adams had a sordid collection of photographs and items taken from neighbors. Trophies, police are calling them."

The basement at 24 Green Street had been empty except for the twin washer-dryer and his weights when Peter left the house five days ago. The images they are showing now on Fox News are staged. Photographs line walls that were nothing but gray breeze block the last time he'd seen them. They now contain photos of his unsuspecting neighbors. Pictures of their children. Most likely taken by the same men who stalked their rooftops.

Other images on the TV show plastic containers filled with underwear. Mostly children's. Boxes packed with stuffed animals.

"Several hard drives," the reporter's voice echoes in Peter's head, *"were also discovered at the home, and once the police's computer forensics team cracked the passwords, they discovered thousands of images of child pornography. Some, the police are saying, that were so depraved they will haunt the detectives for the rest of their lives."*

The footage returns to the facade of 24 Green Street. The reporter is standing with a Monterey detective at the end of Paul Adams's driveway. The Saab 900 is no longer there. Probably in the Monterey Police Department's forensic garage being pulled apart. A slither of Mrs. Harrison's house can be seen on the right of the screen. Peter observes that the curtains of her bedroom are still open.

"I'm joined here by Detective Holbrook of the Monterey

Police Department," the reporter says. "*Detective, can you perhaps take us into the mind of someone like Paul Adams?*"

"*Mr. Adams is what we call an obsessive voyeur,*" the ham-faced detective tells her. "*Or at least that's how he started. He arrived here in Pacific Grove four years ago and quickly went about renovating the basement to how you see it in those photographs. Filling it with state-of-the-art surveillance equipment. So, like a spider feeling its web, he sat listening out for the vibrations of his neighborhood.*"

Detective Holbrook grins. He looks pleased with his use of metaphor. Peter notices the reporter gently roll her eyes.

"*And is this how he honed in on the Hendersons?*"

"*Yes. We believe he became obsessed with them. Neighbors would always see him in close proximity to the family. You see, this type of psychopath starts with stalking his general area. Watching each and every person in that given space. Like a lion stalking prey. Collecting information on possible targets. Then he begins shrinking the field down to a few candidates. Until, finally, he has his victim. In this case Michael Henderson and his mother Kate Henderson.*"

"*What happened last night?*"

"*All hell broke loose is what happened. Paul Adams decided he didn't want to just sit and watch and listen no longer. Like we see with a lot of voyeurs, watching soon wasn't enough.*"

"*But how does that account for the apparent shoot-out on the street?*"

His face going serious, the detective explains, "*The Hendersons had been receiving threatening mail. At their home, we found hundreds of notes we now know were hand-delivered by Paul Adams.*"

"Did they ever go to the police?"

"Unfortunately not. Kate Henderson went to her boss instead. A lawyer at a city law firm, he paid for her to have a private security team watch over the family. It is they who Adams engaged in the street last night. Killing all six men."

"And would this have links to the incidents in San Jose and on the 101 highway?"

The detective's face darkened. "Those incidents aren't covered by this police department, I'm afraid. So I'm unable to comment."

"And are you able to comment on the whereabouts of Michael and Kate Henderson at this time?"

Detective Holbrook took on a solemn look. "I wish I could, but I can't. Nevertheless, that doesn't mean we don't have every available resource throughout the entire country now looking for Michael and Kate."

"And what is the likelihood that the Hendersons are still alive?"

"I believe Adams has a purpose for them. So I do think they are alive."

"Thank you, Detective."

"No. Thank you."

The camera moves away from Holbrook and hones in on the reporter as she steps toward it, making eye contact with the viewers back home—with Peter sitting on the end of the bed dressed like a fat hick.

"Earlier on," she says, "we spoke to the neighbors of Pacific Grove who were only just waking up to the terrible events of last night."

The curly hair and pleasant face of Mrs. Murphy fills the

screen. Sandy held tightly in the crook of her arm like a large purse.

"*I'm like everyone else,*" she says. "*I feel duped by him. I honestly thought he was pleasant. Not overly friendly, but decent at least. Quiet. But, then, isn't that what they always say about these types?*"

She looks into the camera as if genuinely asking.

Peter's blood boils as Jimmy Palmer comes on. He is buried up to his waist in plaster, sitting in a wheelchair, his wife Lyn holding the handles. Both his wrists are heavily plastered and pins poke out of the crushed hand.

"*I always knew he were a pervert,*" Palmer says, a look of triumph on his face like his team has just won the Super Bowl. "*I always saw him hangin' out around the kids. I was the only one who ever had the guts to tell him to his face.*"

He doesn't mention getting his arm broken for the pleasure.

Jack and Kenny Ronson are perplexed.

"*We thought he was sweet,*" Kenny says.

"*Just shows you how wrong you can be,*" Jack adds to his husband's comment with a shake of the head.

Judy and Glenn Chambers always thought something was a little fishy about him. Joining Jimmy Palmer in the "knew it all along" camp.

The Jamesons reminisce about the Hendersons.

"*They were such a nice family,*" Harriet Jameson says. "*Never did no harm. Always good. As for Paul Adams, I can't tell you nothin'. Only that he's truly evil if it was him that killed Carl and took Michael and Kate.*"

"*Utter shame,*" Frank Jameson adds with a sad shake of

the head, his Hawaiian shirt done up to the collar as a mark of respect.

Lastly is the Jenkinses.

"Well, we always suspected him," came the rasping voice of Pamela Jenkins, her red-nosed husband nodding away beside her. *"A month ago we called Child Protective Services on him. We saw a man go around but heard nothing more. If you ask me, the CPS ought to be ashamed of themselves. Maybe if they had done their jobs back then, he wouldn't have hurt that poor family."*

Peter is more sure of everything by the second as he listens to his former neighbors. He is thinking about plan Bs and how *theirs* was to make sure that if he turned on them, they would be able to clean up afterwards and make it all look like nothing more than a single crazy person doing what single crazy people usually do: going crazy. Peter's odd existence in Pacific Grove had leant itself to their version of events, and all they had to do was put a few props in his house and in the Hendersons' house.

Peter is thinking about this when he hears shuffling and creaking sounds coming from the bathroom. The cramped cabin has a main room with two beds and a sectioned-off bathroom taking up a rear corner. A window at the end looks out onto a stretch of dirt that leads to the woods.

Peter sits up sharp when he spots Michael running past it, having escaped through the bathroom window. He sprints out of the room. At the back of the cabin is a bank of dirt that rises steeply to the woods. The kid is almost at the top.

Peter catches Michael when the twelve-year-old trips on a thick root sticking out like a foot and falls onto his front no more than ten meters into the field of colossal trees. He's out of breath and struggling to get back to his feet.

He flips onto his back. His face is red going purple. He looks like he wants to make a sound, but can't. His mouth moves like a suffocating fish. He's having a panic attack and if he doesn't calm it soon he is going to faint.

Peter holds him tightly, the boy trying to push him away, but getting nowhere. He gets down in the leaves with him. The two on their sides together, Peter humming the tune in his ear.

"What'll I do when you are far away and I am—"

The kid elbows him in the ribs. Peter narrowly avoiding the back of his flipping head as it tries to butt him.

"You're having a panic attack," he tells Michael. "You have to take your mind off it. Listen to me sing. Concentrate on my voice. It will help."

And so Peter goes on singing, the kid's breathing gradually calming down. The two of them lying together in the middle of the woods, the haunting song echoing within the trees.

ONE HUNDRED SIX

"Pat?"

"Peter, thank God. What the hell happened?"

It's eleven o'clock the next morning. Peter is standing in the cigarette stench of a telephone booth. It's attached to the outer wall of a roadside diner on the outskirts of Eugene. Michael is in the Mercedes. His hands are zip-tied to the steering column and the minivan is parked where Peter can keep an eye on it.

"They've made me the fall guy," he tells his handler.

"But you had an out, didn't you?"

"Yeah. They just guessed it was all."

"Shit. Where are you now?"

"Best not to get into that over the phone."

"Good idea. We'll communicate further on our usual channel. Speak soon."

. . .

In Eugene, Peter finds a cybercafé that is nestled within the backstreets of the downtown area. So close to midday, the sidewalks are too crowded to leave the kid in the Mercedes. He could easily signal for help. Or worse: someone could spot his hands zip-tied to the steering column. So Peter hustles Michael into the café, a red-and-white-striped sweatshirt hung over the kid's hands to hide the fact his wrists are bound.

The kid stares forward at all times, moving listlessly ahead step by step with each of Peter's prods as they tread out of the late morning sun into the shadows of the café. Booths line the outer walls, the heavy blinds of the windows all closed. A few are occupied by gamers, their faces illuminated in the garish colors of the screens. Close to the entrance, a clerk stands at a counter. Behind him is a polished metal Fracino espresso machine. The gloomy air of the café smells of old coffee and vape pens. On the counter are some unhappy-looking pastries in a glass case and a fruit bowl filled with dry muffins. The remains of the balding clerk's straw-colored hair is tied into a small ponytail that sits at the nape of his neck, and Peter notices that his upper right incisor is missing when he smiles at them.

"Howdy," he says. "How can I help you folks?"

"A booth, please. One at the rear."

In the background a TV news channel plays. Peter catches the reporter's faint voice say, *"Police and FBI are still searching for Paul Adams..."* He can't help glancing over at the television hanging from a wall in the corner. There are grainy CCTV images of himself as Paul Adams alongside a portrait photo of Michael.

"Take number nine," the guy says. "It's over there in the corner." He nods in its direction.

"Thank you."

"You want any coffee? Pastries?"

"Not for me."

"What about you, kid?"

The clerk's eyes are on Michael.

Peter asks him if he'd like something to eat and the kid says nothing. Doesn't make a move. Like he never even registered Peter's voice.

"Jonathon," Peter says, using the prearranged name, "I asked you if you'd like something to eat."

Michael continues to stare blankly ahead, the sweatshirt looped over his wrists made to look like he's carrying it.

"Hey, son," the clerk says. "We got some nice Danishes. Chocolate cookies."

Still nothing.

Earlier in the motel cabin Peter had colored Michael's hair black. All the while he did it, the kid just sat there not saying a single word.

The clerk starts to wrinkle his brows as he stares into Michael's blank eyes. Thankfully, they both look very different to the photos on TV. For one, no one has informed the police that Michael recently had stitches down his face. The bandage hides part of his cheek and nose. Further disguising him.

Placing his eyes back on Peter, the clerk asks, "He autistic or something?"

"Asberger's."

"Oh," the clerk says. "Well, nine's down that way."

. . .

WITH MICHAEL SITTING mute beside him, Peter accesses the computer. He logs onto a VPN he commonly uses and is about to hook onto his and Pat's communication site when he turns to Michael.

"I can't let you go on Facebook or anything like that," he tells him in a hushed voice. "They'll be watching your accounts. But if there's anything you'd like to check, you can."

Michael stays reticent. Just stares ahead. His hands sitting on his lap, buried beneath the sweatshirt. Peter gives it a few seconds before refacing the screen and tapping away on the keyboard. The VPN overrides the parental lock, allowing him to hook onto a pornography site.

Today is a Thursday. The 27th. Odd number. September. Odd month. That means it's Bambi Woods' *Debbie Does Dallas*.

Peter doesn't bother about the porn. He scrolls down to the comments section, looking for GushingGapes69.

There's a message. Six minutes ago. *God, I luv the classics!*

Peter logs into the site and types a message.

BustinBalls88: *u there?*

GushingGapes69: *sure am*

BustinBalls88: *davenport?*

GushingGapes69: *keeps calling. haven't answered. fuck him. we need to think of what to do*

BustinBalls88: *where are you?*

GushingGapes69: *hiding. waiting till fallout over*

BustinBalls88: *I know who client is*

GushingGapes69: *who?*

BustinBalls88: *Fred Wilson*

GushingGapes69: *did girl tell?*

BustinBalls88: *yes*

GushingGapes69: *where she now?*

BustinBalls88: *dead*

There's a slight delay of about thirty seconds. Then:

GushingGapes69: *I told you not to be hero. it makes things very difficult from here*

BustinBalls88: *it was wrong. had to. couldn't help myself*

GushingGapes69: *world is wrong. where you go now?*

BustinBalls88: *Portland safe house*

As he waits for Pat's reply, the computer beeps. Glancing up into the top right corner of the screen he sees the icon of a green bar that has totally filled. It gives him a location.

GushingGapes69: *what are future plans?*

BustinBalls88: *disappear*

GushingGapes69: *good. that would b my advice. I plan doing same*

BustinBalls88: *then maybe we'll meet again in the wind*

GushingGapes69: *maybe old friend maybe*

Peter takes in a deep breath and his jaw tightens as he thinks about the next hours and what he will have to go through.

"Hey! What the fuck?!" the clerk's voice resounds in Peter's ears. "You're watchin' pornography with your darn kid right next to ya? Pervert!"

Peter snaps into action. He quickly comes off the site and out of the VPN. All his search history automatically deleted.

"Jonathon, we need to go," he says to the kid.

Peter gets up from his chair just as the clerk is turning to everyone and bellowing at them, "This son of a bitch was watchin' porn with his kid there."

"Jonathon, come on." Peter attempts to lift Michael by the shoulder. Gently at first, but then rough when the kid just sits there staring forward. "Michael?!" Peter snaps as he grabs him and physically tears the twelve-year-old up off the chair.

It is then that the sweatshirt falls off his wrists, right as the clerk and everyone else turn their eyes on the father and son.

There for all to see are the kid's zip-tied wrists.

"I'm calling the cops!" the clerk bursts out, rushing back to the counter.

Others are on their phones, already calling, some of them taking pictures, the Dwayne Peterson disguise going to shit right there and then.

"Please, Michael," Peter pleads with the kid as the latter refuses to budge. "Please."

Michael faces him. Hate burning in his eyes.

"Please, I'm begging you," Peter goes on. "Please. If the cops come, they'll take you away. And I can't protect you if that happens."

Michael continues to glare at him.

Desperate, Peter says, "Do you want me to punish the people who killed your mom and dad?"

The look on Michael's face changes. Tears well. He nods.

"Then come with me," Peter says, "and I promise the people responsible for their deaths will *all* be punished."

Michael gives in. The two of them flee the shop. No one

bothering to stop them. Just recording them on their phones. When they reach the door, the clerk is speaking to 9-1-1. Michael reaches his bound hands over the counter and snatches the guy's iPhone from his ear. Chucking it out the door into the street, they leave the café.

"Hey!" the clerk shouts after him. "Fucking kid!"

ONE HUNDRED SEVEN

THEY HIT THE ROAD AGAIN, PETER CONTINUOUSLY checking the mirrors. Expecting blue flashing lights. It is only when they reach Salem without incident that his worry dissipates and he's able to concentrate solely on the stretch of gray highway that leads onwards toward revenge.

Michael stares out the window at the smear of bungalows and greenery. The radio plays in the background, Peter waiting for the news to come on. When it does, he turns the volume up.

"KBM News Radio," a harsh voice announces.

"These are the headlines at one o'clock," the newscaster says. *"In further developments in the case involving the abduction of a mother and son from a Monterey suburb, police have now linked the disappearances of two more people to the fugitive Paul Adams. Theresa and Marie da Silva, a* mother and daughter, *were last seen at their San Jose residence on Tuesday night when neighbors reported witnessing similar scenes to those that played out at the same time in Monterey. It is now*

believed that Adams's two neighbors in Pacific Grove, Rosa and Carlos Hernandez, are part of the same pedophile ring that Adams belongs to. The word coming out of Monterey's sheriff's office is that it was in fact the Hernandezes who killed Carl Henderson and the security detail before abducting Kate and Michael Henderson. While, at the same time, seventy miles north in San Jose, Paul Adams was active in the kidnapping of the da Silvas, as well as a bomb that went off nearby killing two men. We'll have more on this later."

Peter switches it off.

For the next minutes they travel in silence. Then.

"Why did my mother say those things to you?"

Peter glances sideways from the road. Michael is staring across the car at him. These are the first words he's said since the night his mother died.

"What was your mother saying?"

"I heard her asking you where you've been. What had happened to you." He let this sink in for a moment. "You're *him*, aren't you?"

Peter frowns. He's confused. "Who's *him*?" he asks.

"The one they used to argue about."

"Who's that?"

"Mom and Dad," the kid says, turning away and staring out the window at the bungalows and trees that flash by. "They used to argue about the guy Mom was with before Dad. She used to get real sad about him. Dad called it the blues. Said it was because the guy had left her all of a sudden and she didn't know if he was alive or dead. She'd go quiet for days. Sometimes weeks. There were times when she didn't even get out of bed. She took pills for it." The kid pauses. "That was you, wasn't it? Because of you leaving her."

"I don't think so," Peter dismisses the idea, eyes fastened to the road ahead.

"She loved you more than my dad, didn't she?"

"She could never love me more than—"

"I heard him shout it at her once," Michael interrupts. "I didn't get it at the time, but I do now. He was shouting that she loved some guy she'd known for a week who couldn't be bothered to stick around more than she loved him, someone who's always been there for her. Does that mean she loved you more than me?"

Peter faces him with a solemn look. "There's no way," he says sincerely, "that your mother loved you less than anything on earth. Not even herself."

The kid is staring back with that burning look again.

"You've ruined my life," he practically spits at Peter. "You know that?"

"I can't begin to tell you how sorry I am, Michael."

"I fucking hate you. It's true what people think about you—about Paul Adams. You're a freak!"

Peter swallows. Stares ahead. He can't say anything from the lump in his throat.

Michael goes on. "You make sure to kill the people who murdered my mom and dad, and then I never want to see you again. You got that?"

"Yes," Peter struggles to say in a faint voice. "I got that."

ONE HUNDRED EIGHT

Patrick Hughes lives in a ten-bedroom beach house just north of Pacific City. The sprawling wood and glass building is perched on a spit of tall cliffs that poke out into the ocean. Wide panoramic windows make up the back walls and they give the perfect view of the Pacific. Fronted by hilly woods, the house is pretty well hidden on one side by trees, and practically impenetrable on the other by a sheer rock wall that rises forty meters out of the bashing waves.

Pat stands at the window smoking a cigarette and gazing out at the endless surf. The Pacific looks angry today. A bank of bruised cloud hovers above it, slowly rolling toward the house, stirring up the waves and turning the water black underneath. Gusting wind sends the gulls into mad loops and the world looks hateful.

Pat's phone chirps in his pocket. He takes it out and holds it up to his eyes. Stamping his cigarette out in a glass ashtray, he answers.

"Peter?"

"We're here."

"Portland?"

"Uh-huh."

"That's good. You're safe."

"Yeah."

"You sound tired?"

Pat listens to him breathe down the phone for a while. His slender fingers pluck another smoke from his pack of Marlboros and he lights it up the second it is clamped between his thin lips.

"I am tired, Pat."

"Then maybe rest will do you good. Sit tight in Portland."

"With the whole world looking for me?"

"For Paul Adams. Not Peter Black."

Neither of them speaks for some time. Pat walks about the vast living room of his house. It practically hangs out over the cliffs so that if you stand in the corner and look out, you feel like you're standing right in the middle of the ocean.

"I guess that kind of worked out all right for them," Peter says in his ear.

"What do you mean?"

"Using my Paul Adams persona against me. It was a perfect plan B. I go rogue and they can fold Pacific Grove up on me. Cover their own work by having it all look like the doings of one depraved monster."

"It's like I always said, Peter. You gotta have a plan B."

"That's right, Pat. You always have said that."

Pat Hughes has wandered into the middle of the room. He stands beside a stone fireplace. A bank of screens sits on the wall in front of him. Satellite footage of a ten-story stone apartment block covers the main one. The other screens are split into footage from the body-cams of the eight armed men who are now entering said apartment block, using hand signals as they file into the lobby and fan out.

"It's good advice," Pat says blankly as his eyes study the monitors.

Peter breathes down his ear. "How long have we worked together, Pat?"

"Since Greece. So, what—thirteen years?"

"That's right. Seven for the agency. Six freelance."

On the monitors, the men move in formation through the apartment block. They split into two teams of four. One team taking the north stairwell, the other taking the south, moving to the penthouse suite that occupies the top floor. It is a fortress with electronically barred doors, Lexan windows and reinforced walls. That is why the eight-man team Pat has sent are packing explosives. Their mission? Blow the door. Kill the targets inside.

"It's a long time, Peter," Pat says blankly.

"We've been through a lot."

"A hell of a lot," Pat agrees. "Kiev. Bogota. Syria. Iraq. Holy shit! I almost forgot Prague. How could I forget Prague?"

"That was a tough one," Peter says.

"It was. I have to say that only you, Peter, would have gotten out of it alive."

"Only me?"

"That's right," Pat says, eyes peeled to the screen as the men reach the front door of the penthouse apartment and begin packing its edges with C4. "You're the best asset I ever worked with," he adds.

"I'm an asset?" Peter says in a hollow voice.

"That's right," Pat says in a tone that's slightly off from his usual one. "And like any asset, Peter," the men run back from the explosives, "you're expendable."

The screens of the eight men's body cams flash. The door flies backwards into the hallway of the apartment, landing on the hardwood floor, blocks of masonry still attached to the hinges. All that's left is a great big hole. The men file into the apartment through it, going room to room, setting off flash grenades; dogs searching the hares out through the optics of their assault rifles. But there's no scent of them anywhere, and soon it is obvious that Peter's Portland safe house is empty. The burrow clean.

"Sir," comes over a speaker in Pat Hughes's living room, the leader of the team speaking, "they're not here."

"Thirteen years, Pat," Peter says down the phone, "and you double-cross me like this."

A shudder creeps beneath Pat Hughes's skin. "How do you mean?"

"How else does anyone ever mean when they accuse someone of double-crossing them? It was *your* Plan B, wasn't it? All of it was *your* plan. *Your* mission. *You,* not Davenport, picked me out of everyone, didn't you?"

Pat Hughes covers the phone. Turning to one of the men by the monitors he snaps, "Get them out of there! NOW!"

The guy starts muttering into his comms microphone.

"Your men are already dead, Pat," Peter says coldly. "The internal walls of that apartment are filled with C4. In case I ever needed a house-shaped bomb."

Pat turns sharply to the monitors with wide eyes. All

eight body cam screens flash white. Then go to static. On the satellite images all the windows on the top floor of the apartment block are blown out by the detonation. The men inside his living room look to Pat Hughes with stunned faces.

"Very good, Peter," Pat says, a slight tremble to his voice. "But I'll tell you this. You really should have just let her inject that poison into her arm. It would have saved so much carnage."

Hugo Davenport sits on a settee to his right, drinking coffee and watching his *boss* with careful eyes. Five other men stand around monitors throughout the room. They are trying to reach the team at the Portland apartment.

"Rainbow Team, do you copy?"

"Come in, Rainbow Team. Come in."

Pat's whole house has been given over as a command center. Being that, as Operation Commander, he himself has been personally running the show from the very beginning.

Peter says, "The Jenkinses never told anyone where I was. Did they?"

"No. They didn't. They only called Child Protection on Paul Adams. Which was bad enough."

"Davenport knew where I lived because you told him."

Pat glances to his left. At Davenport, who cocks his head and sips his coffee.

"Isn't that obvious by now?" Pat says into the phone.

"I'm just glad I never told you about the Lozanos."

One of the men comes before Pat. Some tech guy with pastel purple hair and black-rimmed glasses.

"I'll admit you surprised me with that one," Pat says as he and the tech guy make eye contact. The guy shakes his head. They've been unable to trace the call. "A nice little curveball," Pat goes on. "I knew there'd be some surprise, but I didn't realize it would be that. It was well played not telling me about them living there."

"Rule One. Never drop your guard. I had to keep at least something to myself."

"Yes," Pat says, blowing cigarette smoke out from between his yellow teeth. "That caused me a real headache. Lost a lot of men. Expensive men with expensive contracts that pay out to their families if they die. Now with another eight vaporized in Portland, the overheads on this job are getting seriously out of hand."

"I never did come cheap."

"No, you didn't, Azrael," Pat agrees. "No, you didn't."

"How much is Fred Wilson paying you?"

Pat thinks about it. Glances at Hugo Davenport. *Fuck it!*

"Twenty million up front in cash and another hundred million in the form of shares in his casino organization. A nice little three-point-four million payout every year from that."

Peter is gently laughing on the other end of the phone. "Where is your decency, Pat? The thing that marks us from the common sewer rat."

"I'm a businessman, Peter. The type of man that made this great country. Men who see the bigger picture. Tell me. Why did *you* join the agency, Peter?"

The only reply he gets is the murmur of Peter breathing down the phone.

"I'll tell you, then," Pat says. "It was because *you* were forced to. *You* were nothing but some psycho brat we could turn into a subservient killer. Human trash that no one would care a damn about if we trained them so hard it killed them. No family. No one to worry about them. And if the asset was no good, we'd take the little shit out into the wilds and put a bullet in its head like some mangy dog. You were lucky you did as you were told and were good at it, Peter. So many of those kids didn't make it. Ended up buried in unmarked graves all the way out in Alaska."

Pat finishes for the meantime. For a moment he hears nothing on the end of the line and wonders whether Peter has gone. He checks the phone and sees that the call is still active.

"I, on the other hand," Pat says, "joined the agency by choice. I did it for the career. Went to college. Was top of my class. I joined to make connections and then use them to build the most successful securities company on the West Coast."

Pat stands in the middle of the room. The middle of his kingdom. Proud.

Peter comes back on the line. "Is that why you searched me out when I left the agency?"

"Yes, it was. See, I run a lucrative business offering jobs to men who can't get them elsewhere."

"Makes them easier to burn," Peter interjects.

"I'll agree."

"I take it Luther Bryce is working for you?"

"Obviously. I had to pay the prick a hundred grand just to speak to you."

"All part of the tradecraft," Peter says.

"Yes, Peter. To make sure that whatever happened, all three targets would be dead and there would be no way that any of it could get back to the client. He was very insistent on this."

"And Davenport?"

Pat glances down at the lawyer. "An old friend from MI6 I work with out in Europe from time to time. I needed someone that I could be sure you'd never seen before."

"You said he's an old friend. How long have you known him?"

Pat glances at Davenport. The latter, able to hear every word between them, shrugs.

"I don't know," Pat says. "Ten, maybe eleven years."

"Long enough to form a bond?"

"I guess."

"Then you should take this moment to say goodbye to him."

Pat frowns. So too does Hugo Davenport.

Is it at that moment that the window behind Pat Hughes shatters and the Englishman's head is annihilated. Skull and gore spray Pat and he drops instantly to the floor as more shots enter his living room. Crawling on his hands and knees, he gets behind the settee so that he's hidden from the windows facing the woods.

One by one the five men are taken out. Most before they even know what is happening. Others as they dive for cover. One man almost makes it to where Pat hides behind the settee, but he's hit through the neck before he can get there and his hot blood flies all over the owner and CEO of the most successful securities company on the West Coast.

In only twenty-seven seconds he is all alone in his beach house. Shaking like a leaf. Covered in blood. With no weapon.

The bank of monitors crackles and blinks. He hears the crunch of broken glass underfoot and feels his bladder letting go, the warm piss trickling down the inside of his stick-thin thighs.

Closing his eyes tight, Pat Hughes—more a businessman than an agent—cringes as something hot and hard is pressed against the thinning gray hair of his scalp.

"Just do it," Pat breathes like a man too tired to live.

The rifle comes away. Eyes still closed, Pat imagines Peter stepping back so he doesn't get spray on himself. But instead he feels something loop over his left wrist, the arm dragged around his back, the other wrist secured with another zip-tie and the two placed together behind him.

Ziiip!

Pat almost defecates himself. Snapping his eyelids open, he looks up at Peter with pleading and gasps, "Please, Peter. Not torture. Just kill me outright. Okay? I would have never made you suffer."

Peter crouches in front of him, so that their eyes meet. Pat cringes. Looks sideways. Goes cold when Peter takes hold of his chin and forces him to meet those terrible cold eyes.

"I'm not going to torture you, Pat," Peter tells him. "I'm not even going to kill you."

Pat wears a dubious expression on his sweat-glossed face. "Then what?"

"Do you still settle all accounts in person?"

Pat nods. Already sure he knows what's coming.

"Have you a date arranged with Wilson?"

Another nod.

"Then maybe you can earn your life back. How does that sound?"

A third nod.

Peter hauls him up. Pat is all skin and bone. It means he is light. Using the end of his Barrett M95 bolt-action medium-range sniper rifle, Peter prods Hughes toward the broken window, the curtains billowing and twisting in the heavy wind.

That way leads onto the clifftops, where a pathway hugs the edge of the rocks on one side and the trees on the other. The wooden decking of a veranda ends in a set of steps. Peter keeps the barrel of the gun pressed to the small of Pat's back as they descend them and start down the path. The sound of the waves is so loud it's like they are crashing in their ears. It is why he doesn't hear him.

There is a flash of movement as they pass the wide trunk of a Douglas fir. Flying at Peter from the left comes the figure of a man. Before he can react, the rifle is struck out of his hands and off the cliff by a palm heel smash. A pistol whips around from his sudden opponent. Peter deflects it, the Glock following the rifle into the angry Pacific. He senses further movement low, an arm swinging toward him. He moves his own right arm to parry, but is too slow. He feels the knife enter his belly and shear through the soft flesh just above his left hip bone. Then the momentum of the man takes him off his feet and off the edge of the cliffs. Hurtling down toward the black water.

ONE HUNDRED NINE

THEY TUMBLE THROUGH THE AIR. THE WATER rushing up. The two of them locked together. Peter staring into the dead eyes of Mr. Linton, the knife digging deeper into his stomach. The pain horrific. The whole of him going weak. Bowels loosening.

They hit the water. The air thumps out of both of them. It's like being hit by a car doing thirty. Then comes the shock of the cold. There is cold and black everywhere. The knife is still several inches in Peter, his right hand stopping Linton from bringing it up to his sternum and cutting him in two. They fall through the water, eyes locked in death stares, Linton waiting for the life to go out of Peter's.

Peter fists him weakly in the chest. There is hardly any strength with the pain deep in his belly. A smile purses Linton's thin lips. He tries a head butt, Peter leaning away from it in time. They fight with their free hands. Linton fends off an attempted eye gouge and Peter deflects a Hiraken fore-knuckle punch to his throat that could have crushed his larynx even in the water. Soon their free hands aren't so free, they're trapped together. Linton gets a twist on the blade. It shears into the hip bone and Peter feels sick. A scream bursts from his mouth and is stifled by the water.

Locked together, they float slowly down to the bottom of the ocean. Everything becomes strangely peaceful. Peter shuts his eyes, keeping his grip of Linton, stopping him from gutting him while at the same time controlling the pain, pushing it away into the corners of his psyche. There's a smile on Linton that threatens to rip a hole across his otherwise unremarkable face. His dull little eyes shine as much as they ever have. The act of killing must be the only thing that ever makes this creature feel even a semblance of life.

Then something happens. As they softly hit the rocky bottom, Peter's eyes open and there's a look in them that brings the smile crashing down on Linton's face. It is a look that somehow articulates to Linton that he is not fighting a man, but something else. It is iron will that shines back at him in those jaded blue eyes.

Peter's grip on Linton's hand, the one holding the knife, becomes much firmer, his thumb moving to the pressure point on the underside of the wrist. In acupuncture the point is called P-6, or Neiguan. It can have an effect on the stomach if hit just right.

Peter hits it just right. Digging the digit into the nerves, he causes Linton's stomach to cramp up. The latter's training in pain discipline stops him reacting fully to it. But he does react. Just enough for Peter to find his window, Linton's attention momentarily elsewhere for the first time since they came off the cliff.

Peter lurches forward with his mouth wide open.

Looking like some carnivorous fish. Linton's head is tipped back. His throat stretched out and exposed. Peter tilts sideways and brings his teeth right down on the other man's windpipe. The canines dig in before the jaw clamps down with every ounce of strength and Peter begins ripping side to side like a mauling pit bull, opening up a hole.

Linton unwittingly helps when he tugs his head back from the bite, thus assisting in severing the lump of flesh. He lets go of Peter, of the knife, of everything, floating away into darkness, grabbing at the opening in his throat, the ocean rushing into it and filling his lungs.

The knife still in him, Peter now faces his next battle. Almost out of air, weakened by terrible pain, he has to fight his way to the top of the darkness. Panic thumps through his chest. He starts to fight. His coat weighs him down. He tears it off. Kicks desperately. Claws at the water. Right leg flicking weakly due to the throbbing pain. The flesh moving about the blade with every thrust of his right arm.

It is like trying to tunnel upwards through quicksand.

Peter stops. He takes a few seconds to calm himself. Pushes the pain back to the corners. Pulls the folding knife out, the thing falling heavily down to its owner somewhere in the darkness. Setting himself, he swims properly. The way he was taught. Working through the pain the way he was trained. Peter has been in the water a minute and a half. He can hold his breath no longer than two. Pushing the pain away, ignoring the burn and swell in his lungs, Peter cleaves upwards through the water, the rolling, bubbling surface coming into view.

One minute fifty seconds.

The excursion has cleaned him out. His lungs feel

crushed. There is no air in them anymore. Peter is drowning. His limbs weaken. The pain creeps back into him. His body burns all over from the blows it has taken over these past few days. He should be dead. He should have been dead a long time ago. But something in him always rises to the top. Some will that is beyond even Peter's comprehension. Why, when so many would lie down, does he keep on getting back up?

Two minutes.

His eardrums pound. He lashes at the water, desperation coming back, the water lolling above him. So close.

Two minutes five.

He gasps and salt water fills his mouth. He no longer has feeling in the hands that claw through the water. The numbness is spreading down his arms. His movement becomes almost static. He is floundering so close to the top. Almost dead. His vision tunneling.

Two minutes fifteen seconds.

The storm has made it to the cliffs. It lolls the waves fiercely, and, as his eyes begin to go dead, his chest fixed, deflated lungs twisting up inside him, the water lulls all the way down to where he floats and he is punching through the skin of the ocean.

Peter gasps, filling his aching lungs. He bobs on a wave. Treads water for a while. Letting his faculties slowly return.

The first thing he does when they're back is check his surroundings. He's about twenty feet from the sheer wall of the black cliffs. A figure is standing at the top. He's been watching the whole time. Waiting to see who comes up.

Spotting that the winner is Peter, Pat Hughes runs from the edge.

Apart from the pain and the damage to his hip, the knife

has missed anything vital. Blood loss is minimal. Peter rides a peak and begins swimming across it. The cliffs drop down to a stretch of sandy beach about a hundred meters north along the coastline. That's where several flights of wooden stairs lead all the way back up to the house.

PAT HUGHES WISHES he hadn't waited around. There's no one he can call, being that they're all dead or out of the country. Calling the police would be futile. As well as have consequences for Pat that aren't worth thinking about.

In a panic he runs back into the beach house, his hands still zip-tied behind his back, treading over the six bodies that lie in his living room. There are guns in the house. If he can get his hands free, he can get one and reach Peter before the assassin has a chance to arm himself again. He'll be weak and helpless after nearly drowning. Pat will never get a better chance to kill the man they call Azrael. Otherwise, Hughes knows, he'll be spending the rest of his life waiting for the dark angel to show up and end it.

Pat enters the kitchen and starts with the cupboards, opening the drawers with his back to them. Then he twists around to see which knifes are where, before turning back around and trying to grab one up, flip it around and saw the plastic ties.

This is a waste of time. One that takes him several minutes to figure out as such. He either lacks the skill or it can't be done, but there isn't a knife he can grab up that achieves the goal of cutting through the plastic. Hacking at it. Yes. Cutting his forearm. Twice. Freeing him. No.

It is only when he gives up trying to cut his way free that

Pat Hughes comes up with the idea he should have had when he'd first run into the kitchen three and a half minutes ago. He glances at the gas hob and rolls his eyes.

Putting the largest ring on, he turns his back to the hissing blue flames, lowering his bound hands toward them. Over the next minutes he cries out continuously as he sears the flesh of both wrists like a piece of barbecued meat. By the time he melts the plastic enough to tear it apart, the skin on his forearms and hands is blistered and bleeding.

In a hurry, he runs to the gun cabinet and takes out a Beretta M9, loading a magazine into it with a snap. He runs from the house, out of breath, his tar-coated lungs struggling to heave in enough oxygen to feed the stringy muscles of his stick insect's body. Fifty meters north, the cliffs drop to a beach. Wooden steps zigzag all the way down to the sand. This is the last place he saw Peter heading toward.

He reaches the top of the steps, eyes focused on the water and the beach below. Marches down, scanning the gray sand desperately for Peter. Swings around to the next set of steps and straight into the punch which knocks him onto his back, the Beretta skittling out of his hand.

Peter is already there.

Pat goes to get up and Peter kicks him hard in the face, sending him back down. It stuns the former handler, as well as liberating several of his front teeth. Pat lies on his back mumbling blood as Peter limps around him and picks up the pistol.

Pointing it at Pat, he says in a breathless whisper, "Get up. We're leaving."

ONE HUNDRED TEN

PETER'S HEAVY FEET SHUFFLE ALONG THE UNEVEN ground of the woods. The howling wind of the storm whips his soaking hair about. Warm blood slips down his hip and his wet clothing clings to him.

They have almost killed him.

Almost.

Pat Hughes walks several paces in front. His damaged hands are once more behind his back. His head is hung so low that his chin is almost propped on his bony chest. The Beretta is aimed right at his spine.

They move through the tall Douglas firs, the trees waving from side to side in the squall, Peter clutching his bloody stomach with his free hand. The pain is seizing him up to the point where it's difficult to lift his right foot high enough to clear the exposed tree roots that stick up out of the forest floor.

"You look weak, Peter," Pat says, glancing over his shoulder at him.

"I can still pull a trigger. So shut up."

Michael sits in the passenger seat of a blue Chevrolet Cruze. He's staring at the reflection of the woods in the wing mirror, a nervous sneaker playing invisible kick drum in the footwell. The car is parked off road within the tree line. He spots Pat and then Peter emerging through the bracken. He gets out and runs to them.

"Is that him?" Michael shouts over the wind when he reaches them.

There are tears in his eyes.

"One of them," Peter says.

Michael's face goes fierce. He rushes forward and kicks Pat Hughes right between the legs, bringing the foot all the way up as if he is trying to reach the guy's chin through his torso, or kick the winning field goal at the Super Bowl, the testicles crunching up into the pubic bone. Pat lets out a hoarse scream and drops to his knees. Michael swings the foot again, catching Pat in the mouth and making him bite into his tongue with the jagged ends of broken teeth.

Tucking the pistol into his belt, Peter grabs Michael as the kid comes in for another kick. He takes him by the shoulders and with all his sapping strength pulls the twelve-year-old back.

"No," Peter says weakly. "I need him."

There is ferocious hate in the kid's eyes. Peter recognizes it. He recognizes it and it makes him shudder. The kid tries to push his way past, palming Peter off. But Peter grabs Michael's wrist and stops him. He performs the action with the hand he's been using to hold the wound and the kid notices the blood for the first time.

"He got you?" Michael asks.

He looks genuinely concerned.

"It's only a scratch."

Michael looks at Peter's face. It's bone white and drenched in sweat. He can feel him shivering through the hand that holds his wrist.

"Please," Peter says. "He will pay. Just not yet. I need him to get Marie back."

"The little girl?"

Peter nods.

Michael relaxes and Peter lets him go. He then lifts Pat Hughes back up and escorts him to the Chevy. Michael watches them all the way, wiping tears from his eyes with a sleeve.

"Stay there," Peter tells Pat when they reach the car.

He opens the driver's door and retrieves something from the seat. Pat has little time to figure what it is as Peter turns sharply to him and jabs the needle right into his neck.

"Goodnight, Pat," Peter says, his voice slowly fading along with the world around him. "Sleep tight until you're needed."

Pat Hughes feels himself falling through the world. The trees dissolving all around him.

ONE HUNDRED ELEVEN

CALIFORNIA, 2019

Six days later, Fred Wilson's head of security, a guy named Mathers, picks Peter and Pat up from Wilson's private hangar at LAX. Mathers is some former jarhead still sporting the buzzcut from his days in the Corp. He's waiting for them at the bottom of the boarding steps as they disembark from Wilson's all white Gulfstream G650, the plane having been sent specially to Portland to pick them up.

Peter has the faint whisper of a limp as he steps down with Pat. The wound was easy enough to fix. He cleaned and stitched it in the passenger seat of the Chevy not long after they'd left Pacific City. Still, the slight damage to the bone and the sensitive area of the wound do make movement to some extent cumbersome.

"Mr. Hughes," Mathers says in a growl of a voice when they reach the bottom, "so nice to see you again."

"And you, Mathers."

Mathers has a square head. It reminds Peter of the square watermelons they grow in North Africa. They grow them in wooden crates so that as the fruit stretches out during growth it forms the shape of its container. He wonders whether Mathers was grown in a wooden crate.

There's little emotion in his voice as he tells Pat, "Mr. Wilson sends his apologies for not meeting you in person. But his businesses require him to remain at his Hollywood residence. However, he does await you in his study for the settling up of his account."

"Well, I certainly look forward to that," Pat says with a grin, showing off the dental work he had done yesterday by a Ghanian immigrant working illegally as a dentist out of his apartment in east Portland. He appeared to be unmoved by the fact that Pat's wrists were tied. Only fussed that Peter paid in cash.

"And who is *this*?" Mathers asks, his beady eyes fixing to Peter.

"This is my new assistant. Mr. Black."

"No Mr. Linton?"

"Mr. Linton is unfortunately no longer with us."

"That is sad news. I had heard that the job had become somewhat complicated."

"To say the least," Pat says with a widening of the eyes.

Mathers spreads out a hand toward Peter. It is large. Like the rest of him.

"Mr. Black," he says, shaking with Peter firmly. "Nice to meet you."

"You too, Mr. Mathers," Peter says.

Their eyes meet for a second and Peter wonders whether Mathers sees his own death staring back.

When the handshake ends, Mathers tells them he needs to search both men for weapons. The process is thorough, the man's big paws patting them down, having already checked them over with a metal detector.

Afterwards, and with both men clean, Mathers signals a waiting limousine with a sweep of the hand and says, "Shall we, gentlemen?"

ONE HUNDRED TWELVE

MATHERS SITS IN THE BACK OF THE LIMO WITH them. Some employee of Wilson's dressed in a cap and a tux drives. Pat and Peter are side by side. The buzzcut sits across from them. He's wearing a suit that fits him like a catsuit, his muscles threatening to burst the stitching. It must be well made, double-stitched, to contain him.

Peter doesn't care about Mathers' size. The only thing bulging under that suit that he feels anything for is the Colt Cobra .38 snub-nose revolver Mathers carries in the shoulder holster under his left arm.

The men are silent as the limo cruises through the afternoon sun-drenched streets of Los Angeles toward the tangled passages of the Hollywood Hills. Peter can't help wondering whether Theresa da Silva and the other girl were taken this same route eight years ago. Whether they too stared out of the windows at the tall palm trees lining the sidewalks, the giant white letters of the Hollywood sign bearing down from the crooked hills.

The radio hums in the background and Peter's attention is taken by the sound of the KNX News Radio headline theme kicking in.

"*Here are the headlines at three,*" the newscaster says. "*There has been a significant development in the Paul Adams investigation. Police in the Sierra Nevada have just this hour discovered—*"

"Turn it off, Charlie," Mathers calls to the driver.

"No, keep it on," Peter snaps.

Mathers shrugs and the driver takes his finger away from the radio.

"I guess you like to listen to your work," Mathers says.

Peter ignores him. Next to him, Pat Hughes has become fidgety. His foot taps up and down as he watches Peter out of the corner of an eye.

The newscaster goes on. "*This morning the body of Theresa da Silva was found buried in woodland in the Sierra Nevada close to the entrance of what is believed to be Adams' secret bunker.*"

Peter isn't upset that they've found her body. At least this way she'll get a decent burial. Maybe a headstone. The night she'd died, he hadn't been able to face dissolving her in the drums of hydrofluoric acid he kept in the bunker for waste disposal. It felt like a step too far into the dark. So he and Marta had dug a grave for Theresa in the woods.

It now looks like Pat had tipped the police off about the location and they've discovered the body and the bunker.

"*Ms. da Silva,*" the newscaster's voice fills the back of the limo, "*had been shot multiple times in the torso. As for the bunker, it was supposedly designed for four people and made out of reinforced concrete buried deep in the Sierra Nevada mountain range in what was once the entrance to a mineshaft. Police are saying that the 2000-square-foot space boasted a medical clinic, gym and rumpus room. With reports that they could have stayed there for up to five years without needing to leave. But what went wrong out in those hills and why Adams had to abandon his den is anyone's guess, as detectives keep tight-lipped over the investigation.*"

Peter looks sideways at Pat.

There's no blood in the face of his former handler. Hughes stares out of the window. An expensive Italian loafer jogging up and down in the footwell.

ONE HUNDRED THIRTEEN

Just as Theresa da Silva once had, Peter finds himself being driven down a winding driveway lined with Grecian statues of girlish nymphs and neatly trimmed mini poplar trees. A stone fountain is centerpiece on the carriageway. A water nymph stretches on her toes and squirts a rainbow beam of water from her mouth, filling the overflowing clamshell beneath. The inside of the fountain is lined with mother of pearl and it makes the water glow.

A castle looms over them. A dark stone fortress. Security is pretty lax. Just how Pat had briefed Peter it would be. A couple of guards on the gatehouse. Another awaiting them on the carriageway. That is it. Four guys including Mathers. None of the other three as highly trained as him. Just average nine-to-five security guards with fat bellies and mortgage payments to keep up with. Their training no more than a visit to the local gun range maybe twice a month.

Peter will avoid hurting these men. If he can.

The driver opens the door and they shuffle off the wide leather seating. The guy waiting at the entrance says a few words into Mathers' ear and then leaves them, making his way to the gatehouse to join the others. It is the buzzcut who leads them inside the vast house. At the arched stone entrance, the men pass under a coat of arms with the Latin phrase *parvus pendetur fur, magnus abire videtur* inscribed underneath.

Peter knows the phrase well. It roughly translates as: The petty thief is hanged while the big thief gets away.

Not today they don't.

The hollow staccato beat of their feet tapping across polished parquet fills the tall ceilings of an extensive hallway. Huge oil paintings, mostly portraits of Wilson and his three sons—James among them—line the hallway and corridors. They stare stoically at the men that pass by their impassive expressions.

Mathers leads them down a wood-paneled passageway toward the solid oak door of Fred Wilson's private study. He knocks politely, a cursory act, as he opens the door himself almost immediately, stepping into the room and standing to the side, inviting the guests to go in ahead of him.

They step into a haze of cigar smoke. Wilson has just lit one up. He looks jolly. Like he has just been on the telephone laughing about something.

The smile is due to drop.

Pat moves into the room ahead of Peter. Wilson stands up from his desk. The smile is still there as he greets Hughes warmly. There are two plastic footlockers stacked on top of each other at the end of the desk. They contain the twenty million in $100 bills split into two loads. Each locker weighs at least 110kg.

The second he's passing Mathers on his way into Wilson's study, Peter moves like lightning. Using all his skills in finger-smithery, his hand is inside Mather's suit jacket before the former jarhead has time to react. The next thing, the snub nose is against his temple and Peter is pulling the trigger and Mathers' brains are shooting out the other side of his buzzcut and hitting a portrait of Fred Wilson sitting on a leather armchair that makes the pedophile resemble a king on a throne.

The bang startles the room and shakes the world.

The smile is no longer on Wilson's face as Peter closes the door of the study and locks it. Frederick Wilson is backed up against the window. The cigar drops from his fingers and lands softly on the thick carpet. He stares in absolute terror at his former head of security as the guy sits slumped on the ground just inside the door, blood gushing out of the hole in the side of his head, eyes still wide open.

"What is this, Hughes?" Wilson stammers.

Pat Hughes doesn't care about Fred Wilson. He ignores the billionaire. The man is dead now. There's nothing he can do which can hurt Pat.

Peter, on the other hand...

Facing his former employee, his hands in the air, spots of blood on his face, Pat says, "We cool now, Peter?"

"Turn around," Peter barks.

Ceding to the authority of the tone, Pat Hughes rotates slowly around. "But we're cool though, aren't we? I got you to him, didn't I?"

"You did," Peter says, coming up behind him.

"You said you'd let me live if I did that."

Peter places the snub-nose Colt Cobra to the small of Pat Hughes's back. Right where the spine is.

"I lied."

He pulls the trigger. The .38 goes off like a cannon. The bullet rips through Pat Hughes' spinal cord and continues all the way through his intestines and out his belly button. It practically rips him in two. Pat lets out an animal scream as he's thrown onto his front. There, he remains motionless and groaning as blood pools slowly out of him onto Fred Wilson's expensive Egyptian carpet.

The man of the house is shaking behind the desk. The shooting of Hughes has made his knees go weak and he sits slumped in his armchair. Peter leaps over the fat desk and grabs him by the scruff of his shirt, pulling him up to him.

Jamming the snub nose into his chin, he says right in Wilson's terrified face, "Take me to the basement."

"What basement?"

The movement is quick. Peter places the .38 to Wilson's left cheek and blows him sideways off the chair. He reaches down and picks him back up, gets him upright again.

Wilson's shakes have become violent. A hole goes right through his face from one cheek to the other, exposing the shattered teeth. Blood gushes out. He goes to speak but chokes on it. Swallows. Peter watching the action of his tongue through the holes.

He hisses, "I'll give you twice what I was going to give him."

Tightening his grip on Wilson's scruff, Peter growls,

"Your money can't protect you today, Mr. Wilson. Now take me."

In that moment, for a split second, Fred Wilson is sure that Peter's eyes have gone entirely black.

Swallowing, he nods.

ONE HUNDRED FOURTEEN

THE SECURITY HAS ALL BEEN TOLD TO STAY IN THE gatehouse to ensure privacy in the delicate matter being resolved in the study. So the sprawling manor is deserted except for them.

There's no staircase leading down to the basement. Only an elevator. One with its own power supply. See, the basement is not actually a basement at all but a bunker. Originally built in the 1950s by Howard Hughes as a fallout shelter for use in case the Cold War mutated into thermonuclear war.

Peter spends the whole ride standing behind Fred Wilson. The Cobra pointed right at the small of his back. Pat Hughes is still lying facedown in the study, groaning. Wilson shakes so bad Peter fears he'll have a heart attack from shock before they even get there.

The lift pings and the doors open.

It is completely dark for a few seconds and then light shudders into existence. Wilson is actually crying. Sniffing and trembling. Feeling so fucking sorry for himself it makes Peter sick.

The room is large. The walls are excavated stone. It has metal washbasins like those you see in surgeries. Or abattoirs. There are tools on the wall as though it were some suburban dad's toolshed. Marks outline various surgical implements. A gynecological chair sits in a corner, the leg stirrups jutting out at angles. The floor is smooth concrete and slopes inwards so that anything wet will drain into guttering running down the center of the room.

In another corner are three barred cages.

Peter had noticed something in the far cage stir when the lights went on.

"Get in the chair," Peter orders Wilson.

"Please, whatever you do, please," the billionaire splutters.

Peter cracks him in the side of the head with the butt of the gun. "Get in it!"

Wilson staggers forwards like a man condemned to the firing squad, swaying unevenly in the direction of the chair, his weak limbs carrying him toward his final destination.

When they reach it, Wilson turns around to him and tries one last supplication for his life.

Peter doesn't want to hear it. He hits him with a whip-snap jab to the mouth that sends him falling backwards into the chair. Before he can recover, Peter fastens his arms and legs with the chair's straps. Then, with Wilson secure, he goes to a panel on the wall. It electronically controls the locks of the cages. He releases the end one and rushes inside.

Marie's eyes are filled with tears. She lies on a pancake-thin mattress covered in someone else's dried blood. Peter swoops down to her and checks her over, the girl staring blankly at him the whole time.

"Did he hurt you?" Peter asks.

His heart floods with relief when she gently shakes her head.

Peter pulls her to him, holding the child to his chest. His one single salvation in all of this being her life.

He takes Marie upstairs. In a kitchen he makes her a sandwich and leaves her eating it at a breakfast bar.

"Please, don't go," she begs as he reaches the door.

"It's okay," he says softly. "I won't be long. I just have one last thing I need to do."

Peter marches back down to the bunker. To the sniveling Fred Wilson. On his way to the chair, he snatches a surgical curette from the wall. It is a six-inch-long piece of metal with a small five-millimeter-wide spatula on the end. It is used primarily for the scraping and removal of cysts.

Peter comes over Wilson. Their eyes lock, their faces inches apart. Theresa was right. He doesn't smell of anything.

"No," Fred Wilson says weakly. "Please."

Peter places the flat of one hand on his forehead so that Wilson can't move it. He takes the curette and slides it up the left nostril and into the brain. Slowly, bit by bit. Wilson is dead before it is halfway up, but Peter keeps going until it is buried all the way to the end.

He leaves it there and walks out of the basement.

"That was for all of them," he says over his shoulder before re-entering the elevator. "Everyone you ever hurt."

ONE HUNDRED FIFTEEN

OREGON, 2019

IT IS TWO DAYS LATER. THE NEWS IS FILLED WITH the dead men found at Fred Wilson's Hollywood Hills mansion. Pat Hughes didn't make it. He couldn't hold out long enough for the security guards to finally venture into the house to check.

An added bonus for Peter had been the complete lack of CCTV inside the manor. Due to the house being used for what it was, Wilson had been paranoid that someone could hack the system. Therefore, its wood-paneled corridors were free of prying cameras. It had given Peter ample time to escape the property unseen with Marie and the two foot-lockers.

Fred Wilson had soon been discovered in the bunker. Not reading the situation in a way that would have pleased their deceased boss, his security had immediately called the police. None of this was good for Fred Wilson's reputation or that of the Wilson Organization. Looking for signs of the killer, police forensics had gone over the bunker with a fine-tooth comb. This had resulted in them finding the DNA of at least five missing girls.

Theresa da Silva may get a sliver of justice after all.

THEY'RE BACK IN OREGON, making their way north. Before they reach their destination, however, there's something they need to do first.

Peter drives the three of them through Umpqua National Forest. The road clings to the sides of the Cascade Mountains, leaning in and out of the ridges. In the valley to their left, lakes and rivers shine in the early evening sun like glittering sheets of metal. As they pass a particularly large lake, Michael says, "Here is good. She loved days by the lake."

Peter checks the map of the area. A winding track leads deep into the woods where there's plenty of clearings out of the way of any campsites, but still by the lake. The car bumbles thirty minutes before they're far enough away that Peter stops worrying they'll be caught.

First, they collect firewood. Luckily it hasn't rained for a few days and the early autumn sun has been strong. There's plenty of dry material available, especially with the high winds knocking so many branches off. Marie holds Michael's hand as they collect sticks. The majority of the kindling is collected by Peter, but he is grateful that he has Michael to look after the girl. Though she is healthy, Marie keeps asking for her mother. Sometimes for Natalie as well.

Three hours later, they have a rectangular stack of wood

about two feet high, two feet wide, and six feet long. The sun is dropping below the trees, turning the sky deep purple. A crisp breeze rattles the branches. Marie keeps yawning as she stands with Michael watching Peter pour gasoline all over the wood.

"Tired?" Michael asks the girl.

She nods up at him.

They place Marie back in the car, where she lies across the backseat with a blanket over her. Sucking her thumb, the seven-year-old soon falls asleep.

When she is, Peter pops the trunk.

Kate is wrapped in a cloth sheet. Bags of ice surround her. Her body is stiff as the two of them lift her out. Michael is already crying.

They carry the cloth-wrapped body all the way to the funeral pyre and lay her gently on top. Then they light a torch each and stand over her.

"Do you want to say some words?" Peter asks Michael.

The kid shakes his head, palming the tears from his eyes so he can see.

"Is it okay if I say some?"

"Sure," Michael says.

Facing where her eyes sleep under the cloth, Peter talks to Kate in a trembling voice. "I never told anyone this, but those nine days we spent together were by far the best days of my entire life. I've lived for those days every single second of every single minute ever since. And I know it hurt you when I left, but I did come back. I did. I, eh, I…"

The lump in his throat is so hard that he is unable to go on. Michael stares sideways at him. Beginning to feel a little more sympathy toward this strange man.

Once he's composed, Peter turns to the kid and says, "You ready?"

Michael nods and the two lay their torches on the body, lighting one end of the pyre each. The wood ignites and soon the flames consume her and reach high up into the inky blue.

Peter imagines the smoke as her soul, winding its way toward the stars, and for the first time in his life he genuinely hopes that God exists. He hopes that He exists and that there is a Heaven where she can be at peace.

Peter doesn't expect to join her. If God does exist, there is no place in His kingdom for Azrael.

ONE HUNDRED SIXTEEN

WASHINGTON STATE, 2019

AFTER UMPQUA, THEY HEAD WEST AND CONTINUE driving north up the coast. Marie sits in the middle between Michael and Peter, streaks of sunlight glinting off the silver skin of the Pacific.

In Raymond, Washington State, they park up next to a Chevy Silverado pickup in the dirt lot of a diner. A girl around nine years old with bleached blonde hair sits in the passenger seat. The second they get out, Michael walks up to the window of the pickup and the little girl winds it down.

"Hey, Nikita," Michael says to his former neighbor.

"It's not Nikita anymore," the nine-year-old says with disappointment. "It's Maggie. How boring, right?"

"I'm Joey," Michael replies with a roll of the eyes.

"Well, nice to meet you, Joey," Nikita says, poking a hand out to him.

"You too, Maggie."

"Joey," Peter calls to him, "help me with the footlocker."

"Sure."

The plastic cases are tied to the roof rack of their car. Peter unties one and they carry it down and across to the Silverado, dumping the locker on the cargo bed.

"What's that?" Nikita asks Michael.

He comes right up to her, cups a hand to her ear and whispers, "Ten million dollars. He's giving it to your mom."

Michael and Nikita continue to chat by the vehicles. In the meantime, Peter escorts Marie into the diner. In an end booth by the window an atomic blonde with large sunglasses covering her eyes sits leaned back against the cracked leather, a cup of black coffee steaming in front of her.

"Would you like anything to drink?" Peter asks Marie in a soft voice as they enter.

"Can I have a milkshake?"

"Of course. What flavor?"

"Chocolate."

They order at the counter and tell the waitress they'll be sitting with the woman in the end booth.

"Okay, hun," the waitress says.

The atomic blonde takes off her sunglasses and smiles widely when the two of them take seats opposite her in the booth.

"Peter," Marta Lozano says, the smile showing her white teeth, "you got her."

Peter nods.

The milkshake arrives and the little girl sucks on the straw, draining it while Peter and Marta talk. Every now and then a car enters the sunny lot, the bell above the door jingles, and patrons fill the seats, their voices echoing faintly in the background.

"I thank you from the bottom of my heart for this," Peter tells Marta.

"You don't have to thank me. There's plenty of room at the house."

Peter glances out the window at the lot. Michael and Nikita sit on the hood of Marta's Silverado, their legs swinging back and forth into the grille.

Turning back to Marta, Peter asks how Nikita is taking the loss of her father.

"She won't speak about it yet," Marta says. "She cried at first. But ever since she just shuts her eyes and shakes her head when I ask how she feels."

"She'll open up in time."

Marta nods before picking up her coffee and sipping.

Peter tells her, "There's money for you in the footlocker I put in the back of your pickup. It should cover you."

"How much?" Marta asks casually.

"Ten million."

She gasps into the coffee and spends the next moments coughing into a napkin.

"Wow," she exclaims when her throat is clear.

"It's all in cash. Unmarked bills."

"You didn't have to."

"Yes, I did. You lost as much as I did on this. I'm paying Nikita for the loss of her father and I'm paying Marie for the loss of her mother. The rest is for Michael. I owe him that."

Marie finishes the milkshake, the straw gurgling at the end as the girl sucks up the last of the bubbles. When she is finished she finds Marta gazing softly across the table at her with a pleasant smile.

"This is Marta," Peter tells Marie. "She's the one I told you about. The one who's going to take care of you from now on."

Marta reaches a hand across the table and holds it out. "Hello, sweet pea."

Marie's faces darkens and her gaze falls to the table. "Don't call me sweet pea," she says faintly. "My momma used to call me that."

An apologetic look floods Marta's face. "You don't ever have to worry about that," she says ever so softly. "I will never call you that again. I promise."

The seven-year-old smiles, spreads her hand out and shakes Marta's.

"Now," Marta says, "would you like to go outside and meet your big sister?"

Marie glances out the window, her gaze reaching across the lot and taking in Nikita and Michael. Marta nods through the pane at her daughter. Nikita, who is looking that way, jumps down from the hood of the pickup. She walks across the lot and into the diner.

"Hey there," Nikita says with a smile when she reaches the end of their table.

Marie turns to her. Nikita is holding a hand out.

"Would you like to come with me?" Nikita asks.

Marie turns around to Peter. He tells her gently that it's okay and the little girl turns back to Nikita and jumps down from the seat. Taking her hand, the older girl leads the younger one out of the diner and into the lot, where they join Michael.

"What are you gonna do?" Marta asks Peter once they're alone.

He turns away from the children and meets her eyes.

"I don't know," he admits.

"What about him?"

She's referring to Michael.

"Kate's mom and dad live in San Diego. But he won't go to them."

"Why not?"

"He wants to stay with me."

"But why?"

Peter stares down at the table and breathes out in a sigh. "He wants me to train him."

Marta shakes her head. "He's a child. Doesn't know what he wants or what it entails. What he'll have to give up. He hasn't seen nearly enough death yet."

"I don't know what to do," Peter says.

"Isn't it obvious?" Marta tells him. "Take him to San Diego."

She stares across at Peter and begins to recognize something in his look. A dubious grin stretches her cheeks.

"I can't believe you're even contemplating it," she says.

"Maybe he could stay with me. Not to be trained. But just to live with me."

"Live with you? Where, Peter? You live in the wind."

He's still looking at the table. He glances sideways out the window at the kid. Even though the little brat has shown him nothing but animosity since they've been together, he still feels something growing toward him. The same feeling he has for Kate. Even if she is no more than a memory.

Eyes back on the table, Peter faintly mumbles, "I never had a family."

Though she feels deeply sorry for him, Marta feels the need to insist. "Peter, you *have* to take him to his grandparents. He can't live the life of a fugitive."

Peter looks up at her. There are tears in his eyes.

"But I can be good with him," he says.

He looks so lost. So lost and alone.

Marta sighs. She places a hand upon his. "You *are* good, Peter Black," she tells him. "Don't ever go convincing yourself otherwise."

ONE HUNDRED SEVENTEEN

CANADA, 2019

PETER AND MICHAEL DRIVE NORTH THROUGH Canada. Autumn is here and the leaves have all turned yellow. They're beginning to brown and drop off the trees and the roads are already littered with them.

With the world pitch black around them, the kid sleeps in the passenger seat. He begins murmuring, his feet kicking out, his body tossing and turning on the leaned-back car seat. Peter pulls into the side of the road, gets out and comes to the passenger door. Michael wakes up the second he opens it and Peter crouches at the open door, humming with him.

Michael is still in shock over his mom and dad. Over everything that has happened. Peter wonders whether it isn't the shock that has made him lose his bearings and go off with a complete stranger. After all, he still hasn't told the kid that he's his real father. As far as Michael is concerned, Peter is just some ex of his mother's.

By the side of the road, the occasional headlight beam cutting across them, they hum Irving Berlin's "What'll I Do?" Michael gripping Peter's hand as he gets his breathing under control, his face puffy and red.

Back to normal, Peter goes back around the car, gets in, and they drive off.

"Why did you leave Mom?" the kid asks faintly a mile down the road.

The only non-confrontational conversations they have are about Kate. Though it makes his heart jolt, Peter indulges the kid because it is the only time Michael isn't being mean to him.

"I told you that I was working for the government when I met your mother, right?"

"Yeah. She pulled a bullet out of you. She should have left it in."

Peter swallows. "Well, the people I worked for came looking for me."

"Why didn't you run from them?"

"They were very crafty people, Michael. The types that always lay a trap you can't escape."

"They trapped you?"

"Yes." Peter goes on to tell Michael all about him and Kate coming back to the villa to find three assassins waiting for them.

"So you did it to protect my mom?"

"Yes."

Michael stares at his reflection in the dark glass of the windshield. "Why'd you come back?"

"You mean live in Monterey?"

"Yes."

Peter sighs. "Because your mother was the only thing that I ever felt anything for. Away from her, I just felt numb."

Michael glances left across the car. Peter looks terribly despondent.

"You got them for what they did, though, didn't you?" the kid says.

Peter nods. His face goes fierce and his eyes go dull and he nods. "Yeah," seethes from between his teeth. "I got them." Then he breathes in and out and adds, "But it still doesn't make any of it better."

ONE HUNDRED EIGHTEEN

ALASKA, 2019

THE SNOWS AREN'T FOR ANOTHER WEEK BUT IT'S still bitterly cold. The way being largely clear, they're able to take an all-terrain Jeep up the bending track to the farm. Avoid using the snowcat.

"This is where you grew up?" Michael asks as they pull in front of the log house.

"Yes."

"Cozy," the kid remarks dryly.

They get out of the Jeep and grab their bags from the back. A dark figure fills the doorway of the house and her giant feet creak across the veranda and down the steps. The moment he sees her, Peter drops his bag and holds his arms out. Her hair is now totally gray, but she is still formidable.

"Peter!" Magda announces.

Her thick arms wrap around him and the rosy-cheeked Yakut picks him up in a bearhug. When she puts him down, she swivels to Michael. He is looking up at her with fear in his eyes.

"And this is the boy you told about?" Magda asks.

"Yes," Peter says, eyes on the kid. "Michael, this is Magda."

"Hello, Magda." Michael shivers.

"Ah-ha!" the big woman cries out, picking him up in a hug.

Once he's back on his feet, Magda tells the boy to take his bag to the third door on the left at the top of the stairs.

"I beg you, though, my child," Magda adds, "do your best not to disturb the room at the far end."

"Okay," Michael says with a nod before disappearing inside.

Magda turns to Peter and tells him, "She hasn't been very good lately."

Peter shudders inside. "Does she still have good days and bad?"

"Yes. But the bad are getting longer and the good shorter. Would you like to go up and see her?"

Peter nods solemnly.

On the upstairs landing he passes the open door to Michael's room. He cringes at how loud the kid is as he opens the cupboards and drawers. Recoiling all the way when he practically slams one.

Peter, on the other hand, is creeping light-footed like he always did as a boy. Making sure not to make a peep.

Before he's even at the door, she speaks loud enough for him.

"I hear you out there," comes her croaking voice.

Peter opens the door and steps into the shadowy room.

She sits at the far end in front of the window, her back to the door. Sitting in an armchair, her long fingers spread over the ends of the rests, she watches Magda unload the Jeep, having witnessed their arrival.

"So you've brought me another one," she says without turning.

"Another what?"

"Another child to turn into a killer."

"No, Mother. We're here to stay with you and Magda. You haven't trained boys and girls for many years."

She stands up from the chair, a little unsteady, catching herself. This time, unlike before, she is not playing. This isn't tradecraft. This is genuine old age. The feeble body of someone in their eighties.

She turns to him and he shudders at how much older she looks than when he last laid eyes on her five years ago. There's confusion in her face.

"Why do you call me Mother?" she asks. "I'm not your mother."

"It is what I have always called you. Don't you remember me? I'm Peter."

"Peter?" She shakes her head gently. "You're not Peter. You're some CIA dead-eye come to bring me another boy to train or let die." She steps forward. Again she is unsteady and has to grab the back of the armchair. "I tell you now, you fucking drone, I will not train another of your—"

She stops dead when she spots someone in the doorway.

Peter turns around and sees Michael standing there looking at her.

The old woman's face goes soft. "Peter," she breathes. "Oh, Peter, where have you been?"

She begins walking toward Michael, almost hypnotically. "Oh, Peter," she murmurs.

Reaching Michael, she throws her spindly old arms around him and hugs him tightly. "I'm so sorry I made you do those things," she sobs. "Can you ever forgive me?"

Michael stands there in her arms stunned, the old woman's chin resting on his head. Peter can't help shedding a tear himself.

"Michael," he says, *"this is my mother."*

Don't miss THE MAN WITHOUT A FACE. The riveting sequel in the Peter Black Thriller series.

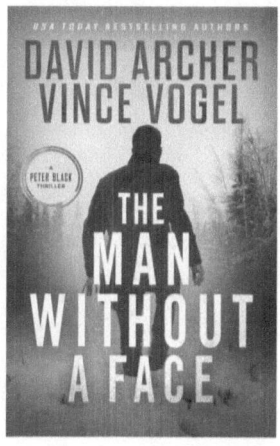

Scan the QR code below to purchase THE MAN WITHOUT A FACE.

Or go to: righthouse.com/the-man-without-a-face

NOTE: flip to the very end to read an exclusive sneak peak...

DON'T MISS ANYTHING!

If you want to stay up to date on all new releases in this series, with these authors, or with any of our new deals, you can do so by joining our newsletters below.

In addition, you will immediately gain access to our entire *Right House VIP Library,* which includes many riveting Mystery and Thriller novels for your enjoyment.

righthouse.com/email

(Easy to unsubscribe. No spam. Ever.)

ALSO BY DAVID ARCHER

Up to date books can be found at:
www.righthouse.com/david-archer

ROGUE THRILLERS
Gates of Hell (Book 1)
Hell's Fury (Book 2)

JACOB HUNTER THRILLERS
The Kyiv File (Book 1)
The Bogota File (Book 2)

PETER BLACK THRILLERS
Burden of the Assassin (Book 1)
The Man Without A Face (Book 2)
Unpunished Deeds (Book 3)
Hunter Killer (Book 4)
Silent Shadows (Book 5)
The Last Run (Book 6)
Dark Corners (Book 7)
Ghost Operative (Book 8)

ALEX MASON THRILLERS
Odin (Book 1)
Ice Cold Spy (Book 2)
Mason's Law (Book 3)
Assets and Liabilities (Book 4)
Russian Roulette (Book 5)

Executive Order (Book 6)
Dead Man Talking (Book 7)
All The King's Men (Book 8)
Flashpoint (Book 9)
Brotherhood of the Goat (Book 10)
Dead Hot (Book 11)
Blood on Megiddo (Book 12)
Son of Hell (Book 13)

NOAH WOLF THRILLERS
Code Name Camelot (Book 1)
Lone Wolf (Book 2)
In Sheep's Clothing (Book 3)
Hit for Hire (Book 4)
The Wolf's Bite (Book 5)
Black Sheep (Book 6)
Balance of Power (Book 7)
Time to Hunt (Book 8)
Red Square (Book 9)
Highest Order (Book 10)
Edge of Anarchy (Book 11)
Unknown Evil (Book 12)
Black Harvest (Book 13)
World Order (Book 14)
Caged Animal (Book 15)
Deep Allegiance (Book 16)
Pack Leader (Book 17)
High Treason (Book 18)
A Wolf Among Men (Book 19)
Rogue Intelligence (Book 20)
Alpha (Book 21)

Rogue Wolf (Book 22)
Shadows of Allegiance (Book 23)
In the Grip of Darkness (Book 24)

SAM PRICHARD MYSTERIES
The Grave Man (Book 1)
Death Sung Softly (Book 2)
Love and War (Book 3)
Framed (Book 4)
The Kill List (Book 5)
Drifter: Part One (Book 6)
Drifter: Part Two (Book 7)
Drifter: Part Three (Book 8)
The Last Song (Book 9)
Ghost (Book 10)
Hidden Agenda (Book 11)

SAM AND INDIE MYSTERIES
Aces and Eights (Book 1)
Fact or Fiction (Book 2)
Close to Home (Book 3)
Brave New World (Book 4)
Innocent Conspiracy (Book 5)
Unfinished Business (Book 6)
Live Bait (Book 7)
Alter Ego (Book 8)
More Than It Seems (Book 9)
Moving On (Book 10)
Worst Nightmare (Book 11)
Chasing Ghosts (Book 12)
Serial Superstition (Book 13)

CHANCE REDDICK THRILLERS
Innocent Injustice (Book 1)
Angel of Justice (Book 2)
High Stakes Hunting (Book 3)
Personal Asset (Book 4)

CASSIE MCGRAW MYSTERIES
What Lies Beneath (Book 1)
Can't Fight Fate (Book 2)
One Last Game (Book 3)
Never Really Gone (Book 4)

ALSO BY VINCE VOGEL

Up to date books can be found at:

www.righthouse.com/vince-vogel

PETER BLACK THRILLERS

Burden of the Assassin (Book 1)

The Man Without A Face (Book 2)

Unpunished Deeds (Book 3)

Hunter Killer (Book 4)

Silent Shadows (Book 5)

The Last Run (Book 6)

Dark Corners (Book 7)

Ghost Operative (Book 8)

JACK SHERIDAN MYSTERIES

A Cross to Bear (Book 1)

The Clay House (Book 2)

Into The Woods (Book 3)

The End is Nigh (Book 4)

A Step Into The Dark (Book 5)

Holier Than Thou (Book 6)

Streetlight City (Book 7)

An Offering for Sin (Book 8)

A Lark on the Wind (Book 9)

A Glass Darkly (Book 10)

Never Came Home (Book 11)

ALEX DORRING THRILLER

Agent 192 (Book 1)

The Hitman's Death (Book 2)

The Wrong Man (Book 3)

Who Dares Wins (Book 4)

The Highwaymen (Book 5)

The Ring (Book 6)

ABOUT US

Right House is an independent publisher created by authors for readers. We specialize in Action, Thriller, Mystery, and Crime novels.

If you enjoyed this novel, then there is a good chance you will like what else we have to offer! Please stay up to date by using any of the links below.

Join our mailing lists to stay up to date -->
righthouse.com/email
Visit our website --> righthouse.com
Contact us --> contact@righthouse.com

facebook.com/righthousebooks
x.com/righthousebooks
instagram.com/righthousebooks

EXCLUSIVE SNEAK PEAK OF...

THE MAN WITHOUT A FACE

CHAPTER 1

VENICE, 2015

LIKE ALWAYS, ST. MARK'S SQUARE WAS CROWDED with tourists. His meeting point, the Café di Biaggio, was nestled in a corner beyond the stone columns of the Procuratie Nuove building. Tables and chairs reached out from the cafés and restaurants that bordered the ancient cobbles. Everywhere thronged with patrons. Waiters weaved in and out of them. The smell of coffee and rich food hung in the air. A three-piece orchestra played Vivaldi on a stage, the music echoing off the tall buildings.

Peter didn't like the position of the café. Sure, it was in a cluttered corner, out the way, but opposite it, at a slight angle, was the Torre dell'Orologio clocktower. Fifty meters across the square, it was the perfect sniper nest, and though he spotted his contact sitting at a table tucked behind a wide column, it was still a little too exposed to the six-hundred-meter-high Renaissance tower.

This was just one of the things that worried Peter as he took a seat opposite a white man in his late fifties, thin face, pale complexion. Dressed like an American tourist in shades and baseball cap, he didn't look much like a man with a gun. More like a man with a desk.

He lowered a pair of Oakleys to reveal a serious expression. To Peter, he looked worried and was trying hard not to let it show. But the leg jogging up and down underneath the table gave it away.

Leaning in, he whispered, "Azrael?"

Peter nodded.

Above the door to the stylish café was a rectangular brass plate. It carried the café's name and had been polished so well it reflected a perfect panoramic view of the whole square behind his seat. This was what Peter's eyes fixed to as he spoke with the contact.

"You look so young," the man commented absentmindedly. "How old are you, son?"

"Twenty-five."

"I've got a daughter close to your age. She's studying medicine at John Hopkins."

"Good for her," Peter said dryly. "Is there a reason I'm here or did you just want to chat about your daughter?"

The man's expression changed. "Of course," he said. Then. "Do you know who I am?"

"You're Walter Smith, deputy director of Central Intelligence. Which is why I find this whole meeting odd."

"Odd how?"

"You're the deputy director. Why are you meeting with an asset your agency officially denies even exists?"

"Good question. I'll answer it. I'm here because there was no one else, son, and because of luck."

"Whose luck," Peter asked, "mine or yours?"

"Yours, son. You see, two hours ago, eight assets in the Fallen Angel program—the same program you are a member of—were terminated whilst awaiting orders at what we thought were secure locations."

As Walter Smith's words washed over him, Peter studied the square through the brass plate. An old man fed pigeons in the center by the fountain, stooped over and scattering seed. The birds kicking up a stink as they clambered for it.

"Who terminated them?"

"GRU."

"How'd the Russians find them—a leak?"

Smith nodded. "A rogue officer that I will do everything in my power to find."

"Okay. So why then is the deputy director of the CIA telling me all of this, rather than, say, another officer?"

"The only reason I'm here is because I happen to be on vacation in Venice with my family. Hence your luck, son. I offered to give you the message in person, because all communication channels are currently corrupted."

Peter took his eyes off the plate. Narrowed them on Smith.

"What about the tracker?"

"That's what's been corrupted. We're sure that the GRU were led to the other assets by their tracker data."

Peter concentrated on the plate, his mind photographing each and every single body around him for any sign that one of them was an enemy asset.

While he did, he asked, "So how in the hell am I going to get it out of my head?"

"You're not. But this will make sure it doesn't work."

Smith slipped a hand in his pocket and brought out a small rectangular device that resembled a USB stick.

"What is it?" Peter asked as he took it and felt around the thing with his fingers. It was heavy, like a paperweight, and bore no other markings except for a single oval button in the center.

"It's an EMP. It lets out a short but very powerful electromagnetic pulse that disables electronics. I need you to place it at your right temple and press the button. It will scramble the tracker."

Peter held it to the side of his head.

"But watch out," Smith cautioned as Peter went to press the button. "I've heard it described as like being hit in the head with a sledgehammer."

With that in mind, Peter thumbed the button.

Pain exploded inside his skull, rushing down his neck and filling his entire body. His teeth clamped shut and his eyelids burst open. His spine arched back with a crack of vertebra. The chair legs scraped the stone as he went into cramping spasms. His face twisting on one side like he was having a stroke.

Right at the moment he thought he was going to faint, it stopped and the pain drained out of him. Sighing loudly through clenched teeth, he was thankful he'd managed to control his bladder in time not to urinate himself.

For a second or two Peter sat panting, limbs weak, sweat dripping down his face.

"It's not fun," Smith remarked.

"No," Peter mumbled. "It isn't."

There was a jug of water on the table. Peter poured himself a glass and drank it down quick. His skull felt like it was slowly shrinking back to normal size.

Smith took his cell phone and checked the tracker. "Good," he said, placing it back in his pocket. "You're no longer on there."

"So what now?"

"Now you come with me, Azrael. The Russians have put their best man on the job. A man they call the Hunter."

Peter had heard of him. A Russian asset who lived just like he did, in the field. The Hunter specialized in the termination of other countries' assets. In the last four years he had personally killed, or was suspected of personally killing, twenty-two active assets. Including five hard assets like Peter.

"Eight angels are already dead," Smith went on. "Killed in a series of attacks. You're to come with me now to a secure location. Once there, I can..."

While he talked, Peter watched the golden reflection of their surroundings. Two children ran in and out of the tables. They almost hit a waiter, who kinked his body into a Z to avoid the tray of food being knocked from his hands.

"The whole program has been jeopardized," Smith droned on.

Peter's eyes scanned the rooftops around the Piazza. For the innumerable time, they stopped on the visage of the ancient clocktower—the Torre dell'Orologio. Something glinted in the sun.

The scope of a rifle.

Peter grabbed Smith by the shoulder. As he yanked him sideways off the chair, a round whipped past and punched a hole through the wooden back of the deputy director's empty chair, penetrating the spot where his heart had been a second ago.

Peter jerked Smith up off the floor and onto his feet as more rounds splintered the table. They needed to move, needed to get away from the X. The shooter was using a high-caliber sniper rifle, at least a .30. The shots came in clear sharp cracks rather than continual pops.

Peter grabbed his rucksack and half dragged Smith through the crowd of people into the café, getting clear of the sniper's vantage. It was at this point, as they entered the throng inside, that everyone outside on the square exploded into a confused stampede and ran blindly into the café.

Peter pulled the deputy director into an alcove as the place descended into screaming, shouting chaos. He removed a Heckler & Koch 45 from the bag, unscrewing the suppressor. He wouldn't be needing stealth for this but accuracy and range.

The front window of the café exploded. A nearby woman took the hit, screaming as the .300 Winchester Magnum round slammed all the way through her back and out her chest.

By the time she landed face first on the floor, she was no longer screaming.

The sniper had moved position and was now firing into the café from an opposite rooftop. A chunk of marble exploded by their feet and Peter used it as a cue to grab Smith once more and run headlong toward the kitchens at the back.

He kept close to the people.

An elderly man tripped and fell under the stampede

rushing for the rear of the building. The surge of bodies carried on like a wave, and the fallen man cried out as he was trampled into the floor.

It was then that Peter spotted something. Or someone.

Over the torrent, one man stood out as the only person not hurrying to escape. Instead, he was standing like a rock in the middle of a rapid river. His eyes pierced at them and he raised a hand: a gun fitted tightly inside. The muzzle flashed. Peter tugged Smith to the left. A man running across them shrieked and spun around, a spray of crimson shooting from his neck.

The explosion of the gun signaled total chaos. The crowd surged behind Peter and Smith, pushing them toward the shooter. Peter threw Smith to the ground and, as a second flash exploded, ducked through the stampede.

The bustle pushed into the shooter, his arm shoved upwards, held aloft by the press of bodies. When he finally managed to lower it, he'd lost sight of Peter, and it was only when the assassin burst at him through the scrum that he finally got a look.

By then it was too late.

Peter swung a chop into the guy's wrist, hitting the tendons and nerves, making the fingers involuntarily snap open. It knocked the gun out of his hand. As he straightened, Peter brought an elbow angling sharply back, catching the guy in the nose and flattening it to his face with a crunch. His opponent tried to change his feet, get a better stance, but the close proximity of rushing bodies made it impossible. His fighting style, the one he was trying to use, needed more space.

Peter didn't need any.

Avoiding the stifled punches and kicks that came his way, he got in several well-aimed blows, finishing with a flurry of palm strikes to the guy's throat—all the way until he heard the larynx crack as the guy dropped to his knees.

While he writhed on the floor, gasping for air that refused to come, Peter found Smith and they continued on their way out of the building.

"Not that way!" Peter shouted when the deputy director went to follow the others out of a back door fire exit. "He'll have the alley covered."

They entered the kitchen instead. The chefs gone, the place empty.

"It's a dead end," Smith complained as he followed Peter to a walk-in fridge.

The assassin ignored him as he hauled the sliding door to the side and ushered the deputy director into the frigid air before getting in himself and slamming the door shut behind them.

Shelves of produce lined the walls. In the frigid light of a low-wattage bulb, Peter went to the rear and began hauling buckets of sauces away from that end of the fridge. It was at this moment that Smith spotted the drainage hatch.

Peter wrenched it open and signaled for him to go down.

A minute later they were walking the Venetian sewers.

Smith asked, "How did you know this would lead us out?"

"You recall the Afrid Hassani assassination?"

"The official thing for me to say is that I have no knowledge of any such assassination."

"Well it happened. And how it happened was that myself and a four-man wet team used the sewers to gain access to the suite he and his twelve-man security detail were stationed in. We got up through a hatch right underneath the hotel's kitchen. During recon I had to remember every detail of the sewage plans in case things went wrong and we needed another way out. I remember that at the Piazza San Marco every café has access to the sewer from the kitchens. Di Biaggio's is in the refrigerator."

They came to a ladder. Peter went up first. Reaching the top, he opened the hatch and cautiously poked his head out, gazing between the running feet that tore past.

"We're as safe as we'll ever be," he said down to Smith.

Having lifted himself out of the sewer, Peter leaned down and called, "Come on."

Smith began making his way up. In the meantime Peter scanned the narrow alleyway the manhole had led to, the HK45 gripped in his hand. Ancient stone buildings towering over him on both sides.

The rooftops. They'll be on the rooftops.

The sun shone in razors of light at the edge of a chimneystack. It was momentarily blocked by the profile of a man. Peter aimed his pistol as the guy rounded the chimney, grasping the stock of an assault rifle.

This wasn't the sniper.

The shooter showed too much of himself as he knelt on the terracotta tiles. A single bullet from Peter's HK45 struck him in the throat and sent him rolling like a rag doll down the roof, long before he could pull the trigger on his AK.

The body toppled off the eaves, landing right at the feet of a runner. It made a resounding slap, bouncing at least a foot, and covered the woman in a spray of blood.

Peter didn't see it. Only heard the woman's scream. He

was too busy pulling Smith out of the sewer. The moment the deputy director was free, a bullet smashed the cobbles close by. The impact sent chips of flint everywhere. Peter spotted the outline of the sniper. He was silhouetted by the sun. Standing on a rooftop about a hundred, a hundred twenty meters away. Beyond his pistol's effective range.

"Come on!" Peter shouted at Smith.

The two of them set off, running toward the mouth of the alley, zigzagging as more shots struck the buildings and ground around them.

At the end, the alley opened out onto the lagoon. A small dock lined its edge. Several motorboats tied to it bobbed along the choppy waves. One of them was occupied, the motor ticking over. Peter jumped onto it, quickly flung the pilot into the water, and, with Smith onboard and the Italians all shouting curses at him, tore out of there, heading into open water.

The runabout had a rearview mirror. As they cut across the lagoon, Peter checked it. At the exact moment he did, a bullet whistled past his head, striking the water a few meters in front of the bow.

When he turned over his shoulder, he saw the silhouette of the sniper standing proudly on the roof.

He was watching them. And not just that. The bastard appeared to be waving.

This, Peter thought, *must be the Hunter*.

CHAPTER 2

CALIFORNIA, 2021

Six years later, headlight beams illuminate the edges of curtains, waking Peter from his reverie. He cocks the silenced HK45 and stays perfectly still in the darkness of the trailer.

Sitting opposite the door disguised one last time as Paul Adams, he has spent the last six hours waiting patiently for this moment like a snake that has infiltrated the warren while the rabbits are away.

The doors of a pickup creak open and two sets of feet crunch down on gravel. One of the men moves with a wide, confident gait. The other shuffles behind like the condemned.

They reach the door. The key scratches in the latch. Next, it is opening and a hand is reaching inside and flipping the light switch.

Jimmy Palmer doesn't notice at first. As he steps into the

trailer, he is looking back over his shoulder at his son Danny. It is only when he is standing right in the middle that he realizes, first, the plastic sheeting covering everything inside his trailer—the floor, furniture, sideboards, ceiling. Second, that his former neighbor Paul Adams is sitting in a chair aiming a pistol at him.

Jimmy goes to speak but the two bullets that hit his kneecaps, one after the other, turn any speech he may have had into a hollow shriek as he collapses to the floor.

Danny Palmer, the man's teenage son, stands on the threshold, wide-eyed and scared. He doesn't have to be. Peter is doing this for him.

During the fall, Jimmy had flung his car keys across the trailer. They'd landed at Peter's feet. He picks them up, rises from the chair, and steps over the squirming Jimmy. At the door he holds them out to Danny. The teenager is still staring at him, unsure.

"Here," Peter says. "Take them."

The teen reaches a trembling hand out and cautiously accepts the keys.

"Tell them what happened," Peter says. "Tell them Paul Adams did it. Tell exactly the truth. *Do not* lie."

Danny nods.

"Take the pickup and go home to your sister," Peter concludes.

"Boy!" Jimmy screams from the floor. "Get my pistol from the truck. Shoot this son-of-a-bitch."

Danny does no such thing. He walks away from the trailer, gets in the pickup, and drives out of there.

Peter closes the door after him. The trailer is in a secluded area of woodland in the middle of Monterey

County. Just as Jimmy does when he brings his son out here in the middle of the night, Peter has all the time in the world.

But Peter is not a sadist.

So the second he can no longer hear the sound of the pickup's engine, he faces Jimmy, locks eyes, and unloads the clip of the HK into the child molester's head. Then he pulls all the plastic down, wraps it around the body, leaves. He fetches a drum of hydrochloric acid from the back of his own pickup and uses a sack-bearer to wheel it to the trailer.

The body of Jimmy Palmer, or any sign of it, will never be found.

CHAPTER 3

ALASKA, 2021

Over two thousand miles north of Monterey, in the wilds of Alaska, a thirteen-year-old boy is busy smashing his fists into the well-beaten wall of a barn. The strapping around his knuckles is pink with blood and sweat. Pain burns all the way up to his elbows, which he does his best not to show to the birdlike, elderly woman who stands behind him.

She leans heavily on a black cane, shouting instructions at him. "Right jab to ten. Left hook to fourteen. Left kick to two," and so on as the kid strikes the thick wood slats with rapid punches and kicks, hitting the numbers that dot the outline of a man with precision. "Now, follow pattern while repeating rules."

"Rule one," the kid says breathlessly as he beats the wood: "Never, huh, drop your guard. Rule two, huh, never underestimate, huh, your opponent. Rule three: don't stand out. Rule four, huh, never assume, only, huh, plan. Rule five: never, huh, hurt an innocent. Rule— Ah!"

His wrist makes a distinct crack that reaches the rafters of the old barn, unsettling the watching birds. The kid buckles over, holding the throbbing limb, whining until the whip of her cane across the backs of his calves straightens him up.

The old woman is in her seventies, withered and senile. But, man, can she hit hard with that fucking cane.

"You must be tougher, boy!"

"I'm sorry. I—"

She whips him again. "Don't whine that you're sorry. You want to be assassin, Peter?"

She's still calling him Peter. No matter how many times they tell her his name is Michael. Lately, they don't even bother. Michael is Peter. And Peter is something else altogether.

"Of course I do," Michael says.

"Then stand up straight and stop whining."

The day is bright, yet cold. Winter has ended and it is now spring. Out here that means little more than longer days and less snowfall. Outside, the frozen drift is yet to melt and it sheets everything.

Michael pulls himself into fighting stance. Faces the wall again. The man's outline. The pummeled, blood-smeared wood. Mother raises her cane, is about to recommence with instructions, when a certain thought comes to her.

"Actually," she says, lowering the stick. "I have an idea. Do you know what it is like to be shot?"

The kid slowly shakes his head.

. . .

INSIDE THE FARMHOUSE, Mother's oldest friend and fellow former trainer of child assassins, Magda, is vacuuming the floors. She is six-five and built as well as any man. Long gray hair, once black, flows down the back of the blue boiler suit she wears and a troubled expression hangs on her wind parched face.

It is only when she is finished that she realizes Mother and the boy are no longer in the barn. She can't hear them. To make sure, she checks.

Standing in the open doorway of the outbuilding and staring at its deserted internals, a thought bites Magda, twisting her stomach. It makes her run to the weapons shed. And when she spots that the small-sized body armor is missing from its peg, the knot in her guts threatens to consume her.

It is enough to make Magda dash into the woods as fast as her thick old legs will carry her, hollering: "Katya, no!"

TOO FAR TO HEAR HER cries, Mother and Michael stand in the middle of the icy trees, the missing body armor strapped to the teenager. They stand approximately ten meters apart in a clearing.

"Today," the old woman says, "we will be performing a shooting test different from what you have done so far."

Michael realizes that the main difference is him being unarmed.

"One day," she goes on, "you will be shot, Peter. Nothing will prepare you for it, but at least this will give you some idea."

Mother lifts a SIG Sauer P226 from her hip holster and aims it at him. The gun trembles in her hand, looking far more heavy than it is in her feeble grip.

Michael flinches.

But Mother doesn't shoot. Instead, she smiles, shakes her head, lowers the gun.

"No. You're expecting it," she says. "Are prepared for it. I can tell you now that when a bullet finally does bore its way into your flesh, it will come without anticipation."

"So you're *not* going to shoot me?"

"Not me."

"Not you?"

"No."

"Then who?"

Mother says nothing. She just remains stock still, the pistol hanging at her side, her steely eyes searching the wide trunk of an Alaskan cedar about twenty meters behind Michael. She stares for so long that he feels obliged to look himself.

When nothing emerges from behind the tree, he turns back to her. It is at this point that Michael begins to hear the faraway sound of Magda calling to them.

"Where is she?" Mother asks no one in particular.

Michael answers anyway. "Who—Magda?"

"Yes. She was supposed to come from that tree."

"I think she's coming now."

"Not enough time."

"Why? What's going to—"

The blast echoes in the forest. The birds scatter. By the time Magda arrives at the scene, Michael is on his back, twisting about in the frozen dirt, trying desperately to breathe, terrible pain filling his entire left side where the bullet struck the armor.

Magda swoops down and lifts him up. "Breathe, Michael," she yells. "Breathe!"

But the boy is going pale.

Scan the QR code below to purchase THE MAN WITHOUT A FACE.
Or go to: righthouse.com/the-man-without-a-face